MIDNIGHT TRIAGE

BOOK 2 OF THE FULL MOON MEDIC SERIES

DANIEL POTTER

ALSO BY DANIEL POTTER

The Full Moon Medic Book 1: Emergency Shift

The Full Moon Medic Book 2: Midnight Triage

* * *

Freelance Familiars Book 1: Off Leash

Freelance Familiars Book 2: Marking Territory

Freelance Familiars Book 3: High Steaks

Freelance Familiars Book 4: Aggressive Behavior

Freelance Familiars Book 5: Pride Fall

Rudy & the Warren Warriors (a Freelance Familiars short story)

* * *

Rise of the Horned Serpent Book 1: Dragon's Price

Rise of the Horned Serpent Book 2: Dragon's Cage

Rise of the Horned Serpent Book 3: Dragon's Run

Rise of the Horned Serpent Book 4: Dragon's Siege

Midnight Triage is dedicated to all the research scientists who dream of punching a disease in the face and spend their years finding the tools to do so.

1
____

Four hours, fifty-eight minutes and eighteen seconds to go on the longest shift I had ever worked. Every breath dedicated to keeping a cage door shut. Noise filled the silence between Cindy and me. Bad techno whispered from the speakers, not quite loud enough to cover the soft smack of lips and the slurping of our questing straws as we hunted for the ice melt at the bottom of our paper cups. I'd closed the windows, shutting out the scents of mud and pine that made both the soles of my feet and my palms itch to run. I breathed through my mouth; it didn't dull the sharp sting of the antiseptic that leeched from every surface, but lessened the sensation that I shared this box on wheels with a frightened rabbit. Cindy functioned fine, but the constant stink of her fear wore on my nerves.

The radio chirped, and I ripped the rectangular microphone out of its holder. The bored tones of the dispatcher drawled out our vehicle number, "MICU-fortee twoo. Do yaa copy?"

I swallowed down a bite of dry burger and squeezed the

talk button, "MICU-42 copies, what'cha got? Over." I asked, my voice high and eager.

"Patient reporting difficulty breathing. Needs transport. Will send details on confirmation. Over." The dispatcher said.

"Confirmated!" I sang, slamming the rectangular microphone back into the cradle and jabbing at the nav screen to lock in our route. Throwing myself against the back of my seat, I fumbled for the seat belt and shoved my half-eaten burger into the brown paper bag it came in. A hunt. Energy shot through my nerves, and I bounced in the seat. "Let's go-let's go-let's go!" I looked at Cindy and found her regarding me warily.

"Abby, down," With that, she serenely capped her thermos and slid it between the seats.

"Shit." I checked my hands. My nails had the crescent edge of humanity, although they were nearly a quarter inch long. They were usually the first things to change, but even if they were human-shaped, they refused to stay short. "Am I slipping somewhere?" I asked, flipping down the visor and checking my face in the mirror there. Rings of pale silver stared back from beneath an unruly mop of black hair that had gone white at the roots. Both of those were new but human; my mother's soft jawline and angled nose remained unaltered. I ran my tongue across the tips of my teeth. They were fine. I was fine. Four hours, fifty-six minutes and forty-six seconds and the shift would be over.

Cindy put the ambulance into reverse and backed out of our parking spot. "You're not slipping yet. You're just acting like a pent-up terrier."

"Am not!" I protested and growled a low rumble, deep and dangerous. Not anything terrier-like.

"Abby!" Her voice sharp with rebuke. "Keep it together."

I could only huff in response to that. She didn't understand, couldn't feel the giant wolf growing inside me. After over forty hours of appearing human, my skin was little more than a rubber bodysuit with a wolf struggling inside of it. As we pulled into traffic, I dug my nails into my palms, blunting the sensation of the paw pads urgently pressing from the other side.

Want to run. Hunt. Hungry. Play with pup. Explore. She, wolf me, whimpered from inside me, too powerful to be contained in either my heart or my head. *Let out! Let out!*

Everything she wanted, I wanted, too. We are two sides of a single coin. *Duty first. Need hands for the duty.* I explained, pleaded, as we bit back a shared howl of frustration. If I let her through the skin, even a little bit, she'd be nigh impossible to pull back. The world changed with the wolf on the outside. Things like the importance of finishing forty-eight hour shifts and paychecks faded beneath Luna's cool light.

Beside me Cindy slammed the gear shift into drive, hitting the lights and siren. Despite her jerky, disgruntled movements, her searing red lips curled up in the corners. We peeled out of the park-and-ride with enough acceleration to push me back into my seat as we ripped out onto the road. A howl of the hunt tore from by throat.

"Jebus, Abby!" Cindy swore at me and hunched closer to her steering wheel. The tang of her stress grew in the air.

"Oh, lay off," I snapped back, panting through my teeth, "I'll hold it in for the patients, but let me have a little fun now." The wolf pressed a little less urgently on the underside of my skin.

Cindy's jaw clenched, "It's loud."

"Merf!" A grumpy feline agreed from the shoe box I held between my feet. Secret, my adopted half human, half cat

Fey pup, lifted her tiny head to peer at me through sleepy slits. In her kitten form, she was about four pounds of cute.

I grinned down at her and prodded her with the toe of my shoe. "You're supposed to be nocturnal."

She swatted at my foot, yawned, her little pink tongue curling, and stretched while making little grumbling noises. "Merf mrrr mew merf." Making it very tempting to snap her up and pet her, but I busied myself pulling on all the PPE required for this call.

Double gloves, face mask, face shield and paper coat to put on as soon as I stepped off the bus. A cap covered my hair.

"You're taking lead?" Cindy asked as we barreled toward the red dot on the nav that was our destination.

"Yes." I said, my voice firm. If I slipped with a patient, that'd be bad. Worse if I was driving, though; giant wolves can't drive. And I wanted to lead this hunt. I stared at Cindy to see if she'd challenge me, but she merely nodded.

We pulled up to a gigantic house in Southwest Portland: Hillsboro neighborhood. A McMansion that looked designed by an architect with multiple personalities: Victorian at one end, with peaked window boxes and a hexagonal turret popping through the roof on the other. Two detached structures marked it as an isolation colony: communities that housed people who had given up on interacting with wider society to protect themselves from the plagues. A small hut marked "Deliveries" and a converted freestanding garage, which would house the colony's quarantine apartments.

In front of that stood one person in a yellow hazmat suit, who waved as we drove up. "You know this one?" Cindy asked.

I didn't. Iso colonies started being founded during the

second plague, Ebola-R. They ranged from clusters of elderly and immune-compromised people to techies who attempted to live entirely in VR.

Some only called in emergency services in an absolute emergency, and others were filled with hypochondriacs who swore that their neighbors had given them the hyperflu on purpose. I hopped out of the bus with a whispered warning at Secret to stay put. As I slipped on the paper jacket, my nose caught a whiff of something sour. Wolf me surged up, and I barely caught her in time. The skin over my skull strained and the bones in my hands vibrated. *Duty,* I thought as I shoved her back.

She whimpered, *Bad smell, bad smell. Find source.*

Sickness, our duty. In truth, I was happy it wasn't something like a stabbing. Had one of those the day before and the blood scent had made me ravenous. Still, the wolf in me sulked as I approached the hazmat-clad individual. I squinted to peer into the dark shadow of his windowed hood. "Are you the patient?"

"Ah-hem," He cleared his throat. "No. He's inside. Would have brought him to the urgent care myself, but we don't have a car at the moment."

He continued as I pulled the stretcher from the back of the bus and wheeled it over towards him. Cindy joined me as he opened the door. That scent redoubled, thick enough to taste as we hurried into a spartan and sterile-looking apartment. Everything was tile and steel, constructed as a hospital is, able to endure being hosed down with disinfectants. Inside, on a fake leather couch, a gray-haired man huddled miserably beneath a pile of comforters. He coughed, a thick, syrupy exhalation with a fading echo that made my hackles rise. Sounded like Covid. I looked at hazmat guy, "Are you all up on your vaccinations?"

"It's not Covid," the sick man rasped before his lungs attempt to strangle him again.

"Ah-hem, we keep them all current." Hazmat guy said, in a voice that didn't sound a hundred percent healthy, either.

I knelt down, so as to be eye level to the sick man, noting that the rise and fall of his chest was faster than it should be. "Hi there, sir, I'm Abby and with me is Cindy. You called 911 for breathing problems. How long have you been having trouble?" Without waiting for permission, I checked his temperature, found it elevated, with pulse ox low enough to be concerned. If it wasn't Covid, he'd have pneumonia. He definitely needed oxygen and to go to the hospital.

"I can't have Covid. I got this year's shot, and I don't break the rules." He lifted his bloodshot eyes to hazmat guy. "Unlike some people."

"Kyle," the hazmat man cleared his throat again. I almost wanted to make sure he wasn't ill with this, but in a colony like this he might have underlying issues to begin with. "No one is breaking the rules."

"Mercy saw you do it. She told me." Kyle rasped and collapsed into a hacking fit, trying to stifle it with his wrist.

"Mr. Kyle," I said loudly, hoping to still their argument. We had no time for their drama. "Please come with us and let the doctors check you out."

Kyle assented, and hazmat man said nothing more. We loaded Kyle onto the stretcher. Once we got him on the bus, I set him up with oxygen and buckled myself in. Vitals weren't wonderful, but nothing indicated a coming crash. He nodded in response to my gentle assurances but made no effort to talk in between coughing spells.

This is how most calls go. There's no dramatics, we just provide transportation to the hospital. The sick patient needs help, but they're not dying on us, so it's a simple, sedate ride. Nothing really to do.

Nothing to distract a wolf from a strange smell. And the sour scent of Kyle's sickness grew with every silent moment in the back of the bus.

Bad smell. Smell it good.

The cold of the wolf's nose pressed behind my human one, making the bones of my face ache. *No, stop it. Not now!* I thought back at her.

But was this simply the scent of a sickness? An entire new world opened when I had a wolf's nose. I'd spent a half-dozen nights in the last two weeks exploring the parks and neighborhood scents, trying, vainly in some cases, to assign human words to the vivid paintings that flowed through the night air. Of which only the brightest strokes were detectable by my human nose. I had detected this one outside his apartment. Why would it be outside his apartment?

With that thought, human curiosity aligned with the wolf's need to know this new canvas and the mask slipped. The scent deepened, gained the earthen texture of deep soil as my mask grew tight against my nose. I slammed the brakes on the transformation and swore, although with my now too-long tongue it came out more "uck."

Kyle's eyes, which had been half closed, opened and focused on me, a question clear in them.

"Everhine's sokay," My voice slurred as I tried to push the partially formed muzzle back into my face with my gloved hand. It had only gotten out about two inches, but filled the entirety of my mask.

Let go! Growled my wolf. *Do our duty. Smell the bad thing!* She hung on stubbornly, flexing limbs that extended inside my own.

Not yet! I pleaded with her. *Few more minutes, he can't see you!*

Kyle started coughing and vitals monitors shrieked with an alarm; our focus sharpened back into one as I looked over the display. It lost his pulse and then found it again as Kyle slumped back against the stretcher, panting for breath.

"Almos zare," I told him. Checking out the back windows, I recognized the road up to OHSU emergency center by the pattern of streetlights and the steep angle.

"Hurts," he rasped, rubbing at his chest. "It's like I'm holding my breath."

"eep reaths," I said, leaning over him, pretending to adjust his oxygen line but really finally getting a good whiff of his breath. Earthy. How could someone's breath smell like sour dirt?

Let me out! My wolf insisted, *let me help!* My toes suddenly jammed into the ends of my shoes. Every bone in my body seemed to slip away from me. I glanced up to the front and saw the emergency drop-off area dead ahead. Had to hold off my wolf for a few more minutes.

Cindy hadn't even stopped when I flung open the rear doors and stumbled out the back. I nearly ripped the oxygen tubes out of Kyle's nose in my haste to pull the stretcher out. Claws broke through the tips of my blue gloves as I charged him into the ER. Nearly rammed the first intake nurse I saw. "Riffivultly Reathing. Poosivial Covid," I told her before turning tail and running back for the bus. My heels slipped over the backs of my shoes, and one flopped off as I dove in and slammed the doors behind me. "RIVE!" I growled at Cindy.

Cindy turned and her eyes went wide. "Abby! What are you doing?!"

"Rust Rive!" I managed before wolf me broke through.

2

Where's the bad smell? Where'd it go? I thrust my nose into the spot the old man had been and sniffed hard. Earth, sour... sweetness? Whispers of other things I did not know. Dank things. Not enough now. Why did human me not let me sniff? Sniffing is better than seeing. Eyes can't smell the insides. Not enough of it now. Pointless. Pointless like... I looked down at the tattered remains of my clothing, hanging off my body. Pointless like clothing. I busied myself ripping stubborn fabric off me with my teeth.

The ground moved suddenly beneath me, and I staggered against the front seats of the bus and slipped on the smooth floor.

Suddenly Cindy loomed overhead, face contorted as she barked words at me, human me so tired that the meanings came slow. *I'm mad at you. Duty broken! You promised to contain your wolf side; now you're a wolf.*

I tried kissing her to calm her. Right in her open mouth.

Cindy squawked and sprang back over the seats. Secret tittered. I stood, and found her lurking over the edge of the seat. Her eyes glimmered, tail tip twitching once before she pounced-hugged, arms wrapping around my head. She squeezed with love, and little fingers found my ears. Her scent is an orchestra of feline gossamer and human notes, all textured with happy vibrations. "Abby, can we play now?" Fey pup sick of box, too.

Play hunt RUN! In answer, I sprang back with a yes wuff. But my head slammed against the ceiling with a loud bang.

"JEBUS!" Cindy howled, cringing in her seat and covering her head with hands. Her scent was always taut, its notes jumbled, fear swelling under stress as I sniffed at her and wagged my tail. She made squeaky noises and shrank away to the wall-door. I huffed and stomped a paw with frustration. Why did she always act so much like prey? Cindy's my friend, maybe my packmate. Licks only made her squeak with distress. Maybe if I make her a packmate, she'll understand?

Secret pulled my nose away from Cindy. "Abby, play with me!"

Yes, let human me worry about my human friend. "Whuff," I agreed, turned to the back door, and pressed. It didn't open. I backed off and stared at it, prodding human me.

Duty... She whined. *Have to finish duty.*

Behind me, Cindy's sounds snapped into meaning, "-taking an unscheduled break. Need to resupply and decontaminate."

Human me feebly tried to press into our flesh. Not enough of her left to even shift halfway. I pushed her back and sniff at the turny things. Handles. Gentle pawing not move them. Locked. Little thingie, next to handle, has to slide.

"Abby, not here!" Cindy scolded. "Let me get us to the park first."

The floor moved, and I bumped my nose against the back window. The park was good. My territory was better, though. Pup slipped up beside me, hugged my foreleg; even in humanish form, tiny fey pup didn't reach my shoulder. I waited.

"Cliff? Could you bring Abby some spare clothes from her locker? She had an accident." Cindy talked to someone not in the box.

"No, no one's hurt. Just slobbered." She muttered the second bit low. "Yes, I know it's not a full moon yet, it doesn't work like that. Look, I'm going to let her out in Marquam Park, or she'll rip the doors off."

The bus stopped. The locks clicked, and with a swipe of my paw the door opened onto the drizzly night. I bolted out. Heard Secret call. Bolted back. Held still only long enough for Secret to leap onto my shoulders before sprinting off down the path between the trees. Secret shrieked with laughter as my claws bit into the earth below me. Compared to human me's snail pace, we didn't run at all, we flew. The clouds above blocked my goddess' light, but I still felt her pull as the trees blurred around us. "Abby, look out!" Secret warned as we charged down toward a flooded gully. I leapt, but the slick mud slipped beneath my paws. The water erupted around us in a glorious splash as I landed dead center in the massive puddle. The muck grabbed hold of my front paws and I heard a cut-off yowl before momentum plowed my muzzle into the water.

Water flooded into my nostrils as I wrenched myself up. Secret thrashed in the water before me. "Ewww! Wet! Wet! Yucky." She flailed a bit farther away from me and stood.

The water came up to her waist. Huffing and spitting, she crossed her arms and glared with her yellow eyes at me. "You did that on purpose!"

I shook my head, then shook my entire body, forcing her use her arms to block the spray. Then once I licked the mud out of her ears, I knocked her down again, with the flick of my muzzle. She came back hissing, claws appearing at the ends of her fingers.

So began the game. We played hard. She climbed trees and pounced on me from above, trying to nip at my ears while I bit at her ankles and tried buck her off. Once that ended, I let my nose explore. The scents were different on this side of the river. My human side couldn't even stop me from rolling in the best ones. She just kept whispering, *duty, we have to finish our duty.* Over and over. I didn't want to go back, feel her worries, or deal with Cindy's stinky fear. Live here, hunt, play, run, raise pup, grow my pack. But human me whispered of the complexities, human forest, and the scents of her aunts. Not a wolf's world. Not yet.

And duty remained; broken duty was a broken promise. So, with Secret yawning, I headed up toward the spot where Cindy had let us out. The road cut along the side of a hill. A wave of guilt washed over me when I caught sight of the ambulance's boxy roof. I'd known that a full 48-hour shift was going to be a stretch to stay human. To save Secret I'd pledged Luna my heart. There had been no discussion of hours or a contract. When I'd run through the streets on that first hunt, there had been no guarantee that I'd ever be human again. I had accepted that risk.

Standing on all fours at the forest edge, my child sprawled limp across my back, fur plastered with mud, and muscles singing from the exertion, I found there was no human me, and no wolf me. There was only this me. Once I climbed up to the road, there'd be two me's, each pushing for time in our respective worlds. As a wolf, the world was uninhibited, primal, and full of a joyful physicality that I'd never known before. But the wider world remained human, and if I ignored it for the wolf's, then it'd only be a matter of time before I'd be dodging silver bullets.

I dallied for a few more minutes, luxuriating in being a united creature again before setting off up the hill. Then froze, spotting the second car on the trail head pull-off, parked behind the ambulance. A low-slung sports car with a long hood. My mind sputtered for a moment, but a sniff confirmed it. Cliff's car.

"There!" A whisper and a movement drew my eyes back to the ambulance. In its shadow stood two humans, Cliff and Cindy.

Why is Cliff here? Cliff is here! My thoughts broke along two parallel paths as I scrambled up the hill's steep incline. Both of them stood with their backs against the Portland Emergency Services logo.

"Abby?! Holy!" Cliff pressed his tall and broad form against the ambulance.

"Uh, I'm not sure that's-" Cindy quickly stepped into the bus, but I ignored her, my attention focused on Cliff. I'd never smelled him with my wolf nose before.

"What do you mean this isn't Abby?" Cliff gulped as I poked my nose at the sling that contained his right arm. His nervous smile flashed in the dim light. The cast that encased his wounded arm was a rich treasure of scent. The sweaty funk of healing flesh accompanied a sharp tang of stress and something else, a deeper, lower note that I hadn't found before. I sniffed, trying to sort it against my memories, but the only two humans I'd gotten this nose this close to were Cindy and Secret. Never scented it on them.

As I snuffled, Cliff's hand shakily stroked my muzzle, muttering, "Nice werewuff, good werewolf. My, my, how big you are." He lifted his hand away and rubbed his fingers together. "What in the hell is this?"

"Mud!" Secret shifted on my back. "Abby rolled in it! She got me all dirty." The catgirl giggled as she rolled off me.

Cliff blinked and looked down into my eyes. "That's really you, Abby?"

"Whuff," I agreed and licked him from chin to eyebrow.

"Albarg!" He exclaimed in such an amusing way, I did it again. The second time produced a less dramatic "Aaah!" followed by a shielding of his face that deflected the third and fourth. I backed off as he scraped the slobber from his face. His grin reappeared, "Damn, Cindy told me you were a big wolf, but I thought like a big dog," He made vague waving gestures at my length, "not like, a horse or bear? Dang, girl."

Another whiff and I found no fresh fear scent on him. Just the stress tang. A flush of happiness moved my tail as I bowed down to him, inviting him to play. Maybe I could nip him "accidentally" and then... if it worked that way, what sort of wolf would he be?

No! The human me broke off again. *Not without permission!*

But my pack's so small!

He won't want me.

But Cindy cut the debate short, popping out of the bus. "Abby, stop showing off. We still have three hours on the clock. Cliff, give her the clothes."

I whined, but she was right.

Cliff laughed, "Glad somebody can be a hard ass. I'm no

good at it." He went to his car and presented me with a wad of fabric.

I huffed as I took them. They had been folded in my locker.

"Hey, gimmie a break. I've only got one hand right now." He said as I walked back down the hill.

"And you, miss toothy smile, are not getting in this ambulance like that." Cindy scolded Secret.

There was a rustle of fabric. "Merf?"

"Better. At least that's a much smaller pawprint."

Out of Cliff's sight, I shifted. Even with both parts of me in alignment, it was shockingly hard. Visualizing pulling on a human costume limb by limb, my bones crushed themselves into the proper shape. Standing, I brushed the remnants of the filth and mud off my skin. Wolf me still filled every portion of me. Our brief run hadn't been nearly enough. My other half needed more time.

The transformation had knocked most of the dirt off my body, but I still felt plenty of grit beneath my clothes and, worse, in my hair. I really needed a shower.

Cliff waved at me as I picked my way up the trail to the cars. Sadly, my locker did not contain spare shoes. "That sounded like it hurt."

"It did," I croaked, my throat felt sandblasted. "I'm fine, though."

"Good! I guess I'll see you back at the fire station. I might as well start my shift anyway." He flashed me a thumbs up and got back in his car.

I almost asked him for a ride, because I had a sudden bad feeling as my mind replayed the morning's events from a medic's perspective.

"Welcome back to the land of the two-legged," Cindy said when I got into the ambulance. Her tone had me recalling the large door of the principal's office, but it was her scent that had the edge in it. Not like the edge of a knife, more akin to the edge of a plank suspended over a tank filled with hungry sharks. I hadn't expected my first encounter with the scent of fury to be Cindy's.

"Jebus Christ, Abby! What the hell was that? You promised me you had it together tonight! I even asked you before we took that call. Then you made me do a runner! Dropping off a patient like we were gangsters after a gun fight. What the flipping fuck am I going to say to that?"

Don't growl, I told myself as I tried to explain. "I had it covered, but there was a scent. A really weird scent."

"You did not have it covered!" Abby slammed a fist on the dashboard. "You didn't get any of his info. Didn't fill out his paperwork. I should have been lead, but I was afraid you'd drive off the road chasing after a squirrel!"

"I wou-"

She cut me off. "Sloppy! You've been sloppy both nights! Worse than that, you stare off into space, sniffing at the air. I've watched you!"

The past 48 hours replayed through my mind as hot spiders crawled up my neck and fought their way across my cheeks. I couldn't refute her point.

"The Abby I know is methodical, organized, and fast on her feet. Now you're like an ADHD probie! We're both lucky we didn't run into anything life or death tonight." Cindy stared straight at the road ahead, not looking at me as she listed every small way I had fucked up in the last 48 hours. Little things: putting the needles back in the wrong spot, forgetting to fill out paperwork, zoning out, getting distracted by a smell. One or two happened to everyone, but not that many things, not to me. "Sloppy," she called me. I'm a lot of things, but never sloppy on the job. The word was a barb of ice through my heart. Tears were leaking from my eyes as we pulled into the station.

Silence reigned as we drove into the harsh light of the garage. Cindy rolled us up to the resupply cabinets, took a long breath, and wiped her eyes. "I don't know how to say this gently," she said.

I gave a little laugh of desperation, "Don't hold back on my account." The wolf wanted to run, urging me to open the door and leave this behind. Secret had crept into my lap during the tirade, and I stroked her now-bristling fur with the back of my sweating fingers.

"Abby, you're not the same person who left the hospital that night." Cindy said.

I laughed loudly, forcing it to stop the indignant growl. "Well, I'm a werewolf now! That's a minor difference."

"That's not what I'm talking about!" Cindy's voice wavered and broke. "We're not talking about when you're that giant monster! It's when you're human!"

"She's not a monster! She hasn't hurt anyone!" I snapped back.

"That you've told me about!" Cindy closed her eyes, squeezing the steering wheel so tightly that the vinyl squirked in protest. "What do you do when you slip out the back door after I go to bed? Hunt squirrels?"

Sometimes, but they were fast little buggers and even

large wolves don't climb trees very well. "I don't hunt humans, if that's what you're asking." I struggled to keep my voice level even as my teeth sharpened.

"Don't say human as if people are a separate species!"

I let the growl out. It was that or sprout claws. "I'm not human, Cindy. I'm never human anymore. The wolf's always there. What are you trying to say, Cindy? That I can't be a paramedic because I happen to be a werewolf now?!"

She flinched. "You need to get your focus back before I go back out with you."

Before I could protest, she opened the door and exited the cab of the ambulance. "Cindy!" I shouted.

She slammed the door.

"Fuck!" I swore, striking my armrest with a fist. Outside, Cindy threw opened the supply cabinet with enough force that it wobbled. Secret gave a sympathetic growl of her own, her puffy tail standing straight up. My own hand started to drift toward my door latch. Instead of opening it, I scooped up Secret and hugged her to my chest.

"Merf!" Secret protested the treatment but endured the squeeze as the wolf slowly relaxed inside me.

Pup safe, run soon. The thought was both mine and the wolf's, that was what mattered. I leaned back in my seat as a realization dawned. There was always part of me watching for threats to Secret, afraid that monsters from the Dream would rear up out of the night. What if that was costing me my focus? Nonsense, there were plenty of paramedics that were parents. Although most didn't take their kids on the bus.

I let Secret relax into the cradle of my arms. "Cindy's still adjusting," I told her. "It's our first shift since all this happened. We'll do better next time."

Secret slow-blinked.

"Glad you agree," I said.

My phone buzzed. I shifted Secret to one arm and checked it. "Do you ever sleep, Victoria?" I asked the surrounding air when I saw the message of her text:

"So how's werewolf life tonight? You okay?"

I almost didn't respond but scrolling revealed I'd ignored several previous texts from her. Since that Christmas dinner, Victoria had been texting me at least once a day. Friendly banalities usually, invitations sometimes for drinks. I found myself torn every time. She fought for us, Secret and me, but I wasn't sure I could really trust the Necromancer of Portland. This time I typed: "It's hard. Cindy just doesn't understand." Then I deleted it and told Victoria I was fine, and I had to finish my shift.

Not waiting for a reply, I stepped out of the bus. Cliff stepped into the bay through the office door and waved. Cindy was putting sheets on a fresh stretcher and pointedly not looking in my direction. I didn't see anyone else; the off-shift crew were still sleeping, I supposed. Returning the wave, I lifted Secret to my shoulder and ran a hand through my hair, grimacing when I found it crusty. I pondered whether helping Cindy would be appreciated or if it would be better to just leave her alone and take a shower. Cliff approached, and the wolf tensed within me.

"Fancy seeing you two so early in the morning," He winked. "Figured I'd come in early before my sister shows up. Get some peace and quiet before the storm hits."

I flashed him my own smile, "Your sister's a storm?"

"Yeaaah." His grin turned into a wince. "She says she's going to help me manage NLR. You'll get to meet her on your next shift. You two going back out?"

Cindy stopped moving long enough to shoot me a glare.

I sighed, "No, I'm clocking out, I need more... Time out,

there." I sort of waved in the general direction of the exit door.

"Cool, cool. No worries. I'll mark MICU-42 as down for maintenance for a few hours." Cliff said.

I heard a soft thump from where Cindy busied herself. "You can't do that!" She hissed.

Cliff shrugged, "Sure I can. I did it for you a few times, remember?"

"That's different!" Cindy huffed.

A sly grin spread across his face as he mimed straightening his shirt, "That's right, it is different. I'm the boss. I can't even get in trouble for it."

"But that's why you can't do it!" Cindy protested, sheer shock on her face, before looking around as if someone might appear in the bay. "It's not fair."

The grin compressed to a tense expression, "I'm not my dad, Cindy," he said while wearing an expression that recalled the elder Gifford. "I'm not going to dock you three hours' pay because of... uh, moon issues." The grin sprang back as he refocused on me. "You still good for your next shift?"

"Uh... I hope so." I said, "48 hours could still be long for me. I'm at my limit here."

"Do your bunk time off base or something. We'll make it work." He nodded.

"Won't people talk?" I asked.

"Let them." He laughed, "Or maul them. Either way works." His eyes flicked over in Cindy's direction; she looked as if she might burst. "I'm kidding, Col-I mean, Cindy, nobody's mauling anyone. Except perhaps my sister Sophie will maul me when she sees the state of the accounting when she gets here." He turned with a sigh, heading back toward the office. He paused at the door. "You're both coming to see the old man off, right?"

The funeral for George Gifford, Cliff's Dad, had been delayed once already because the police classed the body as evidence and were reluctant to release it. Gloria, Cliff's mother, fought a media war to get it back. They'd rescheduled it for the day after the full moon.

"We'll be there," I promised, and Cliff disappeared into in the office with a wave.

Cindy continued to root through the cabinet, pawing aimlessly through the supplies. I paused, watching her before asking, "Are we okay?"

She didn't turn around, "I shouldn't be angry at you. He should be angry at you for me."

I didn't know what to say to that, so I backed away. "I'll see you at home."

I received a curt nod in reply and that's all I needed to take Secret and flee the building.

Morning came before I was ready for my human to come back out. Still, responsibility and a sense of duty compelled me to stand back on two legs, but that stretching sensation of my skin remained. I pondered that as I followed my nose to a parking lot full of food trucks. Clearly, I still had more wolf time ahead of me. Would I have to spend two days in the woods after every shift? Or was wolf me simply unsatisfied with napping on all fours and I needed to get off my tail and hunt to make her happy? On the edge of the lot, I hesitated to enter it because of the sensation of a heavy gaze settling on my back. Stepping to the side, I glanced behind me, searching out the source of the discomfort. Plastered on a billboard, Andrew Millar, the billionaire who seemed to be buying half the city, smiled down on me with a patronizing smile that I'm sure the photographer assured him was grandfatherly. His wrinkled visage had been popping up all over the city in the weeks since I'd returned from the Dream, in some sort of strange PR campaign. "You can't take it with you, so today I'm building Portland's Future!" He declared via speech bubble; this image presided over a half-constructed apartment building. Awfully happy for a man riddled with cancer.

"I'm hungry!" Secret reminded me and tugged me toward the cluster of brightly colored trucks. I turned my back on the billionaire to introduce Secret to the magical culinary travesty that is the sushi burrito. Following a meow of surprise that came with her first bite, "Tuna!" she exclaimed and inhaled the rest of it with a joy that she usually reserved for hot chocolate, licking at her black-furred fingers after the last scrap of it had disappeared. A brisket sandwich stilled my own inner rumblings, but the wolf dreamed of far fresher fare. A bus ride later and we were almost back at the station, where I had parked my car.

I plopped my butt into the driver's seat, started the engine, and sat there for a moment drumming my hands on the wheel. Cindy's disappointed voice echoed. Glancing up at the firehouse, I considered going in and bugging Cliff, but he probably had his own issues with his sister. Still, I didn't want to go home to Cindy. Knowing I would probably regret it, I started the car moving, but not towards the river. I headed to Victoria's house.

4

Victoria had company already; a black limo idled on her circular driveway. Had I seen it before I had committed to the turn, I would have simply driven on, but the ivy-covered wall and the fountain had conspired against me. It wasn't one of those fuck you I'm rich stretch Teslas or hummers, it stood perhaps only a few feet longer than Victoria's hearse, which is an expensive station wagon for corpses. I'm sure it screamed money in terms I wasn't equipped to hear; Cliff would probably wolf whistle at its sleek black paneling and the gleaming rims. Its sheer elegance contrasted to the chaos of construction that had engulfed Victoria's manor.

When Little Nick had avoided our honeyed trap by siccing the Portland SWAT team on us, they'd proved that the old house was no fortress. Bullets had ripped through walls and windows alike. The facade was a mess of blue tarps and naked plywood. The three-story Victorian structure gave the appearance of a patient who'd gotten his teeth kicked in and was now mid-plastic surgery. Meanwhile, the fountain in the center of the circular driveway sported a new sculpture, a winged angel strangling a skeleton, water fountaining from the skull's eyes and the angel's ears. Piles of construction materials flanked both sides of the driveway.

I considered backing right out the way we came, but decided I was being silly. Andrew Millar was far too important to pay attention to unhinged Internet rants that outed a local EMT as a werewolf. He probably wouldn't remember me anyway. I parked close enough to make his driver nervous about the paint on his bumper when Secret piped up, "Why are we here?"

"We're visiting Victoria; you should probably stay in cat form until her guest leaves." I said, offering my hand toward her.

Secret frowned up at the house, her ears flattening "But she's kind of a meanie and smells bad."

Oof, this might go smoother if Secret didn't talk. "Do you want to stay here?" I asked her.

In answer a light force shoved my gaze off her face and by the time I looked back a small black kitten leapt up into my hand. I tucked her into my jacket, so she wasn't entirely obvious and stepped out into the morning gray. Nothing stirred as I made my way up the steps to the white front door that still had stickers in its windows. No doorbell. I reached out my hand to knock and then paused as I heard voices beyond the door.

"I'm not interested in drooling zombies, Victoria." The harsh rasp of Andrew Millar's voice sounded from within the house. "Cheap labor won't cure my cancer."

Victoria's response was too muffled to make out, but Andrew barked a laugh.

"True, but the clock ticks too swiftly for half measures. Since the vampire hasn't been cooperative, that leaves us only one option."

"I can't test that one," Victoria grumbled, her voice coming closer. "It's too risky."

"There are no other options; you will perform that ritual when I pass," answered Andrew.

I knocked, feeling that if I didn't, they'd realize I'd been eavesdropping.

"Who the hell is that? You sent everyone away." I heard the heavy thump of a cane striding towards me over hollow flooring, followed swiftly by the striking of heels.

Victoria beat him to the door and cracked it open. She flinched in surprise, "Abby?" my name coming out in a squeak before she schooled her features into a soft smile. "What are you doing here?"

"Oh, finally on this side of the river, figured I'd swing by." I kept my voice light, a neighbor borrowing a cup of sugar or a wheelbarrow.

"I'll be right with you-"

"-open the damn door, Victoria." Andrew huffed behind her.

Red lips pressed together as she pulled open the door to reveal the billionaire. Braced with both hands on his cane, he peered down at me with piercing eyes set in a face that sagged from his skull. The flesh around those eyes drooped so much that pale pink peeked between the lower eyelid and the white of his eyeballs, like a blood hound's. "Abigale, good to see you again," he rasped, and even standing three feet away, his fetid breath reached me.

Sick! Wolf me hissed with alarm, and combined with my human shock at seeing his decline in the space of a few weeks, I stepped back.

"You, too." I nodded and continued moving so I didn't block the door.

Andrew thumped his way out onto the hastily

constructed porch but didn't continue down the stairs, instead rounding on me. "So, you're a werewolf now. What does that entail?"

I shot an accusatory glare at Victoria as she peeked out of the doorway. She gave a quick shake of her head.

"Oh, she's not to blame. In fact, she's frustratingly closed-mouthed about you, Abigale." He gestured to the surrounding construction. "Wouldn't even admit you were here for this, until I confronted her with the ambulance records."

"I see." There's no legal way for him to get those, but when you own the health care system, privacy rules don't count for much. I crossed my arms, protecting the bulge that was Secret huddled inside my jacket. "It was a harrowing night. I'd rather not talk about it."

He smiled, "You were wounded by a knife, not a police weapon. The knife of the Santa killer. It bisected your iliotibial tract and biceps femoris. Now, less than two weeks later, you don't even have a limp. Combined with facts pointed out in a video by a certain Slade the Ghost Hunter, it's hard to dismiss his hypothesis. With or without Miss Quentin's corroboration."

My stomach twisted as I waited for him to stop his pontificating. He'd pulled my medical records, violating all sorts of privacy laws like so much tissue paper. Now eagerness shone in his cancer-ridden face, like a boy who wanted a cookie for being clever. "So?" I asked him.

Those sagging eyes blinked slowly. "So... There's no need to deny it. I know." Anger trembled in his voice, and he visibly swallowed it down. "Miss Night, be reasonable here. I don't understand the details of your condition, but think of all the good we could do if we understood the mechanics of it." Zeal shone out from him, and those eyes looked straight through me. "All the diseases that could be cured with my resources. You could be the catalyst to a medical revolution!"

"No." I said with firmness.

He refocused that zeal on me, "I could compensate you very well. Do you like Victoria's house here? You could get one bigger. Replace that little car of yours. Think of all the people you could help."

"Like you?" The words escaped my mouth and wolf me pressed up against the inside of my skull, snarling.

Andrew's smile faltered. "Well, if progress was rapid enough, then I would see no reason not to sample the fruits of my labor."

"No." I said, managing to reign in my anger.

His boney hands tightened on the top of his cane. "Why?" The word half strangled.

Oh, there were reasons. I had plenty to choose from: the casual violation of my privacy, the idea of being a test subject, but the truth of it was, it wouldn't work. It'd be a total waste of time. A bone-deep certainty chimed within me. Luna would never allow her gift to be industrialized, and to attempt it would invite her wrath. I stared back into his eyes and said, "Because I can't help you."

His lip curled. "I hope for your sake you believe that."

I braced myself for a torrent of angry words and threats, but he turned instead and thumped heavily down the steps to where his chauffeur helped him into the rear of the limo.

After he drove off, I found Victoria staring at me as she leaned against the door frame, almost bracing against it. She answered my questioning look with a rueful smile. "I'm in awe of both your timing and your diplomatic skills. I hadn't seen him in days, and you show up in the one half hour he's here. Come on in, I'll introduce you to Gerald."

"Do you think he'll do something to me?" I asked her as

I followed her into the house. Inside, the construction appeared to be further along. The plush carpets were gone, exposing unfinished replacement planks.

"Maybe. Not a lot of people have the balls to tell a dying billionaire no. I sure as hell don't." She laughed, and it echoed as we walked around the grand staircase towards the kitchen. "Surprised he didn't demand you turn him into a werewolf on the spot." I caught a whiff of perfume beneath a harsh embalming chemical scent that trailed in her wake, a pleasant dusky musk.

"I have no idea how to make another werewolf," I said, although wolf me definitely had ideas on the subject. "I doubt it's like the movies and even if it is, I guarantee he wouldn't survive a mauling." Secret struggled, and I zipped down my jacket so she could poke her head out.

She gave a little hiss as we entered the kitchen. A zombie stood by the stove staring down at the blue gas flame of a lit burner with nothing on it. His sallow gray flesh contrasted with the pristine whites of the chef's uniform he wore, down to the floppy hat.

"Gerald!" Victoria barked at the zombie, "Turn that off."

The zombie emitted a grumpy groan and kept his slack expression fixed on the flame.

"Yes, I know he was rude, but that's no excuse to light yourself on fire. Why don't you make me and Abby a pair of Bloody Marys." Victoria touched a silver cross hanging from her neck as she spoke with the bright tone of a kindergarten teacher.

"Hrrrrrrm." Gerald moaned contemplatively before switching off the burner and moving towards the fridge.

"Gerald died of smoke inhalation," Victoria whispered conspiratorially to me and Secret, "He's got a thing about fire." She took a seat at the breakfast bar, and I noted that several fire extinguishers had been added to the decor. "But he's a superb cook when he's not being sullen."

"And here I was angry at Andrew for stealing my medical records." I huffed and sat down next to her, wondering why I was here.

"It's consensual!" Victoria protested. "They don't have to take the blood if they don't want to."

"Merf!" Secret disagreed, stepping out onto the counter and lifting her nose.

"It's not a real person. It's a ghost, just a shard." Victoria observed Gerald as he gathered ingredients for the drinks, sitting stiffly in her black sheath dress, looking even more sculpted than usual. Long black hair shone in a tight bun and lightened skin gave her a delicate appearance, compared to her usual rough and tumble goth style. "Hey, easy on the vodka, Gerald. I don't need a hangover for lunch." Rolling her eyes, she turned towards me, and our gaze met briefly, but she swiftly dropped it. Giving a little sigh, she turned back to the zombie chef, "So why you here if I'm still chopped liver?"

"I didn't-" I started but cut myself off with a sigh of my own. "I'm sorry. Cindy and I had a fight. Well, more that; I fucked up and I don't want to head home yet. Sooo... hi." I wondered how much be it be safe to tell her.

"Right, I'm backup girlfriend." She gave a nervous laugh, almost a giggle. "I guess I can handle that. Better than one-word texts; beats waking up at 3 AM wondering why I'm crying."

Three AM? That would have been when Cindy chewed me out. I winced, "The link..."

"Still there. Got a bit muffled when you went to the Dream but if something hurts you, I feel it. I've gotten better at saying, wait no, that's Abby, not me." She shrugged, "Cost of being alive. So, what happened?"

With a heavy clink, Gerald set two Bloody Marys in front of us, each with a slice of bacon. Secret, who'd been washing herself in a typical feline manner, scrambled across the counter and dove into my lap. Now safe, she came up puffy and baring her teeth. Laughing, I stroked her head and picked up the tall glass. Gerald cocked his head; his eyes were milky and stared off in the wrong direction, but I felt his attention, nevertheless. A sniff didn't detect any embalming fluid or stray fingers, so I took a sip. Bloody Marys have never been my favs, but I've drunk a fair few of them due to Aunt Sheryl's brunch habit, and this wasn't bad. "Turns out it's hard to be a paramedic when you're a werewolf," I started, and told Victoria the whole story about my disaster of a shift.

She nodded along and sipped her Bloody Mary. We had a brief intermission when Gerald lit the burner again and used his index finger as a candle. After Victoria banished him to the basement, where I assume there were no open flames, I finished the story and ended with the question, "What if she's right? What if I'm not the same person I was?"

Drink long empty, Victoria pulled her vape stick from somewhere and took a long drag. The smoke made me cough. "Well, if it's any help, you're still an idiot. Saying yes to a Fey's right up there with antagonizing a billionaire," she said with a grin.

"Oh, fuck you." I flipped her off with a chuckle.

Unconcerned, she took another drag, blowing out a ring into the kitchen. "I'm serious. Dead don't change, the living do. I'm not the little girl hunting the ghost of my parents anymore. You're not defined as Jimmy's weird girlfriend anymore."

"Aww, I haven't even thought much about Jimmy since…" I trailed off, thinking. The haunting nasal voice that had bounced around my head for ten years had been much quieter since, well, my hand tightened on Secret and scritched her ears.

"And good riddance, right? Sounds like wolf you gave him the heave-ho from your head. Does she contract? I've got a voice or two that could be pitched out of my skull."

I groaned with frustration. "I have to be able to do my job! What if I needed that… guilt to be a good medic?"

Victoria snorted, "Get a new job. Or don't." A smile quirked the corners of her mouth and her eyes brightened as if something had suddenly occurred to her. "Ya know," She swirled the ice in her glass, "Whether or not this living Pharaoh ritual works out for Andrew Millar, I'm going be pretty set for a bit. I could float ya if you want to go back to school or something."

My brain froze, and I stared at Victoria, my thoughts spinning like an ambulance on black ice. She didn't look back, keeping her eyes on her ice, almost demurely. First, what the hell was a living Pharaoh ritual? And… did she really just flat-out offer to pay for college? Real college? Who does that? The air in the room suddenly felt warm. Shaking my head hard enough to make my brain slosh, I stood up. "I'm a medic." I declared firmly. "It's what I do, Vicky. I don't want to be anything else."

Victoria found her nails very interesting. "Okay, just thinking out loud."

I found the alcohol heating my ears and that strange perfume of hers had the tang of anxiety in it.

"Sorry. Thanks for the talk and the drink." I apologized without understanding why, picked up Secret and drifted towards the door.

I got nearly out of the house before Victoria said, "Hey, Abs." She peered at me from the side of the staircase. "Let me know how it goes with Cindy, right? If you need a place to stay..." She gestured at the upstairs which I knew contained over half a dozen bedrooms.

Wolf me stirred, *not in our territory. Stay in territory.*

"Thanks, I'll keep it in mind." With a wave, I stepped out of the house that would probably house my entire extended family, yet was only home to one Necromancer and however many zombies. Was she lonely? I wondered as I got in my car and drove to face another woman in my life.

5

"You missed it again." Secret observed as we rolled past Cindy's house for the third time. A large two-story house that had somehow grown out of the back of a craftsman cottage. Cindy's little blue Ford hadn't budged. She had to be up by now; surely she'd go out to the grocery store or something soon.

"I'm just looking for a good place to park." I mumbled.

"There's one!" Secret pointed her finger as a car eased out from the curb ahead.

"Yep. You're right." I admitted and slid us into the slot as my internal organs wrestled with one another. *Stop being silly,* I chided myself. She wasn't going to bite my head off... Again.

Sloppy, the word taunted me, this time in Jimmy's voice. *So sloppy, Abby.*

I imagined Jimmy's face being punched in by a hulking werewolf fist and immediately felt better. At least enough to brave the walkway up to the house. "Cindy? Rey?" I called out as we entered the house's atrium, themed with fan art of transgender Link marrying Zelda.

"Welcome home!" Rey appeared in the doorway that led to the kitchen, a petite woman with fox ears and three large fox tails sweeping behind her. Her fur had dulled to an almost yellow orange, a telltale sign that the Fox Fey needed feeding, aka being worshipped. Rey served as my tutor in all things that involved the home of the Fey, the Dream. Although since rescuing Secret from the court of Winter, she hadn't had much occasion to teach me anything. Instead, she'd become that housemate that you could never quite trust and was a bit crazy. "Sandwiches on the table if you're hungry."

"We ate," I said.

"Tuna fish sandwiches?" Secret ducked under Rey's tails as she bolted into the kitchen. Little glutton, maybe she was about to have a growth spurt?

"Where's Cindy?" I couldn't help asking.

Rey's tails stilled for a half second before resuming their cloudlike movement. "Doing some repairs downstairs."

What the heck was in the basement? Not that I'd ever been down there myself, but Rey's hesitation had me curious. "Thanks." I turned to walk down the hallway towards the basement door, but Rey flowed out in front of me, barring my way with both arms and tails.

"She's upset with you. Talking to her right now isn't a good idea. You should wait until she comes up on her own." Rey glared as if it were completely my fault.

I pushed past her with a growl. Rey got more possessive of Cindy by the day. Cindy was my packmate too, and I would not let the Fey control access to her.

Down a set of rickety stairs, I found Cindy kneeling in the harsh white light of a halogen work lamp. She held a trowel with a glob of cement on the blade. Behind her stood an unfinished cinder block wall; she was working on the third row. The wall formed a perfect square in the basement's corner, with a gap in the second row of cinderblocks for a door of some type. *Cage.* Wolf me and my heart leaped up into my throat. Instead of a greeting, the words that came out of my mouth were, "Cindy, what the fuck are you doing?" with a hysterical crack to my voice.

"Aah" In the light Cindy went beet red. "Just been thinking about, uh." She trailed off.

Cage, growled wolf me.

"About what?!" I roared, claws ripped through my fingertips, and my clothing tightened around my body.

Cindy kept her eyes on the bucket of cement. She knelt on a blue foam pad, in her house dress, long blond wig tied in a ponytail. "I-I just thought, maybe, i-in case with the moon tomorrow."

I growled long and low, "You're planning on putting me in a CAGE?!" The wolf surged through my limbs, wanting to seize Cindy by the scruff of her neck and shake her. My human half fought her and lost.

"Ah-" Cindy whimpered.

Grabbing her by her shoulders, I slammed her into the wall and held her there.

"Ow!" Cindy winced, squeezing her eyes shut. "W-what if you need it?"

I reached for words but all that came was that deep threatening rumble. She whimpered. My body pressed close to her; the black nose of my partially extended muzzle pressed to the side of her neck. Her pulse raced beneath it. "No cage." I ground out. Every pore on her skin smelled of terror. I was so tired of living with that smell.

She nodded minutely.

I backed off a few inches, and quick as a lightning strike, softness enveloped my entire body. My vision blurred with pastels of red and black. It parted. Dainty fingers gently caressed my face, soft and warm. Slitted golden eyes appeared: Rey's eyes. I remembered back to the time when I had been clever as her, when I had been her, swathed in impossibly soft fur. I hadn't appreciated just how lovely it had been.

"Oooh, is the big bad wolf angry?" Her patronizing tone caused my anger to flicker but a pulse of warmth smoothed it away. "Relax, wolfie," she purred, kissing me on the nose. I toppled back into a warm sea of cloudlike fur and became lost.

"...there, love, I'm here. Everything is alright." Rey's voice smoothed through the darkness. The absence of her softness creating the first chill through me since I gave a piece of my heart to winter.

"You were supposed to warn me," Cindy said with trembling breathlessness. I opened my eyes to find myself on my knees on the bare concrete of the floor. Rey hugged Cindy, bearing her weight while curling her tails tightly around Cindy's torso.

"Turns out I'm a lousy lookout." Rey kissed her cheek, causing Cindy to release a shivering sigh. After stroking Cindy's cheek Rey turned towards me. "And what do you have to say for yourself, Miss Abby? Attacking poor Cindy as if she were a mouse stealing your dinner."

"I-" The protest died on my tongue. I had attacked her. My wolf probably wouldn't have hurt her but... shame and guilt rolled my guts up into a twisted knot. I tasted bile.

No cage. Wolf me stood firm in my mind, utterly unapologetic.

And from deep in my soul, I heard Jimmy sing, *just like me!* Of course he hadn't gone away.

"Sorry, Cindy." I gasped for air. The basement tasted too

stale. Wolf surged into my limbs, straining to get away from even the concept of being caged. I had to get out of here. Lurching to my feet, I dashed up the stairway and shed my clothing enroute to the back door. Bursting naked into the yard I let go, letting wolf me take over everything. Heedless of the daylight, my world became scents and sound. My paws dashed me from cover to cover until I breathed in more pine than asphalt. Overhead the trees sang with the birds' alarms and the muddy ground squelched beneath me.

I don't need her. I told myself, shoving human me away as she screamed out her impotent hurt that blurred my vision with tears. Only my whiskers prevented me from slamming into the brown blurs that were trees. *Just run. Away from the cage.* It hadn't been surprising that Andrew Millar had wanted to buy me but to see Cindy build... that. A root reached up and snared a paw. I stumbled and the blurry world spun around me as my speed carried me down a hill. I yelped as rocks and roots thumped my hide until the roll stopped at the bottom of the hill. Lying there, belly up, throat bared to the world as I panted, my tongue hanging uselessly out of the side of my mouth.

No one padded over the hill crest, no black noses poked at my belly, nor did anyone gently mouth my muzzle for being silly or dramatic. I had no wolves. My humans would never find me here if I were truly injured. I needed wolves. Would Cliff make a good wolf? At least he hadn't stunk of fear. Without getting up, I howled of my loneliness, lifting my head only to let it fall back onto the soggy earth. Luna had clearly made a mistake in choosing me for her first wolf.

Get up, human me said, hanging haggard in my mind, swirling with all her stupid doubt and guilt. So much of it that even I couldn't escape it.

I growled at her, *go away.*

Can't. Besides, I was here first. She reached for control, and I pushed her back. Easy. I was strong, and she was weak. It was unfair that she made my heart ache so, made everything complicated. Cliff would make a good wolf, good pack, maybe even mate, and she stopped me.

We don't know how, she countered, *and we need permission.*

Huffing at myself, I rolled up onto my paws and shook. Had to go back, if only for the Fey cub. Stupid Rey, I wouldn't have hurt Cindy. Make her understand.

We hurt Cindy. Walls are hard, human me said. *We screwed up... again.*

I growled at human me and dragged in the sodden winter air in through my nose, feeling the texture of my surroundings. Then sagged, as I realized I hadn't even run that far. In trying to avoid civilization I'd run in a circle. I can't even run away from my problems right. Human me's problems, I amended.

Stop sulking and let's try to apologize. Human me said. *Then... maybe take Victoria up on her offer.*

Wolves do not sulk! To show her how wrong she was I went hunting, but she remained a stubborn weight. Only got a very skinny rabbit. As the winter sun retreated over the mountains, I relented and strayed into the asphalt-crusted wasteland that was the majority of my territory. Human me crept back into my heart, filling me with a resolve to pack my and Secret's things and find a new place to stay. One more bridge burned, I thought as I pushed myself back onto two legs in Cindy's grassy backyard. Secret pounced me before I reached the door.

"Abby!" She jumped up into my arms, her weight stag-gering my naked body against the door frame. "Where'd you go? You ran out without me!" Her wilted ears and tiny pout made my chest melt. At least I had her.

Grunting, I managed to transfer her weight to one arm, and ruffled her ears. "Sorry kiddo, I had to go for a run."

She smiled with the physical affection but as soon as I stopped, her expression sobered. "Are you and Aunt Cindy fighting?" she asked, "Are we going to move?"

"Yes, and I don't know yet. Let me get some clothes on," I told her. She nodded, twisted out of my grasp, and landed on the floor without a sound.

"Cindy's still in the basement," she said as she followed me up to our room. I considered simply going to bed, but no fatigue pulled at me and wolf me felt smaller than she had in a week.

If we had to talk, it'd be best if we did it now. For me, at least. Cindy might not be in any shape for conversation. I didn't know how she handled situations like this. After getting dressed, I went down to the kitchen, hoping Rey would be there and I could use her as an intermediary. No such luck. I went to the basement door and spotted a small shadow following me. Secret wasn't much for bedtime, either. Opening the door, I got a rather heady mix of gossamer fox musk, sex, and cement. I'd known that they'd been involved since I'd gotten back with Secret, but I smelled it for the first time standing there trying to dredge up courage. My thoughts slipped sideways, worry for Cindy; sleeping with a Fey probably wasn't good for you, but I had made Rey promise not to feed on Cindy. So, she should be safe. I trusted that the relationship was truly mutual and not glamor-induced. Can a Fey have a "normal" relationship with a human?

I shook the thoughts away. Cindy was an adult, and she knew what Rey was. She'd have to make her own decisions just like I had to make mine. Taking a deep breath, I called down the stairs, "Cindy?! Can we talk?" A mental image of mother calling those words through my bedroom door flashed though my head.

I heard whispers in the depths before a heavy and tired, "Yeah," answered me.

* * *

"I'm thinking of moving out. It might be best for everyone," I said after I had made coffee and joined Cindy at the kitchen table. Rey sat next to her, at least one tail wrapped protectively around her waist.

"No!" Secret whined from the doorway. "We just got here."

I smiled as she scooted to my side. "Secret, it's not your fault."

"Why would it be my fault?" Secret's head tilted before she launched herself into my lap. "I'm cute and blameless," she declared before looking toward Cindy, whose stony expression had cracked into a wry smile. "Therefore! You should let us stay!" As she declared it her body tensed, and the gossamer part of her scent flooded my nostrils.

Shit! I reached under her skirt, grabbed her tail, and gave it a hard yank. "No," I hissed in her ear.

She jumped, "Owwies!" and collapsed against me. Peering up at me, her pudgy face looked wan and tired. "Lemme help." Her voice pitching to a whine.

"We don't glamor our friends." Summoning the same firm tone as my mother. Hopefully it worked better on Secret than it did on me.

"We just slam them into walls?" Cindy asked in a bitter tone as Secret slumped against me.

"Apparently, the wolf really objects to cages. It set me off. That's never happened before, Cindy, but-"

Rey cut me off, "You leapt to conclusions, a room in the basement could be a uh, laundry room or a new bathroom. Or..." Cindy placed her large hand over Rey's, and the Fox Fey trailed off.

"It is a cell." Cindy said. "I thought... after you lost it with a patient last night, it might be a good idea with the full moon tomorrow."

Every follicle on my scalp and head drew tight. The wolf inside me scrabbled for a way to express her displeasure. I pushed her down and held Secret tighter. "That is a bad idea. Besides, the moon is practically full right now and I'm not ripping through the neighborhood."

"We don't know that, Abby," Cindy said, squeezing Rey's hand hard enough to make her ears lower in a half wince.

"You're scared of me. I get it." I chewed on my cheek. "She still wasn't trying to hurt you. Just clarify that... Friends don't put friends in cages."

"Even if they're a danger to themselves and others?" Cindy countered.

Clearly, I would not win this battle. After screwing up in the ambulance, and then tossing her against the wall, I'd used up all my trust-me credit with Cindy. With a sigh of defeat, I slipped off the barstool. "I'll go pack my things. Go find a hotel that takes dogs."

"Waaait," Rey said. "I don't want to split my time between work and pleasure. Surely we can come to an agreement... A promise, if you will?"

I sighed, "I don't see how? Cindy wants me to spend the full moon in a cell! I can't tell you why, but it's a horrible idea. It won't end well."

"What if it's not the entire night?" Rey asked, "Just prove

you're not a rampaging monster and Cindy will let you out. Last five minutes."

But what if I am a rampaging monster? What if that's what Luna wants me to be? It was a horrible thought. The winter queen had warned me of Luna's insanity; if there would be a night when it manifests, it would be tomorrow. Five minutes. Surely wolf me could keep it together for five minutes?

Wolf me howled in protest. *Cage bad. Cage bad!*

The words "fuck it" were on my lips; Secret and I would find a place where we could just be. Then I made the mistake of looking down into her big eyes. Before she'd come to me, she'd spent the last three months being fought over by the Fey. Did I really want to uproot her again because I refused to stay still for five minutes? I'd have the rest of the ten-hour night to do whatever Luna intended me to do. I had no idea what my Goddess would require, but my bones knew that lounging around the house wouldn't be an option. "Fine. I'll do it if we can stay."

Rey leaned close to Cindy, "How's that? She's trying."

Cindy wet her lips and lifted her hands, grasping at the air as if she could pull something from it. "Alright." Then rubbed her eyes with her palms. "I'm just tired, Abby. I keep waiting for the normal world to come back, but it doesn't. You're not the same. You stand too close; you stare everyone down when you talk. Once in a while, we'll have a normal conversation and I get my hopes up. Then the next moment, you're a bear-sized wolf in the middle of the living room with teeth the size of my fingers. Every time I see them, my heart tries to leave my chest. I'm a coward, I know. I don't want you to leave, Abby, I just wish it could go back to normal."

Rey reached over and gently pulled one of Cindy's hands

from her face as I blinked away tears. Cindy looked up at Rey as she pressed Cindy's hand between her breasts. "I'm not part of normal, either." Rey whispered.

"I'm aware." Cindy hooked her fingers on Rey's kimono and pulled her into a kiss. The kitsune's eyes widened in surprise at first, then slowly closed as the kiss deepened.

"Merf." Secret commented softly.

Cindy twisted away first, leaving them both panting. "Don't think I don't know how sharp your teeth are, foxy," she whispered.

To which Rey held the back of hand to her forehead and performed a mock swoon onto the top of the table. "Oh, the drama! The stomach-gnawing tension! I cannot take it anymore. You'll have to take me dancing now."

Everyone laughed along with her yipping chortle.

It should've broken the tension, should have relaxed the spring that was coiling inside me. A memory of the echoing sound of bars slamming; I'd spent a single night in lockup when the police considered charging me as an accessory to Jimmy's crimes. It had been hard enough then. Five minutes might be impossible to endure now, but a promise is not something you wanted to break with Rey around.

The evening passed; I probably would have zoned out watching a show but Secret, miffed I'd gone running without her, wanted my undivided attention. Her choice of amusement for the evening was Jenga, which I usually won, if only because Secret played to make the loudest crash when the tower of blocks fell over.

6

My eyes opened, and I was awake. Completely, totally awake. Not the usual groggy, resentfully awake state of most emergency workers whose bodies drag their minds through get-ready-for-work routines without a conscious thought. Nor the adrenaline-soaked, heart-thundering panic of a city-wide mobilization order. One moment I was asleep, chasing something through my dream, and the next I sat up in bed, head buzzing like a kid on Christmas morning. A rare moment of winter sunshine beamed through the window and Secret lay belly up at the foot my bed, basking in cat mode. The full moon was coming; Luna was coming, I felt her like the breath of a lover on the back of my neck.

I laughed loud enough that Secret opened one bleary eye. "Some terrible creature of the night you are."

"Merf." The eye closed.

Had to go. Had to move. I threw off the covers and the chill of the day greeted me. Giving Secret a scruffle, I checked myself over. Human toes and fingers; it all looked human, if a human whose white body hair needed a shave, that is. I stretched, throwing my hands over my head, and arching my back. I'd been waking up as a wolf so often lately that it was a novel sensation. Wolf me sat safely inside, not pushing but alert, ready. Shrugging, I made a vague gesture towards Secret. "I guess you don't have to get up if you don't wanna, but I'm going to get breakfast."

Secret's tail lashed as she kneaded the mattress, pondering the dilemma between food and sunbeam. By the time I threw on a robe, she was waiting at the door for me.

She'd didn't seem interested in eating at the table with me in the kitchen, so I just popped a can of tuna into a dish for her. I picked up a box of pop tarts from a cupboard, took one packet out, paused, and put it back. Stomach grumbling, I rooted around in the fridge until I found a pound of bacon strips. Then eyed the stove warily. Cooking and I weren't the best of friends. I ate a strip of bacon raw. Not bad, but definitely better cooked. How hard could it be?

As the bacon began to spit in the pan, Rey came in through the front door and sashayed into the kitchen. Her ears and tails had regained their red hue, and she moved with the languid grace of a well-fed cat.

"Was it story morning at the library?" I asked, "You seem... fed."

"Naw," She drawled. "Sadly, they only let me do that on the weekends. I merely tended my garden this morning."

I wondered what she meant by that, and swiftly decided I didn't need to know. "Cindy still sleeping?" I asked.

"Nope. Been up since early morning, trying to get her project finished in time," she said.

My good mood shattered. A growl rolled out of me.

Rey rested her chin on her interlocked fingers as she leaned on the counter. "Remember you promised... five minutes and if you're a good wolfie, she'll let you out." She gave me a sly smirk.

I swallowed, "Listen, what's the chances of her actually finishing that thing by moonrise?"

Her tails waved as she shrugged. "What does a fox know of building rooms? But I know she's very determined to finish. She even sent me away this morning because I was distracting her. Can you believe that?" Rey pouted.

A horrible idea occurred to me, but I couldn't stop myself. "What," I started, stopped, and hurried on before I could have second thoughts. "-if you were more... persistent in distracting her?" I glanced in the basement's direction.

"Oh, I could be very persuasive if I really wanted to be." She licked her lips, "For a favor."

"That depends on the favor, and I have to do it today." Was I going to do this? Make another deal with a Fey? I probed my mind, but the thought of willingly walking into a cinder-block box still made every part of me cringe. It'd be so much better for everyone if Cindy gave up on the idea.

Rey tapped her chin. "It will take effort, so-"

"I cannot imagine it would take you that much effort. She's pretty enamored of those tails of yours," I said, remembering how Cindy seemed to draw strength from the fox fey, and not the other way around.

Rey blushed demurely. "True, but it is different, I cannot taste her devotion while balancing my oaths to you. I will have to show her something that she has not seen before. I need but a small thing."

"And what would that be?" I crossed my arms and felt two paws on my calf. Absently I picked Secret up. She struggled in my grip as I stared at the pondering fox Fey.

Rey grinned, ears perking, "There is a little blond girl at the end of the road. She has a stuffed fox, you'll see it. Without her seeing you, move it to the roof."

"You want me to steal from a child?"

"Temporarily misplace a toy, happens all the time. Do me that favor in the next few hours and I'll prevent Cindy from finishing her project."

"Mew!" Secret protested.

I glanced down at Secret. She looked back at me with wide green eyes and shook her little head. "Yah, I know," I agreed with her. Nevertheless, I looked back up to Rey's smug smile. "Deal."

"Meeeeew! Hissss!" Secret swiped at my face, and I flinched away from her claws. I caught the scruff of her neck and pinned her to my chest.

"Awww," Rey tsked, "Poor little princess. You should really feed her more, Abby. She'll be naught but flesh before much longer."

Worry stung me. "What do you mean?" I glanced over at her bowl and saw it to be empty. "She's eating fine."

"Her flesh part is nourished, but how long has it been since her fey half has eaten?" Rey asked.

Secret twisted in my grip and hissed at her.

Rey only grinned, "Oh, stop. You're always hungry; you can't hide it from me anymore. And you're much more carnivorous than I am." With that she pushed herself upright. "Good hunting. I'll meet you in the backyard when you get back."

I inhaled the scent of burning, Shit! My bacon! In the moment that I glanced at the blackening meat, Rey disappeared from the room.

* * *

"Why can't you tell me what I need to get you?" I asked Secret for what had to be the fifth time since the fox Fey had dropped her little bomb.

All I got was a noncommittal "Merf." from the kitten who pranced along the top of the fence as I walked down the sidewalk. Now that Rey had pointed out Secret's hunger I could see it in her kitten form; her once glossy coat had dulled, and a bit of gunk collected in the corners of her eyes. Guilt chewed at me; had she been sleeping more than she had been? Did Queen Mab feed her while she was captive? Or had Secret gone unfed since she'd been separated from her mother months ago?

These were my worries as I arrived at the house on the corner, a small cottage in a tight lot. I looked over its white and blue trim, seeing no little girl nor her fox. A shriek rolled across the roof, the type that have childless folk like me asking if the kid is having fun or getting murdered. It's simply loud. Circling around to the side, I tried to stand nonchalantly on my tiptoes to peer over the privacy fence into the backyard. Little blond girl, green dress with her hair in two frazzled pigtails, raced around a plastic kitchen set holding a silver teapot above her head. Chasing or being chased by an invisible someone. On the porch a collection of stuffed animals perched on the railing: an elephant, a husky, and a fox. Their glass eyes seemed to stare at me accusingly.

"Tea time!" The girl shouted, spun, and slammed the teapot against the plastic refrigerator, knocking it over with a clang. I ducked back behind the fence. Nothing in the neighborhood stirred as I listened for an adult to be attracted out of the house by the noise. But the only noise was the girl's singsong, "Tea's ready! Just the way you like it!" Followed by more clanging. I really hoped the girl had an active imagination and wasn't mimicking adults. What was I supposed to do now? Hurdle the fence, grab the plush and toss it on top of the roof? Maybe if I turned into a full wolf first? Wolves don't get arrested for stealing kids' toys. Pretend I was a neighborhood mutt, play with the girl a bit, and then snatch the fox to bring it back later? That could work. I stole one more glance over into the yard, but the girl's brilliant blues captured my eyes.

"Hi!" she exclaimed without a single trace of fear. "Would you like tea?" She presented me with the teapot. "It's ready." To demonstrate she tipped the pot and brown liquid spilled from the spout on to the grass.

"Uuuh." I started, then I spotted Secret, struggling to climb the gutter spout on the porch, her teeth clamped on the ear of the fox plush, which was nearly as big as she was. I glanced back to the girl's eager smile and gave her my own. "Sure! I'll have some tea." Hoping to hold the kid's attention for a few more moments. Secret pulled herself up into the gutter as the little blond splashed brown water into a pink teacup. It was a stretch to take the little cup from her hands. I mimed drinking it as Secret pulled the stuffed fox onto the roof. Her little body panted from the effort, although she still preened.

I handed the cup back to the little girl, "Thank you. That was very good. You should give some to your mom."

"Mom doesn't like tea." She declared with a sour note. "She's sleeping! And daddy says she's lazy."

I tried not to wince. Sounded like this girl was destined for large therapy bills if she was lucky. Behind her, Secret jumped down from the roof and onto the fence. I gave the girl a goodbye and started walking down the sidewalk.

Secret had just caught up to me when I heard a high-pitched wail, "Foxie!? Where'd you go?! Foxie?! Foooooxie!"

"Merf," Secret commented as I tasted my own bile. Her glance clearly communicated that this was my fault, not hers. The kid's attention on the fox plush probably fed Rey somehow. Feeling like gum stuck to the underside of a shoe, I power-walked down the street, almost jogging to get out of earshot. Not a great time to have enhanced hearing. Even wolf me huffed with disappointment.

Unsettled, I wandered. I'd never explored what wolf me considered my territory in the daylight. An area about eight suburban blocks wide that brushed Portland's southeast border, beyond which trees dominated. While my scent marked the borders of it, I found Rey had been doing a different sort of claiming. Within four blocks of Cindy's, nearly every other house had a fox something displayed in the yard. A little ceramic fox stalking a garden gnome in one house, a kitschy wooden windmill kitsune with her tails as the blades, and in a house that hung Buddhist prayer flags across its porch, a fox sat among the crowd of figures in the elaborate rock garden landscaping. I wondered if Rey had gifted that fox plush to that little girl.

Did all these people dream of foxes? Were they Rey's garden? I'd been too occupied with myself and Secret during the past couple of weeks to pay much attention to Rey's comings and goings. Cindy and I had repaired the drywall in my room and the next one over, but Rey rarely stuck around for anything approaching manual labor. Did she just wander the neighborhood spreading the word of the good fox or something? If I stopped and asked, would everyone know the girl who spent every day in kitsune cosplay?

A soothing, cool sensation flowed down as my wander became less exploratory and more of a patrol. I kept waiting for Secret to tire of her form so I could interrogate her about her hunger, but she remained stubbornly four-footed. Her mother had fed her human hearts, but I didn't know how literally she meant it.

And if she needed the sort you need to break ribs to get, what would I do about it?

I hunt the meat my pup needs. Wolf me did not see this as anything more than logistics. I didn't want to cross that line but for Secret, I'd do what I'd have to. If it was less literal, that presented even more of a logistical issue. Was I supposed to walk into random bars, make random strangers fall in love with me and somehow carry that love back to Secret? I'd need a Fey's help for that. Specifically, I'd need Rey's help. Is that why she called attention to it?

Worries swirled as I walked, an unsettled sensation crept up my legs as the afternoon stretched from early to mid. Like a tiny rock in your shoe that refused to be shaken out, something was in my territory that should not be.

I had stopped for coffee at a local cafe when I finally figured it out. The same pickup truck drove by three times and as soon as I realized that I saw more. My territory was infested with them. While pickup trucks are not exactly a rare sight in Portland, these were a variety that you don't usually see cruising around a suburban neighborhood in the afternoon on a workday. They were "I'm a real man" huntin'" trucks. The most obvious were festooned with stickers that declared allegiance to their firearms, but others were more subtle, painted green or brown, no stickers, but there were dog kennels in the back. It was like my home-town had come to hunt me down. I haven't noticed silver to have a detectable scent but if it did, I'd imagine I'd have been choking on it every time one of them buzzed by. A minor part of me insisted that I was being paranoid, then I saw a white truck with a wolf decal on the doors, a rough red crosshair spray painted over it. It blasted the theme to ghostbusters to make it that much more obvious. The four men in the truck wore camo and mirrored shades. I bet they'd screamed themselves hoarse shouting "Wolf Busters!" already.

Sudden anger slew my appetite. I had done nothing, I'd hurt no one, just protected a girl from monsters. Now there were men with guns in my neighborhood looking to kill me. Hunting me as if it were a game because one fucker on the Internet had told everyone that I was a werewolf.

Withdraw. Wolf me urged, and I agreed.

I went home to wait for the moon.

7

A knock at the door stirred me from the hypnotic effects of matching fruitcakes on my phone. Cindy's voice came, "It's getting dark, Abby..." Trailing off with an ominous effect.

I furrowed my brow. Maybe she was suggesting I should get out of the house? Rolling up to my feet I pulled the door open to find Cindy. Her eyes immediately fled from contact with mine, examining my bare feet. "What?" I asked, tone not quite a snarl.

"You promised." She said to my toes.

It took me a half second to realize what she was talking about. The cage was ready. But... it certainly smelled like Rey had distracted her. Her house dress hung rumpled on her body as if she'd just flung it on. "You finished an entire room in a day?" Suddenly I felt my skin prickle with sweat.

"I had help." She said with a weak smirk.

Oh, that traitorous little Fox Fey... Numbly I followed Cindy into the basement. They had hung a white sheet in front of the cell. Rey bounced out from behind it and tossed two handfuls of confetti into the air. "Surprise!" Her tails wagged as I did my best to stare her to death.

"I thought you said..." I started.

"Oh, I did! I distracted Cindy from finishing it... by finishing it!" Her face grew a muzzle briefly, just to contain the size of the grin she flashed.

Cindy's gaze whirled from Rey to me and then back to Rey. "What's this?"

"Don't worry about it, muffin. Abby needed a basic lesson in dealing with Fey." Rey swiped dismissively at the air.

"A lesson about the Fey, or just about one called Rey?" I grumbled.

Rey reached out and grabbed the edge of the sheet. "Now may I present one... Foxy Dungeon!" With a whirl of her body, she ripped the sheet away. Gone was the blocky cinderblock construction, instead the cell had transformed into a rounded orb of cobblestone and mortar that adhered to the floor and ceiling like a massive wasp's nest, the single round opening covered by a grate of silver bars. Beside it a sculpted sliver fox head held an oversized key. The inside of it looked so small and dark. Rey ran her fingers along the bars, "Forged from the absolute despair of a child who's lost a toy." With a bat of her hand the porthole door opened. "You'll find the interior much comfier than the original design."

Caged by my own promise, I turned to Cindy for a last-minute appeal. "Don't make me do this! There are hunters prowling the neighborhood."

Her eyes shot wide open. "Hunters?"

"You know. From Slade's video. There are truckloads of hunters looking for me in my territory, Cindy. They're all looking for me. I can't let that stand."

She blinked, "I can't put you in the cage because you need to go face off against a dozen angry men with guns?"

"I-" Well it sounded stupid when you put it like THAT.

Pain. Cindy moved faster than I'd ever seen her outside of work, grabbing my ear and yanking before I knew what was happening. "You are not going out there to face a mob!" She screamed at me as she dragged me towards the cage. Cindy grabbed the waist of my jeans and hurled me into the darkness. I crashed into something soft on the floor. The grate slammed shut, its lock engaging with a dramatic ker-chunk that echoed through the space. Growling, I gathered myself up and flung my body at the bars, wolf me slipping into my muscles and hands.

Cage! No Cages! Wolf me and human me were in complete agreement.

"Let me out!" I snarled at Cindy and shook the bars. They held fast, not even rattling.

"No! Just no, Abby!" Cindy shouted back at me. "Listen to yourself. You're not rational. You're a medic, not a murderer. And that's what's going to happen if I let you out. They'll either murder you or you'll kill them."

"They're in my territory, Cindy. I can't just sit here and let them piss all over it. They need to learn to respect it," I growled.

"That's not how it works, Abby, and you know it. You kill one of these guys tonight and they'll just swarm. They'll show up with double the numbers every night. They have your name, too. We'll be dodging bullets at work before too long." Cindy drifted towards the bars. "You need to stay put. All night, Abby."

Human me thought she had a point, but wolf me gave a sawing growl in our throat. "No!"

"Do you really want to be a murderer, Abby?" she asked.

I wanted to not have intruders in my territory. "They're

coming with silver bullets to kill me when I've hurt nobody. Don't you think for a moment they wouldn't bust through your front door if they knew which one it was."

"What if you lose?" she asked. "What happens to Secret then?"

An image of Secret huddled over my still body jolted through my mind. I let go of the bars.

"Didn't think of that, did you?" Cindy smiled with satisfaction and stepped back. "Let me go get her. She'll make this easier for you."

I said nothing back as she jogged up the stairs. Rey moved to follow but paused at the base of the stairway to give me a wink before hurrying after her lover, tails trailing in her wake.

What the hell did that mean? The halogen work light still pointed at my cage, its harsh white creating vivid shadows, a barred moon on the back wall of the cell. Even here, underground, I could feel the pull of the Goddess as she rose.

Her power flowed into my veins, impossible to hold back. Sweeping wolf me and human me from our perches, into her immensity, we clung to each other, the separation between us dissolving, merging us into a single I. My body shifted smoothly as water, bones and flesh flowing into their proper places. The cell grew small as I heard the urban coyotes raise their voices to her. *Come wolf, come and see the glory that is our Goddess.* My ears bumped against the ceiling of the cell. I sucked in breath through my tooth-lined muzzle to answer them, but fear held my tongue. Would the hunters hear? Would they come while I was in a cage?

My nose drank in the sharp odor that suffused every brick. More gossamer than musk. The cage was nothing but magic. Yet it rejected the wicked claws at the ends of my thick fingers, leaving not even a mark in the mortar between. *Had to get out.*

A shadow with wilted ears appeared in the caged moon. Secret stood outside the bars. "They made me promise not to let you out. Or Rey wouldn't let me have my fingers again."

"Whuff?" I knelt at the bars.

"She locked me in cat form all day." She sniffled. "You shouldn't have taken her deal. She's a meanie."

I sniffed at her; the tang of human stress overwhelmed the delicate spun felinity of my poor hungry cub. So obvious now. Those strained notes in her scent. "Whuff?" I asked.

"Rey is getting stronger," she said.

I growled in frustration. I wanted her to tell me what I needed to do to feed her. Forget Rey.

Does a she-wolf stop hunting and hide when her cub is hungry? Luna's whisper rippled through me, beckoning me to her light. *Come now.*

Secret mewed with surprise when I bit at the bars and yanked. The stupid Fey magic held fast. I threw myself against the wall. The stone had no give whatsoever. Had to get out! I raked my claws over every inch of the cell's walls. Trying to find something loose or weak, anything.

"Abby?" Secret called out distantly.

Why had Rey winked? She'd said I'd needed a lesson. What if this was, too? How could a Fox Fey even make a cage? Unless it was part of a trick? Human me dug through memories of nature YouTube videos I'd watched while waiting for calls. Wolf me explored the scents as I dug through the piles of pillows that covered the floor. Her musk was stronger there. The shape niggled at me. She said she knew nothing of construction but what did a fox know how to build?

There, hidden under a solid two feet of pillows, was an oversized drain cover. It lifted up easily, revealing a tunnel into the earth.

Not a cage. A den. That's what a fox knew how to build.

I leapt at the tunnel entrance; its sharp edges bit at my face. Too small, but I tasted winter's air. Had to pull my human part away; she gave reluctantly, painfully, but went. As a full wolf I slipped into the tunnel. So tight, cold earth squeezing breath from my lungs as I wriggled through. Silver light urged me on. I emerged with a whine of relief beneath a hardy shrub that clung to the back of the house. Luna shone down from a cloudless sky, her light a smile. Stars clustered around her, shining eagerly, as crows might gather in the prelude to a battle. I sang up to my goddess, my howl deepening as human rejoined wolf to become greater than either, monstrous to anyone other than Secret. The wind stirred and brought with it whispers of those who shared the night. They spoke of trucks that wheeled through the streets, of the scent of alcohol and cigarette smoke that drifted from those who lurked on the corners. And beneath the pads of my feet Luna's sister stirred with the slightest tremble as my song died away.

"Abby?"

I found Secret peeking up at me from out of the tunnel. I gave her a lick and gently nuzzled her, urging her to crawl back inside the den. She frowned but obeyed. Then there was nothing else left to stop me.

Am I really going to do to this? human me thought as I put a hand on the fence that separated Cindy's lot from her neighbor's. Pausing, I breathed and closed my eyes. Feeling not only my hulking body, but an awareness stretching out in all directions. Anxious scents danced in my head, human and animal together, my territory unsettled. I would feel safe in my territory. Humans were about to learn to respect it. I leapt over the fence.

Time to hunt.

8

While winter's night had fallen heavily on Portland, we still had hours before the day ended for most residents. The high fences provided plenty of cover and heavy curtains shielded me from the eyes of those in the houses as I skulked across their lawns. I found a truck parked on every corner that led to the false address I had given Slade when he and his brother had found me naked in a park. Before he'd decided I was evil. Beyond that there were trucks roaming up and down the streets, mixing with the late commuter traffic. One of the stationary trucks positioned themselves near a high privacy fence and I caught the reek of weed downwind of it. Figuring it was a safer one to get close to, I crept onto the property and hunkered down in a thicket.

I'd been so eager to escape Cindy's cage that I'd neglected to realize that it would have been prudent to delay until midnight to avoid witnesses. Yet here I could wait. I had a lot of practice waiting.

The pair in the truck weren't the most talkative but

would have small bursts of conversation with each other or someone on their cells.

"Yeah, still nothing on the west corner."

"Rog, this is a cockamamy goose chase. There's no monster here."

"We get paid either way; besides, you heard that howl. That wasn't a coyote."

"Yeah, and nothing since. Maybe somebody got a real big howling dog."

"Make a nice rug, anyway."

"Silver bullet is a really expensive way to kill somebody's dog,"

Paid to be here? Who would pay them? That didn't make sense. Slade might whip up a mob, but he wouldn't offer to pay them, would he? As the hours stretched on, I listened to a few more snippets of conversation and decided I didn't like Rog.

Once all the lights in the house I huddled near went out, I risked peering over the top of the fence at Rog and his compatriot. One sat in the driver's seat with a revolver resting on the steering wheel; his passenger had the barrel of a rifle sticking out the window. My sympathy for the men dropped when I saw the weapons. Checking down the road one last time, I vaulted the fence and hit the sidewalk with a heavy thud. The men jerked up from their slouches but that was as far as they got. Charging up to the passenger window I grabbed the barrel of his rifle and flung it from his grasp. The driver wasted a second to shout "Holy!" And by the time he thought to point the gun in my direction I had his forearm in my fist.

He made a terrified bleat when I pulled him into the lap of his passenger.

My mind split.

Kill the prey! Wolf me howled in my head. *Meat for the pup!*

But I held her back. These men thought they were playing a game. I had to give them a chance to realize that the rules had changed. The bones of my face crackled as I forced them back to something approaching human. "Go home. Tell them all to go home. Anyone who stays is meat."

"Jesus fuck." The passenger swore.

I tightened my grip on the driver's arm, and he twisted in pain. "Do what it says, Rog! Do what it says!"

Rog, the passenger, fumbled with his phone before shouting, "This is Bad Bear. It's here! Its-"

The phone's speaker cracked to life, "ALRIGHT! Wolf-busters here! Enroute, Bad Bear! Don't let her get away."

I growled.

"Daaaah, No! Stay away! Go home!" Rog shouted.

An engine revved down the street and a truck screeched around the corner, its front a phalanx of dazzling bright lights. I snapped my captive's arm and ducked down next to the parked truck. It's eating Rog!" someone shouted, and the air filled with the chatter of gunfire.

Rog screamed. I grabbed the edge of his truck and flipped it up on its side. Men screamed from both trucks. Had to get behind that truck. I dashed for the corner.

"There!"

But the guns barked to life after I'd run around the corner, splintering the wood. I sank claws into the asphalt, using it to pivot and launch my body through the gap in the fence and doubled back behind it.

"It's running! Go! Go!" The pickup's engine told me precisely where it was.

"Where'd it go?" someone called out as they raced by my hiding place.

I answered their question by springing out towards them. My legs propelled me up into the bed of the truck. Two men perched in the pickup's bed. They clung to the light-studded roll bar with one hand, the other holding their rifles. I slammed down behind them. The first's head crunched between my teeth, but I no time to savor the taste or listen to human me's protest. The second tried to jump away, but my claws caught his midsection. His own momentum tore him wide open. The truck bucked beneath me, and I fell back. Caught in his seat belt, the passenger struggled to aim the barrel of a shotgun at me through the cab's rear window. Grabbing both sides of the truck I kicked through the plexiglass. The gun fired, spraying the driver with shot. The pickup lurched to the right as pain lanced up my foot. Driverless, the pickup slammed into a parked car and launched me into the air. The world swung around me; the truck lights flared like an array of blue-white suns. My backside slapped against something long and hard. Telephone pole, part of me commented as gravity peeled me off it and smashed me onto the top of a sedan. The wind rushed out of me with a huff.

Pain.

I knew I should move. My mouth opened to pull in a breath, but nothing came. A strange numbness gripped my foot. Crows cried out in alarm as multiple engines roared towards my location like wasps with long-distance stingers. I lifted my head to see the passenger who'd just shot his friend struggle to jam what I assumed to be a cartridge of silver shot into his gun, but shaking fingers kept fumbling it. If he got it in, he would kill me. That's what the numbness in my foot meant, didn't it? Silver bullet did even the odds.

Cindy was right. I had no pack. Defenseless without numbers of my own.

Get up. Luna's voice was a growl from within my bones. Something popped back into place in me, and the night air refilled my lungs. *My wolf, you are never alone.* A gentle hand caressed my back, and a shiver spurred me to lift my head and shake. My awareness extending into the ground. My territory, my home, thrummed beneath me. Ready to help. *Men believe they are invincible,* The Goddess continued, *that nothing in this world can bite them back. They are wrong. Show them.*

Glass and metal protested as I pulled myself from the car. Luna, I prayed, looking up at her silver light, feeling her healing power pouring through me, I'm a medic not a warrior.

I am both dark and light. Territory must be defended from both the dead and the living, wolf. The breeze shifted and a whiff of sour earth stole into my nose.

It was here, too! Where? What did that have to do with-

My wolf, my lovely wolf. You cannot hunt your true quarry if you are hiding in a Den. End this distraction. Do it in my name.

I came back to the world I hadn't realized I'd left. The engines roaring through the night over the soft desperate curses of the sole survivor of the Wolfbusters. Fresh, bloody meat sang to my nostrils and teased my stomach.

"Work, work, work," the man whimpered, begged his shaking fingers as I approached the cab.

He stopped when my shadow fell over him. I extended my hand through the shattered window palm up. He stared at me for a long moment before hesitantly placing the shell into the black pad of my palm. I waited. The shotgun joined it and I crushed both with a squeeze of my fingers.

So disarmed, I left him there to tremble in the scent of his own piss. The sound of his fellows had faltered, like hounds that had lost the trail. I grabbed the headless body of the first man I'd killed, flung it over my shoulder and dashed away.

Taking down individual wasps would just stir up the others. I needed the queen that held them here.

From the safety of a sprawling backyard garden, I swallowed my kill's heart. It was both a bitter and sweet meat. All around me the trucks buzzed along the streets, not quite brave enough to pierce the fences of their fellow humans. Beams of moonlight reached down from Luna to each individual house. When I howled out to the creatures who I shared the night with, not a single light flicked on. Find me their leader, find Slade, I sang out to them. I dug a lone sliver pellet front my foot, and the wound closed with only slight reluctance. Why would a metal that Luna wears be my bane? I wondered before a soft caw distracted me.

The crows had answered my howl, guiding me up to a safe vantage point on top of a two-story house. A group of three trucks less than two blocks from Cindy's house. They gave off the acrid scent of smoke although I saw no fire. I smelled no Slade, and my eyes did not recognize any of the trucks. The center vehicle was military style, blocky with its armored plating. Its roof bristled with antennas. The two other trucks weren't hunting but guarding this jeep thing. The one in back sported a hunting blind built into its rear, while the one in front sat empty and men milled about it with shotguns in hand. Their fearful scent brought a bucket of spicy chicken wings to mind.

They were positioned away from any tall fences, only open front yards on either side of the street. No cover. One of the chicken wings strayed up to the jeep, scratching his ear as if afflicted by fleas. The jeep's door opened, and the interior shone out into the road, outlining a thin man in the passenger seat.

"Any updates?" The chicken wing asked worriedly.

"What's the matter, got cold feet, son?" The thin man answered.

"Just wondering 'bout the WolfBuster and Bad Bear. They call in?" The chicken wing asked.

A second voice answered from deeper in the jeep, "They're dead. She got them. They were dumb, charged in, didn't wait for the dogs or backup." Fury built in every word.

Chicken wing stepped back, "Dead? Wha? Rog is dead?"

The thin man laughed, a hollow chuckle. "Buck up, son. Be a dilly night yet. She's bedded down somewhere having her snack. Let's stir the pot, eh? Got some gasoline in that truck of yours? Turn up the temp, ya know."

"Mr. Baker, that's not the mission." The other voice protested.

"You want your dough or not? Pick a house and light it up." The thin man, this Mr. Baker said, and I would not let this progress any farther. A growl rolled from my throat.

"Caww?" the crow that perched with me on the roof looked at me with a mischievous shine in her black eyes.

You are not alone. Luna had said.

I nodded at the crow. She took off with a flutter of her wings and glided down to sit on top of the armored truck. Another joined her, hopping across roofs, and pecked at a dark globe nestled between radio antennae. With each of my breaths more crows landed on the trucks. Not attacking, just perching on them. Soon the chicken wings were simply staring at the birds that gathered on every surface their feet could grip.

The chicken wing who had talked to Mr. Baker openly gawped at the crows.

"Aww, fuck this." He turned, bolted for the cab of the front truck. "I didn't sign up for none of this! Load up, we're out!" He shouted at the rest of the men. He hadn't struck me as a leader, but all of his crew seemed to be of the same mind, piling into their truck.

"They're just birds, you lily-bellied sapsuckers!" Mr. Baker shouted as the truck's engine revved. To demonstrate his displeasure, he drew a pistol and fired into the sky.

The crows lifted into a squawking storm cloud, filling the air with black wings. *Now! Flank him!* wolf me barked, and I flung myself over the peak of the roof. A garden gnome shattered underfoot as I landed, running on all fours at the jeep. The swirl of birds opened for me, giving me a clear path to this Mr. Baker.

He'd seen me coming, slamming his door shut the instant before I struck his window with my fist. The glass buckled but didn't break.

"Hoo! She's a big mutt!" Mr. Baker shouted from inside as the engine revved. I hurled myself on top of the truck, raking my claws across the steel, peeling up ribbons of paint. The truck bucked beneath me as it sprang into the deserted road. I grabbed hold of the antenna mount and hung on with one hand, my free fist hammering down on the roof. It dented inward with each thunderous blow and the occupants chittered like a pair of excited squirrels. The driver swerved from side to side, in a vain attempt to fling me off. With the fifth blow, something gave and like breaking the seal on a soda can, I smelled them. A mix of the expected human panic, but also the sour earth and a sweet rot that churned the very blood pumping through me. *Defend the territory from the living and the dead.* This Mr. Baker was of the Twilight, of the dead!

The frame of the roof had bent away from the seal of the door, opening a gap I jammed my fingers into. On the next swerve I slung myself over the door, and so braced against attack from the outside, tore off the side of the vehicle like a piece of cardboard. The men inside cried out an inarticulate scream of alarm. I thrust my arm inside to be met with the popping of that pistol.

"Eat lead, ya flea-bitten floozie!" Baker screamed, as my claws tore the gun from his hand and claiming several fingers with it. A sensation of burning cold erupted across my arm, but I seized his wrist and tossed him down onto the road. He screeched with hysterical laughter as I heard the snap of bones fall behind.

The man in the driver's seat moved with military precision as he raised a sawed-off shotgun in my direction. Instinctively I dodged back, and the bastard slammed on the brakes. For the second time this night, the world ripped itself from my grip. My knee hit asphalt with a crunch that reverberated up through my hip and spine before momentum slammed me bodily into the pavement. My good arm saved me from a cracked skull. As I looked up, its taillights were zooming off down the street, shouting an order to retreat.

A smile reached the corners of my muzzle, and I wagged my tail. I'd squished the queen bee.

9

Luna shone proudly. Her cool power flowed through me as a river. One branch running down to my shattered knee, swirling through my flesh as the bone shards pieced themselves back together. The other fell into the numb abyss that was my injured arm, which hung limply from my shoulder. Baker had hit me twice, the first passing through the palm of my hand and embedding itself in my bicep. I squeezed it out like a bloody blackhead. The second, though, had traveled up my wrist and remained somewhere in the nexus of an icy numbness in the middle of my forearm, swallowing up Luna's might as it whirlpooled into nothing. Its entry wound saturated the white fur with blood to the point that it dripped from the tips of my claws. I considered ripping open my arm to get at it, but decided to endure it for now. My Queen bee's laughter rubbed me rawer than the pain of the silver.

Mr. Baker lay in a tangle of oddly bent limbs. He should have passed out from the pain, but instead he watched me with almost comically wide eyes. I stalked over to him, lifted him by the front of his too big suit, and he simply grinned as if I were the most absurd thing he had ever seen. "You think you got me? You think you can make me squeal? Eh, Miss Mutt?" His breath reeked of that sour earth, a rot. He contained so much of it that black oozed from the cuts on his face. In Luna's silver light, black threads crawled through the white of his eyes in spiral patterns. More sick than Keith had been, more disease than human flesh.

I growled at him, knowing I should shift and articulate questions, but his words about getting some gasoline echoed in my head and my teeth refused to yield, aching to tear out his throat.

"Now, that's not very polite, coming from a lady." His grin was just as predatory as mine. "I'm Mister Baker. See you around." A shadow flickered in his eyes and his body fell slack in my hand. One more bit of mess to clean up. I couldn't eat it either, too rotten.

I let the body fall back onto the ground. Whatever he was, he was gone now. I listened, my ears swiveling to take in the night. No engines, no shouts of men, simply the soft report of the crows and other night residents of my territory resuming their daily lives. I had won. The ground beneath me remained safe and sacred. A howl rose from my heart, and I sang it forth. On the undulating tones of my song visions floated through me. Coyotes dragged off kills from a white truck, crows pecking at escaped bits in their wake. In another space, where I'd eaten my meal, coyotes dug holes as two families of raccoons dragged clean bones to be buried. Crows sailed after myriad trucks scattering out of the city. All except for the armored one missing a door; that one drove towards the northeast section. A fresh wind, crisp and cold, blew down from the north, its scent carrying the promise of snow. My song sung, I collected the door I'd ripped off the armored truck, and the remains of Mr. Baker, and headed home.

* * *

Rey was waiting for me at the back door. "Brought back a toy?" The body was back in the bushes.

"Whuff," I said.

She smiled at my wounded arm; the numbness had waned and now I felt the bullet throbbing in my flesh. "I will go wake up Cindy. Can't imagine she'll be happy about this."

An attempt to shift towards human resulted in a bolt of both freezing and fire lancing up my arm. The double whammy of agony drove me to my knees. I blinked away the sudden multicolored stars. New rule: no shifting with silver in you.

I squeezed in through the door. Inside I stooped to avoid scraping my skull on the ceiling; the floor protested my weight. The rapid patter of small feet on the stairs caught my ear, and before I had gotten past the kitchen counter, Secret shot through kitchen doorway. Her green eyes shone as she leapt up into my arms, heedless of the blood, both mine and others', that caked my fur. I caught her with my good arm, and she threw her short arms around my muzzle and rubbed her nose into my fur. A half second of bliss. Then she sniffed once and her eyes sprang open, pupils narrowing to slits. "You brought me something?!" A hungry growl vibrated her entire body as she bared a mouth suddenly full of fangs. "Gimmie! Gimmie Gimmie!" Her voice full of desperate hunger as her fingers pushed under my lips to stroke my teeth. The sensation pushed a button of instinct and before I could even register my own movement, my jaws yawned open. Secret thrust her head deep inside my mouth. My stomach pulsed and something warm came up my gullet. Secret pressed against me and took the thing from me with an audible gulp. With a pleased sigh, she withdrew and relaxed against me. Shaking myself as a sudden warmth spread across my chest, I looked down to find Secret wiping her mouth with back of her hand before settling back to groom it. She purred louder than I'd ever heard her.

But not loud enough to dampen, "JEBUS! The hell, Abby!" Cindy, clad in her pink robe, stared up at me, her face undulating through terror and rage. "You got out! You killed somebody."

It's hard to defend yourself when you can't speak, I managed a non-committal grumble and stayed still.

Cindy spun in place, fingers plucking at the air. "Uh... uh... This was exactly what I was trying to avoid." She gave this anguished cry and charged up to me. "Don't you see yourself!? What you're doing? The cage was to keep everybody safe! Why couldn't you simply stay there?!" She raised her fist as if to punch me, but it only wavered there, unsure what to do with itself. Rey captured it and pulled Cindy to face her, locking her in place with her eyes.

"Darling," Rey whispered, "It's not fair to ask her all these questions when she can't answer. There's a silver shard in her arm, and she can't shift with it in there."

"Did you let her out, Rey?" Cindy yelled at her lover.

"No, the door is still locked," Rey answered with the most honest smile.

Snorting with impatience, I set Secret down. Clearly, assuming Cindy would help and yell at me afterwards had been a bad assumption. Reaching across the counter, I plucked the big chef's knife from the butcher's block. The blade would be cleaner than my claws, which are more for ripping than cutting.

"What are you doing?" Cindy snapped.

I mimed slicing open my arm with it.

"No!" Tears broke free of her eyes, and I reached out toward her. If I could only explain how I had to do this. How Luna had called for me and the lengths those men would have gone to in order to flush me out. Instead, she slapped my hand away. "Don't touch me! I'll get my kit." She wheeled and stalked from the room. Her footsteps pounded up and then back down the stairs, returning with a large blue medical bag. Face composed and businesslike, she directed me to kneel and lay my forearm on the kitchen table. Blood still spilled from the hole in my palm and she had me hold a wad of gauze as she set to work, clicking open a disposable scalpel. "A doctor should do this," she grumbled at Secret as she watched the scalpel part my flesh. Rey had drifted away.

With my forearm as thick as some human's thighs it took many slices to get down to the bullet. Cindy had to recruit Secret to hold the wound open to prevent it from healing itself closed. Pain ratcheted up to agony as she neared the bullet. I panted through clenched teeth as she dug and twisted with a pair of forceps. As she pulled it free, the disrupted river in my body swept back into a single powerful tide. I howled with the sudden relief and the bones of my wrist made soft cracklings as they reassembled themselves.

"There!" Cindy spat the word as she dropped a bloody pancake of a bullet onto the table.

Wolf me fled inward partially, leaving me hairy instead of furred, but equal to Cindy's bulk. "Thank you." I said around still large canines.

She breathed in and out through her nose, "You're welcome. Now, how did you get out?"

I opened my mouth to lie for Rey but the Fox Fey cut in. "Let's not point fingers. It was a noble idea, but you can't stop what Abby is now. It was in her nature to escape."

"You did it!" Cindy shot to her feet. "I trusted you!"

Rey placed a hand over her heart and her nose in the air. "No one opened the door. It remains locked."

"Don't get too angry with her." I said, "If the cage had worked then she'd be in violation of her oath to me. There was a hole in the bottom I dug through to outside."

"Yes..." Rey winced, "You saw what happens if I break that oath of loyalty; you wouldn't want that to happen to me, would you?" She threaded her way around the table and slid under Cindy's arm, her tails curling around her legs. "I don't make for a very soft statue," she said with a pout, and pushed herself up toward Cindy with obvious intention to kiss.

Cindy grabbed her shoulder and forced her back down to her heels. "No. I'm not happy with you." She turned towards me. "Or you, Abby. I'm going back to bed. I'll sort myself out tomorrow." She strode toward the stairs. Rey made to follow but Cindy stopped her. "Alone, Rey."

The Fox Fey looked like a kicked puppy as Cindy stomped upstairs and slammed her door. After a long pause she drifted towards the TV room, her fur somehow paler.

"So," Secret piped up beside me, "does that mean we can stay?"

"For tonight, at least." I told her, picking up the small pancake of bloody silver that lay on the table. It stuck to my fingers as if magnetic as I rubbed the blood off it. Secret and I slipped back outside where she slumbered against my chest while I listened to the night, my thoughts ranging.

Pondering a man made of rot and what it meant to be a Goddess's monster. Cindy's question circled; I knew my answer to it. Smelled it in the restored vibrancy of Secret's scent, in the peaceful pulse of the earth beneath us, and the satisfaction in defending my family from those who would have hurt us. But Cindy wouldn't like those reasons. To her, to me a few weeks ago, there was no mistake that deserved death, heroes don't kill, they certainly don't eat people. Paramedics showed up both for the mother defending her children and the abusive drunk she stabbed. The enemy was death; anything that avoided death would be Cindy's choice. The sticky morass of Judgment and Justice would be left to others.

What I had to make her understand is that we didn't have that option anymore. Human justice sided with the ones who had power and fought those who'd take it away. It wouldn't give me a space for myself and a pack unless I gave it a reason. Maybe two reasons, one with claws and the other clad in a plastic glove.

10

"You think making coffee will fix things?" Cindy glared from the kitchen doorway, her nostrils flaring.

"I know it will get you in the same room as me." I gestured at the coffee pot. There was a scrabble of small claws over tile followed by a bang as Secret pounced a feathered ball, overshot, and bounced off a cabinet. Cindy's eyebrows went up at the noise. I kicked the ball out into Cindy's line of sight.

"Meeeerf!" Secret's voice exulted as a battle cry, tackling the ball, rolling head over tail, and then viciously clawing the hapless toy with her rear paws. The adorableness was viral video worthy.

Cindy smiled reluctantly, "Well someone has beans this morning," and entered the room.

"Watch your toes, she's vicious." I said, and on cue, Secret broke off from the ball and charged Cindy's feet.

"Hey!" Cindy picked up her foot, dodging the pounce; Secret scrambled to turn but slipped across the floor. "Watch it, you! Coffee before play. What is this, act cute and pretend nothing happened?"

A rustle of fabric and Secret stood on two legs, her green eyes shining brightly in the dim light of the morning. "Is it working?" she asked, flouncing in her little black dress. It had gone from rumpled the night before to free of tatters, and her face bore a tad less baby fat, as if she'd aged a month or two.

"Coffee." Cindy demanded, and I poured her a cup.

She tossed half the mug down her throat like a shot of whiskey before regarding me with eyes asking the question.

I lowered my eyes. "I can't undo last night, Cindy, and I won't apologize for it. Those men were threats, and I made them go away."

"And then what?" Cindy stared down into her mug. "You think that's going to be the end of it?"

"Cindy, it's not just people." I explained to her about the rotten man, how he smelled of the Twilight.

She shook her head, "You can't just kill someone for smelling bad, Abby."

I took her by the hand, "He was already dead. Let me show you." Reluctantly she poured herself another mugful of coffee and followed me outside. By the light of a flashlight, I showed her the corpse that had contained Mr. Baker. Black threads had sprouted from his eyes and mouth, erupted from beneath his nails, reaching toward the ground as if trying to escape. Cindy looked him over with muted horror.

"This smells precisely like that patient that set me off," I told her.

She covered her mouth and backed away. "What do you mean? This is some sort of plague from the land of the dead?"

"I don't know. Yet. But I'm going to find out. Luna told me last night men weren't my quarry, but this is. Things like this are why I am what I am." It wasn't quite a lie, the territory had to be defended from the living and the dead.

Cindy turned, took five steps back toward the house and gave a sound mid-way between a sob and a laugh. "I prayed to God last night. For the first time since... well a long time. I got nothing, no clarity. No insight. We're friends, Abby. We've known each other for what? A half a year now? Now I have to decide if I'm the sort of friend who helps you bury the bodies. That's a big ask."

My hand hovered over her shoulder, unsure if the touch would hurt or help. "I know it is," I said, dropping my hand. "This is still your house, if you want us to go, we will." Wolf me suddenly pressed hard, growling at me. *Our Territory! No leave. We fought!*

With a deep sniff, Cindy wiped her nose with the back of her hand. "That's just it! I don't want you to move out. But I should, right? You're a terrifying monster who, who... murders people. My girlfriend, I'm not quite sure how she works, but she's even more dangerous than you are. I should throw you both out, turn you in, but I haven't. I don't think I will. Does that make me a terrible person?"

I stepped up behind her and gave her a squeeze, pressing my cheek between her shoulder blades, "You're the kindest person this terrifying monster knows, and she's happy to have you as part of her weird pack."

Cindy's back went rigid, and she swallowed hard. "I don't want to be a werewolf, Abby."

Wolf me whimpered, and I translated the sentiment. "Means family, Cindy. No howling required." I let her go, cursing myself for touching her, way to go me. "Since you're not telling us to leave, how about we work on making the world a better place today?"

"Okay," she said cautiously, "what do you have in mind?"

"Hunting a disease."

She laughed tiredly and took a swig of coffee. "I think you're going to buy me a different sort of drink after today."

* * *

"There!" Cindy pointed ahead, and sure enough, we'd reached the Isolation Colony where we had first encountered the lung disease with the sour earth smell: the Rot, as I had termed it. The huge white house glistened in the damp of the early morning; the many peaks of the roof sheltered spots of vibrant green moss. I drove up into the parking space outside the delivery hut and we got out with our official-looking uniforms, Cindy armed with a tablet. After sanitizing our hands, I rang the call button next to the video panel. It flicked blue for a few moments before a thin face appeared on it. He briefly touched his lips with his fist, stifling a burp or a cough before he spoke with a voice I recognized as the man from the hazmat suit.

"Beenmo residence, how can I help you?"

I smiled at the camera, "Hello sir, we're here to do some contact tracing on one of your residents. A mister Kyle-"

"Mason." The man finished, taking off his glasses and pressing his thumb and forefinger into his eyes. "Do you have a word on his condition?" He asked.

"No sir, we're just contact tracing, standard procedure for novel respiratory infections," I said, and it was true, anything with Covid-like symptoms got added to a contact trace queue. However, unless a doctor flagged Kyle's case as priority, it'd be at least a week before they contacted this colony, and they'd do it via phone call, not in person.

He nodded, "Let me get the logs for you. Kyle doesn't get many visitors; his only regular contact with outsiders is when we have contractors come in to help him with the garden. If he caught it from someone it would have to be them." He cleared his throat, a loud, "Ah hem."

As he talked, I took deep breaths through my nose, searching for that tangle of rot and life I had smelled here before. I didn't find it in the air, precisely, but a fragment of it hooked my senses. What in this place was rotting?

"Sometimes with Pneumonia, the bacteria can be found in a variety of products." I said, "Could we get some samples? Doctors might get a DNA match to whatever's in his lungs." This was well beyond the call of duty for a contact tracer.

"Let me suit up and I'll show you the garden shed." He blinked out.

Cindy chewed on her cheek, "What are you thinking?" She asked.

"It's got a kinda earthy smell. And part of it's still here," I said.

We masked up, and I fetched a few swabs from my medical kit. I found an empty plastic baggy that had probably had nuts or something in it long ago. Secret had escaped the car and was poking at a crack in the pavement with a stick.

I was about to ask her to get back in the car when hazmat guy appeared, "Ah-hem. Shouldn't she be in school?" He scowled at her, eyes full of judgement.

"Uuuh," I said in a very articulate manner. "She uh,"

Before I could remember the magic word that is home-schooled, Secret looked up at the man with a glimmer in her green eyes and declared, "I'm not here."

The hazmat man flinched, then echoed her, "You're not here." With a little shake, he turned towards me, "Hi, I'm Ryan, the warden of the Beenmo house. Garden's this way."

Secret's grin shone, while Cindy's eyebrows lifted. I gave a half shrug and followed the warden in the yellow suit. He led us around the back of the house where tidy square hedges framed not only bare flowerbeds but tombstones. Positioned beneath a weeping willow, the polished marble stones pushed out from a layer of wood chips. Five headstones in a grid that could hold twenty. Patches of black mushrooms with a swirl of purple around the edges of their caps had pushed up between the graves. That scent of rot swirled here, and I had to draw to a stop. "That's not what I expected," I said conversationally, buying time to smell, wondering how safe it would be to sneak back here as a wolf.

"It's beautiful in the spring. Ah-hem." Ryan said, "We got through the bola-R without a single case. We all got a bit lax during the hyper flu and paid for it. Kyle set up the garden to remind everyone what can happen if the procedures are not followed."

"Are these actual graves?" I asked.

He pointed at the headstones that read 'Mercy', "That one is. She's Kyle's wife. Coffin and everything. The rest have some of their ashes scattered around but are buried elsewhere."

"Ryan!" A woman called from a deck attached to the house; she wore yoga pants, a jacket, and a hot pink mask. "Have my-" She bent to cough twice into her hand. "Deliveries come yet?"

"Aw, shit." Ryan swore under his breath. "Leena, do you have what Kyle's got?"

"Don't be absurd, it just a touch of allergies. I'm hardly around Kyle." She waved dismissively.

"Leena! It's too early for allergies." Ryan scolded and then stifled a cough. "I want you to isolate now."

"Fine! just like I do every year!" With a huff and a small coughing fit, she went back inside before I could get a sniff.

Ryan turned to give me and Cindy the *see what I have to deal with?* glance, before gesturing at a small shed at the far end of the garden. "Stuff's in there; its unlocked. Take your samples and if you need me, buzz me out front. I have to go take care of Leena before everybody starts panicking." He strode back along the path we'd come down, narrowly missing Secret where she had paused to squint at a bare bush.

"Is it here?" Cindy sidled closer as Ryan disappeared around the corner.

I stared at the door that the woman had gone inside through. "Maybe." Here in the garden, there was a definite element of what had been on Kyle Mason's breath, but to find the source, I'd have to let wolf me have a romp. Probably not a good idea; two gray-haired residents peered at us curiously from the upper windows of the house. We continued on to the shed, pretending to take samples from stacks of potting soil and fertilizer. The scent wasn't in there.

We got back into the car a few minutes later. "Well, that was a waste of time." Cindy sighed.

"Not entirely. I mean if the woman gets worse, we'll know it's contagious," I said.

"This isn't really our job, Abby." Cindy said. "If it is something new, then the docs at the hospital are probably already tracking it. We can't even find out if that guy is recovering or not." Cindy was right; once you dropped a patient off, they were officially somebody else's problem whether you wanted them to be or not. Epic bar stories were spun from finding former patients. From trying to find out if that kid you peeled out of a crushed car survived, to tracking down a cute bicyclist who got doored. The system made it nigh impossible.

"It's not about that guy. It's this connection to the Twilight. That's an angle I doubt anyone at the hospital is considering," I said, but it would be helpful to know how widespread the condition was.

"Let's go back to the station," I suggested after a moment of thought. We had our own paperwork at the station. If anyone in NLR picked up patients with the same symptoms it'd be in the system. While hospital medical records are generally secure, the paramedic companies don't use the same systems, and I knew where Cliff stored his password dongle.

Cindy checked her phone. "Okay but we gotta be fast. Let's not be late for the funeral. Need to go home and primp a bit."

"I'll be quick," I promised, knowing that I'd be stretching the definition of quick. However, when we walked into the office, I found Cliff's dongle missing and the scent of an unfamiliar person lingering in the air. Cliff's sister? A dead end. Maybe I could ask Cliff about getting access at the funeral.

11

———

The drizzle dotted the windshield as we parked at the River View cemetery. Wintry Portland made for good funeral weather, drab and dreary to match the solemn occasion. I shouldered my Secret-containing purse; she had taken one look at all the people streaming in from the parking lot, and practically dove into it. I surveyed the crowd as I waited for Cindy to finish adjusting her makeup and wig. The parking lot was in a lower area from the cemetery proper, so it funneled all the grievers up an ancient set of stone stairs or a far more recent-looking concrete ramp off to the side.

About half the people wore a uniform of one type or another: EMTs, firebugs, and military. The rest wore a range of fashion from stark black suits to vibrant African hues. I spotted a cluster of NLR paramedics up the path, all clad in our dark navy uniforms.

"How do I look?" Cindy asked that dangerous question.

Turning, I smiled and said, "Beautiful." She'd gone as fem as she could while wearing our standard-issue button-down shirt and slacks: choosing a nearly pink lipstick, long blond hair with bangs that softened her cheeks, and with her shirt tightly hugging her breasts.

"Liar," she huffed and turned to stare at the cluster of colleagues, lips pursed sourly.

What the hell was I supposed to say? That she looked a better in a dress? "You look like you, Cindy." I finally said.

That was apparently good enough because she nodded and started walking. "Let's get this over with." I hurried to take the lead; regardless of our current tensions, Cindy was my partner and friend. If anyone was going to give her shit today, they'd have a wolf to deal with first.

"Hi, girls!" Dobson called out at us with a far-too-bright smile. The skinny man always reminded me of a chihuahua, in both his nervous energy and his utter lack of social sense. "It's Cindy and Cinderella." He elbowed his broad-shouldered and heavy-gutted partner, Mitch Fergusson, who resembled the most sullen of bulldogs as his head slowly swiveled towards us. Usually the loudest voice at NLR, Mitch's mother had died a week ago, and the grief weighed down on every aspect of his being. The rest of the group laughed nervously.

"Ha." Mitch responded belatedly to Dobson's joke.

I merely glared at the man.

Dobson pressed on to explain the joke, "You left your shoe on your last call! We pulled the shift after yours and the nurses all wanted to know who the fuck is the Cinderella EMT."

I grimaced hard, "I had a personal issue, alright?" That had all the hallmarks of a nickname that could stick, except I worked with Cindy. Hopefully that would save me. I'd avoided any moniker until now. At least ones used to my face, and I'd rather it stay that way.

As the group chortled harder, Mitch visibly pulled

himself into the present, "Sure you're not hoping one of the ER nurses will be your prince charming? With the contacts and hair, it's like you're giving Colin," Mitch winced when my gaze hardened on him. "I mean Cindy, a run for her money for most changed uh... fashion sense." You could always trust Mitch to walk right up to the line of acceptable behavior.

And have Dobson blunder straight over it. His eyes were glued to Cindy's chest. "Naw, uuuh Cindy's got some uh...," He seemed to detect he was heading into dangerous waters but kept paddling, "explosive growth there."

The group went silent as Cindy's cheeks flushed; every woman's gaze fell on Dobson as heavily as a falling tree. The men quickly stepped back.

"That's horribly rude and inappropriate," I said.

Dobson's eyes bugged out like a stepped-on frog's, "Uh, sorry?"

"Why don't we all find some seats?" Mitch suggested, quickly rescuing his partner, and pulling him down the path.

Slowly we all drifted in that direction. Seats turned out to be reserved for only those who needed them, so we stood amid a crowd of several hundred people clustered in a vague C shape around a closed, dark-wood casket. Pictures and flowers were arrayed in equal measure. Mr. Gifford stared back at us with solemn gazes from official military portraits, and one where he smiled like Cliff does with his three children. Above and behind the coffin stood a podium where a minister greeted us. I closed my eyes and tried not to compare his words to the ones that were said when my own parents were laid to rest. They were similar, containing many variations of cut short and tragic. I recalled Mr. Gifford's hoarse whisper, "Abby, stay away. Call..." His last words cut off by the cackle of a mad fairy. Another death that was my fault.

You killed five men last night. Jimmy's whisper floated among my thoughts. *Where's their tears?*

I shoved him back to the depths of my memories and refocused on the proceedings; the minister had yielded to Mrs. Gifford. She gripped the podium with livid strength. "I first found out what had happened to my husband on the fucking internet! You looked. I know you did." And she gave voice to her rage. She painted a wide and sprawling tapestry as she outlined her brutal circling with officials to find out what had happened to George Gifford. She pilloried the police for letting the Santa killer escape into the night. By the end of it I felt guilty for killing Little Nick myself and not dragging him back to answer to this woman.

Her children came next. Cliff's sisters, Taya and Sophie, each spoke of Mr. Gifford as a good, hardworking dad, telling touching stories that, judging from the nervous chuckles of the family, there was far more to. Then finally Cliff took a turn, flashing that beaming smile of his across the crowd. I shifted over and stood on tiptoe to get a better view.

"I loved Dad. We got along great," Cliff started, provoking muffled chuckles. He soaked it in, smiling. "Look, y'all. I don't have to stand here and tell you Dad and I got along." His eyes strayed to me and the other EMTs, "Especially you guys,"

We all laughed politely, remembering rating their shouting matches on scales of volume and words per minute.

"But Dad always did what he saw as the right thing, and if you were part of his unit, like the NLR, he fought tooth and nail for you. He never ever focused on what he wanted.

Always what his family, his workplace, or his unit needed. And he expected the same of me." He wiped his eyes. "I resented that as much as I respected it. Dad, the world's poorer without you. I'm missing ya." Cliff took a deep sigh before walking down into the arms of his mother and sisters.

I took a moment to wipe my own tears away and clear my nose with a tissue.

And as I inhaled, I found the scent of sour earth. No, just no. Cliff and family had suffered enough; they didn't need to meet this new thing, too. I drifted back through the crowd, trying to get a bead on the scent's source. The wind shifted, and I scented the sweeter rot that I recognized from the garden at the isolation colony. It grew stronger as the funeral progressed.

More relatives and friends were speaking as I reached the edge of the crowd. Beyond it only a lone groundskeeper stood with a cart of tools, waiting for the mourners to move on. Desperately I searched for the source of the scent across the immaculately tended grass. The bright colors of recently placed flowers drew my attention first, but that couldn't be it; the scent didn't vary as I stepped perpendicular to the direction of the drizzle-bearing breeze. I took another step and my boot caught on the flat plaque of a headstone I hadn't seen. And clustered in the corner of the grave stood a clump of mushrooms with their dappled purple caps. The same that had been on the graves at the isolation colony. These were about two inches tall, their thin black stalks supporting inch-wide caps with a black slime dripping from their undersides. I'm no mushroom expert, but I'd never noticed this type of fungus before today. I stooped and plucked one up, holding it to my nose. That was it! The sweet rot odor.

A shadow fell across me. "Careful lass, mushrooms can be poisonous." A hoarse voice croaked.

Startled, I dropped the mushroom and stood to find a groundskeeper frowning at me through dark shades beneath a brim of a wide hat. His weathered copper cheeks had a waxy pallor to them

"Just uh, it's a type I haven't seen before." I gave him a tight smile.

"My, you got some pretty eyes, lass. You be careful; hate for you to fall ill." He spoke with an Irish inflection that contrasted oddly with his dark complexion. Then I got hit with the scent of his breath, sour earth.

As he made to step away I grabbed his wrist. "Wait." It was feverishly hot to the touch. "What are you really doing here?"

He paused, "Only thing I know how to do lass, sowing my seeds."

"What the hell do you mean by that?" I growled, low in my throat, squeezing him tighter.

"Ooooh, Mister Baker warned me about you. The moon bitch. My name's Scully, by the way," he said.

"W-"

My teeth slammed together, and my world exploded into stars.

"Unhand me, you crazy bitch!" I heard him as if his surprise uppercut had blown me down a long, hollow tube. With a jerk of my hand, he rammed my face into the flat of his elbow. The crunch of my nose breaking echoed around my skull.

"Mrrowwwwl!" A feline war-cry reverberated as a black shape rose up between us and latched onto Scully's face.

Staggering back, wolf me found her bearings, then poured into my arms and damaged face. Savage claws tore from my fingertips, shattered bones in my face snapped back into place to join my lengthening jaws.

"Abby?!" Someone shouted my name as I charged, triggering just enough self-awareness to pull back on the transformation and alter my blow from a swipe to a punch. Scully flung Secret away by her tail only in time for my fist to crash into his nose. He rocked back as my own momentum carried me into him. My "training" with Jimmy had only covered firearms; close combat was all from wolf me. I sank my mostly human teeth into his shoulder as I bowled him over. Scully didn't scream or flinch; instead he drove a knee up between my legs as we fell.

Wolf me howled, *Touched pup! Kill!* And the pain of any his following blows was like stones dropping into a distant pond.

"She's biting me!" Scully shrieked belatedly. "She's biting me!"

It took everything I had to keep my form human, but wolf me simply grabbed hold of his neck and throttled his windpipe.

"Abby! Abby!" Hands grabbed me and hauled me off the stinking rot of a man. Wolf me growled and snapped before she realized this wasn't the best look and yielded to human me. I found myself in the grip of Cindy. "Let him go," they urged. "It's okay. Okay."

But it wasn't okay. That man was possessed, and everyone was in the field that smelled of sweet rot. An image of Kyle sitting on the bench in front of his wife's grave, talking to her for hours, breathing that sweet rot. And that other lady, Leena, maybe she did the same thing but not as much. Everyone at the funeral was exposed.

Across from me, Mitch was hauling Scully to his feet, as

the groundskeeper shrieked his innocence like a fox caught red-handed.

Pup. Where pup? Wolf me demanded.

"I saw you punch her, you dirty liar!" Mitch shouted the man down. "Don't give me that shit."

Cindy was still hauling me back, urgently pleading with me to calm down. Scully looked up at me and smiled; the sunglasses had been knocked away, revealing the black veins in the whites of his eyes. Then Cindy blocked the view with her body.

"Secret? Where's Secret?" I asked her, then shouted, "Secret!?"

Cindy shushed me "Calm down, I'll find her," but I was barely aware of her.

Secret found herself, little body charging over the grass and jumping into my arms. I clutched her tiny body to my chest. Cradling her against my thundering heart for several seconds before becoming brave enough to check her for injuries.

"Merf!" She protested as I pinched each of her limbs, and then her claws popped out when I handled her tail. No break, but tender certainly.

Safe. Pup safe. I let out a shaky breath and as the world around me broadened, I found myself surrounded by a fence of navy-clad legs. EMTs held back a surging crowd with soothing words.

"It's okay! It's all over. They're done. No more trouble."

Cindy pulled me up to my feet and clasped my shoulder. "Come on. Let's go."

I tried to shrug her off, "Everyone's gotta get out of here, we've all been exposed to the mushrooms."

She pulled me closer to her side and shepherded me

towards the path. "Mushrooms? Now you're talking extra crazy. Come on."

Trying to explain didn't help. A mushroom that had a scent like a weird pneumonia and the groundskeeper that was like the rotten man from last night. Even listening to myself, I heard a dithering biddy spouting conspiracy theories. "We've got to get everyone out of the cemetery. Everyone's breathing it."

"It's a hunch, Abby. Fastest way for everyone to clear out of here is to wait for them to finish. And I think you have a concussion." Cindy's voice was too gentle, as if I were a child. Her phone buzzed, and after checking it, she changed course from towards the parking lot to a bench beneath a gnarled tree.

I sat down gratefully. My head did throb; he'd hit me so hard, so fast, I literally hadn't even seen the first punch. And if Secret hadn't launched herself at him, he might have killed me before wolf or human me realized what was happening. Certainly, another hit and wolf me might have been the only one left in front of all those people. I petted Secret and soaked in her purrs. "Saved me again, kiddo," I whispered.

She purred louder, proud.

Cindy opened a large black umbrella over us. "Do you smell it here?"

I sniffed through a fairly stuffy nose, "Not really."

We waited, content simply to sit and breathe as my headache waxed and slowly waned. I checked my messages to find a concerned text from Victoria about my nose. Oddly, it was the first message since I'd left her house. I replied vaguely about getting in a fight as I watched the mourners file along the path. Nobody even glanced in our direction. Until at the very rear where Cliff walked with his mother, his head bowed slightly to talk to her. She was a little taller than I, held herself imperially straight, a great mass of barely contained hair in a thick braid. I had always imagined Mr. Gifford's wife to be a meek military wife. One look at her was enough to shatter that expectation, let alone her earlier speech.

Cliff spotted us, and he and his mother stopped, letting the sisters go past them before veering towards us. "Mom, you wanted to meet her, so here she is. Abby, meet my mum."

"Hi, Mrs. Gifford." I stood and shifted Secret to extend my hand. "Sorry for uh, karening up the funeral."

She looked down at my hand until I let it fall away. Then she looked up at me, expression frostier than even the Queen of Winter's. "First, it's Gloria. I know who you are, Abigale Night. George talked about you. I know who you were ten years ago. George believed people like that can change. I don't."

My jaw dropped, it had been years since anyone had picked up my past and hit me with it like a baseball bat. That meant Cliff knew as well. No, no, no.

"Mom, come on. That-" Cliff interjected.

"Not nice? Don't tell me who to be nice to, Clifford. Not today." She spoke without breaking eye contact with me. "You didn't even get probation, did you?"

"No, ma'am." I swallowed. "Just mandated counseling."

"Right, so we're clear. Now show me my son isn't completely insane." She crossed her arms and waited.

"What?" I looked to Cliff. "You told her?"

Cliff scratched the back of his head and gazed into the bushes. "I didn't expect her to actually believe me. She asked how I broke my arm."

"Don't you blame him; he can't lie to save his own

goddamn hide. Too much like his dad." Gloria stood as an immovable object. "He says you killed the creature that tortured my husband to death. Prove it to me."

"Fine. I don't want to be human right now anyway." This little alcove was secluded enough for a quick shift, and wolf me wanted to show her what she was asking. I started undoing my shirt.

"Just show her a little bit, Abby." Cliff glanced around nervously.

"I'm not afraid of a little white girl skin," Gloria said, voice flat and unimpressed as I tossed off my shirt and bra.

"It's more impressive when I shred everything, but I'm really low on uniforms now," I said.

"Yeah, sure." Gloria said, scorn drawing out like a blade.

I stood there, completely naked. Doubt about this swirling; did she have a gun loaded with silver in that purse? But wolf me growled at her projected hostility and forced my human doubts aside. I tore the rubber suit of human skin away and let her see the white fur and muscle beneath.

"God damn hellfire," Gloria swore as I shook the last bit of humanity from my skull a few moments later.

Growling softly, I showed her the teeth I'd ripped off Little Nick's hand with. Good enough for you?

Gloria clutched at her heart but otherwise stood her ground as a cascade of emotions ran over her face, shock plain on her scent.

"Told ya," Cliff sighed, giving me a relieved smile, as if he hadn't fully believed it himself.

She rounded on him. "You stay away from that." Jabbing a finger in my direction. "And whatever you are, you stay away from him!"

"Mom! Stop it." Anger flashed up into Cliff's eyes as he grabbed his mother's arm and forced it down to her side. "I fought that thing, Mom. It wasn't human. If Abby says she killed it, she killed it."

"You listen to me, Clifford! We are not having another closed casket funeral in this family!" Her voice a low hiss.

They stared at each other for a long moment before he simply said "No."

She twisted from his grasp and strode away toward the main path; I could almost smell the smoke she was breathing out.

He'd fought for me, stood against his own mom. Human me babbled doubts as I surged forward and nosed under his good arm. He gave a slight cry of surprise, and I snuck a lick at his cheek.

"Oof." He laughed and leaned on my shoulder. "Just oof. I'm sorry, Mom's having a rough time." He thumped my side and scratched my neck.

The touch stopped way too soon, and I let him know with a whine.

"Sorry, Abby. I gotta go. I'll see you at the office when you two start your next shift. Thanks. Mom's cool; she'll come around." He smelled of exhaustion and sadness. I wanted to drag him to a dark place and force him to rest but he had important duties to attend to now.

Cindy laughed without mirth. "Awkward, the definition of. I don't think either of them saw me."

"Merow." Secret jumped into my open purse and looked at me expectantly.

The smell of that sweet rot nagged at my nostrils. Human me had been wrong; it reached here. How far did it reach? Had to find out what this was, where it was.

"Abby, what are you waiting for?" Cindy asked. "You can't fit in your car like this."

I started gathering up my clothes and dropping them on

top of Secret in my purse as I pushed human me deeper inside myself. Human me didn't resist, weak from both her wounds and Gloria's razor-sharp words, I shrank down to the size of a large mundane canine.

"You now owe me an entire night of drinks." Cindy huffed, "My life..." She bent to stuff the loose clothing into my purse. It almost fit with the weight of Secret on top of it.

"Whuff," I objected when she started to pick it up. I grabbed the strap in my teeth and gently pulled it from her grasp.

She put her fists on her hips. "Really? You want to carry it? You have any idea how ridiculous that looks?"

I nodded once, gave her a quick wag of my tail, and bolted off in the opposite direction of the main path.

"Abby! Aaaah, Jebus!" I heard Cindy shout after me in frustration. When you can't talk, you just have to do.

12

I ran north, sticking to cover where I could, but I had to sprint over the bridge that crossed the interstate. No doubt that I made a social media star out of anyone who was fast enough with a phone camera. Stashing the purse behind a tree in the southern tip of Marquam Nature Park, I started my hunt for the Sweet Rot smell. Secret refused to be hidden along with the clothing, and followed me. I let her up on my shoulders as I wove between houses in Hillsboro. Even though most of the neighborhood is solid pavement, the scent of it leeched up through every storm drain and cable cubby in the sidewalk.

In the drainage ditch along route 10 I found the first clump of purple black mushrooms, sprouting in the shadow of a cross erected on the roadside. Their caps small and tight: immature or waiting for the right opportunity to bloom. As I circled around the town, threading through parks and backyards, I found more mushrooms anywhere a monument stood to grief. They grew in the shadow of park benches that bore the words in "memory of." My ears caught the sound of human coughing outside the armory nursing home, their front lawn studded with clusters of mushrooms, their caps wide open. After sundown we prowled back to the River View Cemetery. They were every-where there. The clouds refused to show me Luna's face, but it couldn't hide a seething movement in their dim shadows.

The scent of the Sweet Rot didn't extend past the ceme-tery, nor more than a mile and a half from the river. North-ward it petered out before reaching the OHSU hospital. Still a vast area: all of Southwest Portland. I became wary of the ground, as if a hand would reach up out of it and grab my paw. There was no denying that something very large and very bad was growing beneath the crust of Portland. Too big for a single werewolf or paramedic to handle. I fetched my clothes and shifted on the edge of the OHSU campus.

As I did, Gloria's words sprang out of my mind like a tiger that had been lurking in the bushes. *I know what you did ten years ago.* I had to take a moment to wait out the wave of guilt that watered my eyes and made my breath hitch as I desperately battled off a sob.

Secret looked up at me, one ear tilted with concern. "What I do?"

I forced a grin. "It's not you, Secret. Just having some feels."

"That lady? She was mean. I don't like her," Secret stated coldly.

"She had her reasons and I'm a big girl. I can take it." I knelt to be at her level. "Now I have to go inside the hospital and talk to someone. You can wait here or..." I offered her the purse.

She shook her head, "Been kitty most of the day. Two feet now. Have my glamor back now. I'm good!"

"Secret, why didn't you tell me you were so hungry?" The question popped out.

Her ears fell. "None of my guardians fed me. And... I didn't want you to know that I'm a monster, like all the rest of the Fey. I was afraid you'd leave me." A bashful little smile appeared. "But... now that you're a wolf, you're a little less good."

I took a deep breath. "I was only defending my... our..." I tried to find a different term, but nothing fit right. "...territory. Those men would have hurt us, and I won't tolerate that."

A predatory zeal lit in her green eyes. "I love hearts like the one you brought me, spicy and angry. Everything layered with frustration. Yum."

I laughed weakly, "So you're not going to ask for children's hearts or anything?"

She blinked. "A kid? Nooo! That'd be like eating, like... tuna eggs. Blech. Older the better but not like old old. If they're too old, if they don't wanna live, then it tastes like when you step in poo."

"You can't take little bits of hearts? Like Rey?" I asked.

She shook her head. "I'm a halfling." She blinked as if that explained everything.

A car's headlights illuminated the branches above our heads, and I decided that this perhaps wasn't the best place for a heart-to-heart discussion. Nor was I feeling ready to deal with the logistics of supplying Secret's dietary requirements. At least it wasn't a nightly or monthly thing. I pushed it all into my overstuffed mental closet marked "later." "Come on." I took her hand and climbed up the steep embankment to the road.

The OHSU, that's Oregon Health and Science University campus, sits on a hill overlooking downtown Portland, and is the best hospital in Oregon. There is a cable car that shuttles people between it and the trauma center on the other side of the highway. I've always thought it was a rather stupid placement for a trauma center because the only way up is on roads that curve up around the hill. More than one paramedic has been in a bit too much of a hurry and kissed the railing on the way up. They tell stories about what prompted them to put up the railing. It's never good when you need an ambulance for an ambulance. I thought about this as we dashed across the road and up to a more pedestrian-friendly access.

More out of habit than conscious thought, we entered through the emergency department, and as soon as the double automatic doors slid open, I smelled the sour earth. The mushrooms hadn't made it up the hill yet, but their consequences certainly had. I peeked into the waiting area and saw that the socially distanced area, which had become a permanent feature after bola-R, contained half a dozen wizened grey-hairs, masked and coughing.

Some of them had the Rot; there was no mistaking that smell.

My paramedic uniform attracted more attention than Secret's ears and tail as I led her into the bowels of the hospital. I'd never been to the place I sought personally, but human corpses have a stink all their own, and even chilling them doesn't make it go away entirely. The steel door had a little blue plaque that read "Morgue."

I knocked on the door.

It opened abruptly outwards, and I had to jump out of the way. "Vhat?" A tall person asked with a heavy Russian accent; she was clad in a hooded suit, face shield, mask, and nitrile gloves pulled over her cuffs. Tall was about the only thing you could tell about Nadia herself beneath all the safety equipment.

"Hi Nadia. Is Doctor Wiggins around tonight? I need to talk to him," I asked.

"You are in luck; we are both working tonight." Her gaze fell on Secret, who straightened, and from the twitch of her tail, I knew she was about to hit Nadia with a glamor. "Oooh hello little one! Would you like to see what happens to a human liver after he's drowned himself with drink?"

Secret blinked once. "Yes?"

Nadia's eyes gleamed as she stepped back from the doorway, holding it open with a foot to allow us to enter. "I'll look after her while you talk to the doctor. Gloves and gowns are on the left. I recommend a face shield, too; Margret will spit at new people."

That did not go at all how I'd expected it to, but I stepped into the hospital morgue. I've been in a few morgues before, mostly tours during training sessions. This one had all the standard things that movies prep you for: large steel tables, a steel wall with lots of body-sized doors that always reminded me of the ancient card catalogs they had at the church library when I was growing up. Cages were a new modern feature; a bank of three of them, taller than wide, stood against the far wall. They had the same stainless-steel gleam as almost everything else in the room. The wide bars were supplemented with a layer of chicken wire. A woman's bloated corpse stood sullenly in the middle cage, empty sockets glaring at me. The pudgy form of Dr. Wiggins leaned over a small microscope in the corner, back turned to the code Z, which didn't strike me as a good idea. They're always stronger than they look.

"Aww, don't be scared. The dead can't hurt you, except for Margret, but we won't get near her." Nadia promised Secret, who stood in the doorway, slitted eyes bouncing around the room. Not scared of the corpses so much as all the steel. "She'll need gloves," I suggested.

Doctor Wiggins turn around, noticing me. "Abby Night! What a surprise to see you in our humble lair." He laughed at his own joke. "I heard your life has gotten a tad interesting."

My mind immediately went to Slade's ranting about werewolves. Doctor Wiggins would be the absolute last person I wanted to know about my wolf side. "Aah," I said filling space as I dug for something to say.

"My condolences about your boss, Mr. Gifford. His son is taking over NLR?" he asked.

A wave of relief washed away the hot prickles that had flared along the back of my neck. "It's staying in the family, for now."

"We'll see if that stays that way," He muttered before sighing. "Anyway, what brings you to me tonight?"

"Right." I tried to organize what I had in my head in a way that sounded less crazy. "Have you noticed an increase of patients with an old man's friend?" That's emergency room code for Pneumonia.

He chuckled, "Uh, not really. Few of the patients I'm working with still breathe at all." The dark skin around his eyes crinkled, broadcasting the smile that was hidden beneath his mask. "You'd be better off talking to the pulmonary department; I'm sure if they've noticed an uptick, they're taking steps and recording it. Usually new things hit Seattle first."

"No," I paused before plunging into, well, the literal twilight zone. "I'm coming to you because this is connected to code Z. It's a new code Weird that looks like pneumonia. And I think it's going to get a lot worse." I kept going, describing the syndrome in as clinical terms as possible, ignoring the slow arching of his eyebrows as I linked its spread to purple mushrooms and finally, "And I've seen at least two victims possessed by a ghost."

Dr. Wiggins stood there, not saying anything as he turned to stare at the corpse in the cage. She lurched forward, pressed her torn lips against the bars, and spat a thick loogie that landed a foot from the cage with a vicious smack. The doctor stared at it as he spoke, "I want to throw my hands up and laugh in your face, Abby. Tell you that your theory about mushrooms and ghosts is impossible gobbledygook. But I've stared at impossible for months now. Right there." He pointed at the zombie. "She's dead. Not just a little dead. Every single cell in her body. Usually when a person dies, it takes some tissues awhile to give it up. That's why hair and nails can keep growing for a bit. I thought code Z might be that, some remnant of life in their muscles and oxygen-starved brains. But I irradiated her, with enough juice to melt any DNA remnants to slag. And still she moves, though there's no charge in her muscles or nerves. No metabolic activity I can find other than the bacteria eating her flesh." Margret rattled the bars and made a wet slurping sound before hawking another loogie. It landed six inches closer to where Dr. Wiggins stood.

He looked down at the milk-white globs on the floor. "And she hates me to boot. So, I'm going to take you very seriously, Miss Night. And then hope very hard that I will find a reasonable, rational explanation for all this in the future. Otherwise, I might start believing that the world is about to end, and everything we've learned about the universe is about the mask it wore." There was a brittleness in his voice. "I'll let you know."

"Oooh!" Secret's delight pierced the doctor's grim mood and deflated it like a balloon. "What's that bubble thing?"

I turned to find Secret standing on a yellow plastic stool, leaning over an opened corpse, a sight that would have made me woozy at her age. Nadia hovered protectively, pointing at the viscera with a pair of forceps as long as my forearm. "Good eyes! That's an enlarged bile duct. If that had burst, he would have found new lands of pain, but his liver got him first."

"Oh gods," Dr. Wiggins sighed, "she got another one."

"It's okay, she's mine." I gave him a quick smile and raised my voice. "Secret, we should get going. Say thank you to Nadia." I decided I didn't want to know if Secret was only the latest child for Nadia to share her work with.

One ear rotated before the rest of her head. "But this is neat!"

"Is no trouble," Nadia added. "Be done in thirty minutes, maybe less."

"We need to get home. Aunt Cindy's going to worry." The memory of running away from Cindy replayed in my mind and hot prickles climbed up my neck. Wolf me needed to treat Cindy better, whether she was afraid of me or not.

Secret pouted, and I felt my resolve crumple; the night was youngish. I wound up hovering over Secret's shoulders as Nadia showed us a liver that looked like it was made of Styrofoam, and I'd probably stumble away drunk if I ate it. By the time Nadia finished giving Secret a lesson on the digestive system, I was salivating so much that it made talking difficult. Wolf me wanted a doggy bag in the worst way. I hadn't eaten since we'd left the house this morning, and I'd crisscrossed the entire west side. So distracted I almost didn't hear Nadia say, "Always so wonderful to meet a non-squeamish child; if not for her steel allergy, she'd have a great future in medicine," as we were tossing our PPE into the trash.

My sharp look was probably all the confirmation she needed. She pulled down her mask, displaying a cat in the cream smile. "Don't worry, I won't tell she Feya." Her eyes dipped in Dr. Wiggins' direction. "He's a mole, sees only what is in front of him but digs deep. I... envy you. Wandering the city as it all happens. Seeing it all change. What does it mean that your eyes are silver now?"

Her own eyes were steely grey.

"Contacts," I said, "I like them."

"As you say." With a brief nod, she backed off, but only to press a card into my palm. "You are homeschooling. I will teach her biology."

As Secret bounced up and down, I realized it already been decided. "Thank you," I said.

Nadia booped Secret's nose, "See you soon kotenok."

Now stunned and hungry, I introduced Secret to the wonders and horrors of OHSU's cafeteria, so I didn't get tempted to take a bite out of some sleep-deprived grad student on the cable car ride downtown. Found a cupcake bakery as my "Sorry I'm a literal bitch" peace offering to Cindy. Although one met a premature demise in the toothy maw of a certain cat-eared child on the tram home. As we neared our stop, I got a surprising text from Cindy. "I hope you're not tired from running around all day, but I'm calling in those drinks you owe me tonight. So there. :P"

13

———

I really hadn't expected Cindy to call in her drinks so soon, but I couldn't say I was opposed. Rey probably had something to do with it. A few did sound nice after a day like today. Cindy wasn't the only one who had a hankering for a taste of normal even if it meant I'd have to wear a dress. Drinking with Cindy wasn't a "throw on jeans and t-shirt" affair. Hopefully she wouldn't mind me slumming it next to her.

"Cindy?" I called out as Secret and I entered the house.

"She's getting ready." Rey's voice sang with pride down the stairs.

I murmured a response and hurried to my room, trying not to imagine what drinking with Rey would be like.

Picking out what to wear was easy; I only had one dress, a standard little black dress that I had picked up the day after Christmas. My wardrobe had burned along with the rest of my apartment. Accented with a few pieces of costume jewelry from the box that Aunt Sheryl had "lent" me, the look didn't seem half bad. Although the white roots of my hair and the paleness of my eyes kinda said cosplayer instead of clubber. The crescent moon that rose above the plunging neckline and the circle of teeth scars on my arm didn't help. "Well, you're either a werewolf or you want to be one very badly," I told my reflection, sucking in the stomach pudge that comes with waiting around for disaster to strike, but grateful I hadn't gone completely pear-shaped yet. My arms and shoulders had a little more tone to them than I remembered; apparently using them as legs counts for something.

Lacking any makeup, my prep hadn't taken long, so I was shocked to find both Rey and Cindy waiting for me and Secret downstairs. Rey wore leather pants that blazed Ferrari red, a black sneaker on one foot and matching medical boot on the other, concealing her stone foot. Her top barely registered because when I tore my eyes off the kitsune's legs they found Cindy.

Long red hair, a pink dress slit to the hip, and a pair of stiletto heels, but that doesn't begin to describe her. The sweep of that dress banished everything I knew about Cindy's body, if I focused, I could still see individual parts of it. The broad shoulders, the rounded curve of her belly but it all disappeared when she moved, subsumed beneath a flowing femininity: vibrant, smooth, and sly. She set off tingles of desire.

"You're f-fucking gorgeous!" I exclaimed but the word that had actually come to mind had been foxy. She looked absolutely foxy.

Cindy glowed under the compliment and hugged me hard, releasing me only after something in my spine popped. "I'll call the taxi, then. Shouldn't be long." She hurried towards the door. In her wake, I realized there hadn't been a whiff of fear on her, just excitement, and I smelled an undercurrent of Rey's gossamer musk that bore a single message: mine. On her back a white fox mask stared out from the center of a bow in the small of her back.

I looked at the Fox Fey, her eyes drifted downward demurely, her subtle smile oozing with a tired satisfaction. "Try not to get all fuzzy tonight. She needs a break."

"What did you do, Rey?" I whispered back at her.

"A question for a question?" She stepped closer and continued once I nodded. "Atoning for my clever trick by making a dream real. Don't turn it into a nightmare for her."

"Less than five minutes!" Cindy called out.

Rey glided past me, but I caught her arm, "Ask me your question."

"Later," she whispered and pulled free, leaving me feeling unsettled. Cindy was an adult and knew that she was sleeping with fire that could burn her. I didn't have to save her from Rey. Rey was the product of two legends: Inari, a benevolent Japanese kitsune who blessed the rice harvest and Reyard, the European fox who was the most bastardy bastard who ever did bastard. Hopefully Cindy would only face the Inari half while the Reynard part played these possession games.

The taxi took us to downtown Burnside Street, and Rey dragged us across traffic, towards a particularly crowded club. Only as we neared the entrance did she pause to collect herself and survey the collection of people lined up behind a red velvet rope. Darker colors dominated the crowd. Me and my little black dress could slip into it unnoticed, but Cindy's pink seemed impossibly girly, a spring flower in the dead of winter. But every eye glued itself to Rey as her tails swirled around each other in an impossible bundle. Drinking their gaze, she linked arms with Cindy and after a moment of whispered conversation, the pair strode up to the small squad of bouncers. I followed them, already feeling like a third wheel.

Yet, with five feet to go, Rey twirled off Cindy's arm and slipped back to my side. And it was Cindy who strode up to the door with a confident sway of her hips, tossed her long, wavy red locks and smiled down at the guard. "My friends and I are here to dance." Her deep voice a lustful purr that reached into my chest and pulled at my heart.

"Murf?" Secret popped her head out of the purse hanging on my shoulder to watch the guards who, slack-jawed, silently removed the rope that barred her path.

"Go." Rey whispered, grasping my arm, and leaning heavily on my side as we went after Cindy. Right before we stepped into the dark of the club, I noticed that Rey's ears had gone almost entirely white.

Inside, Cindy spun around, her face breaking into ecstatic joy and squealing, "That was amazing!" She charged up to Rey, swept the dainty Fox Fey up into her arms and kissed Rey so hard her tails puffed up. When Cindy put her down, a trace of color had returned to Rey's fur; both wore identical love-struck smiles as we all drifted to the bar.

I bought them all drinks. Taking no chances in case my lycanthropy did something to my ability to process alcohol, I ordered a Long Island Iced Tea. One of those and I'd probably be too buzzed to be self-conscious about dancing. I hadn't been "clubbing" since a few disastrous dates that Aunt Sheryl had set me up on after I'd "graduated" from my intensive therapy regime post Jimmy. We clustered at a standing table, the pulsing beat too loud for conversation, Cindy sipped a tall beer, while Rey sucked down a cocktail they'd called the fox and hound before dashing off towards the dance floor.

I lifted my eyebrows at Cindy to indicate the speed at

which she had ditched us. Cindy, still glowing from her pretty lady experience, shrugged and took a long sip of her drink. The world had gained a bit of a slant after I finished my "tea" and we drifted toward the dance floor. Rey didn't take effort to find; she danced in an opening on the floor, pulsing in time with the music in some type of spontaneous dance-off. Bystanders would leap into the circle to challenge her, presenting a new style of dance which she'd copy and then with a whirl of her tails, fling them back into the crowd.

Cindy stepped on the dance floor and instantly a spotlight came down on her. The crowd parted in awe, and with a whirl of her dress she spun onto the dance floor, leaving me facing a wall of people. In steeling myself to follow her, I took a deep breath. In it I tasted sour earth. Instantly my wolf sprang to attention, our ears perking. I sniffed experimentally, and the scent hung there in the air, out of place among the throng of individual human scents. Unable to help myself, I pushed into the throng, cutting my way with a sharp elbow.

I found her. A small cluster of four people near the far wall. Two men and a woman around a second girl in a glittering gold dress who had to be thirty years their senior. Wiry gray hair in a stringy ponytail bounced behind her as her painfully thin limbs whirled in an impressively fluid pop and lock style almost in sync with deep bass of the electronic music. I watched her over the shoulder of a barrel-chested man whose dancing consisted of little more than swaying from side to side and coughing. Sweat soaked through his black shirt and his scent screamed sick. All of them were coughing except for the dancing grandma, I couldn't be sure she breathed at all.

My teeth sharpened as I watched them; wolf huffed with

indecision. This was beyond my territory, but I couldn't do nothing in the face of this sickness. The rotten man had been dead. I backed off and texted Victoria.

"I need you" my thumb sent the message prematurely.

"Oh?" She responded with a wide-eyed emoji as I thumbed in the actual message.

"I need you to meet me in the back of this club. There's a dancing woman who I think is dead. Can you do like an exorcism?"

"Aww. Getting my hopes up. :P" She texted back. As I blinked at the words, a second line appeared, "j/k you way too butch for me. ;) Be there ten minutes."

Butch? Me? Indignation flared as I stared at the texts. "I'm straight," I protested at the screen even as the searing cold of Queen Mab's lips flashed through my mind and kindled a heat in my body. "Straightish," I amended; some allowances had to be made for ancient Fey who held a piece of your heart. Wolf me nosed forward Cliff's shining smile, imagining it on the muzzle of a huge black wolf. Would he have black fur? I wondered; I had been gray before I'd become winter's wolf.

I shook the useless musings away. Victoria had just been kidding around and my trauma-damaged brain was reading too much into it. Right? I refocused on watching the golden granny and waiting for Victoria to arrive.

14

I watched this group of sickness dance from the sidelines, my growl rumbling under the music. Watching their spittle erupt into the air. Could it spread from a person or only via the mushrooms? At the ten-minute mark I thrust my hand into my purse and dug under a wriggling Secret, extracting a pack of surgical masks. With them in hand, I tapped the man on the shoulder hard.

He turned sluggishly to mouth "What?!" at me. The sour earth scent made me blanch even as I shoved three surgical masks into his chest.

"Wear them if you're sick," I shouted back at him.

"Just a cold!" he shouted back before a hacking fit doubled him over.

That gave me a clear shot at the dancing grandma. Stepping around him, I snatched her elbow and her eyes popped open. Too wide, and shot with dark threads, just like Mr. Baker and Scully. "You don't belong here, Grandma," I told her as I searched for an exit, unsure what I'd do with her once I got outside.

"Let me go! I want my last dance! I wanna finish it!" She

whined like a teenager and tried to twist out of my grip, but I held firm to her fever-hot limb.

"Tiffany!" cried her little posse as they staggered after us. I pulled her into a cinder-block hallway that muffled the music down to a building-shaking bass. Fingernails clawed at my hand.

"Let go! It's not fair! I was just dancing! That's all!" Tiffany continued to whine like a naughty child caught by a parent. "They asked me back. They invited me!"

No one stopped me from slamming my hip into the emergency exit door at the end of the hallway. No alarm sounded. I dragged her outside, and she stumbled over the threshold. With a snap of her high heel, she went down to her knees. I let her go as I looked around. We were in an employee parking lot at the back of the building. The drizzle made night under the streetlamps sparkle. Nobody stirred as I wondered if I could shift without damaging my dress. "What are you? Did you make your admirers sick?" I demanded as wolf me pushed out of my skin. White fur slipped over my shoulders and down my arms as my body swelled. Bones crackled like Rice Krispies in milk as my face morphed into a muzzle.

"I just wanted to dance again. Let me finish my dance." Tiffany struggled, those too-wide eyes unfocused as I seized her wrinkled chin and held her mouth up to my nose. The sour earth that clung to her unfolded in my mind; wrapped in rich earthen rot lay a vivid tangle of scents, a mingling of life and death. Yet something lay still deeper in the scent, a wrongness that all words failed to describe. An evil.

An engine's purr echoed off the walls. I took my eyes off Tiffany to see Victoria's black hearse roll into the parking lot. Reluctantly, wolf me pulled back so words could flow. Tiffany made a hissing sound and tried to escape my grip as

Victoria stepped out of the car. With the wolf still in my arms, I pinned her up against the wall. Her eyes finally met mine. "I didn't do anything! Don't tell Mr. Baker." She whined.

"Yeah, that's a possession." Bewilderment rang in Victoria's voice, and I heard a soft rustling, "Get her in this circle!"

I peeled Tiffany from the brick, and turned to find Victoria drawing a circle of salt on the asphalt behind me. With a shove, Tiffany stumbled into its center as Victoria completed it. The old lady threw herself to the side but bounced off an invisible wall. "They invited me!" she shrieked as she collapsed into the center. "My family wanted to see me!"

"Your family's sick." I snarled at her, kneeling. "That body you're riding in is nearly dead. Whose is it?"

"I need to finish my dance!" She wailed.

Victoria stared at the lady, wiping something black beneath each of her eyes. "Anointed with bone, blood, and ash. Show me what is hidden beneath the light of life." Shadows pooled beneath her brows, obscuring her eyes entirely. A tiny gasp escaped Victoria's lips. "This is a Ba!"

"A what?" I asked. This was not the time to be counting sheep.

"Souls break into pieces when someone dies; ghosts are a mere shadow of it, the Sheut. A flawed copy related to the circumstances of their death. This, though! This is an entire person! This could be a breakthrough!" Victoria said with the same breathless cadence that a young girl once used to explain the family dynamics of her unicorn collection to me while trying not to look at the bone fragment jutting out of her leg.

"Victoria," I growled, "we need it to answer questions or get rid of it."

She frowned. "Do you have any idea how long I've been trying to figure out how to summon a Ba instead of a Sheut?"

Tiffany continued to gibber and claw at her cage as I glared at Victoria, "This woman is infected with some sort of disease. A possessed man with the same disease coordinated an attack on my territ- I mean, neighborhood. We need to know where this Ba came from."

That mouth pressed into a thin line as her head bowed. "I wouldn't do this for anyone else," she said, and then started mumbling to herself, "who died dancing?" She reached into her long trenchcoat and to take a pull from her vape stick.

"Her name's Tiffany." I offered.

"Tiffany... tiffany..." Victoria muttered and straightened up. "Tiffany Banon!"

The woman in the circle froze.

"Tiffany Dorothy Banon. Shot at a dance competition by a Herbert Goyle on August 3rd, 2027." Victoria's mouth split into a vicious grin as our captive lifted her head to look up at her. The smile combined with the enshadowed eyes made her look ghoulish in the yellowed streetlamp of the parking lot. "Got it in one. Tiffany Dorothy Banon, answer our questions."

I hear you. The voice came from out of the body as it sat up. *But I will not answer.*

Still holding on to her vape stick, Victoria pulled a long-handled blade from the folds of her trench coat. I recognized it as the same one that had been lodged in her stomach the night we met. With it, she sliced open an inch-long cut on the side of her hand. Blood welled up in the wound, but a darkness flowed up the blade, trailing off it like smoke. "Ah, shit," Victoria muttered before shoving the bloody hand into the circle. "I offer blood for obedience. Partake and answer the living."

Tiffany recoiled from it, pulling her borrowed body out of the way of the dripping blood, but the crimson liquid captivated her eyes. She watched the first drip fall, then the second "No... I..." and on the third she pounced, grabbing at the hand, and trying to bite it like a BBQ rib. With a curse, Victoria wrenched her hand away before the teeth made contact. Tiffany lapped at the pavement where the spilled drops had fallen.

"Now," Victoria said , her voice booming with authority. "How have you come back to us from the land beyond?"

"A crack of agony, a rift of pain. It opened, right there. I was supposed to tell Mr. Baker, but I used it myself. My family wanted me back; grandma invited me in tonight." Wide eyes pleaded with us.

"Who's Mr. Baker?" I asked.

Terror flashed over that weathered face, "He is the left hand of the old King. Chief of the riders and herder of the lost."

The scent of the air changed, from the moist chill to a cool dryness, with a bitter touch in the back of the throat. The world went absolutely silent.

"It is not wise to tease me with your blood, Victoria Quentin." A person stepped seemingly from the corner of my eye and onto the pavement. Wearing a dark gray suit that empathized the sharp features of their pale face. Tiny sparks floated inside their empty eyes. I swallowed, instinctively moving between Victoria and Death.

"You can't have her," I said, and Secret made a small hissing noise from the purse I had left by the door.

Death's mouth did not smile, but the sparks in their eyes danced as they regarded us. "I have not come for her now, but if you were to remove her throat, I would consider it a gesture of goodwill. I would be far more forthcoming than a single frightened shade."

The scent of Victoria's fear blossomed.

"Only over my cooling body." I growled.

"Careful wolf, in this coming age, I am allowed to take sides. I will see her penance served eventually." The sparks focused on Tiffany, and I heard the whoosh of a heavy blade.

The woman fell.

"We're not done with her!" Victoria found her voice.

"You are done with both of them," Death intoned. There, standing over the body, were two translucent figures, one teenage girl in a denim jacket, a bib on the back declaring her contestant 10, a bullet hole right in the center of the zero. Next to her, a mature woman with a sour expression glared back at Death. "Don't look at me," Death said to her. "Your granddaughter forgot how to breathe."

The woman turned her glare on the younger.

The girl mouthed her familiar refrain. "I wanted to finish my dance."

"Down the river with you, girl." Death reached out, and both specters folded into balls of light: the girl just one, the grandmother several. They floated towards Death, who pocketed them. They turned. "Leave Charon's fare if you wish." With those words spoken, the alley brightened without him in it.

"Now that's rude," I grumbled.

Victoria let out a long, shaky breath. "Is that what I think it was? The grim reaper has it in for me?"

I found myself laughing, "What? You didn't believe me when I told you what happened when we pulled you out of the Twilight?"

"Well, yeah, but..." she trailed off and blushed.

"What?" I asked, and her pale cheeks continued to flush redder.

"I thought he'd be hotter."

I stared at her, my mind refusing to process that.

"Look, I read a lot of romance novels." Her smile grew pained, "Meeting him, though, I don't think he's that sort of Death."

"Meeeeerf," Secret said from the safety of my purse, summing up my thoughts entirely. I looked down at the dead body at my feet. Whether it had been Death or simple luck, so far all we needed was someone to come out that door, and we'd be murder suspects.

I fished out two quarters from a side pocket and knelt down next to the woman. Her struggle with me had smudged her lipstick and beneath it, her lips were black, curled with more threads.

Swearing at myself for daring to even touch the body, I put a quarter over each eye, and in a fit of madness or inspiration, I placed a third on her forehead. "For your trouble," I mumbled.

The world dimmed. The ground beneath me rocked once, as if I stood on the deck of a boat, and I heard the splash of Charon's pole as it cut through water.

Coins jingled, and the lights came back. The body was gone.

"The hell?" Victoria breathed.

"Well, Charon still likes me, at least." I smiled at her. "You want a drink?"

She glanced at the door but shook her head, "No, not this club and I was kinda in the middle of something. I'll take a rain check on that drink, though." She smiled before she stepped back towards her car and I had an odd sensation, like missing a step I hadn't seen. I went back inside and found out why Tiffany's posse hadn't burst outside with me. They hadn't made it. They sat in a cluster of chairs, coughing and hacking. Guarded by a trio of security guards with N95 masks. That's Portland night life for you; can drag a protesting grandmother out of a club, but after three plagues, coughing will get you detained.

After a quick stop in a bathroom to safety pin my dress's straps back on, I slipped back into the club with the complete intention of telling Cindy I was taking Secret home.

I took one step inside and froze in horror as a completely insane series of sounds shrieked out of the speakers.

Everyone in the club shouted back, "WHAT DOES A FOX SAY?!"

15

———

Add an industrial strength sound system to the list of things to never let a Fey get near. Rey had gotten on the main stage, her ears and tails so red they appeared to be fused with LEDs. One arm draped over the shoulder of the DJ, hanging off him as they transitioned from What Does a Fox Say to Jimi Hendrix's Foxy Lady.

"Abby! Where'd you go?" Cindy suddenly loomed up in front of me, surfacing from the crowd like a whale from the ocean. A whale with a pair of fox ears poking through her red hair.

My mouth opened to explain the weirdness, the sickness, and why we should probably go home right now, but Cindy simply latched on and pulled me under with her into a sea churning with people. Cindy spun me through it, each note pounding through my brain, each beat inviting me to let it all go.

My feet flailed to keep up with Cindy's, and then the dance caught them. That it wasn't a song that I had ever thought to dance to did not matter. We swayed, we strutted, swishing our hips as we circled, Foxy Ladies! A wave of laughter drowned out the pulse of the guitar for a moment as everyone on the floor shared bright glances that said, *Can you believe we're doing this? This is so silly!* But as Rey commanded, "Foxy!" no one stopped swishing tails that weren't quite real but no longer imaginary, either. "Foxy!... Foxy lady!" Rey's voice floated, adding a hypnotic tone to the song. That moment I had given Rey swelled inside me until my stride became sultry with the weight of three tails pulling on my spine. Cindy's hand captured my waist, and we strode side by side, my tails and her tail curling together.

Distantly, through that small piece of Rey lodged in me, a window opened to the Rey on the stage. My 'I' broke apart, becoming hers, consumed in the task of threading a fine line between effort and an ecstasy that threatened to wash away conscious thought. A delicate web of threads wove through the dancers and back into my heart, Rey's heart. Each note of the guitar a shared beat of fox, of Rey. That heart hurt, straining under the load, but she-I couldn't stop. The rush of all these humans declaring themselves to be us, to be Foxy. Worship had never tasted this good, these unfiltered connections. Too much, too much for the heart, so shriveled from years of hunger. We should stop, had to stop, or we'd explode like an overstuffed star. But we couldn't. "One more song," she and I whispered into the ear of the DJ we hung on, threading the knowledge of another song into his mind with ease.

Danger, growled wolf me. *Move, save packmate.* She pulled at me, and for a moment I became three: human me danced, Wolf me chewed at the threads, while Rey/I marveled at her own accelerating destruction. Wolf and human me snapped back together; I tore myself away from the dance. Cindy simply pivoted to another dancer as I pushed toward the stage through a sea of people who looked more like foxes with every beat.

Rey clung to the DJ, melting into him, the red of her ears bleeding upwards into the air, while her tails had grown long, wrapping around the speakers like fluffy serpents. Through the promise of loyalty she had made to me, I could feel her burning, her entire being on the edge of combustion. I threw myself up on the stage and peeled her from the DJ like a strip of tape from a wall. The revelry continued, the DJ yipping into the microphone and the crowd answering in high pitched keens. She fell against me, utterly limp, giggling drunkenly. "Rey!" I shouted in her fuzzy ear. "Stop it! Let it go!"

"It's one revel," she whined. "A drop in the bucket. Why is it so much?!"

I grabbed her two scalding-hot ears and forced her to look into my eyes. Her pupils were not dark but swimming with images of foxes singing and dancing, most with the too-clean sheen of 3D rendering. Dance, dance, dance with me. They pounded at my skull.

"Loyalty, remember?" I shook her, "Killing yourself... Don't make me say it, Rey."

The threat only made her grin, "Go ahead, I'll pop this time, new foxes will be born from this. They'd be free of you and my promise. Maybe they'll find proper stories of their own."

"And what about Cindy?" I countered. "What will happen to her if you end yourself now?"

The drunken grin fell and the dance in her eyes stuttered to images of Cindy, bent over as she danced with Secret, spinning her around to the beat. Cindy was a distinct flavor all her own in the web that connected us. An astonished delight that radiated through every thread. "Only with her to get back at you?" Rey's voice wavered uncertainly. "Means nothing." She swallowed, tears gathering.

I didn't need the wolf to smell the lie. "If you become some other Fox Fey, you'll break her heart," I said, "and she will cry."

A thin smile appeared as she closed her eyes. "A mortal can't love a Fey without pain." She laughed as she reached out. By the flashing lights of the club, nearly invisible threads gathered in her hand. With a jerk of her wrist, they all snapped. Rey's body rippled, and I held the small head of an actual fox in my hands, her coat so red and vibrant she was more like a cartoon than an actual animal. I gathered her up into my arms. She nipped at my hand halfheartedly and stilled into slumber.

With her in my arms, I retreated to the bar and ordered a drink. Slowly, the club lost its foxy obsession, drifting back to a punky blend of techno and guitar solos. The ears of the dancers were, on second glance, oddly styled hair and the tails revealed themselves to be belts fastened only to a rear belt loop. Rey did not stir from my lap until Cindy came off the dance floor sometime during my third mojito. Secret clung to her back. Both shone with sweat.

Rey's head lifted, and she yawned.

"I wondered where she went." Cindy offered her hand to Rey, and she licked it as Secret slid down from her piggyback ride.

We traded. A fox for a catgirl who was way too young to be in a club. No one said anything as we left and boarded a taxi for the ride home. My phone chirped with a text; thinking it might be Victoria, I checked it.

"All press is good press?" It asked with a link to an NPR story. I clicked it, and the audio played.

"Police are still asking for witnesses to come forward;

anyone who saw what appears to be a running gunfight that left at least three people dead in the Powellhurst neighborhood of southwest Portland. One victim was a known member of the far-right militia Freedom First. Police have no comment at this time, pending what they describe as a very active investigation, but sources within the department have been more forthcoming. While the cause of death of all the bodies found were by gunshots, both trucks recovered showed evidence of a very large animal. They also found silver ammunition. Would these men have been hunting a werewolf IN Portland?" The reporter forced a laugh, as if attempting to convince herself that the very idea was silly. The clip ended. Was Andrew Millar on the other end of this number? He'd violated my hospital records. What would stop him from tracking my phone?

Absolutely nothing.

Turning my phone off, I petted Secret, who was asleep on my lap. Cindy leaned on the window, eyes closed; the heart-stopping glamor had faded, but she radiated contentment as Rey lay belly-up across her lap. So much for a taste of normal. I laughed at myself, returning my attention to Secret; she'd watched a possessed woman die and then danced the very next moment. That brief image of her and Cindy lost in the music made me smile. Exhaustion pulled at me, but wolf me kept us alert, watching the man driving us follow the blue line of his navigation.

I'd play coy with Mr. Millar for now, but as soon as he reached for anyone else, Cindy, Secret, or even Rey, he'd lose his arm.

No sinister force, physical or otherwise, stopped us from reaching home. I shucked off my human skin to sleep. In the morning, an entirely different beast waited for me. Another forty-eight-hour shift.

16

"You sure you can handle this?" Cindy grabbed my shoulder as I reached for the door handle.

I paused and looked at Cindy's stern face. "Same answer as before," I told her. "We got it handled, and thanks to Cliff, I'll spend sleepy time in the park." Wolf me had gotten that romp across west Portland yesterday and currently lounged contentedly inside me. It wouldn't last, but hopefully eight hours among the trees at night would prevent her from causing trouble.

Cindy continued to stare at me. "And?"

I gritted my teeth. "And you're primary until further notice."

"Aaaand I'm here to drive if she can't." Rey hiccupped from the back as she sprawled across the backseat, still in her fox form, grinning drunkenly. Next to her, Secret giggled. Work had officially become a family affair. Mostly because Cindy didn't want to leave Rey unattended. I didn't know which of this car full of bad ideas would sour first, but I hoped it wouldn't be my wolf this time.

Cindy stared at the rear-view mirror, her dubious

expression reflecting what I assumed to be similar misgivings. "Both of you in get in bags."

"As you wish," Rey replied in a sultry tone that shivered through the air before filling the car with a rustle of fabric.

After a few moments of gathering bags and enough food to sustain us for the forty-eight-hour shift, we walked through the open garage door, Secret riding in my purse, and Rey in Cindy's backpack.

All four ambulances were parked in their slots and the bay was a bustle of activity as the shifts swapped. The exiting shift were making last-minute restocks of the ambulances and hoisting their overnight bags onto their shoulders, chatting with the incoming shift. Didn't see Cliff, but I had no idea what hours he kept now.

"Well, if it ain't Cinderella and Cindy." The voice came from behind us, along with a light clearing of a throat. I found Mitch behind me, deep bags under his eyes.

"Hey Mitch, thanks for cleaning up my mess the other day," I said.

He waved it off. "No biggie. I watched him clock you, surprised you're not swelled up like a melon. After Cindy hauled you off, he just collapsed. Said he didn't remember nothing. ahem." Stifled another cough. "I took him into the hospital, and he vomited in my car. Asshole." With a shake of his head, he moved past me with a definite whiff of sour earth in his wake.

"You feeling alright?" I called at him.

He shrugged without turning around. "Didn't sleep well, got a tickle. Don't worry, I'll wear a mask today, mom." And flashed me his middle finger.

I swallowed and stared after him, was it starting already? I checked the office for Cliff, but he wasn't there, I knew Mitch's type. He wouldn't consider himself sick until he was flat on his back. Cliff might be able to make him go home, but it would take a stern order, not a suggestion.

There was nothing for it. We drew a daylight shift and cruised. After a spate of early morning taxi runs for a few elderly individuals, the calls dried up completely. Spurred by Nadia's mention of home schooling, I wound up spending hours in the back of the bus with Secret, trying to introduce the concept of math to her. While Secret could read, numbers beyond counting to ten were foreign concepts. Using the stretcher as a desk, we added and subtracted band aids, at least until she started confusing six and nine. Frustrated, she retreated to cat form and would only say "Merf" for the last hour of the shift. Rey yipped in laughter.

Still, Cindy and I smiled at each other as we drove back to the firehouse, a dangerous spirit of optimism growing between us. Maybe this new normal wouldn't be too bad.

However, that sensation of normalcy shattered when we rolled into the firehouse. A folding table had been set up outside the door to the office, piled high with thick manila folders. Excess paperwork was never a good sign.

The shouting was a return to normal.

"We're not selling!" Cliff's voice carried through the wall.

"Then you 're damn stupid! This is easy money: a lot more than you'll ever get out of this place!" The higher-pitched and equally confrontational tone echoed out through the garage. The office, and indeed most of the walls inside the cinder brick building, were built from drywall so thin that some tissues had better sound-dampening proper-ties. Fortunately, some sleep-deprived fire engineer had insulated the bunkroom.

"That's not the point, Sophie!" Cliff countered. "Dad would never take that money."

"Newsflash: you are not dad. I'm not interested in your little redemption play here, Cliff."

"Let me buy you out, then. Gimmie some time."

"With what? Besides Grandpa's car you've got nothing, Cliff. You want to play at biz shit, which we all know you suck at, then take your share of the money. Then you can go weigh anchor somewhere you won't drag me and Taya down with you. Who the fuck you callin'?"

The door to the office swung open and hit the little brass doorstop so hard the shock of its sudden impact made the wall wobble. Cliff stormed out, his phone pressed to his ear, quickly heading out the open garage door into the waiting drizzle.

Sophie made to chase him but froze when she saw Cindy and me watching. A study in constraint, gold-rimmed glasses held still-smoldering dark eyes, hair held in dozens of shoulder-length braids while several bangle-studded chains hung around her neck. From the neck up, I'd peg her for a librarian. The rest of her was dressed in the Portland standard blue-and-red-checkered flannel combo with hip-hugging stone-washed jeans. She stared at us, eyes calculating, before spinning on her heel with enough speed to whirl her braids, and went back inside the office.

Cindy laughed without opening her mouth as I drove us into our parking spot. "Good to know the local soap opera hasn't been canceled with the change in management," she commented as I locked the emergency brake.

"If anything, the stakes are even higher now." I had a hunch about who was playing the Giffords off one another. Cindy and I drifted to the table after doing a quick inventory. Flipping open one of the manila folders confirmed it. The first words across the top read: Legacy Health Systems. Hello, Andrew Millar. His quest to own everything vaguely medical in the city had finally reached NLR. They were employment contracts, each about an inch thick.

Cindy whistled as she fanned through the pages. "I think you can sell a house with less paperwork."

Sophie stepped out of the office, wearing a plastered-on "friendly" smile. It looked a little worn around the edges. "Hiii, I'm Sophie. Sorry 'bout that earlier. I dunno how much you heard but-"

"Just everything." I cut her off and tapped the stack of contracts. "Looks like these are premature."

The smile faltered, and she shrugged. "You might as well sign them now. Otherwise, you'll have to go through Legacy HR before you can get back to work. It's got a much better health plan than my dad could ever offer."

Cindy dropped the contract back onto the pile. "I don't think it's a good idea to sign an employment contract for a company that only might employ me." Cindy shook her head.

"Ten percent raise if you pre-sign," she countered.

"What?" I narrowed my eyes at her. "That's not how buyouts usually work."

"It's a good deal for everyone except my emotionally-invested brother." Sophie put her smile back on.

Cliff slunk back into my line of sight, shoving his phone into his pocket. "This isn't over, Sophie, Mom will back me up."

She gave him a cool look. "Mom would burn this place to the ground if she had her say. You're outvoted." She patted the contracts and smiled back at us, "I'll just leave these here." With that, she bade Cindy and me goodbye, then walked across the bay to the exit door. Cliff staring daggers at her back as she did so.

I slipped up beside him. Reaching up to touch his back,

the sight of the pale postage-stamp scar between my thumb and forefinger made me pause. Wolf me whined inside as I curled my fingers and let the hand drop. "Fraught night?" I asked, instead of touching him.

He shook himself and flashed a flaccid grin. "Wonderful night. Busted arm and busted family." He didn't add that it was my fault, but he turned and stepped away, as if avoiding my reach. "I'm going to be here for another hour. If you two could get the stuff filed from your run before I leave, that would be a help." And he retreated into the office.

With a sigh, Cindy flipped open one contract and began to skim. She answered my questioning glance. "Taxes are due on the house in a few months. A pause in employment wouldn't be good right now. And well, ten percent."

I said nothing, couldn't blame her for choosing stability over Cliff's pride, but I couldn't bring myself to look at the contracts yet. Instead, I finished up the paperwork from the run and retreated out into the night with Secret.

The plan had been to get some shut eye, but I caught a whiff of an elderly doe and well... it wasn't a hard hunt. Between Secret and me, mostly me, we ate most of it, but I purposely left a haunch untouched. With it in my jaws, I scented out Cliff from the station and tracked him to a free-standing house a few blocks away. Specifically, to the mother-in-law apartment over the garage.

I was slipping back into my clothing behind the station when it occurred to me that leaving a severed deer leg beneath Cliff's doormat perhaps wasn't a gesture of affection he would appreciate. I considered retrieving it, but I'd been out eight hours already. My sleep time was over, and I needed to clock back in.

As we prowled in through the back door, I heard a deep, wracking cough.

17

———

The cough immediately set me on edge. It was nearly three AM, and all the emergency lights were off. The Firehouse comprised the bay or garage, with all the additional rooms next to it. Office, storage, kitchen, bunkroom, and locker room in a row, with an additional hallway between them and the cinder-block wall. A tingle of electricity crept up the back of my neck. I kept my footfalls light as I crept up to the bunkroom.

A half-dozen slumbering forms were scattered through the room's eight bunks. I heard the coughing, but not from this room. The garage? A movement caught my eye in the farthest bunk, a glimmer of yellow eyes under a fold of blanket. Rey peered at me from beneath Cindy's sheets.

I drifted down the hallway, hand slipping down into the bag I carried Secret in, stroking her ears. In the kitchen, I found Mitch and Dobson.

"Heeeey Cinderella, where you been?" Mitch asked, pouring himself a large bowl of fruit loops. A not uncommon sight in the firehouse. Some paramedics have very refined palates, but Mitch wasn't one of them. Neither am I, but my taste for pop tarts had fallen off since becoming a werewolf.

"Around," I said, vaguely gesturing, "Went out for dinner. What you doing up?"

"Not sleeping," Dobson laughed. "No night nanny while Mr. Gifford's brats decide what to do with the place. Fine with me."

"Cliff is not a brat." I huffed.

Mitch opened his mouth to counter and started coughing. He buried his mouth in his elbow. As the fit continued, he warded both me and Douglas off with a hand.

The scent of the Rot had filled the room by the time it subsided. "Mitch, you're sick! Log it and go home," I said.

He glowered back at me. "I just *ahem* choked on my cereal. Don't be such a paranoid bitch, Abby. You're always trying to get me in trouble!" He stifled another cough.

I reeled from the bitch comment, surprised at Mitch's straightforward insult. Wolf me surged forward to fill the gap. I barely swallowed back a growl and twisted it into words. "We have sick days for a good reason, Mitch."

"I'm not sick!" He stood up suddenly, chair shooting out from behind him, arms bowed out as if ready to swing. Had there been another voice behind his?

"Woah, woah. Back off, Abby." Dobson came to his partner's defense.

Wolf me wanted to grab him by the scruff of his neck and grind his nose in the scent of his own breath. But human me recognizes denial; it took a year of very careful prodding by my therapist before I realized how accurate that swastika labeling me had been. Denial is an impenetrable brick wall; you have to go around it or pick at the foundations. Neither of which I had time for.

"Fine." I threw my hands up in surrender and left the

kitchen. As soon as the door shut, Mitch exploded into another coughing fit. I went outside to appeal to a higher power, but Cliff's phone went to voicemail after a few rings. After three attempts, I left a message. Cliff needed to hire a night shift manager yesterday.

"Merf?" Secret asked as I hung up with a sigh.

Secret probably could make them listen but that would risk everyone knowing about her. I heard the garage door open. Someone was back early.

Peeking into the bay, Mitch and Douglas were already hovering like vultures around the parked ambulance. "You're welcome to her, Mitch; we could use a rest." The driver said.

They changed out supplies in record time and as they drove out of the bay Mitch waved, "See ya, lass."

Dread swept across me as he pulled out into the night. Shit. That wasn't Mitch anymore. I didn't know what to do. Did I go after him? Scully had only hit me after I'd grabbed him. But he'd bragged about some sort of bigger plan. Fuuuuck.

Taking a spare radio from storage, I cursed myself for carpooling with Cindy.

Rey gave me a narrowed-eye stare as I approached Cindy's bunk, but I ignored the possessive Fox Fey and shook Cindy's shoulder. She groaned.

I knew the phrase that would get her up. "Cindy we're on."

And like magic her eyes popped open. "Aww, Jebus." She sat up. "Do I have time for a shower?"

"You can roll on into your pants or give me the keys to your car," I said, taking her hand and pulling her from the bed.

Two minutes later, Cindy started the engine of her car after absorbing my suspicions about Mitch. "What the hell are we going to do if we find him?" was her only question as we started moving.

"Stop him. Tell him Cliff is recalling him, any excuse we can think of to get him off the street." I flicked on the radio. Our "radios" have been cellular for over a decade; the dispatch simulates radio broadcasts based on GPS tags. However, during a disaster where the entire city is shitting its collective pants, cell towers can get overwhelmed or simply destroyed. As a backup the city has a network of radio transmitters that are completely independent from the cell network. It's only two channels deep, east and west, but repeaters broadcast everything that passes between dispatch and emergency services.

The radio lit with a garble of chatter. Parallel conversations blending into each other. Really active for 3ish in the morning. Nights can be busy up through 1 AM but from 2 to 5; even night owls were typically sleeping, and even when emergencies happened, nobody noticed until after they woke up. Cindy took us to I5, which ran parallel to the river along the southwest quarter of the city, while I listened for any mentions of MICU #41, the ambulance that Mitch had taken. Sounded like most calls were reports of respiratory distress.

I caught Douglas's voice several times over the course of the next hour, but nothing that would give us a lead on their location.

"Let's stake out the hospital," Cindy suggested. "If they're doing calls, then they'll have to go there."

She didn't say that if they were doing calls, then I had dragged her out of bed for nothing. Cindy drove to the

OHSU emergency room and backed us into a spot with a good view. There were so many ambulances dropping off patients that the scene resembled a school yard 10 minutes before class.

"Jebus," Cindy breathed as we stared at the lineup. "Haven't seen that since…"

"Hyper flu," I finished the sentence.

After ten minutes, only two of the ambulances had departed, meaning either intake was completely overwhelmed, or the hospital was running out of beds. I breathed a little easier when the last two pulled out and the emergency loading area stood vacant. Just a busy night.

MICU #41 rolled up twenty minutes later.

"Okay, how do we do this?" Cindy asked.

"Wait for him to get out of the cab and wheel in the patient," I said, and both of us put our hands on the door latches. Rey gave a little yip of excitement as she hopped up on the dash.

"I could totally help you with this," she said.

"We don't need your help with this, Rey." Cindy said as the back of the ambulance opened, and Dobson hopped out.

He pulled the stretcher out alone with a tiny figure on it, and wheeled it towards the double doors. That struck me as odd; Mitch didn't let Dobson take lead often. I popped my door open and stepped out. This was going to do great things for my rep at this hospital. Adding ambulance jacking to the Cinderella thing.

Cindy and I nodded at each other and strode purposefully toward the idling ambulance. We had made it halfway across the parking lot when Mitch stuck his head out the window. "Oh, you coming for me, lass? It's a bit early to start the show, but let's go!" The electric engine whirred in warning and the ambulance shot forward. The motion was so violent that packages of bandages and saline tumbled out through the still-open rear doors.

"MITCH! What are you doing!" I heard Dobson shout as Cindy and I beat it back to her car.

"Everyone hang on!" Cindy hollered as she slammed her door shut and started the engine. I scrambled for my seatbelt. Knowing what came next. Rey hunched down on the dash, but her claws didn't save her when Cindy stomped on the gas. She yipped as the console tore out from under her and she tumbled into my lap. We zipped out of the parking spot, the little car whirring enthusiastically as we tore down the road and hurtled around the bend.

I caught a flash of white diving into the strip of dark forest that separated the university from downtown.

"There!" I pointed.

"I saw it!" Cindy called back, barreling down towards the corner, and turning hard at the yellow light. We streaked past a line of early bird commuters coming up the hill as the ambulance siren burst through the dark morning. Cindy swerved around a couple of cars just beginning to pull back from the shoulder. Red lights flashed through the trees, streaking down the ramp and into the city. With one arm full of fox, my other hand grabbed hold of the overhead handle as we screamed through a hairpin turn. Then, with a straight shot towards downtown, the little car's acceleration pressed me back into the seat. Still farther ahead were the flashing lights of Mitch's ambulance.

"Question. What do we do when we catch him?" Cindy asked, expertly slaloming down the road as if it were a sparsely populated parking lot.

"We, ah, stop him," I said, groping for words. Hadn't thought that far ahead.

Horns exploded as we shot through an intersection just as it changed from yellow to red. "That's not going to go well for us. Truck vs. compact."

We both knew what that looked like. The new ambulances might be 90% plastic, but they were still tanks compared to Cindy's little Ford. "Just get me close." Forcing myself to let go of the handle, I fumbled with the front of my shirt.

We weren't gaining on him; the flashing lights reflected off buildings, but while a red light only slowed him, it turned into a wall of automobiles the moment we entered the city's gridded streets. Nearing six AM, the city was waking up. Sitting at the light, I growled with frustration and pulled off my shirt, shoving Rey down into the foot well with Secret.

"Jebus, Abby! You can't go running around downtown in wolf mode!" Cindy said.

I wriggled out of my pants. "You got a better idea? Meet me at 4th and Hall."

"Abby, wait!"

"What? I barked, whirling around to fix her with a glare.

She met my eyes, lips compressing before saying, "Be careful!"

Nodding, I grabbed for the door and paused. Was I really doing this? If I went hunting for Mitch in the middle of downtown, the genie would be out of the bottle; Portland would know they had a werewolf on the loose. But that gleeful grin that the shade had worn on the groundskeeper's face, so similar to Little Nick's malice-tainted smile. Whoever that shade had been, they enjoyed hurting people.

Maybe it planned violence now, maybe it didn't, but if it did, then I was the only thing in the city in a position to stop it. Popping open the door, I booked down the street totally buck-ass naked. I imagined every eyeball in a quarter mile riveting itself to my skin as I pounded down the sidewalk, either on my bare ass or my flapping breasts. We were on the fucking state University campus, no alleys to dive down, just buildings the size of each city block and trees too thin to hide a teenager behind. No place to hide, only space for running.

Wolf me eagerly sprang forward; my mammaries tightened into my chest as she surged down my arms and legs. Two more steps and I dropped down to slap my front paws onto the concrete. The transformation flowed up from my paws, every four-legged stride lengthening as human me fell away bit by bit, step by step. The world around me shrank, my lungs taking far more of it in with each breath. My run became a sort of flight as the air streamed across my ears and tugged at my fur. With every inhalation I tasted my quarry, the sour earth mixed with Mitch's sickly sweat.

Mitch hadn't turned, he'd beelined directly into the heart of downtown, sirens and lights blazing as he cut through intersection after intersection. Pumping my limbs, I hurtled after him, leaping across entire streets, dog walkers diving out of my way. I closed the distance, less than a block away when I heard his whoop, "Come and get me, doggy!" With that he turned, not onto a road, but onto the MAX rail line.

Stop! Human me shouted in horror as the ambulance accelerated down the rails towards the blocky MAX train coming in the other direction. Pavement tore beneath my claws as I scrabbled to change my own course. The train's horn blared I as ran after the ambulance. It swerved drunkenly from side to side as if there were a fight inside the cab. Or more likely inside Mitch's head. I closed the gap; the flapping rear door came within five feet of my teeth.

The Train Roared. No time to shift, no time for anything but: BITE!

18

Jumping up, I sank my teeth into the top half of the door and swung my lupine body outward. But instead of tipping the ambulance onto its side, my weight popped the ambulance up into a wheely. Sparks flew from the undercarriage as the rear bumper kissed the pavement. Had I caught up to the ambulance with a little more than a hundred feet between it and the train, I might have stopped it. The train's blaring horn and blazing headlight filled my awareness, blotting out the entire city along with a growing realization of how much this was gonna hurt.

I had thought Scully punched like a truck, but I remember that hit. This one I don't. I'm clinging to back of the ambulance, then I'm flat on my back.

There's a part of me that's screaming in pain, a high pitched eeeeeeeeeee! Blood is flowing down my throat with each labored breath. In front of me lay the joint between the two cars of the train. The impact had thrown me a hundred feet. My entire left side throbbed with what felt like an entire colony of insects as broken bone fitted back together and cords of muscle reknitted themselves to the proper ligaments. The healing was noticeably slower than the night of Luna's glory; she herself peered down at me through a peep-hole in the dense clouds. *I'm getting up, don't worry, I'm getting up,* I growled at my goddess and rolled back up to my feet.

I heard the collective gasp of a crowd as I staggered on limbs not quite ready to support my weight. All along the windows of the train were slack jaws paired with wide eyes, phones held out towards me. At the train's front, the ambulance had punched into the cockpit, but I saw little damage other than that. NLR was definitely down one bus; the front end was completely caved in. Whether I'd slowed the ambulance enough to make a difference, or the MAX trains were designed to take a head-on collision didn't matter as I looked back down the length of the staring faces in the packed cars. They were alright, they were all okay. A relief so palpable rose in me that I had to lift my head in a howl, thank you, thank you!

Lowering my nose from the sky I noticed an SUV driving towards me rather quickly, a long barrel extending from a rear window. The gun chattered to life in a staccato rhythm of three-round bursts.

I flinched reflexively, but they weren't firing at me. Screams answered the bullets punching holes through the windows of the MAX.

NO! Was the only thought in my lupine head as I charged the SUV. Its driver gunned its engine, locking us into a game of chicken. I recalled a terrible accident I'd arrived at once and gritted my teeth. I leapt into the air, twisting my body sideways, the hood of the car passing harmlessly beneath me. Tucking my head, the flat of my skull smashed through the center of the windshield; it bent around me like a piece of saran wrap before I punched through it. There I saw the gunman, an elderly man with bushy eyebrows and wide eyes shot through with black threads. I snapped my jaws around his surprised face as the momentum carried me out the rear window with my prize. I landed with a grace that Secret would be proud of and cracked the skull as easily as a grape. I regretted it immediately; he tasted of rotten meat and a bitter poison. I spat the skull fragments onto the road and turned.

The SUV had crashed into a lamp post and the driver, a white-haired woman, leaned against the open door as she struggled to light the wick sticking out of a beer bottle. It caught. She threw it with a practiced ease, arcing from her hand through the open doors of the MAX right before I snatched her up and shook her hard. Her body slammed against the car with a satisfying crunch. Then I let it fall from my jaws and scented the distinct odor of burning flesh.

I wanted to scream. Why in the world would they do this? But there was no time for playing Sherlock werewolf. Diving through the smoke and flame, I spotted a woman running away, her jacket and hair a blaze of flames. Sirens reached my ears as I bowled her over. She was super grateful, screaming and punching my chest as I smothered out the flames with my body. Instantly I found myself in a circle of phones. Growling to myself as a torrent of curse words circled around my skull with nowhere to go. The bystanders were shouting as I held the woman beneath me: expletives of awe, fear, and everything in between. I had to get out of here so paramedics could access the injured. On duty paramedics like me!

Carefully raising myself, I sniffed at the woman and got a fist in my nose for my trouble. She'd be fine, and I was getting sick of my face getting bashed in. I ran, opting for a side street instead of a busy thoroughfare this time. Our rendezvous location had been a poor choice, trees ran along Hall Street, but they were nothing but bare branches now. A half block away I opted to cut through a parking lot and traded the spectacle of an enormous wolf for merely a large one.

Why did they build a city with so few hiding places? How were you supposed to hunt? I cursed as I ran. So tempting to turn and run for the forests and let the humans deal with their own murderous ghosts, but my nose caught Secret's scent, and I shoved my grumbles aside. A blue car door popped open, and I jumped inside.

"Merf!" Secret welcomed me back.

Cindy opened her mouth, and I greeted her.

She coughed and sputtered, "Close the door!"

Huffing with amusement, I pulled my tail out of the way and hooked the handle with a paw, closing the door. Human me reached for control, spinning with human inanity. I growled at her. How did she expect to do anything without a larger pack? Our bones still stung from the impact.

Soon, she promised. *I'll ask Cliff.*

With that I yielded, and we moved together again, a single I for a brief moment; I imagined standing side by side with a great black wolf. Then human me was outside and wolf was inside. I sat in Cindy's passenger seat, sweating skin adhering to the vinyl seat.

"What happened?" Cindy asked. "Did you save him?"

"I didn't catch him in time." I smiled grimly as I struggled into my clothes, "But it wasn't for nothing. I saved people."

"You did everything you could, Abby." Cindy sighed and presented me with my phone. It had a list of texts. The expected one from Victoria, but also from Dr. Wiggins, and one from Cliff.

That one read: "Nobody come into the station. We're on lockdown until further notice."

Dr. Wiggins requested I drop by the hospital at around noon, and Victoria's: "Did you get hit by a car?!?!?! Ow!" My thumb reached towards the button to call my gothy friend back.

"What do you want to do?" Cindy asked right before I hit the button.

I looked down at myself, at my uniform and hers. "Well, we're in uniform; let's go see if anyone downtown needs help.

Cindy gave a shake of her head and let out a breath; at the next light she pulled a Uie and headed back towards the disaster. I dialed Vicky.

She picked up in one ring. "Abby?"

"It was a train, actually," I said.

"Ashes and Blood. Are you okay? Oh, I guess that's a silly question. You're fine, right?" Her voice sharpened with worry and the tone was doing weird things to my chest.

"I think you'll see it on the news."

"What?! Abby, you have to be more careful!"

Wolf me growled; I hadn't called her to be scolded. "Victoria, stop. There were more of those things, people possessed by Bas or whatever you called them. They were trying to murder people. Why would they do that?"

"I don't know. For fun? You were literally there the first time I encountered a full-fledged Ba. I know they exist." She huffed. "Give me some time to think on it. I'll check some sources."

"Thanks. I gotta go." I hung up; we were already approaching flashing lights. We tried to offer assistance, but all the injured had already been carted off and a pack of reporters were practically clubbing passersby with their microphones. Seemed like downtown had suddenly transformed into a media convention. Next, we attempted to head to the NLR, but with two police cruisers parked in the driveway, we decided to roll on by. Being on shift with Mitch, we probably couldn't avoid making statements forever. "Hi officer. I noticed my coworker was possessed, and I turned into a werewolf to stop him." Yeah, that would go really well. We headed to the hospital.

But it wasn't Dr. Wiggins who met us; instead, only Nadia waved at us from the loading bay where we usually dropped off code Z patients. Since we were officially on call, Cindy elected to stay in the car. If Cliff gave us instructions, she'd text my phone and I'd have to sprint back. Nadia gestured me into a far corner of the loading bay and shoved a set of green scrubs into my arms. "The Docktor is in a meeting, but I will show you what he's found. Put these on."

I did as she asked and followed her into the hospital, trying to match her long, confident strides. She shunned the elevators, and I lost count of how many floors we climbed. At first, I only smelled the normal bite of antiseptic, but when she finally opened a door to exit the stairwell, I gagged. The scent of the Rot hit me like a physical blow. I coughed into my wrist.

Nadia didn't hide her excited smile. "You smell it."

"Just a tickle in my throat." At this rate the entire city would know I'm a werewolf by the end of the day, and then I'd be dodging silver bullets all night.

Need pack. More wolves, wolf me commented.

Human me shuddered; the medical examiner was scary enough as a human, she'd be an absolute terror as a wolf. Maybe that was the point.

Nadia arched one eyebrow but said nothing as she led me onto the floor. We weren't in the hospital wards, this was a university floor; solid wooden doors studded the hallway, each brushed metal handle guarded by a plastic plate where you tapped your ID badge. Nadia looked both ways before pulling an ID from her sleeve and holding it against the plate. A beep and she pulled open the door. I followed her and the scent of the Rot took on a suffocating quality, pressing hard against the back of my throat. Wolf me tried to step forward, but I held her back and she was still too tired to resist. Inside, hospital beds were parked railing to railing. Monitoring machines hung from the foot of each bed. The room wasn't large but there were at least 50 beds, almost all of them occupied, all in rows so tight that you'd have to roll half a dozen beds out of the room before you'd have enough space to even begin to extract one of the furthest patients. One nurse glanced at us as we entered but quickly turned back to her tablet. I wandered up the narrow rows and looked at a patient. The too-wide eyes moved to meet my gaze, but otherwise she lay completely motionless. Glancing down at the monitor at the base of the bed I found impossible numbers. The woman's heart beat four times a minute, and her respiratory rate was even less, and yet her temperature sat at a brain-melting 104 degrees Fahrenheit. Those are not survivable numbers, yet almost all the patients had the marks of age. I'd place the average age well over sixty, maybe seventy.

"There are three more rooms like this one." Nadia whispered. "Most are walking into the ER, but after two or three days they become still. Come," She led me towards the very back corner of the room; the patients there had a far more withered appearance. The whites of their eyes had turned completely black. There were thin black lines branching up their necks, threadlike beneath near transparent skin. Nadia used a gloved hand to peel back the sheets from one man and revealed his entire torso covered in a tangle of black fibers that erupted through red puckered flesh. Nadia recovered the man, and I heard her swallow. "It's eating them, but they're still somehow alive."

I followed her out, wondering if she meant the hospital had three more rooms that were full of patients. So many. Why wasn't this a top story? This had all the makings of a fresh plague. The media should have been swarming all over it. Nadia led me to back to the stairway without another word. I leaned against the wall trying to grapple with the magnitude of it.

"I wanted you to see that before you talked to the mayor," Nadia said.

19

The mayor wanted to talk to ME?! Stunned, I could only stumble after Nadia as she headed down the stairway and led us into a maze of hallways. How Nadia navigated it all was a complete mystery. We cut through a cubicle farm, and she delivered me into a conference room where Dr. Wiggin's perfect teeth waited.

"Abby! There you are. I was starting to wonder if Nadia got lost." He bustled his way over to me and I shook the doctor's hand as if we had just met.

"Just had a to make a quick pit stop. Been a busy morning for the Emergency Services." I gave him a plastered-on smile.

His face sobered immediately, "Ah yes, it was a tragic morning, but not as tragic as it could have been." Then, having given the matter perhaps a second of consideration, the smile returned with fierce brilliance. "Now let me introduce you to Patrick Leary, whom I'm sure you recognize." He gestured from me to the blandly handsome man who rose from across the table to shake my hand. I did vaguely recognize him from various newsclips of him apologizing for some city fuckup or another. They had elected him last year, so he could still blame his predecessor for what went wrong.

"Charmed," he said, squeezing my hand with the ease of a reflex. "The doctor tells me it's you who discovered the origin of this new health crisis. Please sit, sit."

I took a seat next to Doctor Wiggins, somewhat surprised that he was willing to share the credit. "It was a simple hunch I had on my day off. Speaking of jobs, I'm still on call."

"I just need a moment of your time. You must be quite the mushroom hunter to notice the appearance of a new species, Miss Night," he said.

"Uh, I'm not, really."

Wiggins cut in, "Miss Night is one of the city's best paramedics. She was the first to encounter code Z and has since cataloged several events that have not repeated themselves. One could say she has a nose for the strange events that keep happening."

The mayor winced, "I am sorry, that sounds awful, so awful. Miss Night, I just wanted the opportunity here to thank you for your service. The good doctor has made me aware of the depth of the problem. And I want you to know that I am forming a task force today to deal with this emerging health crisis."

"A task force?" I looked to Dr. Wiggins who nodded.

"We'll meet for the first time tonight. The doctors will brief us on all the available research and the task force will, quickly I hope, develop a plan of action. Which the city will implement quickly and head this off. Additionally, the city will financially compensate you for your time as an adviser and your discretion." The mayor smiled, "How's that sound?"

Ahhh, there it was. He didn't want me to blow this thing

up. Two hundred people being slowly eaten by a mushroom made for bad PR. And they'd been keeping this quiet like everything else so far. I had to ask, "Wouldn't this benefit from increased attention? Attract federal help?"

The mayor laughed, but it broke midway into a sad, hollow sound; his jolly cheer slipped and I glimpsed a haggard man behind it. "When code Z first appeared I tried, I did everything I could to attract expertise to study the problem. Even floated evidence to the Washington Post. It went nowhere. No matter how strong the evidence, it hits the same chord as political denial. Whether it's mushrooms invading the elderly's lungs, hospices having to chain patients to their beds in case of a code Z, or you know," he broke eye contact to smile down at his manicured hands, "giant wolves thwarting terrorists. Whatever the situation, Portland is on its own."

He knew. As Andrew Millar had said, it wasn't hard if you had the info. Hell, Slade had laid it all out for everyone to see. With this morning's events, it was only a matter of time before every social media feed declared, "Abby Night, an American werewolf in Portland." While some like Nadia would be fascinated or laud me as a hero, others would see silver bullets as a sound investment. And I had no pack. I needed a pack, or I couldn't defend my cub. Wolf me's anxiety flooded through my guts like a swarm of spiders.

The mayor spoke, but I missed the first words. "-not useful. Therefore, until a plan of action is prepared, let's keep this on a need-to-know basis."

I blinked, cobbling together the meaning of the words. "How can you do that? So many people are sick already."

Dr. Wiggins shifted uncomfortably, "The earliest cases are those without any immediate family in the area. Nursing home residents, primarily. We're just starting to see the demographics broaden."

"It's nothing sinister, Miss Night." The mayor gave me the softest of smiles. "It would be best that citizens see that the full weight of the city's resources are addressing the problem. We don't need a panic or an exodus."

Mitch hadn't been old or infirm. Old for a paramedic, definitely, in his late fifties but nowhere near the elderly who were stacked up in nursing homes. I inhaled, trying to smell the lie. They wanted me to stay quiet for now. The mayor hadn't threatened any consequences, but that didn't mean they weren't there.

"It won't be long, a day or two." The mayor said, taking my silence for consent. They didn't see the second half of the problem, these murderous shades. The only one who had a chance to deal with them was Victoria.

"Fine." The word escaped as a harsh ripping sound, "You do what you think is best, Mr. Mayor. The last thing I want to do is talk to the press right now."

"Perfect." The mayor smiled, completely ignoring my disgruntlement. "I'm sure I'll see you again."

Taking that as a dismissal, I rose, bade them both good day, and made for the door.

"Oh, Miss Night." Mayor Patrick's voice stopped me right before I stepped through the door. "Don't exit through the emergency room; there are a few officers there that do not have my trust."

I nodded and continued on; the mayor's office and the police were often at loggerheads. If the mayor trusted half of the force, I'd be surprised. I threaded through the cubicle farm, questing for the way back to the stairs, when I spotted Andrew Millar's beneficent grandpa face smiling down from the wall. A banner proclaiming his wondrous investment in

Portland's health. A bitter part of me wondered if he'd funded the plague rooms upstairs. That didn't make sense, did it? The man was seeking immortality; the last thing he'd want is a new disease to take advantage of his fragile health.

Once I found my way back to an elevator, I went down to the basement and took the underground route to the loading bays. Standing there, scanning the parking lot for Cindy's Ford Focus, I suddenly found a blue orb of foam thrust at me.

"Miss Night, moment of your time please! Are you a werewolf?" Asked a reporter with a shark's smile on a rich tawny face with intense dark eyes.

I recoiled, swatting the microphone away. Where the hell had he been hiding? I hadn't even smelled him. "Leave me alone!" I turned away, shielding my face, only to spot a cameraman with the local news channel's logo displayed on his T-shirt. "I do not consent to be filmed."

The large camera on his shoulder didn't waver, another sign that this was a cable station and not a YouTube vlogger.

"Do you know anything about the shootings in Puttmann three days ago?" The reporter persisted.

Wolf me reached into my limbs and pressed hard on the inside of my jaw. *Teach lesson,* she growled. I clamped my mouth shut, holding her back with effort. Memories of dashing through a gauntlet of microphones between the courthouse and the car came flooding back. The jeering questions.

Turning my face from the camera forced me to look at the reporter as he sidestepped along, keeping up with my brisk pace. Where was Cindy?

"Why were you in the hospital on December 22nd?" "What's your connection to the Santa Killer? Do you know him personally?" yap, yap, yap, the questions kept coming and the urge to deck the man continued to build. Wolf me urged far worse.

A deep horn sounded. I jerked my head up to see Cindy waving from the window of an ambulance! I didn't question it, I simply sprinted for it. Opening the door, I threw myself into the cab and slammed it closed behind me.

"Looks like you got some local flack," Cindy said, grimly shifting the ambulance into drive.

"Yeah," I agreed. "Where'd you get the bus?"

"Julia and Doc were more than ready for a break when I texted them. We met in the south parking lot. Firehouse is still closed." Cindy swiftly exited the hospital grounds, hopefully faster than the reporter could follow. "What happened?"

My phone chimed before I could answer. A text from that unknown number. "Well handled. Have you done this before? I'm afraid that one's terribly relentless."

"Andrew Millar happened." I turned the phone off and jammed it into my pocket. Before I could give voice to the frustrated scream building in my lungs, Secret jumped into my lap. She purred hard as I hugged her to my chest. "I don't know if I can keep doing this. They all know what I am. I'm not cut out for keeping secrets, Cindy."

"Merf!" Secret objected.

"Not you!" I smiled and rubbed her head. "You're stuck with me. But maybe we should give another thought to leaving. Maybe it is too dangerous to stay." I looked to Cindy, expecting a slow nod.

Instead, she kept her eyes on the road, frowning. "If you weren't here today, if you weren't what you've become, a lot more people would have died this morning. These shades, Secret, and I can't forget what might happen at the next Equinox. It's a flood of change and there's no way to stop it.

You're using what you have to save people and defend your family. Aggressively, more aggressively than I'm comfortable with, but I think this next world is going to be much more violent than any of us are used to. I have to make peace with that. I watched a lot of the footage on the net of the MAX attack. The part where you jumped through that windshield. Jebus, that must have hurt. You just took the hit to get at that guy with the gun."

Honestly, not nearly as much as getting thrown onto the pavement at fortyish miles an hour, but I doubt anyone got a good shot of that.

Cindy wiped her eyes. "This is a long way of saying, I'm sorry for making you get in that cage, and I don't want you to leave. You're still you, Abby. Still charging at the problem with zero concern for yourself." She coughed before continuing. "We got bigger problems and a bigger Abby to match."

I laughed softly. "Thanks, now I suppose there's some grannies out there that need a ride."

"If only we were so lucky." Cindy said.

We weren't.

20

The first call we fielded was for woman beaten to a bloody pulp by a boyfriend who'd already been hauled off. Good thing, too, or there might have been more bloodshed. That was the day's appetizer; afterward we had three opiate over-doses, one of which had Cindy playing lightning goddess all the way back to hospital. Both the grannies we did transport stank of the Rot, and finally was the man whose verbal diarrhea would have been terminal if I hadn't been stuck driving. Cindy took each of his slurs with a smile as she stabilized his broken arms. She asked me to wheel him into the hospital, and when I came back, she was hugging or perhaps restraining a very snarly three-tailed fox.

After we'd restocked from the ER, the bell we had been waiting for finally tolled. Cliff messaged us to come back to the firehouse and give our statements. We spent the drive back trying to get our stories straight, worrying if Dobson had recognized Cindy's car as we'd chased after Mitch's ambulance.

No swat team waited to jump me, despite all my worrying. Cliff greeted us with eyes so bloodshot they were more red than white. Standing next to him was a flannel-clad man with a salt-and-pepper flattop, whom he introduced as detective Garza. He smiled at me and scowled at Cindy, referring to a tablet.

"You prefer Ms. Maveri, then?" he asked her; when she answered affirmatively, he tapped on the pad. Then he shot Cliff a sour glare. "I cannot believe you are still on duty after what's happened. This is a very tragic situation, neither of you should be out there today."

Sympathy had been the last thing I'd been expecting from this stern-looking man. All three of us shifted uncomfortably. "I process trauma by working," I quipped.

He acknowledged me with the smallest of nods before launching into his procedure for taking witness statements. Within moments I was alone with him in the office, describing the morning, leaving out only the fact that Cindy and I had chased after Mitch, instead saying that we had gone out for an early morning snack. It was clear to me that Detective Garza thought the whole wolf thing was pure BS. He squarely focused on what I knew about Mitch's family and home life. Not a single question about the Santa killer or a comment about how my eyes were the wrong color.

I had thought I'd somehow won the lottery and had the most incurious cop in existence dropped in my lap. Until I caught a whiff of gossamer felinity on him as he opened the door to wave me out of the office. Secret perched on those piled up contracts, staring intently at the officer, who didn't appear to see her at all. Suddenly it all made sense. I smiled at her. Maybe we could weather this storm, after all.

Cindy breezed past me, her scent mingled with fox, looking taller, fuller, and more confident. Her voice was silky as she asked how the detective's day was going. I didn't need to see where Rey hid to know she was smiling. One detective would be no match for her. Cliff, though, he didn't have that sort of protection. He hunched in a folding chair, staring sourly at his broken arm.

"Hey," I said softly, braving myself to touch his broad shoulder. "You holding up?"

"First thing outta that bastard's mouth was, you've got a record." Cliff's head shook as he let out a huge sigh. "First dad, now this. I should walk away. Mom's gonna be impossible now."

Wolf me perked up. "You could join me in the woods," I said and laughed, wishing I hadn't said it so seriously.

"What's that supposed to mean?" He coughed once before sitting back and turning so he could smile up at me. It was a sad thing, that smile, so far from the brilliance of his usual expression.

Wolf me pressed against my teeth. *Take him, bite him, make pack.* The teeth sharpened as wolf me reached down into my limbs.

"Aaah," I covered my mouth, trying to hold wolf me back, "That's where I'm going next. Gotta blow off some steam." His scent danced on my hand, singing with stress. "You could come, bring a..."

Nothing, I'll show you how to run beneath the moon, to curl up together in the cool shadows. Wolf me tried to use my tongue, but I swallowed her words.

"Frisbee or something?" My voice sounded strangled as wolf me pushed everywhere at once. My shoes grew tight. *Not here! Not now!* I pleaded with wolf me. There was a cop in the office, for Luna's sake.

"Really?" His face lit up, and that smile shone again. "That'd be something, but I can't pull a disappearing act right now." He nodded towards the office. "Can't be suspicious." His brow furrowed as my limbs shook from the strain of holding wolf me back. "What's wrong?"

"Fine." I tried to smile, but I bared my teeth instead. "Gotta go! Tell Cindy I'll meet her at home. Come on, Secret."

Need pack. Smell his hurt. Help him. Heal him, wolf me growled, pleading in my head as I hastily retreated into the hallway and ran for the locker room. Fur sprouted as I took off my shirt.

"Secret, get clothes," were my last words before I lost them to the muzzle. I got everything off but my socks; their remnants encircled my ankles as I burst out of the back of the firehouse, Secret clinging to my neck as I sprinted through the thin forest corridor. Wolf and human thoughts warred as I ran. *Cliff was alone. I was alone. I could pull him in. Start a pack, not a weird pack, full of human and Fey. A real pack that hunts together. Have pups.*

No! Not without permission. I told myself. *I don't know how it works.*

Try everything: bite, blood, and sex, another part of me answered, and somewhere in the mix I heard Jimmy's laugh.

I growled at myself, *Never!* Stopping, I futilely tried to shake out these voices, making Secret squeal. *I'll take prey, take territory, but not family, not pack.*

Need pack. The voice countered. *Sick of being alone.*

I had no answer to that. Other than running, letting the cold air flush out Cliff's scent. Secret giggled as we crashed through the trees, their low branches slapping against my face and chest. Resolve against that selfish voice grew with every step I pounded into the forest floor, the good ache working through my muscles, and the tapestry of scents even in this contained forest struck me with its beauty. A smile split my muzzle as I crested a hill and slowed to a stop. Closing my eyes, I breathed it all in. The rich damp of forest dozing in this Portland winter and the scents of the sharp tangs of the city playing around its edges. The Rot was there too, a sinister undercurrent beneath the life and death. It didn't detract from beauty that no human would ever perceive. Maybe this is what I should tell Cliff about.

"Why we stopping?" Secret whined and slid off.

I snapped at her playfully, and soon my troubles were forgotten as she attacked back with the serious viciousness of kittens. Her green eyes glowed as she ran up trees to pounce me from far above. Even in her human form, I could catch her in my jaws and toss her away. No matter how far I threw her, she bounced right back and charged with a hiss, clawing furiously until I pinned her. Only once I had savaged her with licks would she surrender with a giggle.

The sun had retreated and only the barest hint of light teased the sky when Secret and I came down from the wooded hills. I powered up my almost-dead phone. That unknown number had been very busy. Notably, a number with a lot of zeroes attached. I texted back. "You can't pay me to be your guinea pig. If money mattered to me, then I wouldn't be a paramedic." I added an ambulance emoji to be cute.

We were on a train approaching our stop when the phone vibrated again. "You should consider the benefits, then. In your case, legal representation is going to be very important to you and friends of yours soon."

I looked at Secret, who was playing with a silver coin next to me, flipping it between her furry fingers. At least Andrew Millar hadn't realized that he was tangling with a bit more than he knew about. "Secret, what you did with the police officer today?"

"Ya-uh," she said distractedly.

"How many could you do that to?" I asked. "And what is that?

She flipped the coin and caught it between two fingers. "Not many. I can hide us though! Easier when you're smaller, though. Big wolf is big." Then she showed me her coin. "Found it in your fur." It wasn't a coin; it was the pancaked silver bullet Cindy had pulled out of my arm.

As I stared at it, the thing jumped from Secret's hand on to my arm, and stuck there as if magnetic.

"Aw, it likes you better," she pouted. I plucked it off and gave it back to her. She played with it contentedly until our stop, leaving me to puzzle out how to answer Andrew's threat. We walked home with my head hoping he was all talk and my twisting stomach knowing better.

It was a good thing we were walking instead of driving, because ducking back around a corner with a car is difficult. Three police SUVs were double-parked in front of Cindy's house. This had to be Andy Millar's flexing of his atrophied muscles.

I looked down at Secret, who frowned in the general direction of the police. "Can you sneak us in?" I asked her.

"Maybe? That's a lot of people looking for you."

Well, I'd told him I wasn't afraid of him. Time to prove it... somehow. The problem with cops was that if I sent this group packing, then I'd have a SWAT van crashing through Cindy's front wall. I walked down the sidewalk away from the house and skidded to a stop at the corner. I'd been intending to sneak in the back, but I spotted two more cars parked opposite the house Cindy's shared a back fence with. Watching to see if I'd run.

Wolf me growled as I stepped back behind the fence and pushed claws out of my fingertips. I could go wolf and fight, or walk away. That seemed to be the extent of my options. I considered the fence I leaned up against. Plain light mud-colored slats that extended about a foot over my head.

My phone buzzed; a text read: "Will you handle this the same way you handled the hunters? Hard to cover it up with all those body cameras."

Dammit, he was definitely tracking me. I turned it off.

When the full moon had shone, the crows and coyotes of the neighborhood had helped me. Was that only a full moon thing?

Only one way to find out.

After telling Secret to go hide, I reached back to that night; I found the notes to the howls I had sung. Clear as crystals in my mind. Bringing wolf me to my lips, I tipped my head back and released the song to the cloudy sky. *Intruders here.*

The ground stirred beneath my feet as sharp caws of alarm echoed from all the directions. Several sleepy-sounding coyote howls sounded off as black wings lifted from everywhere, creating a noisy chorus as they gathered into a storm of black overhead. As the sky became more crow than cloud, a single bird swooped down from the flock and perched lightly on my shoulder.

"Caw?" she asked, sparks flashing in her bright black eyes. The same bird that had met me on the roof as I'd watched Mr. Baker.

"Thank you for coming. Shall we show these folks they are not welcome here?" I asked with a smile.

"CaCaaa!" The bird called enthusiastically. The wind kicked up as she launched herself back into the air. The flock dove to meet her, forming into a great black snake that slithered across the sky briefly before diving towards Cindy's front yard.

I withdrew my claws and took off my EMS jacket and T-shirt before walking down the sidewalk and turning onto Cindy's street. On the power lines overhead, on the low fences that lined the sidewalks, on the gutters, perched thousands of crows, each watching the three police cars with the intensity of hawks. Time to pretend I knew precisely I what I was doing. I sauntered toward the cars. Two officers weren't in their vehicles. Instead, they stood on the front porch of the house. A phalanx of crows blocked their path back to their car. Their mirrored shades scanned across the yard as their hands rested on their guns. The cars were all lined up facing away from me. I couldn't see through the tinted glass of the rear window of the first car, just had to hope the occupants didn't have a gun trained on me.

"Hello, Officers!" I called out in a cheery voice.

The shades of the pair on the porch snapped to me. "That's her," the taller of the two whispered, which was really the only noticeable difference between the two men, both cut from the same cloth, lean and athletic looking. They hadn't sent the donut squad.

I heard the snaps pop from the straps that went across the back of their guns.

The crows responded with a cacophony of raucous calls that made both men flinch.

"I'd put those back!" I shouted to be heard over the noise, "You shouldn't antagonize a murder of crows this large. If you want to keep your eyes."

The two stepped closer together, lips pressed into grim expressions as more cawing crows fluttered down onto the porch railings. As suddenly as it started, the crows stopped their calling. The crows on the path to the house hopped out of the way. The two of them spared each other a single glance before hurrying back to the sidewalk, where they stopped and faced me. "Portland Police Department, Ma'am." The larger of the two stepped toward me and flinched when the crows nearest to him hissed a warning. "We have a warrant for your arrest. Why don't you come along quietly, and we don't have to add threatening a police officer and resisting arrest to the charges."

"On what charges?" I asked. "I talked to a detective this afternoon, and he didn't mention any charges."

He started, "We can discuss that-"

"You know what?" I cut him off. "I don't give a damn what string Andy Millar pulled to try to scare me. You two can get back in your cars, drive away and never come back."

"I can't do that, ma'am. It doesn't matter how many pets you have, nobody's above the law." The muscles in his arms tensed.

"Ha-ha." I said as stepped closer, "Do you live in the same world I do?"

His arm jerked up, but the crows were faster, black blurs mobbing his hand before the gun cleared its holster. He cried out, and the gun tumbled out of his grip, clattering to the ground. He clutched at his wounded hand as the birds flapped away, and stared at me with disbelieving eyes. Doors opened on the other squad cars and four more officers tried to push their way out, but the birds mobbed them, driving them back into their cars with sharp beaks and scratching talons.

The officer watched in slack-jawed shock before his face tightened with anger. "You think you're real smart, don't you? All I have to do is call for backup and the department will squash you like a bug."

"I'm trying to save as much of this city as I can. I don't have time to go dance with you and a billionaire with a wounded ego. So get back in your car and drive away before

I have to show you how little those guns of yours matter anymore."

He chewed on my words for a moment and his partner spoke up. "Come on Tony, this is above our pay grade."

Slowly, reluctantly, Tony followed his partner and got in his car. The crows took off, swirling above the cars until they drove out of sight, and then broke off and scattered back into the neighborhood. Only the young female stayed perched on the fence.

"Would a jumbo bag of peanuts tossed into the back yard be sufficient?" I asked her.

She shook her head.

"Two bags?"

Again, a negative before preening her wing.

"Okay two bags and a package of cashews for you personally."

Her head snapped up and let out an enthusiastic "Caw!" She pecked my offered finger to seal the deal, eyes flashing. Then took wing while I headed inside.

"What did you do now?" Cindy asked as I came in the door.

"Aborted a battle, now I gotta stop it from becoming a war," I told her and then grunted as Secret tackled my waist. I scuffled her ears and hoisted her up to my hip.

"You just scared away the police, Abby. In what universe is that going to be a long-term solution?" Cindy asked.

"This one. I just have to make it clear to a certain someone that he's not as untouchable as he thinks."

Cindy started twisting her fingers with worry. "Jebus, Abby, that doesn't sound good. Maybe we should all go stay somewhere else for a bit. That way you don't have to murder anybody while things calm down."

"I'm not murdering, I'm defending us. My pack needs a

home and I need everyone to respect that home." I said hurriedly.

"Abby, you're doing it again. You're talking like you were before the full moon." She scowled. "Why don't we make some dinner first?"

I looked down at the stool. I considered staying, talking this through, but every second that passed would give the police longer to build momentum for a response. If they weren't told to stand down soon, then there wouldn't be any stopping it. "Sorry. I gotta go."

Secret merfed and tightened her grip on my leg.

"Secret," I smiled down at her, "I'll be back soon."

Her slitted eyes narrowed, "Nope!"

"This is going to be dangerous. Steel still hurts you." I tried to peel her off, but she clung harder, wrapping my leg with every limb except her tail. "Ugh, come on, let go. Don't make me scruff you."

"I can help! Take me with you." I opened my mouth to object, but she thrust out her bottom lip and I swear her green eyes doubled in size, "Pleeease!"

"Alright" I gave in. "But if something goes wrong, you come back here. You don't defend me like you did at the funereal."

"Kay!" Victorious, she released my leg as I headed to the backyard.

"Be careful." Cindy said.

I nodded, then shifted, wolf me eager to lead the hunt.

21

———

With Secret hunkered down between my shoulder blades, nobody gave us more than a passing glance as I trotted across the river in my smaller wolf form. Good to bring her. Human me fretted but her decision is sound. Can't expand territory if den is unsafe. Rich man is like a pup poking at a porcupine, needed a nip. Where to find? I knew his scent and his odor of sickness, different from the Rot, his was of flesh warring against flesh. So many humans in the city, notes of their scents smeared together as I stepped through the park on the other side of the bridge.

The trail had gone cold, and I shifted tactics. Where would a sickly billionaire be in the early dark? Home? Or at the sick place? *King's Heights,* human me whispered. Up the hill I went. Wealth doesn't have a smell of its own but has a definite medley, a sparseness compared to downtown. Human scents separated into a perceivable palette, although some tried to hide beneath perfume. I walked along the edge of the road, nose to the ground, straining to find a scent shaped like the familiar. A trace of the Rot's mushrooms tickled my nose, a whisper compared to a cemetery in the city's south but still here, lurking beneath the ground.

How far has it spread? human me wanted to know, but one quarry at a time. I am only one wolf. I sat back on my haunches, cleared my nose with a snort, lifted it to the wind and inhaled. To my surprise, there was Andy Millar's scent on the breeze that traveled up from downtown. I ran down the hill, led by my nose. When the scent disappeared, I doubled back, finding myself nose to the ground on the black pavement of a driveway that led to a large house. Yet I found the strongest part of him in the bushes, coupled with a sour bite of stomach acid. He'd vomited. Beyond that I couldn't find him, had he gone into the house? Or out?

"Merf!" Secret complained after I'd circled the pavement nearly a dozen times, gathering all the scents I could: rubber, exhaust, and oil. Fixing them in my mind, I followed it out into the street, and after a block I knew I had it. The scent of his limo. I let myself howl out the thrill of the hunt and ran down into the city.

It led me to a building encased in opaque white scaffolding a few blocks from city hall. This area of downtown essentially had one building per block, and they weren't large. I'd driven by it before, and it had been a prestigious office building before the scaffold went up. Now as I studied it from across the street, human me noted that it had no signage whatsoever hinting at what was growing within, simply Andrew Millar's face and his slogans.

With a rustle of fabric, Secret stood next to me, breathing hard.

"Can't hide us inside." She gasped, leaning against my shoulder. "No dogs allowed."

I huffed understanding and leaned back against her. She'd done great.

The lowest level had been fitted with a chain-link fence and covered with white plastic; access was controlled by a motorized gate, with no other visible entrance. Could wait for him to come out or dig under the fence.

"Wait here. I'll open it," Secret said before darting out into a gap in the slow-moving traffic. I snapped at her dress to try to stop her but only caught air. She reached the opposite sidewalk as a cat and dove through the gap beneath the gate. I would have screamed her name, but I could only bark my protest.

A car honked, brakes screeching as I ran out in front of it. I slammed into the gate, making the entire fence jangle as my bulk bounced off it. Dancing back and shaking from the impact, I inhaled, preparing myself to shift. I'd simply rip the gate open.

My digits had lengthened into fingers when I heard a light buzz from inside and the gate started moving. Human me quickly pulled herself back, letting myself fall back to normal wolf size before the opening widened enough for me to see Secret smiling from inside a security booth on the inside of the gate. Next to her sat a guard with his eyes almost closed. "There she is! Thanks, Mister, you found my doggo! Why don't you take a nap? You look very tired."

The man nodded and slumped back in his chair as Secret came out of the booth. She wiped away a trickle of blood from her little nose and sniffed. "It's easy when they're sleepy."

I growled my disapproval, but she merely grinned cheekily, displaying her sharp canines. What an irrepressible cub. Human me would have words with her later, but for now I turned my attention on the building standing before us.

The scaffold had no wall beyond it. The sole building on

the block occupied the center fourth of it or so. Five stories in height, the red marble facade was a collection of classical pillars for the first two stories or so before transitioning to swooping art deco patterns of swirls around a trifecta of long stained-glass windows.

Standing between the building and us stood Andy Millar, immortalized in the same stone. Bearing a shirtless torso with a radiant six pack of abs, he wielded a lumber ax in one hand and a judge's gavel in the other, both raised as if to do battle.

We walked beneath Andy's legs, to the twin golden doors centered between a pair of columns. A small brick held one of them open, and the scent of industrial solvents made me sneeze. Secret opened the door and held it for me as I padded through onto smooth polished tiles. An unlit corridor stretched before us, the arched ceiling making it seem like a tunnel with a softly lit room beyond it.

"It's certainly uh, grand overall," someone who sounded familiar said as I padded forward, cursing each click of my claws on the tile.

I heard my quarry's soft voice echo as I poked my nose around the corner, "That's the idea, Patrick. I know it feels a little... ostentatious while I'm standing here. But with the death of my son, it's left to the city to remember the Millar clan, and these days you need something more than a bench named after you." Andy Millar stood straighter than I'd ever seen him in a cathedral built solely to himself. Looming above him, his likeness lounged on a throne of timber and gold, so large that if the statue stood, its beneficent smile would be put through the skylights that tiled the ceiling.

He coughed once; the sound drew my eyes back to the men, five of them in total, arrayed around Andy. The mayor stood closest, staring up at the mosaics that ringed the top of the walls. Big men in dark suits, doing their best to not look bored, made up the remainder "Public reveal isn't too far away. At least I get a front-row seat." He gestured at the giant's feet where a large stone box lay open, a sarcophagus.

This man might think he can conquer death, but I wouldn't let him conquer me. I shifted as quietly as I as could, but even though wolf and human stood unified, I had to push hard to stand and stretch. The reshaping of my bones betrayed me.

"What's that?" a gruff voice asked as I finished the shift and shook out my hands. I watched the head of his shadow approach my hiding spot, then rushed around the corner. The big man's eyes widened, his gun pointed down. I swatted it from his hands and charged past him. Two others raised pistols, while a third man scooped up Andy Millar like a babe and made to book it on the heels of the mayor. The guns popped as I sprang across the distance and back-handed the pair of them hard enough to send them sprawling, their guns skittering across the warm red and white tiles.

I growled a warning to the running men, but they didn't stop; the mayor had nearly reached the door marked emergency exit. It'd be so easy to end the problem. Both the Mayor and the Billionaire: wouldn't that be enough of a message to the city to leave me alone?

You're not a murderer. Cindy said from before.

Not yet, I agreed, and sprinted across the tile, shooting past the grunt carrying Andy Millar and reaching the mayor as his hands impacted the door. Catching his shoulder, I jerked him back before he'd entirely passed through. The man carrying Millar made a high-pitched warble of distress, narrowly avoiding crashing into the mayor. He turned to run towards a different exit, but I grabbed the back of his head, and he froze in my grip. I pulled both him and the mayor in front of me and squatted down, shielding most of my body from the other bodyguards who were getting up.

"Put me down," Andy Millar wheezed as he stared up at me, and started blinking as if I would disappear into the dark of his eyelids. "Abigale Night? Is that what you are?"

"Don't shoot!" The mayor warned the help as they regained their weapons. "What do you want?"

I pulled my muzzle back into my face and without Luna overhead, the agony reached root canal levels. I ignored the mayor, moving my nose to within an inch of Andrew Millar's face. "Want you to know that I can find you. Anywhere." I ground out, sniffing for emphasis. This close, I heard his heartbeat in his chest. "Next time anyone brings guns to my home, you will pay."

"You... can't threaten me." His mouth twitched up into a spastic smile. "I've been facing down death for years. Killing me would be signing your own death warrant. The executor will-"

I interrupted him by bringing a claw into his field of vision, "I will eat your sickened body, choke down your bones. Hard to be mummified without those."

His sagging face broke out in sweat, eyes narrowing down to fearful pinholes. He gulped, and in the cavernous silence of the mausoleum, I heard the rapid beat of his heart falter. Pain suddenly twisted across his face as one hand clawed at his chest.

Heart attack! The medic in me screamed, and trained instincts kicked in. Catching him as he fell, I guided him down to the floor. *No, no, no!* I had just intended to scare him! Not kill him.

"What did you do!?" The mayor shouted in my ear.

"Harrr tack! Harr tac!" I managed though a deforming

mouth as the sudden flush of fear and mortification caused wolf me to surge forward. "Neee niro!" He needed nitroglycerin. I supported his head and shoulders with one hand as he stared up at me.

What do I do? My mind spun. Scoop him up and run for the hospital?

Run, said wolf me.

Have to call 911 first. But how? What phone, had to shift back first.

Run, insisted wolf me, *Run.*

I can't run! I did this! Andrew Millar's breath rattled below me.

Belatedly I saw the nearest bodyguard step around the mayor and level a pistol at my head. I jerked away as the thunderclap sounded in my ear and the bullet stung my neck. The back of my hand slapped him away. A second shot, with its muffled pop, bit at my ribs.

The pain kicked the fear into sheer panic, yelping I threw myself backward against the door I'd prevented them from escaping through. My head slammed against the top of the door frame. My body fell towards the wolf as I struggled to fit through, more bullets stinging my backside before I tumbled outside. Feet found the ground, and I ran despite the pain. Halfway to the edge of the block before the thought of Secret pierced the panic. *Pup!* I barked, *Come!* As I ran back around the front of the building, she dashed up to meet me, swinging up on to my back. I jumped the chain link fence and ripped through the white webbing that surrounded the block. Horns exploded around us as I charged through the city streets.

Parts of me shouted for me to stop, to shift, but I ran instead. Up the hills and into the woods. Sirens howled behind me, seeming to chase us up the slope. *I didn't mean to!* I wanted to howl back at them. It was supposed to have been a show!

I wanted to run all the way out of the city. Wanted to dig a hole and lie in it forever. Human me pulled herself farther and farther away as I ran, radiating failure, taking with her the reason for my run. My pace slowed deep in the forest. Secret lay heavy on my back in her human form.

"You got him; you got the bad man." Secret said, slipping down beside me.

But that wasn't it. I reached out to human me, inviting her understanding, but all she offered was a mournful sadness.

Fine, then. I'd do what I wanted to do.

22

Secret skipped along beside me as we threaded down the tendrils of forest that reached through southwest Portland. The scent of the Rot's mushrooms was stronger here than up north, and we steered wide of the occasional clusters of mushrooms forcing their way up between tree roots. The sirens had grown distant. We paused on the edge of a human yard, the trees and underbrush suddenly yielding to cut grass.

"Where are we?" Secret whispered as we peered at the house set on the yard, windows glowing with their yellow light.

Unable to answer, I nuzzled her softly and told her to stay put with a huff. Which she ignored as I worked my way around the side of the house to the garage. One window over it glowed softly with a spray of undulating color. After a wary glance at the main house, I crept forward to the stairway that led up to the den over the garage. The metal groaned beneath my paws; at the top of the stairs, I could smell Cliff, and it brought to mind that beaming smile.

Secret followed behind me, arms crossed as she eyed the metal railings.

I scratched at the door, licking my chops in anticipation. The bite was part of it. I knew that. Felt it in my bones, but it couldn't simply be that. Luna would not want careless accidents. Would she?

No movement inside, just sharp murmurs of TV dialog. I scratched again, my dull claws stirring up the plastic scent of the paint. Secret slipped up beside me and poked the button beside the door with a little smirk. A chime sounded. A deep weary groan answered it. Cliff's heavy footfalls and then an odd, soft note, like that of a tuning fork, sustained and constant.

Open! I urged the door. Blearily, Human me uncurled. Had to do it fast. I tensed, ready to charge, just a nip.

What are you doing? Human me asked.

The seal around the door cracked as it pulled inward. I lunged, but pulled short as a pair of narrowed silver eyes confronted my own. *Who? Who dares protect my Cliff from me?* I growled.

Reflection, human me laughed. A gleaming blade across the crack of the door at my eye level. High above, Cliff squinted down at me, and the scent of sadness filled my nose. "Woah... Abby. Secret?" his tired voice croaked, and he pulled the door open. The blade moved with an undulating note that stood all the fur along my back. The blade was about a foot and a half long, broad as a woman's hand until it narrowed at the tip. As I stared at it, the scents of wildflowers and roses snuck into my mind. It was the sword of the Fey Knight who had died in my ambulance. We had found her amid a field of severed limbs, and in Cliff's hands it sang of sharpness.

How the hell had he gotten it? Still growling, I stepped

back from him, pressing my tail against the slats of the railing.

"Heh," he breathed. "I don't get much company that I can't see through the peephole." He forced a dull grin and waved the sword, "Neat though, right? Won't go through steel but just about anything else. Figure if any of those red caps come again, it will be different with this. Just gotta get my good arm healed up and I'll be all Rurouni Kenshin, samurai badass. Cool, right?" His smile regained some of its shine.

But the sword still sang its hungry song, and I growled again. It could hurt me; it promised it would.

Cliff's face fell a bit. "I'm not going to stab you with it. Come on inside." Gesturing with the blade into the dimness of his den. I considered running back down the steps.

Secret had also retreated back to the stairs. "It is a sword of Summer, and we are of Winter. It sings for our blood. Put it away, please."

"Aww, okay. Right." He frowned down at the sword, forehead furrowing as if he found something about the sword concerning. Then he slid the sword into something behind the door frame, his face scrunched into a grimace as his fingers slowly peeled away from the hilt, one by one. As soon as he let go, the sword's song stopped.

Shaking out his hand, he turned his back and walked into the dim interior. We followed him in, and the place reeked of grief, sadness, and stale pizza. The sword resided in an umbrella stand, sheathed in a scabbard wrapped in green silk. Next to it a garbage can overflowed with the remnants of take-out meals. Through the kitchen was a small living room, where brightly colored characters twirled and fought on the TV screen. The plush couch had a blanket and a pillow. It creaked when he sat down on it.

"Welcome to my castle. Princesses not included." He looked to Secret, "What you here for?"

"Dunno. Followed Abby." She said, peering up at the bookcase where plastic figurines dueled in front of thick manuals with precise drawings of cars on their spines.

Now. I had to do to it now. Reaching forward I caught his good wrist with my jaws. He made a surprised grunt.

No. Human me surged forward, finally reaching out from her ball of misery, but she couldn't stop me. I'd finally have a pack! All I had to do was bite down. Let blood flow. Wouldn't hurt him much. Bite down, I told myself as Cliff started to pull away. I tightened my grip; his sadness, his pain, was a flavor. Hurt him. Make pack. He'd forgive me.

But I couldn't do it. Couldn't add to his pain. When he wrenched his wrist away, I let go.

"The hell, Abby?" he asked. "Are you trying to play?"

Let me explain. Human reached, extending herself through our limbs. I shoved her back, she always made a mess of things. If I let her out, there would just be more guilt. I didn't want her guilt. I wanted...

With a whine I laid my head in his lap and my tail gave a hopeful wag.

Cliff gave a frustrated huff. "Abby, are you stuck or something? I was sleeping, you know. What am I supposed to do?"

I continued to look up at him.

"What?" He shrugged.

Stupid dense human. I hopped up onto the couch, licked his face once and very pointedly laid down across his lap.

"You've gotta be kidding me. Abby, you're a werewolf, not a lapdog," he chided, but his fingers started threading through the fur at the base of my neck. Touch. Slowly he began to scratch me, dragging rough fingers down my body. When they brushed the spots where the bullets had stung me, the memories of the pain made me whimper, but the itching of skin soothed it away. "I cannot believe this," he grumbled, but his fingers spoke louder. *I accept you. I'm not afraid.*

After some time of simply being, Human me slid out through my body and I didn't try to stop her. I rolled off him as my bulk swelled and her worries became mine again. Oh Luna, what am I going to do? I prayed.

"Oh, are we done?" Cliff laughed, a real rolling chuckle that contained sun.

There was a bedroom, and I trotted into it, hiding myself as I eased wolf me back inside. It smelled of Cliff far less than the living room: Ikea wood laminate bed and dresser, white sheets. Nothing on the walls but their off-white paint. It was definitely bold of me to open his drawers and put on one of his t-shirts. It covered me down to my knees. I slipped back out into the living room. Cliff was standing at the bookcase pointing to all the figures and naming them for Secret.

"Thanks. I needed that," I said.

His eyes momentarily bugged like a frog's when he saw me standing in his shirt. "Heh, well that's a look."

"Would you rather I stand here naked?" I smiled, wondering if that counts as flirting.

He stood, leaving Secret jousting with a race car and a samurai with a sword longer than the car. With darkened cheeks, he looked down at the floor. "You needed petting?"

"I... needed somewhere, someone safe. I fucked up real bad this evening." Did I tell him he was the closest someone that the wolf considered pack? Do I say what she really wanted to do? What would he do if I walked over and hugged him? How weird would that be? Wolf me had gotten her touch, but human me still ached for it.

"How bad?" He stole a glance back at the door.

"Bad enough that it's going to be on the news. Could you give us a ride back home?"

"Yeah, let me find my keys and piss." A weariness had entered his voice; with a nod he ducked into the bathroom.

I squatted next to Secret as she made clashing sounds. "Who you got there?"

"I got ummm, Hot Car and Samurai Chaploo." Her shoulders slumped and in a softer voice she said, "I could have done that."

"That... wasn't really what wolf me wanted, but I took what I could get." I whispered.

"Oooooh." She brightened, turning to me with comprehension brimming in her eyes. "You wanted his heart. Don't worry Abby, even mother missed sometimes."

"Uuuh," I was still searching for words to explain when Cliff came back.

* * *

The news confirmed my fears as we pulled into Cindy's street.

"Portland's Greatest Philanthropist, Andrew Millar is in critical condition at OHSU after what is rumored to be an assassination attempt. It is said that Mayor Leary was a witness to the assault, but he offered no comment at this time. The confrontation happened at about eight this evening, and we have two witnesses who claim that they spotted a giant white wolf near the capital building at the same time. Could the same being that thwarted this morning's MAX shooting now have assaulted one of Portland's most generous persons?

"This is KVAT sponsored big news today. Tune in at 6 AM for more on this developing story."

Cliff sighed and turned down the station as it launched into a commercial. "Well, he's not dead yet."

I flashed him a wan smile, "I still hurt him, Cliff. It wasn't supposed to happen like that." I told him the story.

"The dude was stalking you. You were totally within your rights to go tell the bastard off. Not your fault if he can't take a tenth of the shit he's flinging." Cliff ambled his car up in front of Cindy's house; there were lights on the first floor.

"Thanks." He had a point, sure as the hunters with guns, I had to do something about Andrew, but to watch him have a heart attack and then run away struck me as so wrong. That'd be the medic, not the wolf. I reached for the door, "You want to come in?"

"Not if the Fox lady's home. I'm staying wide of her if I can."

"Understandable." I lifted Secret from my lap and climbed out of his low car, briefly wondering how he even fit in it.

"See you at work in a few days." The window rolled up with a whirr of an electric motor and the red car grumbled to itself as it slipped down the street, leaving me there with Secret.

I looked down at her, "Alright, now let's explain to Cindy why we should probably all go into hiding tonight."

"Merf," she responded, jumping out of my arms, and bouncing up the walkway to the front door. She gave me an annoyed glance when I paused, realizing that I didn't have my key and I needed to go around to the back.

I wasn't surprised when it opened on its own, but seeing

Victoria stepping out from the doorway was a complete shock that doubled when she hugged me. A tight squeeze, friendly and warm. I returned it instinctively with a breath of surprise.

"This is what you needed," she whispered before stepping back, "And I need to do this."

Her hand slapped my cheek, not particularly hard, but it made a sharp clap. "What were you thinking, Abby!?"

23

My cheek stung, "Vicky, what?" Human and wolf reeled in equal measure as anger twisted Victoria's face and tears threatened to escape her dark eyes.

"He's dead. You killed him. I just got the call." Her hands grabbed the front of my jacket and clung there, staring down at me, teeth bared, lips quivering as I felt the heat of her churning emotions. Her breath sweet somehow, grief without sadness but a whole lot of fear.

"My condolences?" I managed to breathe out as a rote instinct.

"Ha!" She spun away, gesticulating up at the stairway. "I'm not sad! The man is... was a bastard through and through." Victoria rounded back to me, the tears had not escaped her eyes, but they remained wet and manic. "But it's the timing, Abby! I needed one more week. One month maybe."

"You're upset about the money he's paying you?" I blinked in confusion.

"No! For him to die from natural causes!" She exclaimed, slipping by me to slam the door shut.

"I didn't touch him." I protested, hearing my voice climb defensively.

"Doesn't matter! If he blames you for his death, it changes everything. It gives his spirits focus and purpose. And since I'm connected to you, that means I'll have to do the entire damn purification ritual before I start. 12 hours of chanting and ritual bathing. I'm going to be on that altar looking like a prune!" She ranted. "Bastards are recording it!"

"Victoria, uh. You're not making any sense." I looked down at her shoes, avoiding her flashing eyes. She wore black high-top sneakers.

Pale hands encircled mine and squeezed hard. "Abby, I am contractually obligated to attempt a ritual that will return Andrew Millar to life." She spoke with deliberate slowness, "We had three options. One was the Vampire, whom nobody can find. Two was to create a revenant, simply rebind a soul to body, that's the zombies, and third is the Hail Mary, the ritual to create a pharaoh."

"And that's bad?" I said carefully. On the upstairs landing, Cindy had appeared and rested her elbows on the railing.

She hissed through her teeth. "A revenant is a walking corpse, no more or less frail than a man, a Vampire is clearly a monster, but the Pharaohs were gods, Abby. Cities of people worshipped them, and that worship provided their power. He always liked that option but it's not one you can test, and I didn't understand how it worked until recently."

"What do you mean?" I asked, peering up at her.

She licked her lips. "When we met that girl possessing that grandmother? Death came for them both when the grandmother died, because we had trapped them together. I know the Ba exists now. She claimed the others had come through in the wake of Little Nick's killings. That makes several references in the Book of the Dead make sense."

"You know how to make it work now?" Several things clicking.

She shook her head. "No. He doesn't have a city of worship calling him back, but magic is forged from bonds and agreements. You are my friend, and my... blood bond?" A nervous smile surfaced before being weighed down into a frown. "You killed him, and I'll be calling him back; our connection will strengthen his hunger for vengeance. That makes it more potent, much more potent than if he had died of a faceless disease. Some part of him will come back, and it's going to come after you."

"Then don't do it. You don't have to do this ritual." I countered.

Disappointment washed across her feature. "Abby, I gave my word and signed my full name, in blood. You out of anyone should understand why I can't back out. The dead can't trap you in a contract as easily as, say," she glanced down at Secret, "but the penalties for breaking agreements can be even more severe."

"Vicky, Andrew's just a man." A growl crept into my voice.

"And if I break my word, I'm just another scammy, gold-digging medium. I won't be that. Not even for friends." She drew herself up, thrust her shoulders back, and looked me straight in the eyes, the challenge clear, "So unless you're going to physically stop me, I'm heading to the Millar residence next."

Was that a request? Did she want me to lock her into Cindy's basement? I stared back at her, wolf me's hackles rising. "What about these shades that are loose in the city? Or the Rot?"

"I know nothing about the Rot, Abby, but if you find more shades riding bodies, do what we did with the dancing girl. Trap them in a circle and then kill the body; Death will come for them both." She shuddered, breaking eye contact.

Wolf me pushed, stepped me forward, reached around her back, and grabbed her long black hair. With a yank I forced her head back, exposing her cream-colored throat. My head cocked to the side and only as my mouth opened did I realize what I was doing. Trying to make her submit as a wolf! I shut my teeth with a click and shoved Wolf me back.

Make her not go! Wolf me gnawed at the mental hand that held her back.

Biting people's throats is not how you make them do that! I huffed in my head as I quickly stepped back from Victoria with a mumbled, "Sorry."

Victoria's chest heaved as she gripped at her own heart, her cheeks flushing through her makeup. "Yeah. Look, hopefully, I'm like, wrong, and the ritual's a total bust, right? I have to honor my contract. I took the man's money." She hurried around me and down the stairs, and I got a whiff of spicy excitement and a musky smell... canine? I watched Victoria hurry down the path to her car, scanning the bushes and gardens for a lurking canine shape.

But I saw nothing, other than a fox-tailed shadow creeping into the light from the kitchen doorway. "Tsk, tsk," Rey tutted, "That one will cause you grief. Glad she's not mine."

"And what do you mean by that?" I turned to face the Fox Fey and found her sly smile.

She avoided the question with a half shrug as she leaned provocatively in the door frame. Her human form had filled out, hips flaring beneath her kimono, which was open in a V that proudly displayed deep cleavage. A body far closer to what I assumed Jimi Hendrix had been picturing when he composed his foxy ode. "Lady Abby, given your public appearances today, Cindy has asked me to protect this house as I would a den of my own. We have bargained and agreed terms." She smiled with satisfaction.

"What terms?" I asked automatically, looking up to Cindy on the banister who wore a similar, although slightly more bashful, smile.

"The terms are private," Cindy said, "But anyone who tries to find the house without letting us know first will be very confused when they find themselves driving back across the river. Current residents and friends will not have any trouble."

Residents, something about the way she said it struck a note of sadness in me. I had begun to think of Cindy's house as a home. Resident sounded more temporary than that. "That's probably wise, so long as the price of the protection was reasonable," I said carefully, wishing, not for the first time, that I had some way to determine what happened with the pair while I was elsewhere. Did Cindy even have any idea how close Rey had gotten to exploding at that club?

The pair simply shared a look and nodded. I expected Cindy's next words to have her own take on my frightening an old and infirm man to death but instead I got only a kind smile. "Abby, you look dead on your feet. Why don't you get some rest?"

Neither human nor wolf me could argue with that. I'd been up since... how long? The attack this morning. I clearly was no good for talking, and hunting would be better after a rest. Secret and I would hunt rot and ghosts in the morning.

Except I woke to a different call to action. An alert declaring a city-wide emergency and for all currently unassigned EMTs to report to downtown for duty at 7 AM. A shared text group among NLR's paramedics showed nobody had a clue what was going on. No news outlets were reporting any explosion or active shooter event or anything else out of the ordinary, other than repeating more nonsense on how generous Andrew Millar had been to our "great city." Yeah, generous to the radio and TV stations. The address we were to report to wasn't even the hospital. Curiosity drove me to answer the call more than anything else. Secret and I took my car so I could make a judgment as to what form I worked the emergency in.

Downtown had exploded, alright. Exploded with construction, not demolition. Workers in yellow day-bright vests swarmed the streets erecting signs and statues which all depicted a single face, Andrew Millar's, but this wasn't Grandpa Andy; no, this Andrew wore a stern expression of disapproval, narrowed eyes lit with white LEDs. The signs declared, "Portland Remembers and Honors Andrew Millar."

"I don't like this." Secret gave voice to my own sentiment as goosebumps prickled along my arms and legs. Victoria's words about Pharaohs being literally gods with entire cities worshiping them rang like bells in my head. Andrew Millar had clearly understood that part, better than Victoria had given him credit for. The activity centered on the mausoleum I had hunted Andrew to, the white mesh that had surrounded it had been torn away and crews hastily pulled down the scaffolding. In the dim light of the winter morning, the jutting shape of the tomb stood as an alien object compared to the office buildings that surrounded it. They had assembled tents in the nearby park where the messages had told me to report to.

I parked on a block that had no evidence of construction

and reached into my glove box for the pair of mirrored shades I kept there. "What are those?" Secret asked as I slid them onto my face.

"These are my 'I'm an asshole' glasses. You wear these and nobody wants to talk to you," I explained as bitter anger tightened my shoulders. They'd used an emergency call-to-action protocol to summon up staff for a rich guy's funeral.

"Oh. I can do that!" Secret giggled and then put on her own mirrored shades, the lenses vaguely shaped like cat heads with rhinestones around the ears. I snorted with laughter; she looked like a tiny movie star. She grinned and went skipping from the car before I could suggest an alternative, leaving me to chase after her and her flouncing dress.

Each of the emergency personnel groups had their own tent, police, firefighters, and emergency medical personnel; they were tiny compared to the tent next to them, so huge I feared they had to cut down half the trees in the park to put it up. It read: "Mourners. Earn 500 Dollars a Day." Busloads of people were striding through the park toward its entrance beneath its white top.

I gawked at that, more money than a single shift, quite a bit more. I was curious about what awaited me in the EMS tent. A sign inside cut right to the chase, fifteen hundred dollars for a 12-hour shift at one of the dozen medical tents, 2k if you were an ER nurse. A man in a white lab coat gave a quick spiel about available shifts and locations before they directed us to the back where staff slapped down a quarter-inch thick contract with one hand and a stack of hundred-dollar bills with the other. I'd never seen anything like it. People swarmed up to sign. I wasn't the only one to hang back; a small cluster of people eyed the easy money warily.

The "Doc" came over to them.

"What's the catch?" A gray-templed woman asked with a light accent. "That's stupid money."

The Doc shrugged. "Billionaire died with no heirs. He'd rather you have it instead of the government." He pulled a copy off a nearby table. "Standard contractor thing. No big strings, I even read mine."

"I'll be the judge of that." The woman snagged the contract from him and started paging through it.

The Doc grinned, "Better hurry, we only got so many slots for today."

She continued to read, but a few of her group sauntered toward the tables. With an eyeroll he turned toward me, eyes pausing on my chest after bouncing off the mirrored glasses. "How 'bout you, hon? You want a special deal?"

"Already signed!" Secret cut in before I could cut him down, and fanned out a spread of hundred-dollar bills in her hand. The scent of her glamor tickled my nostrils as the Doc's eyes went glassy.

"Uh, yeah." I sputtered, "Where do I get my assignment again?"

He blinked, his smile going up to gigawatt level, "Right! My mistake, just talk to Cedric over there." A finger guided us to a man with a tablet and printer. He gave us an assignment, three twelve-hour shifts over the next three days, without looking up. First shift started in less than an hour. I walked out frowning at my ill-gotten schedule, Secret bouncing proudly beside me, still holding the money in her fist. I hadn't seen Cindy; maybe Rey warned her off somehow? Something about this smelled dangerous.

"Secret, make that money go away." I said, mostly to stop her distracting cavorting; no one had even glanced at her.

"Awww, but there's nowhere to spend it here," she

whined. "I guess you can have it. Got no pockets." She collected the money into a neat stack and held it out to me.

I cautiously took the bills, they felt real. "Aren't these like your glasses?"

"Nope!" She preened as only a house cat with a mouse can. "I stole them! Stole from the dead. Don't worry your head but I stole from the dead!" She sang and danced around me.

"Sssshh," I shushed her, kneeling down to her level. "Why?"

"My Momma said, don't bargain with the dead." She continued her singsong. "Ring the bells, dig'em up, throw'em on the pyre. That's how ya quench a dead that desires." Trailing off to a hum, she twisted from my grip to jump up on a half wall, using it like a balance beam. I walked beside her, pondering the wad of crisp money in my pocket, along with her words. Secret never liked direct questions, but maybe that really was the best way to deal with the dead. Dead like Andrew Millar, or like Mr. Baker and Scully.

Need pack. Wolf me grumbled.

Don't have one. I had to decide what I was going to do. Run around the west side hunting for mushrooms and the mushroom-riddled, stay here and figure out what Andrew Millar was attempting to do, or try to dig up a bunch of ghosts that I didn't have complete names for? I texted Cindy to stay wide of downtown if she could, and headed toward the tomb to report for my shift.

24

In the middle of the misty, chilly, dreary afternoon, Andrew Millar's voice boomed, seemingly from everywhere, a deep tender rasp. "Hello Portland." Looking up from my phone, my neck popped; Andrew smiled genially down on me from a screen suspended between buildings on opposite sides of the street. Me and four other medics I didn't know had been staffing this joke of a first aid booth for almost five hours now. We had two palm-sized first aid kits, three cases of water, and a stack of pamphlets on the wonders of the Legacy Health System. Nothing to do but watch the trickle of paid mourners, each carrying a square of black fabric with beaded edges, some wearing it as a veil as intended, I guessed; many others had it draped on their shoulders or stuffed one end in a pocket. One group of teenagers whipped each other, the beads lending welt-making force to the fabric. The mourners ranged from the young, to the old, not too many folks in between. The exception being for those with large backpacks or carts full of belongings. The city's homeless population couldn't say no to five hundred bucks, but they didn't trust it either.

"Thank you for honoring me with your presence today." Andrew droned on from above, spinning a whimsical tale of his love for the city, eyes squinting as he struggled to read from a teleprompter.

Secret had gone into cat mode to hassle a cluster of pigeons, but didn't protest when I plucked her from the ground. Her bright green eyes asked, *What's next?*

Not that I knew, but wolf me pawed restlessly at the back of my eyes. My companions had no objections to me going for a walk. Cradling Secret, I stepped forward with half-closed eyes, breathing deeply through my nose and straining my ears. My senses provided no revelations, only illustrated the swelling of the crowds as the day progressed. My medical tent nestled among stands usually seen at state fairs and farmers markets, hawking everything from jewelry to funnel cakes to booze and weed. If you could drink it, eat it, or smoke it, free had replaced the prices. The clothing and other things advertised eighty percent off. This carnival formed a ring of revelry about three blocks from the tomb. The streets closer were marked "Mourners and Staff Only." As Secret and I drifted closer to see what we could see, a heavy drum sounded, *Dumm... Dumm... Dumm...* A heartbeat that slowed my steps as the powerful sound insisted that the world move to its deliberate pace. The crowds traversing the street appeared to ignore it, but as the beat came, they slowed their step and paused their conversation. Closer, voices rose in song between the beats, melodic and beautiful. It emanated from a stage constructed in front of Millar's tomb. Two bare-chested drummers each stood before a great leather drum, their faces covered with black veils, and in each hand, they wielded a large wooden mallet. They struck their drums in perfect synchrony, twirling their mallets by the leather throngs that secured the sticks to their wrists. On either side of the drummers, a chorus of black-robed men stood on risers with their heads bowed within their deep hoods. Arrayed on plastic benches the mourners lounged. They smoked, ate, and drank among their fellows. Many of them seemed to ignore the stage, but as those mallets crashed into the heads of the drums, every single one of them gave a small nod.

From them I perceived a heat that wasn't; it warmed the pelt that I held inside my skin. A tenuous kindling of power that steadied with each beat and wavered in between. A far cry from the crashing wave of dancing bliss that Rey had brought to that club, but this heat was of the same ilk. Worship and devotion building without direction but growing nonetheless amid Andrew's retellings of his family's story over the speakers. He planned to return from the dead using these people as his power source, buying their attention and devotion. Would that work? Or was this all for naught and this would be a one-time tribute to a man's vanity?

The wind shifted and a whiff of the Rot roused me from my ponderings. Wolf me perked as I scanned my surroundings for threats. Only then did I see all the guns. Scattered among the mourners were clusters of men with pistols on their hips. In front of the stage stood a row of security guards, some of them with longer weapons slung over their backs. Watching for me?

Was Victoria in that marble box performing the ritual now?

Charge in, eat his meat, wolf me prodded. *Fix problem good.*

And how many silver bullets can I take? I answered myself, remembering that spreading numbness from a single pistol round. As if called by the question, I found my fingers playing with the silver pancake of that very bullet. It clung to my fingers, reluctant to leave my touch. With a flick it sailed away, bounced once with a pinging ring and rolled into a sewer grate. Good riddance.

"Meeerf," Secret mewed with amusement.

With a huff, I decided this was a waste of time unless I wanted to find out exactly how many bullets it took to kill me. Let the old man and Victoria play with death. I had a disease and a bunch of murderous ghosts to hunt. Inhaling deeply, I tried to home in on that sour earth smell. Wolf me could do it so much easier, but that would produce plenty of its own problems, so I fought off that urge, stepping through the crowd while breathing deeply through my nose.

There were people here with the Rot, elderly mourners, mostly. I didn't see any purple-black mushrooms peeking between the sidewalks or around the trees that lined the streets, so at least there were no new infections happening here. Maybe it was still only a southwest problem. Only as I resolved to leave and started drifting towards my car did I get a breath so full of rot that I coughed in surprise.

I followed the scent to a triple-sized booth with an exhibit of the founding of our great city. The source of the contamination: three white-haired men in ill-fitting black suits clustered around a model of what had to be early Portland.

"Dis is all wrong." One jabbed with a bony finger at a series of buildings along the river. "Dose were bars, and the mills were up here."

"Feh," another harrumphed, then continued with a light Scottish accent, "Yer daft, Clemins. This here's twenty years after you been dumped under the fir." The voice was different, but I recognized the accent and the cadence...

"How you know? You can't read nothing, Scully." Clemins lifted his chin.

"Careful lad, or you be talkin' out the back of yer head. This here's eighteen-nine-six. We both riding for the old king then." Scully tapped the table. I stepped behind a poster to listen.

"Both a yez should shut ya gobs," the third grumbled. "Baker told us to lie low."

"Baker can't see no better than the rest of us in the goddamn sun. We stayin' away from the hairy lass and keepin' our powder dry till midnight." Scully's voice dropped low.

"Talk about screwing the pooch," Clemins huffed. "My brothers should be here for this."

The thud of a hand striking wood made me jump. "We're not talking 'bout the thrice-cursed train, Clem!" Heads turned toward the group, and they all fell silent for a moment before Scully continued in a whisper. "We'll do tonight with the five of us, no prob. Fish in barrels. And we got silver for the dog."

I listened for a few more minutes, but they resumed quietly bickering over where things were supposed to be. I slipped back thinking, five of them. Did that include Mister Baker? It didn't really matter; I had to stop them from whatever they were keeping powder dry for. Too bad they hadn't been freer with their full names. Under the fir had to be the Lone Fir Cemetery on the east side of Portland. The earliest residents of Portland are buried there. I considered buying some salt and surprising the shades but wolf me had been too public already.

What I needed was a way to draw them to me. I walked among the various vendors, called Cindy and Cliff, but neither picked up nor responded immediately to texts.

Maybe I'd have to go to Rey. Secret purred contentedly in my arms as the wind whistled between the buildings and a gleam caught my eye.

In a glass case sat a tarnished teapot, two cups, and a circular platter. A little sign declared it to be a hundred percent silver.

Thoughts and memories of what I knew of the dead snaked through my head.

The dead want one thing.

Ring the Bell.

And the image of that dancer's shade, salivating over a few drops of Victoria's blood.

The plan crystallized in my head swiftly, its simplicity and insanity completely clear. I bought the tea set with Secret's ill-gotten money. Then took it home to introduce the antique silver platter to Cindy's power tools.

25

It'd been at least ten years since I'd gone anywhere near a gravestone at night and driving up to Lone Fir Cemetery had my memories stirring. The sensation of Jimmy's hot breath on my face and the sucking chill of marble against my back swept over me before I could hold the images back. All I could do was grip the steering wheel and growl as my mind replayed the scene. How giggle-proud we had been of our defilement as we traded drags on a cigarette. So bravely we dishonored dead who couldn't defend themselves.

I wanted to reach back through time and rip the giddy smile off my mouth. It took me a few minutes to shove those memories back into their cages and assure wolf me that the precious little bitch I had been was long gone.

"Aren't childhood memories the sweetest?" Rey smirked from the passenger seat.

"Mine are more like leftovers that have gone sour." I told her. Rey had volunteered to come along for this adventure, but I couldn't be sure if she intended to help or merely wanted a front-row seat for the train wreck. Together we had managed to convince Secret to stay home with Cindy. I didn't want to be distracted worrying about her. A chill prickled across my skin as I stepped out of the car. The breeze carried angry murmurs on it as I pulled a cardboard box out of the trunk. Rey followed me without a sound down a paved path that seemed to shift beneath my feet as if things beneath it were tossing and turning. I doubted that teenage me's crime would have gone unpunished in this place.

The cemetery comprises two heavily wooded city blocks, scattered with ancient tombstones stretching back to the very first white settlers to push the natives out and die here. Yet it wasn't a discriminating place. From Portland's first mayors to thousands of Chinese laborers buried without even noting their names, the ground held them all in their slumber. As tall as the trees were, they were younger than most of the dead that resided beneath them.

We went to its center, standing beneath a fir tree, the scent of its old life balanced against the sweetness of the decay that pervaded the soil. Rey shivered from the chill, her tails wrapping around her legs for extra warmth. "Fox magic will not work in this place," she announced, "We are of life and living. So I will teach you a human charm." Extending a claw, she bent over and drew a precise hexagon on a patch of dirt. "You need to bleed into the center."

I frowned at it. "Do I have to make it a stop sign?"

"No," she said simply; her mouth wrinkled a bit, as if the word tasted wrong. "A drop will do. This is a simple warning. It's best to use symbols people will understand. Your blood is much more potent than any mortal's. That's the only reason this could even work." She looked up and shot the waning moon a jealous glare. Luna peeked back down at us like a slightly sleepy eye.

I took a box cutter from my pocket and slit the tip of my

pinkie. It took effort to squeeze a drop of blood onto the center of the hexagon. As the blood soaked into the dirt, the breeze paused, and the night sound quieted for the briefest instant before continuing on.

"Now mortals will mind their own business," Rey said, "unless they're purposely looking for us."

I took out one of the six canisters of salt I had in the box and opened its spout. "You're being suspiciously helpful," I said.

A tight-lipped smile answered me, "You're a wolf; you couldn't do this without help. If not me, then Cindy would be in harm's way. While some Fey revel in the trappings of the Twilight, once a mortal steps over that line they are lost to us. Even winter's court has waged war on the undead."

With a nod, I walked out the main gate and began to pour a line of salt on the sidewalk. As soon as the first grain landed, I heard disapproving muttering from among the trees. They grew louder with every inch of salt I poured. It took the five of the six canisters before I came back to gate where I'd started. The graveyard had filled with gibbering whispers punctuated by wails that made the trees shiver. Rey had not moved, but her dainty hands choked the pommel of a broadsword, holding it as a batter holds a baseball bat. Her yellow eyes flashed in the moonlight as they darted from side to side. "Hurry up and do it," she whispered.

I swallowed and took the remaining objects out of my box. First, the silver teapot: I'd drilled two holes in the bottom and looped a heavy sterling silver chain I'd found in my aunt's box of donated jewelry through the holes. I handed it and a silver spoon to Rey. She took it with steady hands, her sword nowhere to be seen. Next came the object I had spent most of the afternoon failing to put together and then the evening sharpening. A right triangle of tarnished metal, two inches wide at the base and half a foot long, was bolted to a longer strip of steel, the excess length wrapped in black electrical tape. An oversized prison shiv made for a far larger hand than my human one, the edge gleaming with a hungry shine. Finally, I placed an empty plastic washbasin at my feet.

My simple, stupid, plan was to summon every single soul buried here. The hope being that in that wide net I'd get Scully and his crew of murderous shades. I stood there, studying the decorative whorls in the blade.

"Ready?" Rey asked.

I nodded, placing the blade against the underside of my scarred wrist. *Ring the bell.* In the corner of my eye Rey struck the upturned teapot with the spoon. It didn't sound like a bell. It went *clack!* a but the murmurings of the dead stilled, the world falling into an attentive silence. The heavy weight of many eyes fell on me, Luna's cool affection was but one. The shiv, large and crude compared to the single-blade razor I had used the last time I had watched my blood bloom out of my vein. In those seconds before the red obscured the view it was beautiful how the blood extended itself through the water. In the swirls of that memory, I recalled how Secret had used her own blood to open the way to the Dream, how she had danced as two beings, and the power that whirled around her words. I needed to get those right, too.

I took a breath and spoke. "My name is Abigale Night and tonight I call out to those who rest beneath these trees..."

Who? Came a slithering whisper that stirred the needles of the pines.

"She who has walked among the dead. She who bears

the scars of Luna's teeth. She who loves a child of the Dream." As I spoke, the night drank my words; my keen ears heard the trees groan softly, the grass rustle, and the stones in the wall that ringed the cemetery shifting as the world itself listened.

I drew the blade across my skin, it sliced eagerly into my flesh. Vivid red swelled up from the wound, bright against the muted colors of the night. The pain, like fire and freezing ripping through my entire arm, shocked me so I barely swallowed back the scream. Breathing through clenched teeth I watched the blood pool in my palm. Luna's reflection floated on its surface, her power contained within it.

Clang!

"I... Call you in the name of Luna and the blood of her first wolf." The ground beneath my feet squirmed as an icy gust of wind rushed into me, carrying a low-lying blanket of fog that poured over the top of the stone wall.

Clang! The closed gate shuddered from the force of an unseen blow. "Come!" I barked at it. "Attend me now."

Wolf me whimpered as the scent of my blood mingled with the cloying sweetness of death. The blood overflowed my palm and dripped into the basin. The gate opened with a thunderous clang and a flash, not of light but of dark. A glowing mist rushed through the opening, vague shadows of screaming faces and grasping hands roiled within it.

Clang! The sound jarred me out of my own fear as the spirits flooded over the ground. I held up my bleeding wrist to them as a priest holding up a crucifix. What had Victoria said? "I offer blood for obedience. Partake and, and obey the living!"

They fell on the basin like a ravenous river. Then flowed up the dripping stream of blood. I felt icy tongues and teeth against my skin before they slipped their coldness inside my ragged wound. The shocking cold spiked directly into my heart.

Clang! "No!" I shouted with the same note as the silver kettle. "Back! Protect me!"

The spirits whirled in an ethereal melee. Brighter souls of the fed, pushing back a greater tide of those still unsuppered. "Allow them to approach one at a time."

Clang! I straightened my spine and growled at the ghosts as I re-extended my hand over the basin. My wrist was still bleeding in a constant drip, drip, drip. The cold of both the silver and the ghosts had spread up to my shoulder. Those spirits in the ring separated out into vaguely human shaped individuals, watching me with cold blue embers for eyes. "I seek the shades and the bones of ones who answer to Scully and Clemins. Along with all who serve the old king."

Clang!

The spirits beyond the circle of ghosts cried, "*Let our bones taste your life, let us all share of it and they will come. They will come.*"

The basin had been a mistake, that had provoked a feeding frenzy. I kicked it out of the way and let the drips fall into the dirt. The graveyard itself let out a sigh of satisfaction.

It didn't happen immediately; I stood there, feeding the ground, an ache growing in my bones as my mouth went dry. The ghosts around me grew more substantial with every drop. The clang of the teapot marking the time.

Three darker shadows stole through the gate and the ghosts hissed, *They come.*

One shadow darted forward, snatching a drop of blood before it hit the ground. *Oh, I came alright, ya hairy bitch. What you gonna do about it?* It was Clemins' voice.

I swung my bloody knife straight through the shadow. He only laughed. It had been worth a shot.

"You're going down the river tonight." I growled, "You took my blood, now tell me where your bones are."

Beneath the ground. Deep. Go ahead and dig, doggy. He and the other two shades laughed. All the other ghosts shrank away from them. Red eyes glowed in their wispy forms. Behind them Rey stole over the fence, a canister of salt in her hands. Now or never; guess Scully wasn't in this patch of dirt.

"Spirits of my call!" I shouted to the night. "For my final ask, remember your loves and defend them from this evil!"

The ghosts of the cemetery surged toward the shadows, rushing them like water eager to fill a void. I saw only a swirl of light and dark as the spirits clashed. Muffled gunshots echoed as if from a distant TV set. I finally allowed myself to clap my hand over my wrist.

In seconds the shadows consumed the light and they again separated into three figures as the acrid scent of spent gun powder drifted through the air.

We be riders of the old King, and his kingdom is a-coming, Clemins declared. *Now open that gate back up. Don't think we need bodies to hurt you.* His form shivered with effort and a cross-shaped tombstone pulled itself from the ground.

Shit. So much for this plan. Now would be a great time for Victoria to appear out of nowhere, I thought with fervent hope as I ran for the back gate. My lungs sucked in air, but they couldn't fill entirely. Wolf me stepped into my limbs but my bones barely responded to her presence, screaming with pain and twisting with jarring cracks. I stumbled on misshapen feet into the low wall that surround the grave-yard. A hardness struck me from behind, propelling me over the wall. I saw the glistening line of salt on the sidewalk as I fell toward it.

And... Softness caught me.

"Silly wolf, you almost broke the line." Rey whispered from somewhere above.

The softness went away, depositing me on the pavement, just beyond the sidewalk, thick tails lifting off me like a curtain revealing the world. The ache of my bones had grown into a throbbing pain. My wrist had stopped bleeding finally, but my body felt empty. Luna's power still flowed, but as a river trying to fill an empty lake. The ghosts had taken more than I had realized.

"Thu angs rrrRey." I forced the words through a half-formed muzzle.

"I don't know what you said but I remind you that you shouldn't thank Fey," Rey scolded before taking my hand and pulling me up to my feet, which were still squeezed in two sneakers about four sizes too small.

Burning red eyes watched us from behind the low wall. *Let us out. Now.* Clemins' voice rattled with menace.

I growled back. The salt would at least hold them till somebody jogged on it.

"Hey, Lass!" A voice called out behind me, "I got ya a present." Scully! My brain shouted. My body was slower on the uptake, whirling around instead of diving for cover. He wore the same body he had at the funeral and held a black pistol aimed directly for my head.

Red blurred across my vision with the first pop of the gun. I staggered back as weight thudded into my torso.

Pop, pop, pop, pop, went the gun, each pop accompanied by a yip of pain. The red in front of me was the fan of Rey's tails, the weight, her body clinging to my torso. The gun clicked empty. "Now we're even for the club," she hissed in my ear before rolling off me. Silver bullets fell from her tail, jingling as they bounced on the asphalt.

Scully swore a blue streak as he fumbled to get another clip in his gun. "Goddamn, ya freak shows! Bullet proof tails? I'll show ya. Had to run all the fookin' way! I'll plug ya all good."

Out of the corner of my eye I saw the salt canister that Rey had been carrying. I snatched it up with a clawed hand and threw it. It arced through the air leaving a trail of salt.

The clip clicked into place simultaneously; Scully fired. The canister exploded 2/3rds of the distance to him in a spray of salt. Scully screeched, dropping the gun to claw at his eyes.

I knew one way to dispose of shades. Didn't know if it would get the rest of them but it would definitely take care of Scully. Throwing myself onto my feet, I charged; it was more of a lumber. He stopped wiping his eyes in time to scoop up the gun, but I caught his wrist. The gun thundered in my left ear as I sank my teeth into his shoulder. He hammered my skull with his free hand but the pain of that couldn't compete with the searing foulness of the Rot spurting onto my tongue. It didn't matter, I wouldn't let them win. This bastard would pay for Mitch and everybody else he'd hurt. Wrapping my arm around his waist, I lifted him up from the ground and started carrying him towards the circle of salt. *Luna give me strength,* I prayed as he started kicking at my shins.

"Put me down, ya whorey bitch!" Scully screamed, slamming his knuckles into the side of my head over and over.

Get out of here, Scully! one shade hissed. *Go back to Mister Baker!*

"I can't! Salt's not lettin' me out! Gnnrah!" He let out a roar of pain as I pressed him up against the circle. His arm twisted suddenly, firing the gun wildly at the sidewalk. Pain ripped through my calf as it caught a ricochet. With a roar, I shoved him with all my might, and he went through. Feet kicking up as he tumbled back over the wall. The gun clattered to the ground on my side.

I picked it up and emptied the clip into him. Three shots and he lay still.

Aaah, crud, we chicagoed, the shade muttered, and I heard the swing of a heavy blade.

I waited, listening, but nothing stirred. The cemetery was completely dead still. Slowly, I released a breath. *Pleasure working with you, Death,* I thought as I eased myself to sit on the wall, head throbbing; a numb sensation reached from the tips of my fingers and into my heart. My body ached for sleep.

Rey came over to me, absently combing fingers through her tails. I waited for her to say something snide or judgmental on how that had gone. "I'm going home to Cindy. She'll take care of me." With that, her form shimmered, and a three-tailed fox bounded off in the direction of Cindy's house.

Leaving me there with the question, if Cindy was taking care of her, who'd take care of me?

Myself of course. That was the answer. I went back to my car, pulled a steel shard from my leg, wrapped both it and my wrist with bandages. Then I had nothing left and collapsed into the driver's seat. I should go home to Secret, but I couldn't bring myself to lift my hand up and turn the key. The adrenaline of the fight faded, leaving me with the pain and an emptiness that went far deeper.

Wounded, wolf me pushed into my lips and howled uselessly to the car interior. A howl for help, for a pack that didn't exist. Staring out through the windshield, I watched the cemetery sit in its peaceful stillness, not bothering to wipe the tears that were leaking down my face.

Later, a muffled ping broke the quiet. Then another. And another. I blinked and stirred from my fugue and clawed at the glove compartment. My phone tumbled out and its screen lit to display the most recent message. From Victoria.

"R U Okay?"

"No." I told it and let my head fall back against the headrest.

You don't need help. You're just being pathetic and weepy. Jimmy's voice taunted me.

"Shutup," I mumbled, and started the car.

26

"Bloody fucking ashes, Abby." was the first comment Victoria made when she opened the front door. Clad in black satin pajamas, she frowned elegantly; without her concealer on I could see the pattern of freckles on her pale skin, clustered around her cheekbones and the corners of her wide, staring eyes.

I ran my tongue over still-sharpened teeth; no words came at first, lost to that void of numbness that had settled on me. When the words finally came, they were slow and hollow, "I'm not... okay."

Fear quickened her breath as she shifted to peer over my shoulder, "Where's Secret?" she asked, not moving out of the way.

"Home. Safe with Cindy," I mumbled, stepping forward, pushing with my eyes, but she held her ground. Why didn't she let me in? Why wasn't she helping me?

Victoria's throat bobbed, staring at me, challenging me, her hands closing into loose fists. "Abby, could you stop trying to scare me and tell me what's going on? I started bleeding during the ritual!" She held up her wrist to display a bandage across its underside.

Anger sparked in the hollowness inside me, and I growled, "It's always about you."

She answered with a snarl of her own, lips curling back from teeth, and eyes alight with challenge. "It's a self-inflicted wound! Were you trying to ruin the ritual?! Because you almost did! Now put those awful fangs away!"

"Awful fangs..." I echoed, my anger igniting into rage. "So I'm an inconvenience to you? You'd rather I'd have just died tonight instead of interrupting your precious ritual?" In the back of my mind, Jimmy cackled, and I knew this was all wrong, but I couldn't stop the boiling frustrations. If she would only stop staring at me. "Why don't I show you my real fangs, Vicky?" I reached out and shoved her back into her house.

"Abby!" she squawked. I slammed the door behind me.

Eager to answer her challenging eyes, wolf me slid up into my body. My clothes tore as I burst their seams; Victoria shrank before me, tripping over her own backpedaling feet and tumbling down onto the freshly laid carpet.

My stomach howled with the sweetness of her abject terror. Exhaustion clawed at my body. The prospect of a good meal coupled with a long sleep made me lick my lengthening muzzle. Who'd would miss the necromancer other than Andy Millar? Victoria defiled the dead with a casual callousness that sickened me.

"Come on, Abby!" Victoria pleaded as she scuttled backwards "I didn't mean- ah!" Her head rammed into the wall, and she swiftly pressed her spine against it. "Please don't kill me! Whatever I did, I'm sorry! I just tried to protect..." She lifted her chin as far as she could, offering her throat.

I seized her with my teeth, but something in the taste of

her skin made me pause. She whimpered softly, a high-pitched canine sound that spoke through my anger. *You win, don't hurt me. Please don't hurt me.*

Not prey, wolf me decided, and I let her go. She toppled onto the floor, arching her back and neck in submission. I lowered my nose to the base of her throat and pulled in her scent.

Human fear sweated from every single pore of her skin but there beneath it, that dusky scent that had teased me every time we'd met, lay plain as day to my black nose. Lupine musk; a wolf lurked inside Victoria, and she had begun to come out, she just needed a little help. *Pack?* Was it almost too much to hope for? I drank in her scent and licked at her neck. It had to have been the transfusion. Luna lurked in my bloodstream, and I had given it to her fresh off that first touch. Beneath me, Victoria shuddered and gasped, her eyes cracking open to show gold ringing her dilated pupils. "What's happening? Hurts."

I picked her up from the floor and curled my body around hers, holding her tightly to my chest, grooming her wavy black hair. Her skin glistened with sweat as the scent of her wolf grew stronger with every breath. All of our interactions replayed through the prism of a wolf inside her. Her want to be close and informed, the odd sense of longing every time we parted company, and just now, she'd been defending her territory against another wolf.

Tenderly, I pulled open her shirt enough to expose her shoulder. I lathered it with my tongue. With the contact I finally felt our link, like my connection to Rey, but born of blood instead of obligation.

"Aaaaaaaah!" She screamed as my teeth punctured her flesh. "Abby! I don't-"

I bit harder, feeling the bones in her shoulder strain to

their limit. "Aah! Aah!" She panted before erupting into a howl of pain. I released her, and she scrabbled away, black fur spreading from the bloody mess of her shoulder as her bones crackled like a tree trunk bent too far. She made it about ten feet away from me before the change locked up her back. All she could do was dig her nails into the plush carpet and hang on as her spine extended, exposing more and more midriff, as her pajama top had barely covered it to begin with. Her lengthening tail tented the rear of her pants. I crept forward and pulled it free, slipping the waistband down around her knees. She rounded on me suddenly, ramming her face into my side. At first, I thought she was attempting to bite me, but she just pressed insistently into my thick fur. I gathered her up into the long arms of my hybrid form, tore off her top, and stroked the black fur as it spread down her spine. The sharp snaps of her reforming bones quieted to a soft grinding of gears. Where my body swelled with the change, Victoria's extended, remaining lithe, her black fur short compared to my thick winter coat. Only once the change reached her face did she lift it from my shoulder. "Why is it Good?" grinding out the words through sharpening teeth before her nose raced away from her face, dragging it into a long narrow muzzle. Combined with a pair of tall, pointed ears, she more resembled a massive black jackal than any wolf I'd ever seen. But to my nose she had a dusky lupine musk that called to mind my parents and my aunts. *Family, Packmate.* I shifted to my own big wolf form and settled down on the floor beside her. She looked cold with that thin fur, and she huddled against me. I settled my head across her shoulders and slipped into slumber with that hollow part of me filling with the warmth of her body.

I woke to sunshine streaming in through a myriad of

curtained windows, inhaled Victoria's dusky scent, and if I had a hand instead of a paw, I would have slapped my forehead so hard I might have given myself a concussion. Instead, I sprang up from the floor like a startled cat and rushed over towards the door, sniffing desperately at the tattered remnants of my clothing until I found the one that contained my cell phone. After a little frantic pawing, I remembered fingers were kinda required, and I shifted to my human skin. Wolf me yielded for Secret's sake, but her reluctance to leave Victoria made it painful. After I'd told Cindy I was okay and wished good morning to Secret, Victoria's curled up figure stirred. I paused to stroke a hand down her long spine and thread nails through her glossy fur. She stilled back to sleep with a soft huff.

My stomach grumbled, and I wandered towards Victoria's kitchen, looking at the house surrounding me as I went. All traces of the bullet holes that had shredded the house had been removed. Everything had that slightly nauseating brand-new smell; the fresh paint was the worst of it. I noted fist-sized dents in the huge stainless-steel refrigerator that were new. Several cabinet doors had been torn off and the faucet had been replaced. I remembered the full moon nights before I met Secret, and the anger at myself and the world that had led me to wreck my apartment. Why didn't she tell me? I wondered, but my own denial had been formidable. It had happened three times before I admitted to myself what had really happened. If this full moon had been the first time...

I open the fridge; it was hardly full, but had more than enough food for a family on a high protein diet. I pulled out a package of organic bacon that probably cost at least as much as my hourly wage, and turned to find Victoria standing in the doorway to the kitchen.

I had a momentary surge of fear seeing a four-footed creature large enough to look me in the eye. Pushing away human me's instinctual reaction, I looked more critically; she might be nearly as large as me at the shoulder, but her weight had to be much less. Built more like a greyhound than any wolf I'd met. Incredibly elegant lines, although a vicious, petty part of me was pleased that while she had a human body many women would kill for, I was the better-looking wolf unless the viewer had a bias in favor of Egyptian mythology.

"Good morning," I greeted her intense golden eyes that quickly looked down and whined.

"It's hard to say how long you'll be stuck," I told her truthfully. While there wasn't her human voice speaking in my head or anything like that, I still knew precisely what she wanted. "For me, sleeping as a wolf will usually allow me to be human for breakfast, but generally I have to keep it close to fifty-fifty. Also, make sure that the wolf has some time to be a wolf. Otherwise," I recalled my difficulties earlier in the week, "you'll find yourself on all fours at a moment you really don't want to be."

She yipped and shook her head. The shake traveled down her body to the tip of her tail. Once it passed, she sat down heavily, blinking with surprise at the sensation.

"Yes, that is more than once a month. Might be different for you if my hunch is right. You're a two-touch wolf; I'm three." I opened the package of bacon.

She growled, but not about the food.

"Luna had marked me before I gave you the transfusion: blood, one touch. Then I bit you last night; that's two," I said.

This time, she snorted.

"No. Sex isn't the third touch." I snapped back and

popped a strip of bacon into my mouth. Chewed a bit to give me time to think about it. "I made a deal with Luna herself. Actually, no. I didn't make a deal at all. I simply gave myself to her. So the whole touch theory could be utter bullcrap. Now come here and eat something."

Those great big ears of hers laid back and her answering growl was defiant.

I had to smile. "Fine, stay right there and watch me eat it all if you still think raw is gross." I made a show of savoring the next strip of bacon, then another. She drifted towards me, mouth hanging open, eyes locked on the food. I dangled a strip in front of her nose. She sniffed it desperately, body vibrating as the human and the wolf fought for the first time. For me, raw had been an easy transition but I was willing to admit Victoria was starting out much more civilized than I.

With a snap of her long jaws, she snatched the bacon from my fingers.

"Good Girl!" I exclaimed, and she gave me such a glare that I had to laugh. "Want another?"

Nod.

We ate everything out of her fridge, and it was glorious. While Cindy often cooked Secret and me dinner, this proved to be a different experience entirely. We gorged ourselves like wolves at a kill. At first, I divided the chunks of meat between us after warming them a little in the microwave, but she could eat so much faster than I. Giving up, I tossed everything onto the floor and gave in to wolf me. By the end, our bellies were pleasantly distended and as we cleaned the last bit of the juices from each other's muzzles, my tail was wagging almost as rapidly as a dog's with the joy of finally have another wolf to share this with. I couldn't wait to show her the glory of the run and the hunt. To fill that sad and lonely piece of me that howled out every time I did it alone.

And why wait? I led her to the back door and grabbed the doorknob with my teeth.

Victoria let out a plaintive whine and stuck her head between me and the door.

Watched, the house was watched. Course it was. Andrew had expected to come back, and perhaps he had? Either way, he'd want to know Victoria's whereabouts, and they certainly didn't need to know what Victoria had become. We backed away from the door. Victoria bent down, craning her neck to look at her paws, huffing with effort.

I reached into myself to human me. Found her still tired and worried, but she answered my request, pushing her limbs down mine and while I took the change slow, I stood up on two feet within a minute or two, rolling bare shoulders.

Meanwhile, Victoria whined anxiously, and literally ran in a circle before pounce-slamming her front paws into the floor repeatedly. "Vicky! Stop it!" I rushed towards her, but she stopped me with an accusatory snarl, showing a muzzle packed full of gleaming white fangs.

"Yes, I did this to you," I admitted. "I'm..." I found I couldn't say sorry. Victoria wasn't my first choice as a pack-mate but just her dusky scent made me want to sing praises to Luna. "Let me help you change. It will be easier if you're calm," I amended, offering her the palm of my hand. While the angry baring of teeth remained, I took the small wag of her whip-like tail as permission to touch her. I slid my hand over the top of her muzzle and swept it down the length of her neck. She growled, but I ignored it, kneeling and wrapping my arms around her. Combing my fingers through her fur, I softly explained how I managed the exchange of human me and wolf me. Slowly the growling subsided, and her tail made audible thuds against the floor.

I had to laugh when the growl came back and the tail stilled; she must have noticed it. "You can chew me out when you can talk. I know you're angry and scared, but I need you to relax right now." I spoke with my medic voice and raked my fingers from the base of her skull down the length of her spine. She shivered and closed her eyes. Then whined with pain as a sharp snap of bone echoed in my ears, and with it, all the fur on her body pulled back into her pale skin at once. It left her strangely naked in my arms as the change radiated out from her hips. I watched her tail wither without a sound as her spine cracked like a frozen lake during a spring thaw. Her skin grew sweaty and slick, but I held on even as cool rivulets of her sweat ran between my breasts and down my stomach. I didn't dare let go as I whispered encouragements and kissed the feverish skin, tasting the salt. Her arms clamped around my torso and pressed her chest against mine. Breasts swelled back into existence and pressed against my own as her ribcage flattened. She rested her head on my shoulder until the change had almost finished, but then she moved, suddenly capturing my lips with her own. Soft, warm, full of want. The opposite of alone. I pushed back, not wanting it to end, feeling the retracting of her fangs with my tongue.

She broke it off with a quiet, "Aw, fuck." Her head fell back to my shoulder, her arms squeezing me tighter. Damn, you Abby." she swore. "Why does everything about you hurt so much?"

I held her, still tasting her on my lips, feeling confused. I ached to kiss her again. It had been so quick and instinctual that its meaning seemed ungraspable, unlike the sizzling cold of Queen Mab's questing tongue.

I shook myself a little, refocused on Victoria. "It's okay," I mumbled. "You're okay now."

She lifted her head to look into my eyes; hers were still gold, human-proportioned but so bright, as if a jeweler had embedded gold leaf into her irises. "Okay?" Her voice cracked. "You have a weird definition of okay." she closed her eyes and pulled out of my grasp, standing up. A few paces away, she sighed and ran her nails through her long black hair. When I become human, I retain an almost shocking level of white body hair, but her thin body appeared to be nearly hairless. I chuckled at my own jealousy.

"It's not funny!" She turned on me. "You were going to kill me last night!" Her eyes met mine and the anger there snuffed out suddenly. She looked down at the carpet. "I didn't do anything to you."

Shame finally broke through my jubilation at finding a packmate. Our wolves didn't care about the how, but our human sides did, and I realized that unless I was very careful, I'd lose her as fast as I had gained her. "Victoria, it had already happened. Your refrigerator was full of meat and I'm going to guess you don't remember much from the last full moon."

Victoria crossed her arms and stared at a display case with a collection of carved skulls. "That doesn't excuse you from barging into my territory-" she cut herself off and stomped her foot into the floor, "Home! Barging into my home and scaring me and then hugging me and... Ugh." She made as if to rip out her hair. "Now it's loose in my head; it won't let me even be angry at you."

I reach out to hug her but pulled my hands back. "Victoria, I'm really sorry it happened like that. I really needed someone to... be with, I guess. That why I came, and then when you challenged me instead, I snapped. I wanted to scare you into doing what I wanted. I wanted the fangs to make a difference for once. Then you submitted like a wolf. I couldn't stop myself."

"You came to my door with your claws and teeth out... Because you wanted a hug?" She laughed wetly and sniffed hard.

"I'm not good at this, alright?" When she didn't respond I sighed, "Look, you need some time and I need to get home. Could I borrow some clothes?"

"Upstairs, second room on the right is my wardrobe. Take what you want. That seems to be your M O," she said, looking at the carpet. Her inner conflict was so strong it had a scent, none of the sour notes of Cindy's fear, but bitter tension so thick I could almost strum it.

I went around her and followed her directions, finding she had converted an entire bedroom into a walk-in closet. There were racks and racks of elegant gowns that barely had any scent on them at all. The more casual clothing of her usual red-on-black style smelled of more use. It was tempting to shower, but instead I just squeezed into a pair of stretch jeans and grabbed a t-shirt that didn't look well-loved. Yet I couldn't resist letting my nose guide me to a door set in the wall where you might expect the room's original closet to be. I opened it to find a bedroom, its air heavy with Victoria's human scent and rose-flavored air freshener. The four-post bed with red velvet curtains, its frame painted black, of course. The dark wooden dresser with the skulls and roses motifs carved into every surface, but most impressive was the wall of framed portraits dominated by a single oil painting of a reclining couple I recognized as her parents, while smaller framed photographs were tiled around it. A section of them had cracked and broken glass as if they'd been ripped down and put back up. Whether they smiled or scowled, all bore a name and two dates. I found Jimmy's evil smirk among them. These were all dead people, and what she woke up to each morning in this huge house. I had no idea what that meant, but feeling like a dirty voyeur, I stepped back into the "closet." Vicky is a necromancer, she's allowed to be weird, I told myself.

I heard the crack of glass downstairs. "Vicky!?" I shouted, bursting through the door and leaping down the staircase. I found her close to where I'd left her, her hand now covered with blood, a spiky hole in the glass display case. "W-what are you doing?"

"Blood," she said, as if it were the obvious answer. I could feel her roiling emotions, despair, anger, and a tiny bit of awe as she studied her hand. "It's been in my blood since the Twilight."

Pup being silly, wolf me huffed, but I took a gentler approach.

"What do you mean, Victoria? Talk to me."

"You used your blood last night. Same way I do. That's why you cut yourself." Victoria kept her eyes on her hand, the cuts sealing as she watched.

"Yeah. I had to summon a pack of ghosts, to stop them from doing something at the funeral. I would have asked you for help, but you were kinda busy last night," I said.

"Did they come?" She refused to look at me.

"Yes. They practically drained me dry, that's why I was so... strained last night."

"Dammit. It's not fair." She finally moved, fixing me with her shining rings of gold. "It was you all along. Things started working, doing what I asked them to do when I got out of the hospital. I thought I'd picked up a little piece of the Twilight, or just that the walls between the worlds were thinner, but it was your blood! The only reason I could do anything this entire time is because you infected me!"

"It's not an *infection!*" A sawing growl followed my words as wolf me pressed into my features.

Victoria jerked her eyes away. "Sorry." She winced "Wait, why am I-"

"Because it was rude to say." Rolling my shoulders and letting wolf me fall back, I relaxed. "So your magic isn't from where you thought it was. So? Luna is the light within the night. She watches over the Twilight, the Dream, and Crossroads. I'm still trying to get a handle on it all, but it's not bad. Together, we can figure it out. Why don't you come back with me to Cindy's?"

"Like a pack of wolves?" She spoke the words as if they were bladed. "So we can run around and howl at the moon?"

All that warmth from the morning drained away, and I blinked back tears. "Kinda. It's like a family." My words were small and hurt.

"I thought, maybe we had an attraction or something, but it's just your blood messing with my head." She crossed her arms. "My family's long dead and I'm fine alone."

She lies. Let her wolf out, urged wolf me. *Make her see. She IS pack.*

No. I'd done enough damage here. "Right. I'll leave you alone, then." Ducking around her, I headed for the foyer. She followed right on my heels, breathing hard as if laboring with a weight. I exited the front door, and she only stopped when I went down the steps.

I had opened the door to my car, and she spoke. "It didn't work."

Turning, I found her standing completely naked at the top of the three steps of her unfinished porch, bloody hand resting on the railing. I waited for her to say something more, my eyes on the long scar that bisected her belly button and my lips remembering the softness of hers. Anything to avoid the rage and hurt in her eyes.

"I did the ritual almost perfectly, embalmed his body and separated the organs. I felt its power. But he didn't come back. They called me a fraud. So you don't have to worry about any mummy billionaires anymore."

"Thanks for letting me know," I said. "Anything else you need to tell me?"

Don't go. Wolf me tried to push into my arms and I shoved clawed fingers into my pockets.

She turned her back, balling hands into fists. "No. Don't come back."

"If you change your mind, call me." I ducked into the car and slammed the door before she could answer. I drove out of her little estate with blurry vision, wolf me howling in protest.

27

She'll come around; she just needs time, I told myself and hoped to Luna it would be true.

As I walked through the door to Cindy's place, Secret came running down the stairs, calling my name. I scooped her up, kissed her between her fuzzy ears, and squeezed her until she squirmed. "So glad I have you, kiddo." I told her on release.

She gave a happy mew, hugged my thigh, and rubbed her cheeks on my waist. How could a girl who ate human hearts be so sweet? "You're lovey this morning." I scratched her ears.

"You're sad." She purred a bit before looking up with a pout. "And I'm hungry."

"How 'bout some tuna fish?" I asked, taking a step towards the kitchen.

She held onto my leg and her ears wilted a bit. "Abby, it's the other type of hungry." She whispered in a hushed voice.

Hunt? Wolf me stirred from her depression as I froze. I shouldn't be surprised; she'd used her glamor to hide me while we had hunted Andrew, and again at his funeral.

Magic had costs, and I'd been allowing Secret to use hers on my behalf. "It's only been a few days. How hungry?" I heard myself ask.

"It doesn't have to be right now." Her shoulders hunched. "But if there's a meanie you don't like..."

Get pup meat, wolf me growled, unbothered by the prospect of hunting a human being that wasn't a direct threat to us. The cops hadn't even hassled me after I'd given Andrew that heart attack. Although maybe that had more to do with Rey's protection on the house and the fact that I hadn't used my name at Andrew's funeral than anything else. And, well, Secret had been protecting me, using that energy.

I knelt down, put my forehead against hers, and whispered. "Thank you for telling me. I will find you a heart, but we have to make the next one last a little longer, alright?"

She nodded timidly, "'Kay. Just hungry, not starving."

"I'll find something for you tonight." I hugged her, mind whirling with how the hell I was going to feed her. Would the heart of Scully's host have worked? Had I wasted a perfectly good heart? Or had the heart been as foul to her as his blood had been? Then I remembered I had just left the body in the graveyard and the pistol was still in my car! Criminal mastermind, I am not.

I let Secret go and called out for Cindy. Nobody answered.

"She went to work. Rey went out." Secret said.

"Cindy left you here?!" My voice climbed high. No wonder she hadn't texted me back earlier this morning.

"I can be alone." Secret sniffed and wandered off into the kitchen.

My throat grumbled at that as I checked my phone. There were quite a few messages. A new unknown number suggested we have a chat and claimed to be Mayor Leary. Cliff said that the NLR was critically short-handed and begged me to take another shift. Cindy, meanwhile, was up at the funeral party for a shift, citing needing money for redoing the kitchen counters.

I made coffee and debated what to do. I considered; Baker was still out there, but maybe I'd gotten most of his servants. Andrew Millar had stayed dead, which was a relief. That left the disease itself. How do you fight a mushroom? Hopefully, the mayor and his task force were working on that. I pondered trying to find Baker the same way I'd found Millar, but wolf me slumped down in the depths of my being, uninterested. She wanted to go back to Victoria, but I couldn't sit here and brood. I took the shift from Cliff on the condition he'd watch Secret. Afterward, I'd let wolf me try again with Victoria.

Cliff stank of stress, and after thanking me for coming in, he was all business. Within five minutes of walking into the firehouse I was driving out again with Patricia, a newer EMT who was still on probation. She acted like I was going to bite her at first, but warmed up quickly, filling my silence with stories about her three kids and her clueless husband. I didn't have much to say as we transported back-to-back overdoses up at Millar's carnival. The weak flame of power had grown overnight to the point that it made my skin itch throughout downtown, weighing on my brain, searching for an outlet or perhaps its owner. The mourners had grown in number and now marched through downtown carrying black banners printed with Andrew Millar's face. The radio was all about the funeral; some stations made fun of it, others complained about the traffic and noise, while ads invited everyone down to get paid to party in a billionaire's name.

Calls then took us south, and there I could feel the tug of Victoria's turbulent heart. I couldn't tell what she was doing precisely, but her anger towards me glowed red hot. Trying to ignore her, I focused on the road and didn't like what I saw. Zero green; even the evergreens that dotted the land-scape had turned brown. The moss that usually creeps over winter Portland's sidewalks had disappeared. Every time I stepped outside the ambulance, I scented the sweet rot beneath the ground when I didn't simply smell it in the patients. We ferried nearly a dozen elderly folks with the sour earth smell to the hospital, all complaining of difficulty breathing. Patricia had already been out with someone else before me, so we went back to the firehouse when her shift ended at four.

See pack, Wolf me urged, *help her.*

Maybe I was done, too.

Cliff didn't come out to greet us, but I scented a spicy anger so strong that it was only a few steps down from snorting cayenne pepper, not just Cliff's, but his sister Sophie's, too. Secret didn't appear as I helped Patricia restock the bus and I didn't see anyone else in the bay coming to finish the shift with me. I walked to the office with trepidation and heard someone cough as I opened the door.

My eyes found Secret first. She lay sprawled out across Cliff's lap as he stared into a monitor. Sophie sat on the opposite side of the room. Both swiveled their heads toward me with an eerie synchrony. The siblings' reactions parted then, a relieved smile growing on Cliff's face while Sophie's eyes narrowed in suspicion.

"Hey, Abby!" Cliff said, beating his sister to the punch, "You're back early. Something wrong?" One of Secret's eyes popped open.

Sophie visibly swallowed back whatever had first come to her lips.

"Patricia's shift is over and unless you got someone else to ride with me, I guess mine is, too." I said, stepping into the room. Wolf me squirmed, and I sniffed the air.

"Uuuh," Cliff's forehead wrinkled as he clicked with his mouse and squinted at the screen. "Douglas ain't here?" he asked, stifling a cough.

"Called in to use his grieving period, remember?" The last word stretching out with Sophie's scorn. "You okayed it. He's probably up working the funeral for easy money like everybody else who didn't show up today."

"Did I?" Cliff answered mildly and rolled his eyes. "Can't fire someone for taking sick time." He straightened up, coughed once into his elbow. "Let me hit the phones again."

In my mind's eye, Cliff lay like a corpse in a hospital bed, torso wrapped in fine black fibers. "Cliff, I don't like that cough. Can I check your breath?"

He laughed, "Considering the amount of coffee I'm drinking today, that's really not a good idea."

Not caring, I bent over and stuck my nose right in front of his lips; wolf me was so preoccupied with Victoria that she didn't even stir. "Exhale," I instructed.

He obeyed, pursing his lips and blowing at my face. Thick with coffee, the acrid flavor of stress, his own heavy human scent and beneath it, buried, was the Rot. "We're taking you to the hospital."

"What the what!" Sophie went off with a sputter.

I ignored her and focused on him. "I can smell the Rot on your breath. It's what made Mitch do what he did. We all got exposed at the funeral. Mitch got a stronger dose somehow."

Anger drew in Cliff's broad features, "Exposed to what? By whom?"

"All this pneumonia outbreak. Look, Dr. Wiggins can explain it better than I can."

"The code Z guy? What the fuck is this, Abby?" Confusion plain on his face.

Secret answered, suddenly a girl perched on the desk. "It's a mushroom that eats you," she said, swinging her legs. "It's the ghosts that are really mean, though."

Cliff looked at Secret, then to me and back to Secret. "Are you telling me that Mitch was possessed when he drove an ambulance into a train yesterday?"

Secret nodded, "Uh huh."

Not bothering to ask me for clarification, he gripped his forehead with his good hand and dragged his palm down over his face. "We've fallen into a bad movie, haven't we?" He laughed without humor. "Where's the cameras?" He looked around and flashed that wonderful smile of his, but his eyes remained shrunken and tired.

"I'm sorry, Cliff." I wanted to hug him, but the way he just slumped into his seat meant I'd have to throw myself on top of him first.

"Naw, its fine. Figures; I go through all that trouble, get that magic sword and what gets me? A mushroom. You can't stab a fungus." He stood.

"Cliff! Sit right back down. You cannot just believe her like that!" Sophie exclaimed, breaking her silence.

Cliff shrugged. "Abby's always straight with me. She smells something wrong, then something's wrong." With his eyes on me, he nodded towards his sister. "Wanna check her too?"

Sophie's narrowed eyes had gone wide. "Oh no. I am not gonna let the crazy racist chick sniff me. No fucking way.

Clearly you drinking what she's selling, little bro, but that bitch is not coming near me."

I mentally flinched back from the sudden bile and wolf me stepped up into the gap with a warning growl.

"And what's that? A threat?" Sophie stared me down through her gold-rimmed glasses.

"Simply letting you know that I've had a shitty morning. So maybe you'd like to rephrase that?" Wolf me slipped out further, eager to vent frustration on a yapping dog, and my clothes tightened around my limbs.

"Woah, woah! Abby, calm down!" Cliff sputtered; his hand clapped on my shoulder. I jerked out of his grip.

"Wow, Mom's right. You really are a freak." Sophie stepped up and her hands came up into a loose boxing stance. "I'll rephrase: you're fired. So don't bother signing one of those contracts in the bay."

"What?!" I half barked the word. Cliff's arm hooked around my chest and hauled me back. The world spun as if I'd been sucker-punched. "You can't do that!"

"You bet your ass I can. I own a third of this company and you threatened me. Cliff, you gonna fight me on this one, too?" She glowered at Cliff.

My job, I needed my job. Another rolling rumble came out of my throat. She couldn't take it away like that.

"Abby that's not helpful. Calm down." Cliff dragged me further from his sister. I made to escape but his grunt of pain stopped me. He had me pinned against his injured arm. If I struggled, I'd hurt him, and if I shifted further, my borrowed clothes were going to be scraps. "Calm down," he insisted.

"Why are you holding her back, Cliff?" Sophie taunted. "I thought you trusted her."

"Sophie! Shut the hell up and leave right now!" Cliff boomed.

"Sure. Be right back with her walking papers!" The door slammed shut and the entire room shook from the aftershock.

28

A few thundering heartbeats later, Wolf me belatedly stepped back and my snowy fur pulled back into the soft copper of my skin. Still, Cliff did not release me. "You going to let me go?" I finally asked.

"Are you calm enough?" Cliff responded, a bit of his father's steel in his voice.

"I would never hit her." I responded, hoping it was true.

"Fooled me. I'll let you go when you stop growling," he told me, grip loosening a tad.

"I'm not-" Then I heard it, a very soft rumble. I looked over toward the sound to see Secret standing on a desk in the far corner, glaring at Cliff, claws extended, fangs bared and ears back. "Way to go from hero to zero, Cliff." I sighed.

"Back at ya." Cliff let me go with a grunt.

With a disgruntled merf, Secret crossed her arms and turned her back on Cliff as I stepped away from him. "So you're just going to let her fire me, then?"

Cliff rubbed his arm and grimaced, "You just wolfed out and almost attacked my sister."

"She called me a bitch!" I countered. "Am I supposed to stand here and take that?"

He slumped back down into his chair. "I don't know! I can't even stop her and Taya from selling the company. Dad split it three ways. Both my sisters blame you for Dad's death. Sorry, I'm overruled."

With a note like threatening a supervisor, I'd never get hired again as an EMT in Portland. "What am I supposed to do? Apologize for a fight she started? Would that work?"

Cliff made a series of uncertain noises before saying, "You know, Abby, maybe Cindy was right the last time we talked about this. You weren't ready to come back to work yet."

No, no, no, no. I clutched at my head; if I wasn't a paramedic, then I'd only be a werewolf. Sanity and balance did not lie in that direction. Not that sanity and balance had much to do with being a paramedic, but I knew I needed to fill my calendar with things other than the phases of the moon. Too late now, though, if Cliff wasn't willing to defend me, then this bridge was doused with napalm and flaming to the sky. "Fuck it," I declared and went to the door. "I guess I'll go beg for my job. Why don't you get your things?"

"What?" Cliff asked. I didn't turn around to look at his face.

I spoke into the door, "I know you're mad at me and I'm upset with you, but that doesn't make anything I've said untrue. So you need to go to the hospital today and because I care for you, you're going even if I have to carry you in my slavering jaws." I didn't wait for him to answer before exiting the office.

Sophie was the opposite of difficult to find, already unloading a torrent of words into her cell phone at the opposite end of the hall. Secret growled in my arms along with wolf me, but I silenced them both, Secret with a stroke of my fingers and wolf me got shoved back down inside me. Steeling myself against any verbal slings that she chose to hurl at me.

I walked down the hall and Sophie watched me, lips twisted into a sneer. "Oh, here comes the freak, stay on the line, Taya." She slipped her phone into the outer pocket of her purse. "You want round two? Do you expect my brother to save you again by yanking back on your leash?"

I stopped a good twenty feet from her, staring at her chin so as not to stir up wolf me. "No. I'm just here to say sorry. That was unprofessional of me." I choked back all the excuses that flurried up into my mind. How she'd been goading me from the get-go or how I was only trying to help her? Those didn't matter.

"You think that's going save your job? You think that's something you can kiss and make better? Huh?" She kept her hands at her sides but balled them into fists.

That would have been the dream, but I'd settle for not getting a black mark on my record. "Not really, no."

She scowled, tongue pressing on the inside of her lips as she thought. "Okay, because you're so sorry I'll make you a deal, Miss Night. You turn your ass around. Write up your resignation and turn it in."

"Okay," I started, but she held up a finger.

"Nah-huh! I'm not done. After you do that, you walk out that door and you stay the hell away from my family. You don't talk to my brother ever again." She looked at me over her glasses. "Got it?"

I didn't need a single second to consider. "Yeah, no." Nobody was going to blackmail me into leaving a friend. Cliff had insisted on getting involved against Little Nick, even before the creature had brutally tortured and killed his father. If he didn't want me in his life, then that'd be his decision, and I would never shut that door.

Sophie arched one eyebrow, perhaps waiting for an explanation for my refusal or a counteroffer but I simply turned and walked out of the building. Anything I said to her would simply give her more ammunition. It was easy to pick the screaming red of Cliff's sports car out of the line of gray vehicles parked along the side of the street. A light rain had drifted in, and it felt cool on my too-hot skin. I walked over to the car, low and sleek with a hood so long that I could lie down across it and my head wouldn't even touch the windshield. I considered siting on it, but the red metal was beaded with a garden of droplets, and I had a sponge wrapped around my legs. So I stood by his car and waited, wondering if Cliff would force me to make good on my threat.

To my relief he didn't. Cliff appeared after a few more rounds of cinder-brick-muffled shouting and stalked toward the car, his face a grim mask. He seemed to see me at the halfway point and forced a fake plastic smile. The locks on the car doors popped, surprising me, I'd thought Cliff's little red monster was too old for power locks. I circled around to the passenger seat with Secret, and together we got in without speaking. The car reluctantly rumbled to life, and we pulled out into the street. We both released held breaths and started talking at the same time. I gestured for him to go first.

"So," he began, "about that deer leg I found under my door mat. I assume that was from you?"

"Uh," I peered through the passenger window to hide the sudden hotness in my cheeks. "Well, it's either that or you've got a lovesick bear in your neighborhood."

His chuckle was low, a laugh taking cover, "If it's a bear, then they're awfully sneaky."

"Meeerf," Secret commented, an audible eye roll.

Don't screw this one up, Abby, I chided myself. "Cliff, in case you haven't noticed," I petted Secret a bit harder than strictly necessary, "My wolf side, I call her wolf me, really likes you. You're not half as afraid of her as Cindy is, and you fought with us. She's lonely and wants you as a packmate."

"And what does human Abby think of this crazy idea?" A small bit of amusement slipped through his neutral tone, and it made my heart speed up, spreading the heat into my ears. Wolf me pressed forward, eager to explain what I wanted in very unsubtle ways.

"Human me has, is, a sucker for a big smile on a big man, but her history is very fraught and has enough baggage to require a forklift." Distantly I heard Jimmy's laugh.

"Forklift, werewolf, about the same lifting capacity."

We laughed, and I breathed deep. Beneath the sharp sourness of various cleaning agents was his scent, everywhere in the car. Like being inside of him, almost. Nervously stole a look back at him. The laugh had given way to a glum expression and ripped all the hope directly out of my heart.

"Don't take this the wrong way, Abby, but I think it'd be a real bad idea. Had you asked before this craziness started, I'd be like hell, ya. I'll sign up for all that howling and hunting right away," his voice briefly echoing geeky enthusiasm. "Cool, awesome werewolves." Then he sighed, "But it's fuckin' done a number on you. Before, I could barely imagine you throwing a punch unless somebody got in between you and a patient. Now, you got in a fight at my dad's funeral, now…"

"Cliff I-," I protested.

"Whatever, she's fine. This ain't about that. I know you could have ripped her to itty bits. This is about what would happen if you made me a werewolf. If you have trouble not hauling off. Well... I think half my family would be dead in a week and the other half would be werewolves."

"It takes more than a bite," I said.

"Oh, so it won't be the zombie apocalypse but werewolves, then? Too bad, that'd be an interesting way to go." He sighed. "Better than being eaten by a mushroom."

"I understand," I said.

Good packmate. Puts others first, wolf me insisted, completely undeterred by our highly rational and human conversation that had left me with a heavy lump in my throat.

The car tilted back as we drove up the ramp to OHSU and we lapsed into silence.

Finding Dr. Wiggins proved to be distressingly easy, I didn't even need to go ask Nadia where he was. I smelled him on arrival to the hospital's basement and tracked him to a lab I hadn't been in before. When he answered the door his face had a sheen of old sweat.

"Ah, Miss Night!" A grin appeared on his weary face. "Good to see you!"

"Hi Doctor, I was wondering if you could help us." I swiftly introduced the Doctor to Cliff. Doctor Wiggins was swift to offer Cliff his condolences for his father and ushered us inside. The interior proved to be an airlock, one wall stuffed with scrubs and other safety gear.

"Better to talk here than in the hallway. Now what's this about?" He looked up at me expectantly.

I told him and then changed partially to demonstrate why my sense of smell might be more acute than others. He gave me the same look of loss as the one he had eyed his captive code Z with. "Yes, let's throw some casual violations of thermodynamics on top of everything else," he muttered under his breath. "Miss Night, Mr. Gifford, if you would excuse me for one moment. Quickly strapping a mask to his face, he stepped through the far door of the airlock.

From beyond the door, I heard an excellent imitation of Charlie Brown's scream of frustration when Lucy pulled the football away. "Aaaauuuuurrrgh!!"

"Uh, is this guy okay?" Cliff whispered.

"He's having a rough week," I admitted, but had no time to elaborate as the door reopened and the doctor came back, stripping off the mask to reveal a tight smile. "Screams are better out than in. Now why don't you two follow me, and we'll all go make the radiology department furious with me.

Hospitals are complex organisms that use routine and scheduling as blood, and bureaucratic red tape for almost everything else. Dr. Wiggins bludgeoned through it all, citing a bewildering variety of codes and proclaiming that Cliff and I had been exposed to some horrific chemical, and if we didn't get CAT scans, we might die where we stood. He clearly earned the enmity of the front desk staff, but it worked. We were ushered out of the waiting room. I barely had time to say over five words to Cindy over the phone before we were both very professionally poked, X-rayed, and scanned.

29

"Right, then," Dr. Wiggins rubbed his hands together as we huddled in a cramped office that had definitely been a janitor's closet in recent history. Secret was "playing" with Nadia in the morgue as the doctor turned his laptop to show us a display of Cliff's lungs and pointed to a patch on the bottom right. I didn't see anything at first, other than a few darker dots among all the nebulous gray. "Now I'm not a pulmonologist, but I'd bet my doctorate that these are not supposed to be there." He slid his finger over the scroll wheel of the mouse and the plane of the scans moved in and out. The dots moved; they weren't dots at all, but small continuous threads weaving through the lung.

Cliff hissed and rubbed at his chest. "Yuck. How do we get it out?"

"Don't panic; we've got options," Dr Wiggins said.

"So, first of all, this is the earliest we've caught it. Usually, these threads are all over the lung by the time the patient realizes they're in trouble. You're also younger than anyone else admitted for this thing so we can test the antifungals at a higher dose." He smiled warmly.

Cliff rubbed his short hair, "And if it still grows?"

"Then it's a cancer we don't have many treatment options for. I've found one chemotherapy drug that kills it in the dish which we can try, but it's a harsh one. If it works, you'll still be in the hospital from the drug for two weeks. Barring that, we burn it out with radiation, or cut it out and hope we get it all."

Cliff nodded and looked at me. "What do Abby's lungs look like?"

Dr. Wiggins hit a button, and the view changed to a chest x-ray of a smaller frame, mine. White stripes decorated my ribs. "Miss Night's lungs are fine, but her condition seems to have its own costs. Healed broken ribs have marks like these," He pointed at the brighter bands. "I'd be careful using your... alternative anatomy too often or your bones might get brittle."

"It doesn't work like that, Doctor." I gave him a weak smile.

"Then again, what do I know? Nothing. Absolutely nothing. Unless you want to tell me more." A little bit of hope shone in his eyes.

"Not today, Dr. Wiggins. My condition isn't trying to kill me."

"Just your social life and career." Cliff cracked with a laugh.

Finally sitting on his left, I smacked his good arm.

"Ow! Don't break my other arm or I'll be as useless as dad always said I was." Cliff's laughter had a desperate edge to it.

"Cliff! Do you know the meaning of the words 'too soon'?" My voice went high, Mr. Gifford's last raspy words echoing through my mind.

"Too soon's better than too late," he snapped back, his

rich voice breaking. "Broken arm! Mushroom cancer! What's next? Spontaneous combustion?!" He stood so fast that his chair fell over behind him as he rushed from the room. Doctor Wiggins jumped at the bang of the door hitting the wall in his wake.

"Sorry, one moment," I smiled at him, getting up.

"No need to apologize; you're looking at a man who put a bucket on his head to scream into it not two hours ago. I understand." He grinned broadly.

I paused, "That was through a bucket and a wall?"

"I have good lungs," he chuckled as I hurried after Cliff.

He wasn't hard to find; he stood in a corner where the hallway bent, his nose maybe three inches from the wall. I approached him cautiously, watching his shoulders rise and fall, his breathing heavy in that universal way that men did when the emotional barriers they'd spent a lifetime building came crashing down.

"It's okay, Cliff." Speaking softly, I placed my hand between his shoulder blades and rubbed gently. "We'll-- you'll get through this."

He sniffed hard and choked out, "don't touch me."

I dropped my hand. "Sorry. I'll give you space."

In response he turned. Tears leaked down his cheeks from lost eyes. "Yes," he said, but his left arm reached up and I stepped closer. His hand curled around my back and pulled me to him. Threading my own arms around him, I hugged him the best I could without putting pressure on his busted arm. Pressing up onto my toes got me just tall enough for him to rest his chin on my head.

"Mixed signals," I murmured; wolf me desperately pawed at the underside of my skin but I couldn't let her out here, not in the hospital.

"Add it to the list of things I can't do right." Cliff

squeezed me tighter, voice hiccupping. "It's either hug you or put my hand through this wall. My luck, I'd break it, then Mom would have to spoon feed me for months." His laugh drowned in hitching sobs.

"Don't be so hard on yourself." I tried to look up at him, but he held me tight to his chest.

"Can't say it's not true, though. I'm useless, couldn't get hired by anyone but my pa, can't run his business, get beat up by an overgrown garden gnome and can't even stop a friend from getting fired from a company I own a third of."

I pushed away so I could look up into his sad eyes. "Cliff, that gnome was nine feet tall, and you faced him down with an iron toothpick. And I lost control, not you. I deserve to be fired." Adding a firm growl to my voice.

He smiled down at me and sighed, "Yes, Ma'am."

"You listen to me, Mister!" I grabbed his shirt with both of my hands and wrenched him down to my level. "I don't care if you're a lousy accountant. You are both brave and kind. That's all I need. I'm not going to let you die to a fucking mushroom. If the drugs don't work, you're joining my pack. Understand?!"

"Abby, uh," he stumbled, as wolf me breached my skin.

I kissed him, I only meant to do it lightly but wolf me pressed her paw down on an internal gas pedal. Heat passed between our lips as my teeth sharpened; our jaws worked, opening and closing against each other, the tips of his fingers digging into my shoulder. He kissed back just as hard. I could have him; I could take him right now. Let wolf me slip out a little bit farther.

"Abby?!" Cindy's scandalized voice stabbed right through my building passion.

* * *

We broke off the kiss at the same time. Turning our heads in opposite directions to catch our breaths. Cindy watched me with a nervous smile beside Rey, who looked positively gleeful.

"Aaah, S-sorry to interrupt." Cindy stammered with a sudden flush to her cheeks. "And, uh," Her voice dropping to a whisper, "You're a little long in the ears."

I looked down at myself and found that the situation had gotten more than a little hairy. It took next to no effort to pull back to human, wolf me already howling a victory in my head. "It's okay. We were finishing up here. Right, Cliff?"

He cleared his throat and tried to pull his shirt back into shape. "Yeah. Finished." Then laughed... "Oooh boy. Finished."

"Cliff I'm sorry, I shouldn't have..."

His huge hand cupped my cheek, his eyes warm and bright. "Yeah, well... Yeah, takes two, and stuff." Turning away he blew out between his lips, "And wow, I'm good at words."

"I know that what you said in the car still stands, but maybe think about it?" I reached up and gave his hand a squeeze as he started to lower it. Telling myself to ignore the feeling of my heart trying to visit my stomach.

"I will. S-see you later, Abby." He started down toward the door to Dr. Wiggins' office, moving stiffly. I tore my eyes off his back to take in Cindy and Rey.

"Thanks for coming to pick me up." I told them.

Cindy wouldn't meet my eyes, bashfully twining a lock of her long red wig, which matched the color of Rey's ears perfectly. "Let me guess, you have a complaint about our timing?"

Rey nodded from Cindy's side, almost melting against it, "We would have been slower, but someone was worried you were hurt. And here you are on a date." Rey yipped with laughter, enduring side eye from both me and Cindy.

"Let me go collect Secret," I said, and they followed me to the very end of the hallway. Cindy made a low, "Uuuuh," sound as I approached the morgue. The door flew open as I reached for the handle, and a black blur shot out, circled around me, and slammed into my rear with a "Merf!"

My hand instantly moved to grip Secret's shoulder protectively as Nadia loomed in the doorway spurting Russian like an angry volcano spurts lava. She skidded to a halt in front of me, gray eyes blazing from behind her facemask.

She spit a torrent of angry Russian at me.

"Uuuh, I'm guessing Secret's behavior was less than ideal this time?" I asked.

Nadia said something more in Russian before taking a breath, "I turn my back for one moment and she ate a heart! Ripped it right out of the open chest and made a mess."

I looked down at Secret as she huddled behind me; she had something dark smeared around her black lips, in contrast to her wide, innocent-seeming eyes. "Secret, did you touch something you weren't supposed to?"

Her fuzzy ears folded down against her head. "She didn't say I couldn't..." Her voice pitched up to a whine as the smell of stale blood reached my nose.

"I was not even done with that one yet, child!" Nadia huffed.

"Tell Nadia you're sorry." I told Secret firmly.

"But I was hungry, and it was almost stale!" Her mouth opened to a long, "Uurrrrp!" She burped, hunching against me, the copper of her skin tinting towards green. "It was a little stale."

"Well, maybe you shouldn't do that." I tried to scold her

but the best I could manage was a gentle chiding. "I hadn't forgotten."

"But now you don't have to get me one!" She stuck out her bottom lip in a heart-breaking pout.

"Don't change the subject," I insisted. "Say you're sorry, or Nadia might not invite you back."

A force tugged on my eyeballs as she attempted to shift but I had been ready for it and kept my eyes glued to hers. Her skin rippled a moment, but she stayed a little girl and winced. "My momma never apologizes to mortals."

"That heart wasn't yours to take." I said, having no clue if having this debate was a good idea or not. Keeping a hand firmly on her shoulder I stepped behind Secret and knelt, preventing her from running away from Nadia. "Now be a good girl." Adding under my breath, "It's just a mortal apology, you won't owe her anything."

She made a tiny feline groan, "I'm sorry." She said so softly that I opened my mouth to make her repeat it, but Nadia leaned down to her level.

"I forgive you. This time, kotenok. But those corpses are mine. You make lot work for me tonight. Understood?"

Secret gave a tiny shake of her head.

"Good." She rose, dismissed us both with a wave of her hand. "I'll be in touch." With that she went back into the morgue, muttering under her breath.

I gave her a hug from behind, "There, was that so bad?"

"Terrible. Cats don't say sorry." She sulked as she flopped against me.

"You're half human. Humans say sorry." I argued.

I let the wave of her magic push my eyes off her this time and heard the rustle of fabric as soft fur suddenly pressed against my arm. Secret the kitten made growling noises, every strand of fur on end to illustrate her anger with me.

Cindy appeared ready to swallow her own tongue, mouthing, "She eats human hearts?"

"Only the bad ones," I said with as much confidence as I could scrape up. "How 'bout we go get some dinner? I haven't eaten anything all day."

"Not even the man!" Rey giggled and pulled the still-huffy Cindy along. Secret kept up her upset hedgehog impression as far as the first floor, when my fingers coaxed out a reluctant purr. We piled into Cindy's car and started heading for a good Korean BBQ south of the hospital.

Cindy chatted about her kitchen plans during the drive, but I had a hard time focusing on the conversation. Victoria's dusky scent rose in my mind; I had to fix that relationship before I let myself get carried away with Cliff. I'd approach her as a wolf tonight. Maybe that'd be easier? Or should I wait for a call? What if she created another pack instead? Or what if she didn't like Cliff? My mind spiraled out, trying to think of all the possible ways this could go horribly wrong.

"Abby!"

I jumped, blinked. We were in the restaurant, there was food on my plate, and Cindy reached across the table and grabbed my arm, her nails glittering gold and blue on my wrist. Concern etched in her face.

"You were whining like a dog, well, wolf, I guess." She said softly.

"Sorry." I pulled my hand free of her grip. "Worried."

"Cliff will be okay. It didn't look like he was worrying about dog breath." She smiled.

"Heh," I wiped my mouth, but I really did it to sniff at my wrist. I hadn't smelled her at all in the car, Rey's musk overpowered everything else, but there she was on my wrist. The fear hadn't faded, the anxiety was less, but I doubted that would be the case after I told her about Victoria. I needed to tell her before she found out.

I opened my mouth, "So, about Victoria."

As if the universe was waiting for me to utter her name, my ear caught the sound of a distant howl, singing of fear and pain. Victoria's voice.

30

Rey's head jerked up from her languid slouch, ears turning toward the howl. "Been busier than I thought."

Secret hurriedly slurped in a long noodle from the plate in front of her before asking, "Who's that Abby?"

I opened my wallet and slapped my emergency cash of five twenties down on the table. "That's Victoria. I gotta go."

Cindy, the only person at the table with purely human hearing stood as I did. "What about Victoria?"

"She's a wolf now." Rey said.

"And in trouble." Secret added.

Cindy stared at me with a combination of shock, fear, and disbelief that all added up to say, *Jebus, Abby! What the hell did you do now?*

"Pack happens?" I shrugged nervously and threaded my way out of the restaurant, mumbling, "Sorry, family emergency," to the concerned hostess I passed.

Cindy was right behind me as I pushed through the door and ran to the car. Rey and Secret slipped into the back seats as Cindy started the car. "It wasn't planned," I told

Cindy as we backed out of the parking space. "The process had started because of that blood transfusion I gave her. She was already like me before I went into the Dream."

"But you made it worse," Cindy whispered between her teeth.

"I fixed her. I brought it out," I huffed.

Cindy stomped on the accelerator, making her tired car growl, sending us shooting through a yellow light. The traffic on the four-lane road was thickening as the sky dimmed toward the early dusk. Cindy drove as fast as she could, but without our sirens and flashing lights we were confined to the current of the commute. At every red light I considered jumping out of the car and bursting into a run. Not knowing what sort of trouble Victoria had found herself in stopped me. I didn't want to wolf out on animal control. So I sat, straining my ears for another howl as we inched closer and closer to her house.

Finally, we broke free of the main commuter street and tore down the heavily wooded road that Victoria's house sat on. Light peeked through the heavy curtains that guarded the lower-story windows. The repaired porch with its bright new paint looked out of place, as if the rest of the house resented the new patch. I had the passenger door open before Cindy had entirely stopped the car.

"Victoria!?" I called out as I stepped onto the surface of the circular driveway.

No answer.

I ran up to the door, rang the doorbell, and tried to peer through the windows. No movement as I hammered the bell again.

Nothing.

"A ward is breached in the back." Rey said from behind me.

I turned to find all three of them standing at the foot of the steps leading up to the porch. Both Rey and Secret squinted as if they were staring into a bright light. Cindy had a first aid kit held in her hand.

"Let's check that, then!" We all rushed around to the back of the house and sure enough, a window had been shattered, the bush beneath it decorated with shards of shattered glass. It had been a large single pane of glass that let in the morning light onto Victoria's kitchen sink. Standing on tiptoe, I looked into Victoria's kitchen, immediately spotting a variety of clothing strewn on the floor. Both her human and lupine scents mingled in the air.

"She shifted inside and wanted out," I said out loud, backing away from the window and pulling off my own top.

"I'm coming with you, so don't run ahead," Cindy said, and I heard a metallic snap. To my shock, Cindy held a shiny pistol in her shaking hand, colored the pink, white, and light blue of the trans flag. Maybe half the size of the jet-black numbers on the hip of a cop, it looked tiny, the barrel extending maybe two inches past her finger.

"You hate guns," I croaked.

"Still do. But," she blew out a breath and pulled back the slide, cocking it. "It's a required fashion accessory this winter." Turning it to and fro, she found the safety and clicked it on before slipping the thing into the broad pocket of her house dress.

A sour sense of guilt churned my stomach. How long had she had that? And had she been so afraid of me that there were silver bullets in that clip? I nodded at her, appreciating that she wasn't coming with me entirely toothless.

"Teeth are always a last resort, but it's important to show everyone they exist." Rey patted Cindy's arm, her yellow eyes including me with everyone.

I didn't have time to suss out the fox's game right then; I kicked off my pants and sneakers and shifted into big wolf form with more relief than pain.

As soon as I did, the Rot's scent greeted my sharpened nose. The breeze that blew out from the tree line carried both the sour earth of an active infection and the sweetness of the mushrooms.

Secret clambered up onto my back and then we trotted into the trees, me sweeping my nose across the ground. I found a nervous scent marking of Victoria's. *This mine?* Then another a few paces deeper. That was it.

But a paw print in the muddy ground gave me a direction. In minutes, I found myself up against a high wooden fence that utterly stank of the Rot. Beneath it, a hole had been dug, large enough for a bear or... a werewolf. I slipped beneath it, or tried to. Secret giggled when I got stuck. I jerked up and the 2 by 4 that made the bottom of the fence snapped, and the entire section fell apart around me like so many toothpicks.

I amended my opinion of the hole. Big enough for a small werewolf. Grumbling as even Cindy stifled laughter, I stood partially and eased my way though, the broken planks tumbling off my back. Beyond the fence the scent of the Rot strengthened to a stench. Yet we weren't in a yard; trees blocked the view of anything else. Padding forward, the forest swiftly thinned out into a garden, with green blocks of shrubs, but in what should have been empty beds waiting for the spring flowers to push through the sodden mulch, huge clusters of black purple mushrooms bloomed. I didn't recognize the building beyond it at first, because the first story of the huge manor house appeared to be painted black.

"Jebus. This is that isolation colony." Cindy whispered from behind me. In a blink I recognized it. The windows where the residents peered down at me and Cindy as we collected bogus samples were dark holes. The black that covered the stonework and the path was a dense weave of fibers. With a scrape of my claws, I peeled some away from the base of a statue. The stone beneath it was pitted, the threads working their way into the very rock. The entire place was still.

I heard the lightest sound, like a soap bubble popping. Down at my feet, I found a cluster of mushrooms whose rounded caps had become flat tops, and black dust eddied around my ankles. I might be immune, but Cindy wouldn't be. She'd come with me as far as the trees, and I turned around, put my head to her chest, and forced her back.

"I see them, Abby." She didn't resist as I herded her to the hole in the fence. "Wait here and I'll go get some masks for everyone. I saw a box of them in your car. I'll be right back." She ran back the way we came.

With Cindy clear for now, I went back to the manor, finding both Rey and Secret peering at the threads on the building's wall. Rey broke off a piece and sniffed at it.

I barked a warning at them. Rey's nose wrinkled in distaste. "I know it is dangerous, Miss Abby. It's not from the Twilight. Not entirely."

Cocking my head, I shot her a questioning stare.

"The seal of the nine was never intended to cut either the Twilight or the Dream off from the Crossroads. It protected the Crossroads from a third world, called the Corruption. This," she held a bundle of fibers out to me, "is a corruption of the Twilight."

That sounded bad; I still didn't really understand how

the seal worked, but a bunch of Fey and undead used it to protect the mortal realm from something worse than both of them combined. I nodded, but this got me no closer to finding Victoria.

I'd been immune to this stuff so far, but that didn't mean I wanted a lung full of spores. If Victoria had been here, this stuff was drowning her scent in its stench. Instead of using my nose I carefully looked over the mats of threads for signs of disturbance. I found a series of not quite footprints, but depressions leading up to the central door. Threads had found their way into the building through the corners and beneath the bottom seam of the screen door. I grabbed the handle with my teeth, it opened easily. The threads covered the latch mechanism and only the door's spring had been holding it shut. The solid inner door was wide open. Within I caught a whiff of Victoria.

Inside, the threads crept across every surface, sparsely on the walls and furniture, a network of black cobwebs, but the strands were moist and slippery instead of sticky. Following the smell upstairs was like walking on a bed of ramen noodles. On the second level they were even thicker. The threads squirmed beneath my paws as I looked up and down the hallway; on one side were a series of wooden doors. Exit signs and narrow red lights by the side of each door provided the only light. Those doors were odd; each had a slot in the middle of it, like a prison cell, maybe, and those red lights had letters on them: ISOLATION, they declared. Every single one of them had fibers pushing beneath them. One had been wrenched from its hinges and fallen inside.

Against my better judgment, I peered into the room; a small, darkened apartment greeted me, the door opened into a living room area, with a massive entertainment center, and in front of that, a plush leather sofa, a figure covered with a bright pink blanket sunk into its cushions. Threads cascaded from under the blanket and down the front of the couch like a still waterfall. They snaked like a river towards the door.

A cold voice whispered across the inside of my ears. *Let me out.*

Its chill cut through my thick fur generating an involuntary shiver that turned into a full nose-to-tail shake. I hurried on down the hall, where the scent of Victoria strengthened along with a sharp scent of gunsmoke.

Past the row of isolation apartments, my paws found bare carpet, and I ran down the rest of the hallway. It seemed to stretch out as I traveled along it. What I had judged to be a few strides left me nearly panting by the time I reached the end of it. Sharp, jagged lines grew into the edges of my vision as if my eyes had cracked. The pungent taste of a bouquet of decay in the air roiled my stomach with its sheer wrongness as I nosed open the door.

There was only one thing that smell could be. The Twilight. There on the floor, a pool of black ichor sat, leeching into the hardwood floor. A bundle of black fibers as thick as a man's arm ran from a vent in the wall down into the pool, slowly undulating as if pumping something from its depths. Not a pool, not a puddle, a hole. The one living note in the twisted vapors was Victoria's dusky scent.

How? Had the hole been here, and she'd fallen into it? Or...

Pulling my attention away from the abyss I scanned the room. A double-barreled shotgun gripped by a severed arm clad in the yellow of a hazmat suit lay inches from the hole. The rest of Ryan, the administrator of the colony, lay in a puddle of drying blood beneath a massive corner desk, the walls above it practically paneled with dark monitors.

No answers here. Only more questions. Questions that only Victoria had answers to.

I dove into the abyss.

31

Total darkness filled my vision as the scent of death overwhelmed my nostrils. I had just enough time to think about how it might have been wise to tell Cindy and Secret what I was doing before the very world inverted around me with a lurch.

I landed hard, legs collapsing beneath me, or perhaps above me. The darkness fell from my eyes like a curtain, and I found myself in the same office I had left, devoid of color, except for the hole, which shone with a rainbow opal shimmer. The black threads branched out from their bundle, extending roots out along the floor and up the wall towards the same vent that the threads had entered the room by on the other side. No sign of Ryan's corpse.

The sensation of being upside down faded as my ears caught the whisper of a growl. Victoria! I ran from the room and down the strangely stretched hallway. No threads impeded my claws from digging into the floor, but anguished wails assaulted me from the open doors of the isolation apartments.

HELP! LETMEOUT! HURTS!

Pressing my ears against my head, I ran past without looking through at the trapped souls, leaping down to the first floor. One paw broke through a rotted plank, but it barely slowed me down. I hurled myself through the open door.

I narrowly avoided crashing into Victoria's rear end. She crouched on the edge of the porch, facing out into the garden where over fifty figures stood against her. Some stood slack-jawed and stumbled out of the trees, eyes glowing the dull red of sputtering embers. Others had eyes of cold flame. These wore clothing marred by the marks of violence and brandished weapons.

Victoria's long head turned in response to my barked greeting to regard me with a single eye. The pupil glowed with the same cold fire as the ghosts, while a silver chain looped around her neck, secured to the ground with a spike of black metal.

Her whip-like tail gave a small wag of recognition before a shambler crossed an invisible line and she pounced on it with the speed of black lightning. Jaws clamped over its head and ripped it from the shade's shoulders. The shambler's body fell as a pile of dust; another lurched for her and met the same fate as her flashing teeth ripped out its midsection. She dusted five more before reaching the end of her chain and dutifully returning to her spot in front of the porch. None of the more advanced shades approached her, watching both of us with caution.

I crept up next to her, putting myself between her and the stake she was tied to. A touch of my nose revealed warmth radiating from her body. Still alive. I huffed with relief.

Her ears flicked in annoyance. *Busy, serving duty.* Before baring her teeth at the assembled shades.

Home, I gave a soft howl, *Come.*

The flames in her eyes flickered, but she didn't budge. *Protect home.*

I bumped her shoulder, a clear *No.*

When she didn't respond I reached down to grab the black metal stake in my teeth.

"You should consider the consequences of freeing my guardian before you do that, Abigale Night," said a voice as smooth as silk that sheathed a knife's edge. Death reclined against a wall of the manor, dressed in a dark suit and a red tie, tiny sparks dancing in the empty sockets of their eyes.

Growling with annoyance I shifted my body back to humanish form so I could grind out words again. "Let her go. She's alive; she doesn't belong here."

Death smirked, "Two high-caliber slugs shredded her heart and it ceased to beat. A mortal wound. She was dead."

I blinked in shock. She'd regenerated from that? In the Twilight no less. Praise Luna, I guess; covering my surprise with a swallow, I smiled back at him. "Not for us. Not anymore."

"Did you and Luna do this to spite me?" Death asked.

"It wasn't part of my plan, but Luna doesn't share her grand designs with me." I bent for the stake.

"You pull that, and the hole will be unguarded." They moved their hand to encompass the gathered shades, all of which were shying back, away from Death. "Nothing to stop these wretches from bubbling out into the Crossroads."

"Except you; doesn't look like they're too eager to try anything with you standing there. This is your purpose, right? Keeping the Dead and Living on the right sides of the wall."

"Do not presume you know my office and duties, Wolf." The sockets narrowed. "I cannot remain in this place for long. It's far better for a guardian to watch over this rift until it closes on its own. It's fitting for her to serve in this way, since she is the one who thinned the barrier in the first place."

"You made that Rift dragging her down here! You can't force her to protect the mess you made. In what universe is that fair?"

The corners of their mouth turned up and a twinkle flickered in the back of their eye sockets. "I will never be accused of being fair. That rift is one of many that will open in the coming days as certain factions within the Twilight make misguided grasps for what they will never have. This parasite they have unleashed seeks to knit the Crossroads and the Twilight together. The only reason you are not over-whelmed already is that your doctors have mostly prevented it from joining the souls together and thinning the walls so that a single death will open a gate. Here though, they panicked, locked themselves away and died. They gave it their despair, allowing it to feed and grow. Unchecked, countless shades will cross here to slake their hunger and spread even more despair. This, *Rot*, as you call it will grow. In a short time, it will consume the city."

My brain ground to a halt trying to imagine what that would be like.

"Do not worry yourself, wolf. It would hardly be the first time an entire city moved to the Twilight." No humor to their voice, a simple statement of fact. "Once Gaia awakens, she will pop it like an infected pore."

"No." I shook my head hard, shaking away my crawling sense of doom, "I won't let that happen."

The illusion of flesh fled their face, displaying the grin of the skull. "Then leave this errant child with me. I will task her with guarding places like these. A bit of my power added to hers and she can withstand all but the most focused assaults of the old king. Her howl will alert you to any rift, and give the living time to defend themselves."

My attention shifted to Victoria, my first packmate. Her entire being was focused on the crowd of shades as they withdrew to the gnarled trees. "And what would happen to her? What sort of life would she have here?" I asked.

"She will have what she wanted. Each time she falls that chain will pull her back to her duty, stronger than ever." The sparks in Death's eyes whirled. "That chain was tempered in the Lethe itself; it will consume her memories one by one, until she remembers nothing but her duty."

Victoria let out a keening whine that jangled my heart.

Death's gaze shifted to her. "Fight hard and the process will be slower, be good and I might allow you to keep your name. Victoria has a charm that Cerberus lacks."

I stepped out in front of Victoria, blocking Death's gaze, "She's not your dog! I won't let you press her into your service. She's coming back with me."

The skull did not waver, "It's not as if you would never run together, oh hound of Winter. It is a just fate and you know it. Victoria Quentin, the reckless Necromancer who's endangered the entire city. You've been frantically attempting to contain the fallout of what's she's wrought. Now she's a wolf purely by accident, and has scorned your precious gift, which is the only reason she lives in the first place. You owe her nothing, let alone the risk she's taken with Andrew Millar. Don't think that his threat to you and yours has lessened. Step aside and go home, Abigale Night."

They made sense. I could lay all of this at Victoria's feet. That first call that led us into the Twilight where I had come to Luna's attention. If I took her back, Death would just let these holes fester. They didn't promise to fix the problem if I left, but would make it manageable. Victoria wasn't who wolf me had even wanted; I didn't even realize that she was ours until she was right there.

Victoria whined at me. *Please, please don't.*

I turned; her eyes remained fixed outward, cold flame blazing inside her golden eyes, wet ichor oozing from where the silver chain bit into her neck. That dusky scent brought the taste of her lips to my tongue, and I remembered her wounding Little Nick with my mother's frying pan. Andrew Millar had had to ask me very basic questions; Victoria hadn't sold me out to him.

Death spoke, "You leave her with me, and you gain Death as an ally. But if you take her, I won't lift a finger to ease the pain the Old King inflicts on your city. Even if you survive, your territory will be overrun with the energies of this place and Luna's first wolf will be shamed."

"No." I ground out the word, but as soon as I did, I felt lighter. "She fought with us."

"Only because her life depends on yours," Death said. "There will be more wolves. Let me have this one. No one has to know. Even your little charge isn't here."

"No one has to know." I laughed; it mixed with a growl in my throat. "Your lies stink, Death. Luna would know I traded her second wolf and trapped her in torment because I'm a petty fool. Secondly, I'd always know. And, because I'm a terrible liar, so would everybody else." I reached down, seized the stake, and pulled it from the ground.

Death crossed their arms, "I see. Very well then... Victoria, kill."

32

———

A brief growl was the only warning I had. My left arm managed to get between Victoria's head and mine; her teeth sliced it to the bone. With a brutal shake, she lifted me up to my tiptoes before slamming me into the planks beneath us. The wood cracked against my skull. A sluggish *What?* was my only thought before the plank flew away from me. Hardness slammed into my boneless body. The wall. Gravity followed up, reintroducing me to the concept of the floor. With my body silent with shock, I beheld Victoria's too-lean body crouching to pounce, that ghostly flame jetting out of her golden eyes. She came at me: a black blur with a streak of the deadly white of her teeth. Instinct swept my clawed hand across my vision; it struck her lower jaw and snapped her mouth closed. Instead of teeth, only fur brushed the side of my neck. Her long neck reared back like a serpent's before diving back at my stomach. I kicked up a knee and she bit into that instead and hoisted me into the air. I drove the palm of my hand straight into her flaring nostrils. She flinched but didn't let go. I hit her again, this time grabbing it, digging my claws into the thin flesh of her muzzle.

A yipe, a shake, a wet ripping sound, and I was left holding her nose. I stared at it, blinking in horror as she backed off, head held low as she pawed at the exposed bone at the end of her snout. *Fight!* Wolf me surged out into my body, deepening my growl as I swelled with her power towards my hybrid form.

Death snapped their fingers, Victoria's head jerked up to snarl at me. She charged while I was still struggling up to my shifting feet. Sliding under a swipe of my claws, she clamped her jaws around my ankle and jerked hard. With muscles still squirming to accommodate my shifting skeleton, I could only hang on to the wall behind me. I slammed down onto my still-growing tail and engaged in a tug of war, with my leg as the rope.

I saw Death watching from the corner of my eye, as I struggled to pull my leg back from its full extent. She tried to break my ankle with a death shake but it held. Off-balance, I pulled her in and made a grab for the chain on her neck. Sheer agony ran up my arm like lightning made of bees. I released it with a yip. What sort of silver was that?! It had never burned me before.

Victoria surged up, going for my neck, but I parried her jaws with my own. We locked together, a snarling kiss of teeth. She bore me down, pinning me to the wall, our strength evenly matched; she had the leverage but while she had paws, I had hands. My injured arm mostly healed, both hands reached up, drove claws into the thick neck muscle and froze. Death had taken a step closer. I could kill her right here.

Dammit, Death wasn't trying to kill me. They were trying to force me to kill Victoria!

Fuck that.

Kicking out with both legs I slammed my paws into

Victoria's rear ankles, sweeping them wide. Her rear fell into an inelegant split; with her leverage gone, I pushed her to the side. She tried to withdraw, but I followed her, wrapping my arm around that long neck, trapping her in a headlock.

Her eyes flared with power, and she ripped herself from my grip. Scooting backward, she growled, heedless of her missing nose and the crimson blood flowing from her neck, vivid against the grey of the Twilight. She wasn't healing; she was bleeding out. I needed to get that chain off her now.

I tackled her. Her teeth claimed a chunk of my thigh, but it didn't stop me from encircling her chest with my arms. Death had strengthened her but not made her any bigger. With a twist of my body, I forced her down onto her side where she could only kick and snap at places I wasn't. Growling with effort, I lifted her upright so her rear claws scraped the floor. Squeezing her as tightly I as could, I hauled her back through the door. The chain sizzled against the fur of my neck but didn't flash into agony as it had when I had attempted to remove it. It trailed on the ground in our wake. Death walked towards it. Afraid they'd stake it into the ground, I swung Victoria around, jerking its length into the air. Hungry thing swung around and tagged the back of my calf; the flash of pain made me stumble against the stairs. Victoria exploded from my arms. I grabbed for the only thing available: the chain.

Victoria jerked short, body swinging up beneath her head and landing hard on her back. Grimacing against the burning bite of the heavy links on the pads of my hands, I hauled her back to me and dragged her up the stairs.

Death's silhouette stepped into the doorway as I struggled to get a solid grip on the scruff of Victoria's neck. "You again deny me my first desire in this new age, Abigale Night.

An age where I am allowed to have desires. I am out of sympathy for you and your city."

I huffed, putting as much derision into the sound as I could. Hard to be a witty heroine when you can't talk.

They snapped their fingers, and the chain fell from Victoria's neck. "You can leave that with me. It will be waiting for her." They glowered there for a moment before adding, "While the strength of Luna shimmers in those veins of yours, I hear the heart of a martyr beating in your chest. See you soon, Abigale."

Death's form blurred, expanded, and flowed into the surroundings, as if my eyes could no longer focus on them, but everything else remained as clear as the dim light allowed. Outside, a chorus of hungry moans sounded. The shades! I had forgotten about the shades. I grabbed up Victoria's limp form and tossed her over my shoulder. She whined a soft apology as I ran towards the office. I blew past or through several shades that had wandered out into the hallway from the apartments as I heard the pounding of an army scrambling up the stairs. Down the stretched-out hallway, I walked as fast as I could, refusing the urge to fall to all fours. I only risked a glance behind as I ducked into Ryan's office. The swarm of shades had blended together into a mass of hungry light as it charged towards us and the living world.

Taking Victoria with both hands, I spiked her into the shining light of the hole like an out-of-bounds soccer ball. The threads had grown over most of the back wall. I severed them with a single swipe of my claws and jumped into the brightness with all the elegance of a cannonball.

Warmth. Brightness embraced me before that stomach twisting inversion of gravity.

I landed on something soft. It yipped and my nose filled

with Victoria's dusky scent and sour fear before the white drained away. I rolled off Victoria, careful to avoid the hole to the Twilight. The office wasn't much brighter than the one I'd left, lit only by the red of the emergency light. Victoria's golden eyes shone with the brightness of panic as she scrabbled towards me, tail wagging so hard it made it difficult for her rear legs to work. She crashed into my open arms, tongue trying to find every crevice of my lupine face. *Thank you thank you thank you.*

Safe now. I squeezed her tight, answering her flurry of love with my own. Relief made my entire body shaky.

I inhaled to howl when a skeletal hand erupted from the pool of blackness beside us. We both froze as it flopped down onto the edge, clawing at the floor. It found a purchase, and its form shimmered, straining as the dome of a head pressed out of the ichor like a bubble. I tried to smash the hand with my palm, but I felt nothing but a slight chill.

Barking an order at Victoria to follow as I sprinted from the room, I ignored the pain that lanced up my arms every time I slammed the palms of my paw-hands into the thread-covered floor. I grabbed hold of the wall as I approached the stairs and launched myself down to the ground floor. A hazmat-suited figure screamed and ducked as I narrowly avoided landing on top of them. Two more stumbled back from me.

I had no time to reassure them, rushing down the hallway, checking the rooms off as I passed them. Gym. Dining room. Kitchen. I howled a note of prey found. Storming into the kitchen, I ripped off the doors of the cupboards one by one, searching for the one thing I needed. Victoria skidded into the kitchen, took one look at me, and then joined in the ransacking.

A dome of a hazmat suit peered poked around the doorway.

"What are they doing?" One asked.

"Hungry?"

"Wouldn't they open the fridge first?"

"Maybe they're restaurateurs who really hate home cooking?"

I had to snort at that. And there it was. Not in a cabinet, right in plain sight in the counter's corner, cuddled up with the side of the huge fridge. A canister of salt. I grabbed it and beat it back upstairs. A different shade was pulling himself out of the pool now, a cowboy hat adorning his transparent head. He redoubled his efforts as his blue-flame eyes caught sight of me, tearing his legs free of the ichor and flowing out through the wall of the office. Not bothering with the spout, I poked a hole in the bottom of the salt canister, wrenched the thread bundle away from the edge of the hole, and drew a circle of salt around it.

Nothing happened at first. The next spirit pulled himself from the floor; the angry sneer on his lips was impressive since half his head was missing. But once he was free, he didn't go anywhere; he just floated, staring at me with one eye.

It worked. The salt plugged the hole for now.

A win. It was something, tilting my head back, I sang out an undulating howl of relief and victory as Victoria joined in, her tone high with anxiety, following my lead before adding her own verse. Falling to a dirge before rising to hope, leaning against me, singing her thanks.

Before I could add my praise to Luna, a new voice joined us, a howl spoken like a word, "AAAwwwoooo!" It had no song, but my tail wagged to hear Secret's call from outside the house.

Victoria tilted her head at the call. I nosed her to follow; there was still work to do. We trotted past the hazmat team and back upstairs as they gave us a wide berth. I went into each apartment and ripped the almost corpses from the webbing of the thick black threads. They died as soon as they were disconnected and were little more than rotting meat when we piled them up downstairs. Their ghosts screamed in our ears. Death might refuse to help, but they had told me how to stop the thinning. The hazmat team scents were bottled, but from shape and height, the one in charge appeared to be Dr. Wiggins. He kept them out of our way until my nose couldn't find any more humans in the threads of the Rot.

Outside, we found Secret standing on the hood of my car in the colony's front courtyard. Cindy glared at me from the driver's seat over a respirator mask. I ducked my head in apology, knowing she'd be giving me an earful soon. Maybe shifting to human would be a good idea, give her much smaller ears to fill. I chuffed with laughter at the thought.

Secret pounced as we neared, throwing her arms around my muzzle, and squeezing hard while rubbing her nose into my forehead. I rumbled back. She let go of me to eye the black wolf with an uncertain squint, ears half turning back.

Victoria huffed in greeting; her flesh had closed over the tip of her muzzle, forming two snake like slits instead of a proper canine nose. Her eyes caught mine and her own ears wilted a bit before rolling onto her back, submitting.

I gave Secret a nudge; she mewed in wordless protest, challenging me with a stubborn gaze.

I bared my teeth at her for the first time. *Do it.*

Her little lips pushed forward into a pout, but she averted her eyes. "Fine." With that she knelt before Victoria, whose jaws were half as long as she was tall, and began to knead her black-furred hands over the ridges of Victoria's ribs, spreading her scent into the short fur. "You're soft." Secret remarked.

Victoria craned her neck to sniff at Secret's tail and froze when my cub hugged her head. Secret put her lips and most of her face to one of Victoria's giant ears. I heard the murmur of a whisper and Victoria bristled. Secret stepped back, declaring with a sudden smile, "Welcome to the family!" and scratching the top of Victoria's head.

Secret retreated to my side as Victoria regained her feet and shook herself out.

"Please don't make me call it a pack. The court of cats will never stop laughing at me," she whispered.

I gave her a long wet lick and laughed when she "Ewwwww! Wolf slime!"ed in protest.

Cindy shook her head at us. "Now that everyone's out and accounted for, let's let Dr. Wiggins and his team do their work," she announced before adding in a quieter tone, "And get the hell out of here before they start asking questions."

Victoria sat on the rear bumper of my car, flexing and unflexing her now-human hands as if she'd forgotten how they worked. We were parked in the round in front of her house, but she had made no move to go inside once I'd coaxed her back into human form. I sat sandwiched between her and Secret, my own blistered palms covered in gauze. Cindy bent over Victoria, applying ointment to the oozing burns that encircled her neck. The punctures of my claws into her neck had healed, but the scars showed red and angry, like a series of small gill slits on either side. More shocking than that was her continued lack of her formerly prominent nose. Remaining two slits in an unnatural flat of skin in the center of her face.

Cindy finished and stepped back, grimacing at the viscous gel she had spread. "Victoria, you should really go to the hospital for these burns; they're edging up to the third degree and could get infected. As far as I can tell, they're not healing any swifter than normal."

"I'll get it looked at. Thank you," Victoria said, not

glancing up, and pulling the hood of the sweatshirt Cindy had loaned her over her head.

"You want to tell me what happened?" I asked.

"Not really." Victoria leaned against me, and my arm wrapped around her waist. "You can probably figure it out." She sighed, "I spent the day tearing through my library looking for a cure for Lycanthropy. It was all ridiculous. I couldn't sit still; I had to smell everything. I had a voice in my head that wouldn't stop whining. It kept telling me to call you. Howl for you."

I gave her a sympathetic squeeze. "I term mine: wolf me. She can be pretty insistent."

"Well, she's got me all sorts of confused. Abby, I..." She hung her head, "I was so angry with you this morning because I... Because I..." lapsing into silence, she turned and pulled my bandaged hand tighter around her. It was the most natural thing in the world for my other arm to encircle and hug her from behind. The sweet decay of the Twilight still clung to her hair.

She relaxed against me. "This, for a start. I wanted this and I've never wanted that before. I wondered whether with that bite you had killed the real me, the person I had been before." Long fingers closed over my wrists and squeezed my arms to her body. "Then Death showed up and showed me what the term 'controlling' really means." A shiver ran through us both. It paled compared to the nexus of warmth and comfort that flowed from the contact between us. An uncoiling of tension for me as I rested my forehead against the back of her neck and her fear eased away within my arms. "That's twice you've saved me from the dark. You could have left me there." Her voice quavered, "Things are going to be worse because you didn't."

"First time it was my job. This time it was personal.

You're my friend and I'm not giving up my first packmate to a skeleton in a suit." I tried to release her, but she tightened her grip on my arms.

"Not yet. Don't let me go yet," she whispered.

"Tell me what happened? How'd you get, uh, down there?" I asked. Cindy had wandered away, giving us space, but Secret had done the opposite. Slipping into her cat form, she purred aggressively as she rubbed against my thigh.

"The wolf got too loud to ignore. Kept on bringing up your contact on my phone and tossing it away. I tried drowning it with three gin and tonics. I noticed the claws first and then my clothing tried to strangle me. Things stopped making sense then. I... my house was a cage all of a sudden. I broke out and then there was this scent that was just... wrong. I wanted to find you, but I smelled nothing other than the wrongness." A huff of frustration, "Stupid, but I couldn't think of anything other than killing it, fighting it somehow. I went to that house, and it was everywhere, those threads, coming out of people, and their ghosts were... screaming. Then I found someone who was still alive. Coughing his lungs out in that suit... and he shot me," Victoria rubbed her chest.

"I think I attacked him and then I blacked out. I remember slipping or falling. There was a man and he," her fingers probed her burn and she sucked in air between teeth. "Put that chain around my neck. It was so cold I'm not sure I'll ever be warm again. Everything in me froze, except for the duty. The Duty was like a bonfire, the only warmth in the midst of a blizzard." Her voice went soft. "It was so heavy, nothing else mattered. It trapped everything else beneath it. No time for sorrow, no time for thinking, just the task. I barely remember what it was. Protect something. I fought for it. When I smelled you, I struggled, tried to push it aside. I couldn't, I wasn't strong enough. You know all those stories where the hero is possessed or turned into a monster? They hesitate or stop themselves just in time? That wouldn't have happened; if you hadn't blocked that first attack, I would have killed you. And that would have been it for both of us. Hello, eternity."

"Vicky, it's okay. Luna would not want you to be anyone's hound, even Death's," I said. "You're safe now."

She gave a breathy laugh, "I wanted to solve the mysteries of death, determine what happens to a soul." She inhaled sharply and that flat place where her nose had been bowed inward, outlining the triangular shape of her nasal cavity. "Now I know my fate. To be a guard dog and slowly forget I had ever been anything else."

The grinding of tires turning on asphalt drew my attention to the entryway of the property; a black SUV turned into the driveway.

"Who's that?" Victoria flung my hands off her and stood, snuffing hard through her damaged nose.

"It's okay," Cindy raised her hand toward us, "I called him, it was the only thing I could think of after Abby went into that colony."

"Him?" I asked, rising from the bumper and straightening my hair.

In answer, Dr. Wiggins stepped down from the driver's seat of the SUV, bearing a smile that was clearly a plea for help. "You rang, Miz Maveri?" His eyes sought Cindy, "I am here, and I have come alone. Am I to be mauled now? Ripped to tiny, teeny weeny pieces, perhaps?"

Cindy gave a nervous laugh, "No one's mauling anyone here. Right, Abby?"

"Not planning on it," I said, wondering if Cindy having

the Doctor meet us here had been the greatest decision on her part. Everyone might know I'm a werewolf, but Victoria still had a shot at hiding it.

"That's a pity, I really don't want to be the one to tell the mayor that we have to send hazmat crews to every isolation colony in the city and check up on them." He grinned at me, "I highly doubt the mayor will be screaming into a bucket. I don't suppose you know precisely what happened there, Miss Night? I assume the white, nine foot tall, wolf creature is you, at least. Perhaps you can explain that abyss in the circle of salt upstairs?"

"It's not good, doctor." I explained to him and Cindy that if the fungus was allowed to bind its victims together, it thinned the border between Death and Life. I suggested watching the hole carefully and seeing if it closed. Once closed, burning the house to the ground might not be a bad idea. I concluded with, "But I can't tell you why this is happening."

"I'm guessing that the dead are not coming back to invest in the real estate market." Dr. Wiggins laughed hollowly. "Nadia and I have made some inquiries; we have had several disappearances from the plague wards, so there is some evidence for your possession theory. They're full anyway, now. Comatose victims are overflowing the wards, and the staff are cramming their beds into normal rooms; those who haven't reached that stage are going to be fighting for space with those who are within a day. There's talk of constructing shelving but after seeing that colony..." He shook his head. "We've got your friend Clifford hooked up to an IV cocktail with every antifungal I can safely hit him with at once. If it's effective, I might invite you and your nose to work at the hospital as an early screening test. There have been some spontaneous recoveries: ten percent or so."

"Anything special about those who recovered?" Hope stirred my voice to spike.

"Nothing in the clinical notes, but I'm not the one seeing them. I'm in the lab and in the morgue. They don't technically die so..." He shrugged. "This isn't a nationwide plague. It's purely a Portland problem. We're starting to see cases on the east side, too. After seeing that Iso Colony, though. I think the task force will have to consider evacuating the entire city."

It feeds on despair. Death's words echoed, all those people fleeing could trigger a feast for the Rot. Or maybe it was the sensible thing. The Rot lurked in the ground; removing people from its reach might be the best option until we had a cure. Or would we simply be carrying it with us? "There has to be a way to stop this," I said more to the world than to Dr. Wiggins.

Dr. Wiggins straightened his short body. "Science can stop it. Most of the victims so far are elderly, but not all. If there is a pattern, I will find it." Then he coughed into the back of his hand; it came away to reveal a grimace on his face. "But science needs time. Years, maybe. Years that none of us might have. You say there are intelligences behind this? Then we have to find them. Make them tell us how to fight this thing."

I nodded; there was still this Mr. Baker out there somewhere. He had all these answers. I glanced back at Victoria; she had her hood up and had turned sideways so the doctor could not see her face. Wolf me wanted nothing more than to take her home and show her our territory but that had to wait; we had a shade to find tonight. Victoria had seen ghosts long before Luna's power had entered her bloodstream... perhaps there was a reason beyond the transfusion that she had become the second wolf. I turned back to the doctor, "We'll do what we can."

"I know you will. Meanwhile, I'm going to try to find the mayor, he's been rather distracted by the festivities in downtown. Once they're over and we get through this, you might need to keep a low profile." He stepped up into his car.

"I'll take care of it," I said, meaning it.

He responded with a weak smile, "Patrick Leary's not a bad man. We've had far worse." With that he closed the door and started the SUV before I realized he had shaded my negotiation style. I was going to have to bring my Aunt Sheryl into the fold, but not tonight.

"Who was that?" Victoria asked.

"Doctor who I'm friendly with. He's been helping organize the response to the Rot. Which so far is to stack the victims up like cordwood," I told her.

"He smelled..." Victoria pursed her lips and narrowed her eyes in concentration, "Stressed?"

Giving a nervous laugh, I answered, "I don't think anyone's having a great week."

"I am!" Secret piped up, with a shine in her eyes. "I made a friend who's gonna teach me how humans work! And I ate some goodies and danced. We're all happy at Cindy's house now. It's a good week."

Cindy barked a laugh so sharp that it stung my ears. "At least someone's having fun."

"Well, it hasn't been all bad," I conceded; my eyes found Victoria's, and she lowered hers as a smile played on her lips, furrowing the freckles at the corner of her mouth.

"So, we have to find this Baker?" Her smile turned into a frown of concentration. "We have anything other than a name?"

"He led the group that tried to hunt me a week ago. Was apparently the one funding the operation. Spoke like a gangster from an old movie, said dilly a lot." Had that really been a week ago? Felt like I'd been running flat out since then.

"Like a gangster... That sounds familiar. Let me go grab my phone." She danced up the stairs and patted down her empty pockets and gave a canine whine. "Oh! Left my key on the kitchen floor; we'll have to go in through the back." More nervous laughter: she turned, eyes shining with her wolf. "On second thought, I don't really want to see more messages from Andrew's lawyers. Could I uh... use yours."

"Sure?" I pulled my phone from my pocket, and in the time it took me to unlock it, Victoria not only returned but pecked me on the cheek. Wolf me rumbled tenderly, overriding my surprise.

"Sorry," she huffed, "Not usually so touchy but-"

"Wolves are touchy," I finished for her, handing her the phone and sliding an arm around her as she hunched over the little screen.

"And nauseatingly cute," Cindy commented with a shake of her head.

"Says the woman whose Fox Fey girlfriend practically melts all over her," I sassed her back, and in the harsh lights of Victoria's driveway I could see Cindy's blush. "Speaking of, where'd foxy lady go?"

Cindy gestured. "I dunno, she noped out as soon as I called Dr. Wiggins. Said she'd meet us at home, but if you're going hunting, then I might go see if Cliff is still having a labor shortage."

Victoria interrupted, flashing me the screen of my phone displaying a black-and-white photo of a broad-faced man with impressively thick eyebrows. "This might be him! George L. Baker! Portland's Prohibition-era mayor and listed as the city's most corrupt administration." His thin-lipped smile stretched his entire face and something about it called to mind the mad talking corpse I had held in my claws. If that wasn't him, they were definitely related.

"And it's even listed where he's buried." Victoria scrolled to a different tab. "I doubt George here knew he was on the Internet. Let's take my car."

Good packmate. Wolf me huffed with pride.

34

———

I was truly surprised that the address was on the lower east side of the city instead of Riverview where most city bigwigs were. However, once I saw The Wilhelm Mausoleum, I wondered if the city's most corrupt mayor had died richer than most. I don't know what I was expecting, but the adobe facade with large arched windows wasn't it. Behind the squat roof of this first building loomed a much taller structure, blocky, in the way some cathedrals are, but aggressively not a church. It had its own somber thing going on. Somewhere in there were the remains of George Baker. We parked across the street. Far behind it, spotlights played over the clouds as Andrew Millar's funeral continued long into the night. A very different sort of memorial that I hoped would draw all the city's attention while we did this.

I stared up at it; the thing had to be eight stories tall. "When you said Mausoleum, I assumed you meant we'd have to break into a small family crypt or something. A place like this is going to have security," I said, looking at Victoria as she frowned at the building beside me.

"We're going to need to find an index, too, or we'll be here for hours," she said.

"How are we doing this?" I asked. This place had to have cameras, at the very least. Then again, what the hell were cameras going to do to us?

"I don't know. I'm a necromancer and now a werewolf; if we were a heist team, I think that falls under distraction more than breaking-and-entering expert," Victoria said.

"I've broken down plenty of doors, but I've always gotten an invitation first." I scowled at the building.

"I can help," Secret volunteered.

"You need to conserve your energy for emergencies." Not wanting to explain Secret's exotic diet to Victoria, I popped open the door and stepped outside before she could argue. The chill air nipped at my nostrils and the breeze held the prelude of a storm. Pulling my hood up over my head, I made my way across the road, Victoria following behind. A wall prevented access to the compound except through the main entrance, which I definitely did not want to use. I touched its artfully patterned surface and let wolf me press into my body until the waistband of my jeans grew uncomfortably tight.

"How do you do that?" Victoria huffed besides me. "I feel like if I give it an inch it will take it all."

We didn't have time to explain how her wolf wasn't an "it," so I just said, "practice." I jumped up, grasped the top of the wall, and hauled myself up. It had no spiky bits, so I straddled it and offered a clawed hand to Victoria. Glancing around first, as if one person on the wall wasn't something obvious in and of itself, she took my hand. With wolf me in my arms, I easily lifted her, and together we jumped down into a garden on the other side. Broad-leaved plants guarding burbling pools were out of place for the season. A touch revealed them to be too smooth for actual leaves: plastic. Victoria and I paused on the edge of the garden; the soft patter of rain filled in between the sounds of the city. No security guard hustled out to confront us. There were plenty of windows and doors to get into the building. The only question was which one would be farthest from the security desk.

"So how are we going to do this?" Victoria asked, crouching by the edge of the fountain. Feeling like an asshole teen once again, I picked up a rock about three times the size of my fist and showed it to her.

She hunched further down. "You'll set off an alarm, and what do we do when the cops show up?"

"You ever gotten burgled before?" I asked with a smile.

"Not really." Victoria shook her head.

"Unless it's a real quiet and it ain't," I pointed at the whirling spot lights, "cops will take at least a half hour getting here. Tonight, we have at least an hour." Also, I doubted they'd be coming with silver bullets. If onsite security challenged us, I'd simply shove them into a closet.

"That long? How the hell do you know that?" Victoria's voice climbed up from its whisper.

"Professional pride and rivalry; we EMTs keep our response time under nine minutes." I grinned, "Come on." With a wave of my hand to indicate for her to follow, I darted toward the closest window.

Flinging the rock with a sideways hurl produced a satisfying crash and a rock-sized hole with arching cracks radiating out to the corners of the glass. Not safety glass! I nearly whooped and brought my elbow down on the glass. A wedge of glass fell inward, making an opening more than big enough to scramble through.

With that, we were in. Glass cases were arrayed in three

rows, which made me wonder if we'd broken into a museum instead. A reception desk stood at the far wall. Moving towards it, I saw the contents were a variety of urns. I swore at myself; we'd broken into their showroom. It was certainly alarmed, but I heard nothing, so maybe it was silent?

Vaulting over the desk, I found the equipment behind it to be sparse: a computer and a few drawers. Dammit, had they digitized everything?

Victoria moved slowly through the room, eyes lingering on the contents of the cases. "Does anyone really want to be buried in something so gaudy?" She paused, focused, "Oh, now there's a nice one."

I growled at her as I pulled open the drawers, "Vicky, this isn't a shopping trip!" Second pull and I found a leather-bound book as thick as my arm.

"Sorry, I just can't believe I've never been hired to do a seance here. I mean I haven't done one since I signed on to be Andrew's immortality consultant, but I did plenty before that." Victoria straightened

Whipping out my penlight revealed the words "Directory, 2010 edition" in swoopy lettering across the cover. I slapped it onto the counter and opened it, flipping through the pages of names. There were pages of Bakers, but I found him, with a number for the sky room. If I only knew where that was.

Cautiously, we crept out of the showroom into a main hallway. Illuminated only by the green exit signs, the murk hid all the details of its columns and arched ceiling. As we stepped towards a double-wide stairway at the end of the hall, my ears perked to the sound of murmured whispering. I froze, listening, but the speech articulated no words. Victoria had crept ahead of me, approaching the stairway with something dangling from her raised hand as if it cast a light she could see by. "I'm guessing you can hear that?" I whispered, joining her at the base of the stairs. In the shadows above us figures clustered at the edges of my vision but refused to be there if I turned my gaze.

"Yeah. And they're riled up, too." Victoria whispered as she placed her foot on the first step.

Something flew down at us from the top of the stairs. We flinched out of the way; it sailed between us and shattered on the floor. A large vase.

"They angry we broke a window?" I asked.

"Ghosts don't care about that," Victoria said with the shake of her head. "But there's your answer on the security. This many ghosts would wreak havoc with any electronic sensor. Come on, let's go find Mr. Mayor."

As we climbed the steps, I felt the ghosts' presence like frost creeping up the back of my neck. Cold icy stares burned at my back as we reached the landing. It branched off in three directions, through archways that opened into blackness...

-don't belong- The whispers clarified as I caught a slender shadow flowing back into the right hallway.

"You will not stop us." Victoria announced in a ringing tone. "The Dead yield to the living, and you hold no power over us."

The whispering stopped abruptly, collapsing into a hostile silence. With that, Victoria strode forward with a confidence I hadn't seen since she became one of Luna's. I tried to copy her stance, but every step felt like I was walking deeper into my own grave. The hallways had no windows and were lined with columns of marble panels that each bore a three-digit number in the corner. Engraved names decorated some, other had photos or flowers attached like refrigerator magnets, others had nothing but the number, no indication if they were merely empty or sadly forgotten. The strangest combination of a hallway of PO boxes, a morgue, and a grand old church.

"So, question." Victoria broke the hostile silence. "What would I use for Luna's holy symbol?"

"Uhhh, maybe a circle?" My fingers moved to press on the crescent moon mark above my heart. The Ghosts weren't throwing anything more at us, but were making it perfectly clear we were not welcome. Threatening footsteps echoed behind us while emergency exit lights winked in and out. "She's not big on instruction."

Victoria tsked, "You mean she's not sending you instructional thirty-second videos every five minutes?"

"She speaks when she wants to." I recalled her words during the full moon and added, "I'm never alone." Even here as we walked among the dead, I could feel her constant presence in my body, my blood reflecting her power as a calm river does her light on a cloudless night.

"I was trying to make a joke." She peered at a directory posted by the side of a stairwell.

"Religion isn't funny to me. My parents were kinda like Seventh Day Adventists, mom always telling me that the world could end tomorrow. Church had no humor." Then I chuckled despite myself, "Course, Dad used it as an excuse to play video games until he fell asleep in his chair. Then he'd drag himself up from the basement and mutter, darn, not today, then."

Victoria's laugh boomed as we entered the stairwell, and the heavy dark shrank back some. "Opposite of mine. They believed in the plan and made sure I knew that the plan included me getting straight As and going to Harvard."

"And captain of the cheer leading squad?" I teased as we jogged up the stairs

"Hey, I was never captain! Didn't get to senior year, remember? Besides, I liked cheerleading! Saved me from actually having to chase balls." She whirled as she reached a landing "And don't you make any snide comments about that!" Her golden irises shone brilliant in the feeble light.

I yelped in surprise, stumbling into her. Her arms folded around my back, and I found myself suddenly very warm, "Wasn't gunna make that... very obvious joke you set yourself up for," I said, but I couldn't keep the smile from cracking my expression. Suddenly I was very aware that we were completely alone except for the ghosts. With my penlight trapped behind her back, I could barely make out her silhouette.

She growled playfully, and it sent heat rushing all over my body, "Lets lay off the ancient history and talk about something more recent. What's pack*mate* mean?"

"Uh..." The moisture in my mouth suddenly fled. "It's like a family, but Vicky, is this really the time?"

"You said we had an hour; you can give us five minutes." Victoria swallowed, "And I don't know when we'll be alone again." As we breathed in each other's breath, sparks tingled in my body. "Did you know that ever since you pulled me back from the Twilight, I haven't been able to stop thinking about you? You telling Death to get out of the way echoed through my head. I know lots of powerful people, Abby, from occult circles, shared drinks and more with them, but I woke up alone. I didn't know anyone who would do that for me."

My tongue scrubbed the roof of my mouth to find enough moisture to speak, "We went over this. That was my job, and this afternoon was be-"

She kissed me, a simple motion, and I lost myself in the sensation of her. With it came a familiar shriek, *You shouldn't do this! You're straight! You're fucking everything up. She's confused. You need Cliff, not her!* I shoved the voice into my mental closet, muffling my doubt.

Our lips separated. "Victoria," I gasped.

"Sssh. I'm only going to say this once because it's pathetic. When I figured out that I experienced your pain, that we were linked, I was thrilled. It gave me a hook into your world, to you. My heroine."

"I'm not-" I started, but she muted me with a kiss, a peck to silence me.

"Not done. I've been crushing on you since that Christmas dinner. Flirting went straight over your head. No biggie, I've crushed on straight friends before, I get over it. I'm fine being alone, except I'm not anymore. Not with this wolf in my head. She'll follow you to the end of the earth, happy to be part of this pack thing." She rested her forehead against mine; her golden eyes had their own shine in the dark. "But I want us to be more than that."

"Well," Is this what I wanted? I asked myself, my memories recoloring as I ran through them, finding attraction beneath the flare of jealousy when she stood in her striking trench coat and black boots on my doorstep. The cuteness of the freckles she hid under that makeup. Or was I simply smarting from Cliff's rejection, and she was here? Or worse, pairing up because she was the only option my lonely heart could see, like I had with Jimmy? No, I smacked that thought away. Victoria didn't deserve to share the same thought as that monster. Impulsively, to prove it to myself, I pressed my lips to Victoria's with a small growl, and she yielded to my tongue, letting me taste her depths. When the seal between us broke, she raised her chin and offered her throat. She shivered as I gave her the lightest bite. It took an effort to stop from going further and let my head fall against her shoulder. "Well, I think there's something mutual here," I said, panting into her as I marveled at my articulation.

"Good," Victoria whispered. "Does this screw things up? I have no idea how wolf packs work." Her hand stroked my hair, and I loved the sensation. Savoring the whirling spice of her dusky scent, I composed my thoughts.

"We're not wild wolves, Vicky; there are no rules for what a pack needs to be. We can make it any shape we want." I kissed her on the cheek; it felt right. "I can't say I know what I'm doing. The only rule I've got is we protect our own and our home. We have to do that, then figure out the rest along the way."

"Then why'd you stop?" A hiss of frustration in her voice.

"Because we're in a graveyard! And that's not a turn-on for me," I said.

"Oh!" Victoria made the sound as if that were a revelation to her. She let me go, a note of embarrassment ringing out from her, not a smell but through a connection between us. "You mean you don't find a huge wealthy mausoleum romantic?"

I forced a bit of a chuckle, "I'm more of a roses and steak dinner girl." I said, although after ten years where the closest I got to romance were occasional Hallmark channel binges, I didn't know what I liked.

"Noted." She took a deep breath. "Let's go find our dead mayor."

35

If the dead had been listening to our heart to heart, they didn't appreciate it. Our breath appeared thick and white in the penlight's narrow beam as we stepped out onto the fourth floor. In the Sky room, a starscape had been painted across the ceiling, and beneath it sat a perfectly circular depression in the floor, painted to vaguely resemble a pool of water. Baker's panel had no adornments, just a number. As Vicky traced her fingers around the edges, trying to find a latch, my pen light sputtered out.

"Blast. Do you have another? I wish I had thought to bring some glow sticks," Victoria muttered from the darkness. The red letters of the exit signed glowed, beckoning, its light only hinting at the door frame below it.

I slipped my hand into my pocket and found nothing but a coin.

"What was that light?" Victoria asked. I hadn't seen any, but I'd been staring at where Baker's panel had been.

"Where?" Looking around in the dark, I could almost make out the outlines of people standing just out of arms' reach.

"From your pocket," Victoria whispered.

I stuck my hand back in and grabbed that coin; a soft pale luminescence glowed around my wrist. Pulling the coin out and opening my hand, I found that flattened bullet sitting in my palm, shining with the light of Luna herself. It had gone down a storm drain; I had watched it bounce in. Yet it sat there and shone against the dark, bright enough to see the number on Baker's tomb and the dozen pale figures that stood in the room with us. The ghosts did not have the bright cold fire flame eyes of the residents of the Lone Fir Cemetery, but dark patches in their misty forms.

"Don't look at them. It will just rile them up further. Bring the light over here." Victoria turned back to the panel, tugging at the edges. The room rumbled with a deep murmur of threat.

"You all have to lighten up," she chided the spirits as a vague face appeared on the panel, mouth open in a soundless scream. Frost spidered across the marble from its edge.

"Vicky..." I whispered as it made to bite at her hands.

"Is it bothering you?" Victoria slapped the face with an open palm; her skin clapped against the marble with a solid smack. "Nothing to worry about. I'll tell you when I get worried." She flashed me a smile of supreme confidence and I heard a click. "And there's the latch!" She pried off the marble panel, revealing a collection of pewter urns inside. Peering in, "George Baker, which one are you?"

A harsh whisper answered.

"Gotcha." She grabbed one and my stomach squirmed with wrongness. Something deep in the mausoleum shrieked and the door to the room slammed shut. "Okay, now you can get a little worried." Victoria shook her head with disapproval "Ghosts don't judge; this could be a serial killer and they'd be just as angry." Her golden eyes fell on the glowing disk I held. "What is that? They don't like it."

"Silver," I told her, and had to suppress a possessive snarl when she plucked it from my hand.

Its light dimmed to half its previous strength; more oddly, I could feel her fingers on it. "It's a little moon. Can I borrow it? I'll give it back."

Wolf me wanted to snatch it from her and bite her scruff for her rudeness. It took effort to huff out a "Yes." Immediately it regained its brightness.

With reverence she elevated the glowing disk over her head and thrust it towards the door. "We stand here in Luna's name, she who shines brightest in the night. It is her work we do this night! You will not bar our path!" She covered the distance to the door in two strides and shoved it open. "Come on, Abby, let's get out of here."

I certainly didn't disagree, and I followed close on her heels as we made our way back to the stairs. The residents didn't slam any more doors, but instead battered us with every object that wasn't nailed down. Mostly plastic flowers, vases, and an entire storm of brochures that did their level best to leave paper cuts on my eyeballs. It seemed acceptable to Victoria; she held my flattened bullet as a lantern, and with the urn in the crook of her arm, took the brunt of the ghosts' rage without complaint.

The scent of her blood had grown thick by the time we made it back to the main stairs. She laughed as we hurried down them. "This will be a rich story to tell later on."

I coughed as we stopped in the hallway to catch our breath. "I hardly see why we should tell anyone about this. Grave robbing is hardly something I want to brag about."

Victoria curled her arm around my neck and pulled me

close, her eyes shining with their own amused light. "Someday I'm going to brag to a horde of your grandpups how the Queen of the Werewolves cowered behind me as I faced down a storm of angry ghosts."

My brain froze. I wasn't quite sure which concept shocked me more, Queen of the Werewolves or MY grandpups. Together they combined into a double-barreled shotgun firing into my head, splattering the remains of my thoughts on the inner walls of my mind.

Victoria kissed me. Lips tasted of her own blood and adrenaline as she slipped my pancaked bullet back into my hand. Pulled away before I could even do anything about them. She took my hand and tugged me toward the showroom as I sputtered, "G-grandpups? But Vicky..."

"It's not going to be only us forever, right? Or even for long." She babbled with a sorta manic lilt to her voice. "I think I saw her, felt her, when I called her name. That's never happened before. I've called out to many of the gods for protection, but they've never answered, not like that. Something held my hand, something massive, that's her, isn't it?" Victoria led my very numb self up to the broken window we'd entered by. Outside the patter of rain whispered.

"Yes." I remember that sensation of feeling Luna's pull on the full moon, and started to feel less like a fish tossed onto the shore. "You'll meet her."

"Do you think she could save me from Death?" She laughed, high and nervous. "That's too much to ask, though, isn't it? Artemis, the huntress, that's her too; she and death are probably pals, right? If I'm good, maybe Death will take me for walks through werewolf heaven." With a heavy sniff, she knelt to slip through the window.

I caught her waist and squeezed her gently to me.

Anxiety danced in her scent now, and her pulse thundered beneath her pale skin. "Vicky, what's going on? You walked through... that like it was nothing."

"You can't show them fear, no matter what they throw or say. They called me Death's pet." She leaned back against me and wiped at her face. "It hit me, though; this is all real. This is our lives now. Not since my parents died have I doubted that there's some existence beyond life, but I don't enjoy knowing what mine's going to be."

"One day at a time," I whispered and shifted my tone to a growl. "Oh, and if you ever call me Queen of the Werewolves again, I will bite out your throat."

She laughed softly. "Promise?"

I nipped her neck and pushed her toward the window. "Get moving!"

"As you command." She dove through the hole before I could swat her. I followed, unable to stop the rueful chuckle from creeping out.

Victoria hissed as we walked out into the rain. "Fuck sakes, that's cold," she muttered, pulled up her hood, took one step forward, and fell directly onto her face.

"Holy shit," I cursed in surprise, and my own foot nearly betrayed me as I stepped out towards her. The walk shone slickly with a thin covering of ice: freezing rain. How wonderful. I braced myself and offered a hand to Victoria. She grasped it and nearly pulled me down on top of her, so slick had everything become. After half walking, half skating back to the car and Secret, Victoria risked driving a very treacherous block away from the Mausoleum. We had talked of doing the summoning at Cindy's, but after the hearse slid halfway into an intersection when Victoria braked for a red light, we reconsidered. Secret watched with interest as Victoria drew a chalk circle and then surrounded it with a circle of salt but left an inch-wide gap. The back of Victoria's hearse felt appropriate for summoning; it had a lingering scent of decay. Victoria's nose-less face gave her the appearance of a golden-eyed skull in the dim illumination of the streetlights. She set the urn in the center of the circles and folded herself into a lotus position. As she breathed, the lights of a passing car filled the cabin, and as they retreated, the darkness that rushed into the light's wake seemed deeper.

"I hold the ashes that bear your name, George Baker." Victoria spoke in a low monotone. "With an offering of my-" she sliced open the side of her hand with a small Swiss army knife, "-blood, I reach through the world and command you to attend me." Reaching into the circle she squeezed out a few drops of blood onto the urn before the cut stopped bleeding. "Come, taste the life you once knew."

The urn first vibrated, then shivered, as grains of dirt and sand rose from the carpet within the circle, hanging in the air.

"The bones call, the blood calls. Let us speak, George Baker." Victoria reached out, fingers extended and curling, pulling on invisible threads as her forehead furrowed in concentration. "Come to me. Or these ashes are going into the river." Her hand snapped closed and with a grunt she jerked hard on the invisible thread. The pewter tipped up on the edge of its base before falling back with a loud clink and I smelled the sweet the decay of the Twilight. A pale shape coiled protectively around the urn.

Of all the nights to snatch a fellow away. I'm busy tonight.

"In a hurry, are we?" Victoria's lips split into a predatory grin. "Perhaps if you answer my friend's questions, I'll think about letting you go." Grabbing the container of salt, she completed the outer circle.

I owe you nothing, witch, and you got nothing to offer me.

"That sounds like a shade who's looking to get his ashes spread over the river," Victoria said calmly.

Go ahead. I don't need them anymore. I have a body waiting for me, Baker hissed back.

Mitch and his cough reared up in my mind. I had to cut in. "You know, maybe we should go do something else. Let Mister Baker here rest a bit."

Cold flame sparked within the circle, and I felt a gaze bore into my chest. *Well, well, if it isn't Miss Mutt. This plain dilly, then. Exactly who I've been looking for.* His voice suddenly oozing confidence.

"What do you mean you're looking for me? You've known where I was from the get-go. You attacked my territory." Wolf came to the surface to growl as the headlights of trucks blazed in my mind.

Oh, I've been far too busy to come visit you again. After our little introductory tussle, my associate thought the dog would sell herself to him. I told the fellow he was barking up the wrong tree, but he got his moola stuck in his ears. The ghost let out a chilling chuckle.

"Andrew?" Victoria gasped, "You worked with Andrew?"

You ain't figured that out yet? You're a thick one. Tell me witch bitch, how else would he know that a Pharaoh needed to buy himself a party or bind the population with an oath of service? You left that out. He had to scramble to get all those new contracts out.

"Contracts?" I blinked; that pile of paperwork in the NLR office, the papers they were having everyone sign who worked at the funeral.

Oh, Miss Mutt gets it. You've slipped that collar, didn't take that bait, but we got plenty who did. Gotta hand it to ya. My timetable's a wreck. Hassling my boys, icing Andy weeks before I was ready. So I wanna take this opportunity and offer you a deal. The shadows within the circle shifted to the silhouette of a man's face, red embers for eyes.

"What deal?" I heard myself croak.

You gave me no time for sowing our seed on the east side, so how bout we call it where it is and do it like the Egyptians? East of the river, you live. That's where your turf is, anyway. Then west of the river is for the dead.

"You're full of crap." I lost my patience and snarled, "We've shut you out. You're the very last piece I need to shred. The Pharaoh ritual didn't work, and we know how to stop your Rot from thinning the barrier. Now we have you and you're going to tell us how to get the Rot out of those people."

His ugly chuckle grated on my nerves. *You got most of my guys, plugged a hole and took me down to the last ace in my sleeve. But if we're here jawing, then you not where I don't want you to be. The Pharaoh's coming home tonight, and he'll rule in the name of the Old King.*

Outside a rumble roared, so loud it rattled the windows. The ground shook, jostling the car; the urn tipped over, spilling gray ash onto the red-carpet interior.

And now it's a damn dilly day! Baker whispered, *Go look at the bridge, girls.*

Both Victoria and I scrambled to open the back and stepped out into the freezing rain. Secret opened the front door but didn't step out. Against the gray clouds, illuminated by both the city below it and Luna above it, a soot-black plume of smoke rose into the sky. The buildings blocked my view of its origin, and acting on panicky instinct, I ran for the river. Slipping and skidding over patches of wet ice, I heard both Victoria and Secret call my name, but it didn't matter. I had to see.

Finally, after two blocks of running, I broke through the city and into the riverside park. There I stopped. Orange and red flames leapt from the lower deck of the Marquam bridge and turned to smoke at the upper deck. Portland's largest bridge had just been bombed during an ice storm. Help would be long a long time coming in this. Three or four miles away. If I sprinted, I could be on the bridge in less than ten minutes. I pulled off my hoodie as Victoria caught up with me, her breathing ragged.

"Abby, what the fuck?" she gasped, bending nearly double, revealing the black kitten that had adhered herself to Victoria's back.

"Merf!" Secret seconded.

I pointed at the bridge. "Get changed, we're going there."

Victoria stared at the plume and swallowed hard, "Abby, I know you have a love affair for public acts of werewolfery, but I really don't think I'm ready for my debut yet."

"Secret, gather up our clothes, will you?" Ignoring Victoria's protests, I kicked off my sneakers and peeled off my jeans. Standing naked in the rain, I felt Victoria's frantic helplessness lap at my heart. I turned to her. She gawped at me, panting, the golden irises filling the whites of her eyes as she challenged me despite quivering with uncertainty.

"Abby, don't make me do this. I-I have no idea what to do-in that."

I reached my hand out toward her; steam rose from my sopping skin as I stroked her trembling jaw line. "Do you trust me?" I asked as I stepped closer, holding her gaze.

"What if there's a trigger-happy cop with a clip of silver bullets, Abby? If we go there, they'll blame us!" Tears welled up as she growled from the strain of keeping her eyes on mine.

I stopped; it hadn't even occurred to me that we could

choose not to go. Yet she was right, running towards that disaster was a choice. We could take the shade's deal, go home, and declare it good enough. My, our, territory only extended through a dozen city blocks and the wooded park it connected to. "Victoria, we are monsters," I said softly as the choice before me crystallized. "But this is how we decide what sort of monsters we are. I won't be the sort that lurks on the edge of civilization and eats children who explore too deeply. We have to be the devils the city knows. The ones they leave gifts for on their back porches. How long do you think we'll last if the only thing we do is defend ourselves? If they only see the bodies of those who hunt us? If that happens, Secret won't make it to adulthood, and you'll never tell stories to any grandpups."

"When you put it like that," Victoria closed her eyes and lifted her chin to expose her throat. "As my queen commands," she said with a small smile playing on her lips.

I nosed her offered neck, accepting her submission, "Now change," I growled, pushing the order through our bond.

"Grrck!" Victoria flinched forward as if I'd thumped her in the stomach, smile stretching into a sharp-toothed grimace as her face pushed out. "Ah, gods," she gasped, frantically clawing at her clothing to get it off before it tore. I set my hands against the grass and stretched into my hulking wolf form, my flesh flowing with ease and grace compared to Victoria's painful snapping of limb and muscle.

Secret giggled as she helped Victoria out of her pants; they saved everything but her scarlet T-shirt, which tore across her chest as it barreled out. When the change finished, Victoria rolled up onto all fours, tongue panting from her long mouth. *Showoff*, her glance said. Secret bundled the clothing up and sandwiched it between herself and my back.

I flashed Victoria a doggie grin and took off towards the disaster.

Within a few paces I could smell the death in the air.

36

Wolf me ran, propelling me toward the bridge with a speed that blurred my eyes. My claws bit surely into the ice when we ran out of the park. The scent of oily smoke and charred meat grew with every pound of my paws. Yet if I was fast, Victoria was warp speed, her lean form outpacing me, the remains of her T-shirt flapping against her back, a tiny superhero cape. Human me, whirling through a storm of emergency protocols, paused with a sudden idea.

I veered off a block into the city where a paint store sat in a red brick building. People scattered like a flock of pigeons as the automatic doors slid open to admit me. Secret shrieked as we skidded more than halfway down an aisle before the friction between my wet paws and the glossy tile finally stopped us. Luna must have smiled at the idea because it was the right aisle. I grabbed a red-capped can of spray paint and tossed it back to Secret.

"What this for, Abby?" She asked, her tone curious.

"Whuff." I responded, hoping she'd at least hang onto it until I had time for hands. I ran back out of the store and let out a howl, letting Victoria know where I was.

Marquam bridge is not the longest of Portland's bridges, but it's one of its major arteries, conducting I5 traffic traveling north and south through the city. It loomed over the east riverbank on pairs of concrete pillars. The roads it carried swept towards the north, where they deposited the roads back onto the earth. Victoria streaked towards those on and off ramps. Scattered reflections of flashing lights lay in that direction, but the only light on the bridge was the hellish glow of the fire on the lower deck. Sirens screamed from both sides of the river but didn't sound like too many had reached the bridge yet. If cars jammed the exit and on ramps, they'd have to work their way up them slowly, provided someone didn't declare the scene itself too dangerous to approach entirely.

I ran up to the closest concrete pillar and forced my body to stand, shifting into my hybrid form. Secret hopped down as her perch went vertical, and looked up at me with her green eyes. "No getting shot again," she pouted, tail lashing behind her.

Nodding, I held out my hand, and she handed me the can of spray. It felt stupidly tiny in my awkward hands, but I managed to paint a rough red cross on each shoulder. Hopefully it looked a little like the universal symbol of first aid on the white. An echoing howl let me know that Victoria was already racing up one of the ramps. I reached up, dug my claws into the pillar's seams and started climbing. The lower deck, carrying northbound traffic, was mostly empty but the upper deck reeked of blood and terror. I had to stop and stare at the heaped shapes before I could make any sense of it. The highway was a solid mass of cars. No road visible except for a clear hundred feet to the edge of the crater in the middle of the bridge. The explosion had happened on this level; it had blown back a row of cars against the flow of traffic and then, thanks to the icy conditions, no one could stop; the chaos carried on around the bend of the on ramp.

From the sea of twisted metal came the thumps and pounding of fists on windows and doors. Hoarse voices screaming for help, mothers desperately calling to children. I shook off the sensory overload; couldn't just stand here, had to make it better.

I jumped down to the tan sedan in front of me, its front and back crumpled. Punching through the passenger window, the coppery scent of clotting blood greeted me. Inside, a balding man slumped at the wheel. Not dead, but not going anywhere on his own, either. I reached in to grab him, but stopped myself. I had no medical supplies with me. Moving him now wouldn't help.

Reverse triage, human me barked. I had to save the people most likely to live first. Then if they're lightly injured, they can help or at least get out of the way. Most of the cars were pinned so closely together that none of the doors could be opened.

Jumping to the next car, I heard someone scream from inside. Good sign. I punched my claws through the roof and peeled it back. A young woman shrieked and cringed in the driver's seat while struggling with the steering wheel pressed to her chest. She didn't smell bloody, hopefully only pinned. Her scream reached the pitch of a sonic weapon as I grabbed the back of her seat and wrenched. The mechanism snapped. She shut up when I threaded a hand under each armpit and lifted her free of the car. I carried her like a baby with a dirty diaper to a small island of pavement.

Victoria came running up the ramp as I set the woman down. She took one look at Victoria and must have decided I'd rescued her for lunch, because she immediately collapsed into a fetal position. Stepping over her, Victoria looked me up and down, taking in my hybrid form. *How do I do that?* she whined.

I huffed back at her, *later*. And waved my hand for her to follow. She watched with an anxious vibration to her body as I punched out the back window of an SUV and then cut another man out of his seat belt. Her head cocked as I moved on to the next car, a black Lexus. Man in the front was barely breathing, but two kids in the back in seats both struggled desperately to free themselves. Growling with effort, I had to rip through much more metal and foam to get at the kids. They didn't make a single sound as I pulled them out.

A crack sounded as I deposited the children with the shell-shocked woman. Victoria had punched through a rear window by a slamming her front paws through it. I chuffed with approval and rejoined her. We worked down the line, Victoria breaking all the windows while I pried open the doors and roofs for those that needed more assistance. A few of the humans started helping. A dark-skinned man followed Victoria, assuring car occupants that the "dogs" were here to help. I had worked through five full rows of cars when Victoria let out a warning growl. She stood four rows ahead of me, perched on the side of a rolled SUV, nose pointed down the bridge. There, among vehicles so twisted together I had no hope of survivors, movement. Things were forcing their way out of the wreckage and standing up on the cars. Human bodies, crooked and twisted. The wind shifted, bringing blood, bile, and a fetid stink of perforated intestines. Code Zs. Dozens of them.

With a growl rising in my throat, I stretched myself up for a better view. The emerging horde began to stumble towards us; the movement wasn't coordinated enough to call it a shamble. Yet with every movement, whether a flop, a step, or a crawl, they gained speed. The red eyes broadcast a bottomless hunger, leaving no question as to their intentions.

The injured would have to wait. I howled out a challenge to the dead, a song promising their destruction. Their gazes rose from the cars to me, answering me with groans that chorused together into a terrible roar.

Victoria and I charged out towards them baring fangs and claws. I leapt into the middle of a pack and separated one's hips from its spinal column with a single swipe. My other hand tore a head from misshapen shoulders and tossed it into the river below. Their fellows didn't flinch or pause, but reached out towards me with misshapen and maimed hands. They were the mangled victims of the crash reassembled by something that only had the vaguest notion how humans were shaped. Feet were commonly stuck on the ends of arms, skin inverted, and intestines used as tendons. No matter how I slashed or tore their limbs from their bodies, they refused to stop moving. The severed limbs used whatever means they could to slip back beneath the sea of wreckage. Beside me Victoria bounded from foe to foe, ripping skulls from each and crushing them with almost mechanical precision, pounce- rip- crunch, pounce-rip-crunch. Skull-less, the meat and bone assemblages fell, but only to squirm away.

A human scream of pure terror broke through the growing cacophony of sirens and shouts behind us. I turned my ears and then my head. Two huge gorilla-shaped assemblages were reaching into an SUV. I charged, hurdling over the cars so fast the wind whistled in my ears. Leaping towards one, my jaws opened to take its arm. Its head swiveled, displaying a mouth bearing a mishmash of teeth, jagged bone splinters, and fingernails. Horror cut to the quick of my heart and the world stuttered. Glass broke and metal protested as I impacted the wrecked sea and rolled. Memory of the blow to the side of my face replayed as I staggered up to my feet and shook the stars from my vision. Victoria had fared better, spitting out a chunk of squirming flesh. The woman's screams cut off with a wet splorch.

Claws and teeth may break bones, but you cannot hurt the servants of the Pharaoh. The things taunted, their arms swelling with the addition of new flesh. Victoria and I gave rise to twin growls. One turned to face each of us, smiling with their terrible faces.

Victoria glanced at me, *Any ideas?*

What do you do with the dead? The answer came swiftly; you bury them. *Follow my feint,* I told her with a flick of my ears as I lowered into a crouch. With a bellowing roar, I hurled myself at the closest flesh gorilla. It opened its arms as if my teeth were coming in for a kiss, but I hurdled over it to the other side of the car. The other meat puppet gurgled in surprise as I clamped down on the back of its neck. Sharp, jagged bone embedded in the flesh bit back into the roof of my mouth, but I held on, wrapping my arms around its torso. I heaved with every muscle I had. Stepping out I pivoted, spinning once before hurling the monster like a sack of potatoes. It sailed over two lanes, landing on the undercarriage of an upturned SUV, and rolled over the side of the bridge.

One down, one to go.

Nice trick, doggies. Will only work once. The remaining thing's voice vibrated around us.

Victoria yelped as I turned from the bridge's edge. She pinwheeled through the air, legs outstretched, flying away from the first creature, and crashed into a van. The metal bent from her bulk, but she bounced from the impact, landing on all fours. A huge strip of flesh wriggled in her jaws, and she tossed it out into the river. She licked her bloody mouth and snarled back.

We hit it front and back, Victoria going in low while I went high. Not to slash or bleed, but to rip off the largest chunks we could. It swung hard, clubbing at us with its heavy fists. For each blow that knocked me away, I claimed a chunk of grisly flesh to throw over the side of the bridge. Its wounds closed quickly, but it diminished in size until we cast the entire thing into the dark waters below. The river took it without complaint. Yet as we watched the indifferent bubbles sweep downstream, my eyes caught an odd streak in the river below. Spreading out like an oil slick, it both ate what light there was and reflected more in its ripples. As if I had slid the contrast up for that one part.

Leaning further out and looking up the bridge, I saw the dark liquid falling into the river like a chemical runoff. The origin of it, the burning lower level of the bridge. Finally closing my panting mouth, I breathed in through my nose and found the air stinking of the Twilight. The realm of the dead was literally leaking into ours.

37

The blue brilliance of halogen headlights casting down the length of the bridge heralded the arrival of the emergency crews.

Still things squirmed, but we'd kept these puppets from marching down the bridge and causing more chaos. We had to get to the root of the problem, or we'd have to throw every scrap of flesh into the water. We'd done what we could here. With a frustrated growl, I took off down towards the crater and its pillar of smoke. Victoria followed on my heels as I bounded over the wrecks to the very end of the sea of wrecks and scrambled over a rise of charred wreckage three cars high. On the other side, the blast had cleared fifty feet of bare concrete before a chasm opened across all four lanes of highway. Thick black smoke rose from the lower deck, but it couldn't obscure the circle of utter blackness that floated in its midst, or hide the ichor pouring out of its bottom. Its surface writhed as shadows escaped its depths and streamed into the sky with the column of smoke.

The hole was so wide that my nine-foot-tall form could jump into it spread-eagle and not touch the sides.

"HALT!" The bridge itself called out, the word ringing through the steel girders that surrounded us. "This is your first and only warning. Begone." Despite the distortion I recognized the voice. Smoke broke off from the plume and composed itself into the hovering shape of a man: the eyes flared with cold flame and illuminated the larger-than-life features of Andrew Millar.

I growled, long and low.

He smiled at me, "Don't be angry at me, Miss Night. It's your fault it comes to this. If not for you and Dr. Wiggins, then the city would have passed peacefully in its sleep; there'd be no need for the..." He waved behind him, "dramatics of an invasion." He floated closer, sneering down at me. "Those claws and teeth of yours mean nothing to me now." Opening his arms, he invited me to strike his smoke-filled body.

The crackle and pop of bones briefly overpowered the hiss of flames as Victoria changed. Andrew's shade focused on her. "Victoria?" he asked when she stood human and naked, one arm clamped over her breasts.

"A-Andrew, l-listen to me." Her teeth chattered as she pushed a lock of wet black hair out of her face. "The Egyptian Pharaohs ruled over the dead and advised the living with their consent. How long do you think that will last if you pull the entire west side into the realm of the dead? Those people downtown shouting your name will abandon you once they realize you've trapped them."

Andrew's laugh shook the bridge, jostling it beneath our feet. Victoria nearly stumbled into the fires below. I grabbed her and pulled her into an embrace, trying to shield her from the icy rain. The shade in the graveyard had struggled with a single tombstone. Just how much more powerful was Millar compared to the other shades?

"Oh, Victoria, you put on such a speech on how words and promises matter now. That they have weight to them. And yet, no one even understands half the agreements they sign. A single line inserted in a contract and its bound them to me in life or death. It's right there in the text which few of them read, and those that do, figure it's impossible and sign anyway. Between the festival and employment contracts, over a hundred thousand souls are pledged to my service. Souls, bodies, and obedience: I'm cashing in on the surplus stupidity of the masses." He laughed again.

Cindy had signed a contract to work at the funeral and was working a shift on that side of the river! I had to get her out.

"Andrew, listen," Victoria pleaded from my arms. "Baker told us about the employment contracts and I'm certain he's lying. Entrapment, whatever power that has, it won't last. It will take more power to enforce than you'll gain."

He tsked, "Dear Victoria, you think this is for show?" He gestured to the shades pouring out of the underworld. "As you trade your blood to ghosts for their obedience, I trade the blood of the city for their loyalty and service. From this day Portland will be reborn into a port not on the Willamette but on the Styx, the river of the underworld. It's as you told me over drinks, the meeting place between the living and the dead." He floated down to our level and extended his hand towards us.

"Besides, our contract is much more explicit and signed in blood. It is very interesting what you've become Victoria Gabriella Quentin." As he spoke her name, Vicky stiffened in my arms. "I require your services now."

Victoria made a weak attempt to break out of my arms, but I held her, pulling her back from the shade. A possessive growl rose in my throat. He couldn't have her. Vicky belonged with me now, we were Luna's, a greater power than one ghost with an overinflated ego would ever be.

Those flaming orbs focused on me, brightening in surprise as if he had forgotten that Victoria didn't stand alone. "Let her go, Miss Night. As my, I believed we termed it, immortality consultant, she is bound to assist me in all consultations with the supernatural, and I call her now."

In my arms Victoria shook, alternately whining and growling. Distantly I felt a sensation like a hook in our flesh, pulling insistently. "No. H-help me, Abby," she pleaded.

Pushing my cheek against hers, I searched for the mental lever I'd found when she'd balked at coming to the bridge in the first place. I followed that distant pull to find her, her entire self at the edge of my mind, two separate selves, a woman who clung to a jackal-like wolf, trying to resist the force of the barbed hooks in her back and head.

Change. I touched her wolf and gave her a push.

Victoria threw back her head and howled a song of defiance. *Not yours! I am mine.* She shifted in my arms at the same speed she had last night when we'd arrived in our territory for the first time. She shifted entirely, submerging her human self deep within her wolf. I let her go, and she shook out her short black fur, looking small next to me.

I pulled in my muzzle, "Go back and find Secret beneath the bridge. Then go to Cindy's. I'll meet you there once I find her and Cliff."

Victoria nodded her long muzzle, growled once at Andrew, and ran off full tilt towards the east.

"You..." Andrew's voice groaned out of the steel.

Not waiting for another word, I ran for the still-intact railing of the bridge and skirted the edge of the flaming chasm.

"I AM NOT DONE SPEAKING!" Andrew roared like a

giant-sized petulant child as I landed on all fours and booked for the far side of the bridge. "You cannot run from a god!"

The bridge rumbled beneath me, and the steel screamed. A pair of giant girders curled up on either side of the road and swept down toward me. I jagged around one and jumped over the other.

A bellow of frustration sent a fissure in the pavement racing alongside me. As it overtook me, Andrew's outline appeared ahead of me as a haze of light. He raised his arms as if lifting a great weight, and chunks of pavement tore free of the road. Ice visibly coated them as they hovered.

With a throwing gesture, he sent them all rocketing towards me. Stupid! I growled at myself before a coffee table-sized piece of asphalt struck me edge on. The blow tore the ground from beneath my paws and I tumbled backwards, flipping head over tail, and slammed into the concrete. A sharp ting perked one ear as I rolled up onto my feet. I had no time to find its source as the bridge tilted beneath me. Even on all fours I staggered and swayed.

Concern and worry prodded the edge of my awareness: Victoria's.

Go! I thought at her and shook myself out.

Ahead of me, Andrew hadn't moved, making grabbing motions towards the ground as strips of rebar peeled out of the concrete. "You think I cannot see how brightly you shine? How much life you contain?" With a metallic ring a half dozen lengths of rebar snapped off at their bases and floated around him in an arc of twisted metal.

Still shaking off the dizziness, I looked past him. I still had a good two hundred feet to run or about fifteen to the edge if I wanted to see whether werewolves would swim.

I feinted for the river, and a spear of steel shot across my path. I dodged the second, jumping up as it parted my belly fur. But the third pierced my front paw the instant I landed, pinning me to the road. Instinctively jerking away, I pivoted around the paw to avoid the next.

The fifth spear pierced my side, bringing a sudden awareness of the contents of my rib cage. As I sucked in a breath, I felt rusty metal tearing at both my lungs.

I let out a wheeze and made to grab at the metal driven through my side, pawing uselessly at it before pushing out a thumb. As soon as it closed around the metal shaft, another rebar came down on it like a nun's ruler from hell. Bone cracked.

I had no breath to yelp with, so as the rebar sliced through the air, the only sound was the shallow reverberation of steel against skull. "No silver here, but let's see if asphyxiation can't dim that light of yours," Andrew hissed, the voice no longer shaking the bridge, instead becoming a bitterly cold whisper in my ears.

He rained blow after blow into my head, the pain dull compared to the burning roar in my lungs. Yet even in the dark of my eyelids, Luna's cool light shone from above and below, coolness at my ribs, and I breathed in a desperate breath. "No," he said in the way you'd scold a dog. The rebar that he'd been rearranging my face with clattered to the ground. His ghostly hands gripped the rebar he'd skewered me with and began to saw it back and forth through my ribcage. I screamed without breath; what little air I possessed bubbled out between my ribs, my left side collapsed, and I fell hard onto my side. There in front of my nose sat the silver pancake, gleaming with eagerness.

Seizing it with my broken fist, I shoved it into Andrew's shimmering outline as he reached to grab the rebar in my side. Pale light shone out between my fingertips and the ghost shrieked as his form scattered into translucent bits. No time to consider what that meant; I bit down on the rebar and ripped it out.

You will not defy me again, you bloody bitch. My servants will hunt you to the end of the earth and their weapons will be loaded with silver. So quiet his voice that without the ears of the wolf I might not have heard it, but it still made me shiver with the power of its oath. The weight of his presence lifted.

For a long, panicky moment, I still couldn't breathe. My vision swam, and I worried I'd gotten too much air in my chest cavity.

That panic notched up a level when I saw Death leaning up against the railing of the bridge. They waved, "What a mess. Not very good at this, are you? Not that he's any better, exhausting himself like that."

Passive aggressive bastard. I knew the price for their help. Something in my chest constricted, the hole in my side passed a wet bloody fart. A gasp filled my lungs with sweet, wonderful air and with my first breath I said, "You can't have her."

Death shook their head, a small smile on their lips. "I get everyone in the end. The only thing that changes is the timing."

With my second breath, my eyes opened onto the same scene I had seen with them closed, except Death had disappeared. My impaled paw had changed to human in shape, decorated with blood-dyed fur and a fierce set of claws. I'd gone from big wolf to near human; perhaps that's how I'd squeezed the air out of my chest? Didn't matter; I focused on breathing. I opened my fist to look at the small silver disc and whisper a "Thank you," to it. Silver was supposed to be the thing that could kill me with ease. It had certainly felt that way when it had been embedded in my arm. A holy symbol, Victoria said. Why would the one thing that could hurt me, also be holy? It had certainly hurt Andrew, even if it hadn't destroyed him. Luna volunteered nothing, although judging from the sensation of soothing coolness on the back of my neck, I had her attention. When I reached over to free my other hand from its rebar spear, the disk stuck to my palm.

I had to get up. Had to find Cindy and Cliff before Andrew could make good on his promise of silver-armed minions. Yet I couldn't move on until I acknowledged this little miracle. Pure silver is soft, it folded in half easily, and just by rolling it between my palms it stretched out to a small bar of metal. As I twisted it around my third finger, a gentle hand touched my head and stroked down my back. Luna approved of my new jewelry.

With a smile, I stood and brushed myself off. It had been a mistake to challenge Andrew alone. Had he started with the rebar act I'd be pinned to the bridge like a butterfly. Much longer without oxygen and Death wouldn't have visited for a chat. That now familiar hollowness echoed within me, my body calling for food and rest. Get to Cindy and Cliff first, then we can rest, I promised myself. And with that thought, I shifted to wolf form and ran for the hospital. *Hang on, Cliff, I'm coming.*

38

I caught a whiff of Cindy's scent as I rushed down off the bridge. I'd planned to rush to the hospital first, since I knew that's where Cliff was. But with a mass casualty incident here, she and every medic in the city would be on either side of this bridge. Or rushing between it and the hospital.

Maybe I could hitch a ride, but the sound of gunfire punctured that optimism. The deserted highway slowly curved its way back down to the ground over a length twice as long as the bridge itself, where it joined a complex network of exits and on ramps. Even in full wolf mode, I wondered why there were no emergency vehicles approaching up this way by now. Even if they didn't know about the portal to the twilight, fire trucks could reach the fire easily. The cascades of gunfire came in waves. I ran along the outer wall of the road, planning on jumping it if any of those bullets started coming my way.

The end of the ramp came into view. Police barriers spanned the lanes, backed up with a gauntlet of blue-and-white SUVs four vehicles deep. Behind them an array of fire trucks and ambulances lined up like race cars itching for a green flag. The ramps straddled 405, another eight-lane highway, and across it I saw a similar blockade set up on the bridge's on ramp. The shoulders of the road were strewn with abandoned civilian cars that looked as if a bulldozer had pushed them off the highway. Behind the barriers a line of police officers knelt, the muzzle flashes of their weapons reflected off the shiny plates of their face shields. Figures ran down the ramp at them through a field of abandoned and wrecked cars.

This side hadn't had a pair of rescue werewolves. The paramedics had probably encountered the zombies and had to pull back, abandoning everyone on the bridge. Maybe the other side was like this too, now, without me and Victoria occupying the attention of the shades. I swallowed back the guilt and kept running.

Doors on the police SUVs opened. I took that as my cue to hop up to the railing and jump down onto the grassy median below. Landed hard but didn't break anything. The city had stopped all traffic through this section, so I didn't even have to dodge cars as I ran to a row of evergreens that attempted to shield the city from highway noise.

Using them to cover my approach, I scanned the lines of ambulances and spotted one from NLR; our electric ambulances have a more rounded design and are easy to pick out. Only question would be if Cindy was inside. The back was open as firebugs and paramedics milled around the vehicles. I paused behind a tree, considering whether a rapidly moving wolf or a naked woman would attract more attention.

Deciding on speed, I dashed out of my cover and sprinted across two empty four-lane highways. I heard one person utter a surprised, "What the-" before I leapt into the back of the ambulance and very nearly into the lap of a surprised Douglas instead of the stretcher I had assumed would be there.

"Holy F-" The curse cut off because his head slammed into the ceiling. He fell back into the seat hard, the interior of the ambulance ringing. They had secured the stretcher to the wall, to make room for a second seat in the ambulance's rear.

"Abby?!" I heard Cindy exclaim from the front. The other occupants of the bus gave their own cries of shock. Patricia sat open-mouthed next to Douglas as he clutched his head. In the driver's seat sat Doc, Patricia's usual partner. I grabbed the door handle nearest me with my teeth and yanked it closed.

"Give her room! She won't bite!" Cindy assured everyone as the scent of fear flooded the enclosed space. I pushed human me forward, but the process refused to go as smoothly as it had on the bridge. All the paramedics stared at me in mute silence as I slowly became the woman they all knew, although not usually this naked.

"Christ on a stick." Douglas summed it up as I grabbed a spare sheet off the shelf and opened it for modesty's sake.

"Hi everyone!" I gave them all a smile, "Care to give me a ride to the hospital?"

"Abby, what are you doing here?" Cindy asked and then quieter, "Couldn't you have just called?"

"Sadly, my fur coat doesn't come with pockets." I cocked my head to see the back of Doc's bald spot as he watched me through the rearview mirror. "How 'bout that ride, Doc?"

"But the bridge," Douglas protested as the cracks of guns sounded.

"There's nobody on that bridge who's still alive. At least on this side. OHSU is about to have or is having a code Z outbreak," I said.

To my surprise, I heard the whine of the ambulance's engine. I hadn't expected it to be that easy.

"Close that door," Doc barked.

"What are you doing?" Douglas squeaked while I flashed the elderly medic a thankful grin.

"Transporting a patient with acute lycanthropy to the hospital," he deadpanned, "Also I'm sick of sitting around. Hang on; rain's eased up but these roads are still slick as hell."

* * *

I explained the situation as simply as I could. The bomb on the bridge had opened a portal to the underworld, ghosts were scrambling out of it, and OHSU had victims of the Rot stacked up like cordwood, waiting for a ghost to turn them into a weapon against the living.

"Why are we going there?" Cindy asked at the end of before anyone else could get a word in.

"They kept Cliff there overnight," I told her.

Cindy dialed her phone and the whirr of the engine increased.

"This is nuts," Patricia commented, pulling out the de-animator, aka the double-barreled sawed-off shotgun from its holster. We had it just in case a patient went code Z and couldn't be safely restrained.

Douglas just about swallowed his lower lip before arming himself with the battering ram we used for forced entry. I love paramedics. Not a bloodthirsty bunch at all but never ones to back away from trouble.

I heard Cliff pick up the phone, a heavy cough sounded. "Oh, hey, Cindy!"

"Cliff, are you in the hospital?" Cindy asked. "If you are, you need to get out of there. Its-"

"Like the night of the living dead but they're a lot faster?" He laughed uneasily, "Yeah, I know, I've got a chair in front of the door to my room, but I think they tore apart my nurse."

"What floor are you on? We're coming to get you," Cindy told him with the tone of a professional dispatcher and glanced back at me. "We've got Abby with us."

"They got me up on the... tenth or eleventh?" A crack sounded, "Aw, that ain't fair; zombies aren't supposed to use tools! And where the hell did he get an axe from?"

Shit. How the hell was I supposed to get up there in time? Climb the side of building like King Kong? "Cliff!" I shouted across the ambulance, "Break your window!" That would show me where he was.

"No time for that. I guess I shouldn't have wished so hard about wanting to try out this poker I got. Yeah, so, would have been cool to have gotten to know ya better, Abby. You, too, Cindy. I kinda need my hand now. Bye." The phone made a bip boop of a hung-up call.

"Jebus," Cindy swore and looked up ahead. "Almost there." We were climbing the hill.

Wolf me growled, but I held her back. Cliff had that fairy sword with him, surely that counted for something.

Doc swerved, throwing me against the cabinets as he calmly corrected out of the fishtail. "Where the hell are all these yahoos going? That's the third bus coming down this hill as if lanes don't exist."

"Fleeing the zombies?" Douglas suggested.

I recalled the crowd of shades that were trying to get by Victoria when I rescued her from the Twilight. A portion of those shades seemed intelligent, while the majority were scarcely more than appetite on two legs. I had a hunch that they loaded those busses with the more intelligent zombies, but I didn't voice it.

People were streaming out of every opening the hospital possessed when Doc pulled up to the curb. I hopped down from the bus still wrapped in the sheet, the scent of the Rot a choking presence.

39

As if sensing death's approach, mushrooms were rising from every possible crack in the concrete-covered landscape: between fissures in the pavement and gaps in the sidewalk. The people hustling out of the doorways trampled them as their spores joined the night air. Everyone here, even if they got away without injury from the shades, would be contending with the Rot within a few days. "Mask up!" I called back to my small crew, who were stepping out of the ambulance behind me. We had to keep moving; I approached an entrance that had fewer people streaming out of it.

My little pack of paramedics followed me in, slipping through the flow of frightened patients, some assisting others in their green patterned gowns. The less addled ones had worn their sheets around them for warmth. Inside, a klaxon blared, and bright lights flashed from small alarm boxes near the ceilings. "Code Z, Code white," a calm female voice announced. "Levels eleven through nine are overrun by aggressive code Z. Please evacuate the building. Patients, if you are able, do not wait for assistance to exit the building. All Security personnel report to level seven. All other staff, reverse triage protocol." That meant patients were being evac'd in order of mobility. A very deep shit response.

"Come on!" I ran for the sign marked stairway right beside the elevator bank. As I did, one of them opened, and the stench of the Rot hit me so hard that I stopped in my tracks. A group of seven patients, clad in their pale green gowns, stepped out, their eyes too wide and shot with black. One had black threads weaving in and out of his cheeks. Several of them had their mouths open in awe as they scanned their surroundings.

"Stop gawping; we got work to do." A man shouldered one of the others and they moved toward the exit.

I shook my head and pushed open the door to the stairs. That entire crew had been possessed by shades. How many more would escape unnoticed during the evacuation? Briefly I considered turning back and attacking them, but getting to Cliff was more important than stopping a single group of Andrew's minions. I didn't need to add a code Werewolf to the announcer's load.

The stairway smelled of both blood and rot. Adjusting the sheet, I pounded up the steps, letting wolf me into my legs. Everyone behind me sounded like a pack of winded elephants but they almost kept up.

"Ma'am, you're going the wrong way." A well-intentioned security guard tried to block the stairway, gripping both railings.

"We have a friend up there!" I panted.

"We'll handle it, Ma'am," he answered. I didn't have the breath to argue with him and plowed into him without stopping. "Hey!" He protested as I lifted him from his feet and drove him back against the wall of the landing he stood on. Swiftly I pivoted off him and let my sheet fall from my shoulders before continuing, ignoring his shocked expression. With every step, I pushed wolf me out further towards my hybrid form.

"Sorry about that!" I heard Cindy tell the guard behind me.

"She's on the good side! Don't shoot her!" Patricia called, her voice echoing up and down the stairwell.

Above me, urgent voices shouted at one another. "Hold them!"

"I'm trying! They're heavy!"

"Tase them! Tase them!"

"Give mmmmeaaat," a deeper voice moaned.

Rounding a corner, I saw a cluster of four security guards desperately trying to hold back a mass of Rot victims. Unlike Baker's gang, nothing drove these shades other than hunger. Two guards braced a hospital bed against the tide of flesh, but they were being shoved back. Another pair used IV stands to fend off the zombies that were trying to climb over their fellows and the barrier. A fifth held a taser in shaky hands in the doorway.

I took the IV stand from the closest guard and shoved him into mister useless with the taser. He staggered back, eyes threatening to spring out of his head. No time to explain; I reached over the head of the nearest guard and swatted a shambler reaching around the bed. The skull popped like a brittle eggshell, spraying its contents: a mass of gray and red.

A guard shrieked as the gore rained down on him and ducked away. The bed toppled towards us.

"Get back!" I tried to say, but it might have just been a growl as I thrust myself into the space. The shamblers rushed down on me like a burst pipe full of bitey people. Teeth chomped down on my arms, as my claws ripped into bodies. Grabbing necks and spines, I flung the animated corpses down the central shaft of the stairwell. Or tried to; there wasn't much of one. Most of them landed right on the stairway below me. Douglas's battering ram fell on anything still groaning, and the rest of them used gloved hands to shovel anything large further behind them. The plug of bodies dwindled to a stairway slick with blood; my fur had never been so wet as I pushed on. The guards stared at us mutely as we continued our climb against a trickle of shamblers, one or two at a time. These at least didn't get up after I hit them. I stopped to sniff at the door to floor nine, but didn't smell Cliff; at floor ten I heard him.

"You heard the lady! Let's go! Let's go!" He sounded... happy?

Ducking through the door, I stepped out into the hallway to a chorus of screams.

A group of about ten hospital staff and patients staggered to a stop in front of me, several of them piling into each other's backs Scooby Doo-style. "I don't think the central stair is clear, Cliff!" A man in scrubs shouted as they all scrabbled to run in the other direction.

"Well, it sure as hell ain't clear this way!" Farther down the hall, Cliff stood; his hospital gown had come open, displaying his own full moon and everything else as he swung the glittering Fey blade. Shamblers crowded the hallway in front of him, but they hung back, afraid.

Backing away from the entrance to the stairwell, I let out of a thick wuff to get Cliff's attention. He glanced back, doing a double take. "Woah, somebody had a bad day!" His sunny grin flashed. "That's the backup, keep moving!"

A shambler picked that moment to lunge at Cliff. The sword swung almost without Cliff's attention, cleaving through the shambler's chest as if it was no more substantial than air. The shambler fell in two pieces, spraying blood. Yet more than that. I felt a twist in my heart and a flare of light within the blood.

Cliff laughed, brandishing his sword at the monsters. "Ooooh, so close, anyone else want to try?"

"Give us life." They moaned as a chorus, their eyes brightening with a red light. "Give us our due."

"Okay, that's creepy." Cliff took a step back, sword twirling in his hand.

A bang at the other end of the hall attracted my attention; a new group of zombies poured out into the hallway. A set of feral grannies, black eyes lit with an eerie red light.

Cindy stepped out from the stairwell, assessed the situation with a quick glance up and down the hall. "Alright, ladies and gentlemen, if you'd please follow me! Don't mind the werewolf; she's here for your protection," she announced in a calm and level voice, gently patting my hip.

"Go!" Cliff added when the group didn't budge. Then the group surged toward the stairway.

The shades piloting these bodies weren't the brightest tools in the Twilight, but they understood when they were about to lose out on a meal. Shamblers surged from both ends; Cliff slashed and sliced, but had to give ground to the sheer mass of bodies. Meanwhile the feral grannies sprinted directly at me, one having enough wits to grab a parked hospital bed and wheel it at me like a battering ram. Praying to Luna that Cliff could handle his end, I squatted low and spread my arms like a goalie at a high-stakes soccer game. About half of Cliff's crew were in the stairway when I caught the first granny and hurled her headfirst into the second. The bed came barreling into me next; I grabbed it with both hands, planning to pick it up and swat the entire squad with it. Even braced against the impact, my paws skidded back a few inches. The granny driving it didn't stop; she spun to the right and launched herself past me, dodging beneath my awkward backhand. Panic seized me. I kicked the bed back into the oncoming two grannies and whirled in time to see the clever one spring like a feline towards an elderly man in a Red Sox cap. He swung up his cane like a batter bunting. She knocked him flat on his back, but he got that cane between him and her. In the half-second it took me to crouch in preparation for leaping towards him, Patricia slammed the deanimator into the granny's temple and fired. Head instantaneously emptied, she collapsed on top of the poor guy.

I flattened the remaining grannies as Patricia hauled the old guy onto his feet. With no one else heading in my direction, I tried to take a step towards helping Cliff. He was in a full fighting retreat now. Still slashing but the Shamblers in the back were throwing debris, including previously severed limbs.

"Abby! Abby! There's a big wave coming down the stairs!" I heard Douglas cry from the stairwell. The last few patients continued to hobble into the doorway, blocking it.

Momentarily torn, I glanced between Cliff and the stairwell. Cliff was still over twenty or thirty feet down the hallway. If he broke and ran, they'd catch him. I grabbed the bed, hoping that Cindy and the crew could defend the stairs long enough that I could help Cliff. Letting out a bellow to warn him, I hoisted the bed over my head and charged. Attempted to charge, at least; they didn't build the hospital to account for nine-foot-tall werewolves, let alone ones dramatically carrying furniture over their heads. I took out three lights and lost the mattress, but Cliff heard me coming. He stepped back when I smashed the bed down on the front row of his mob and shoved it hard. The shamblers piled up in front of it like bulldozed bodies.

"Damn." He eyed me up and down, smiling with a manic edge. "I don't think covered in gore is a great look for you, but it really highlights those moons you have in your head."

"un," I grunted, hoping he'd get the hint.

"Thanks, Abby." He reached out and squeezed my thigh before turning and running back towards the stairs. I peered over the mass of bodies; I couldn't count them all. They filled the hallway, and more were joining them through another stairway.

"Abby! Help!" Douglas and Patricia both called out.

I howled in response. Searching for some way to wedge the bed in their path but finding nothing, I gave the shamblers a final push and abandoned it; my hands kissed the floor as I caught back up with Cliff at the stairway. Right before I ducked through, another group arrived from the same door the grannies had. Different faces, but they moved identically. Same shades, different bodies.

I found a very crowded landing; one of the security guys had joined us and brought a fresh stretcher, which shamblers were enthusiastically piling themselves up against. Douglas was swinging the battering ram like a bat to crush skulls, but there was nowhere for the meat to go. Other shamblers were trying to crawl over the railings and drop down on us. Patricia shoved fresh ammo into the deanimator. Below, both Doc and Cindy kept their voices controlled as they guided people down the blood-slicked stair.

Taking the stretcher shield from the security guy, I shoved it against the horde as hard as I could. The mass of them all didn't budge. Hundreds of bodies packed the stairway. No give to it at all. How many people had the hospital stashed with the Rot? Growling, I slowly retreated down after the last of the group. A few steps and the bodies had room to fall to the ground. Fresh shamblers would crawl over those.

Cliff stayed right next to me, or more accurately, left of me, thrusting his sword into every shambler the blade could reach. For those he couldn't reach, I crushed arms and skulls with my teeth.

Together we'd kill until only inert meat leaned against me, retreat a few steps, and kill the fresh wave. Down we went. Either every shade I evicted was circling back to the seemingly endless stockpile on the floors above, or the number of shades that were coming through that rift was endless. It was like wading down a river of blood. With the steps too small for my feet, I kept losing my footing, smashing my knees into the steps again and again. Finally, as I prepared to slip by another door, Cliff nudged me. "We're here. Ground floor."

I practically fell out the door.

40

My human and wolf halves both tried to retreat into myself at the same time. While my strength and stamina are supernatural, holding back the weight of hundreds of zombies for however long it takes a bunch of hospital patients to get down nine flights of slick stairs took the last of it. Cliff was safe. My form wobbled, uncertain where to go until I let the wolf retreat. I needed to be able to talk. I regretted the decision instantly. Wolf me doesn't really mind tasting her enemies, but with her withdrawing so completely, I gagged on the various flavors of blood, brains, and rot coating my tongue.

"Woah, woah, woah!" Cliff knelt at my side as I shifted. "You can't stop here. They're still coming, Abby! You gotta get up." He set down the sword.

"I just need a moment." My voice mixed with a canine whine.

I lifted my head. They were right; I had picked the wrong time to become a defenseless human. The ground-floor lobby looked like a battlefield. Shamblers had reached it before we had; barricades blocked the hallways to the right and left. The only direction to go was out of the building.

"Are you the last ones?" somebody asked.

"They are!" Cindy answered him. Next thing I knew I was being lifted. It took me a moment to realize that it was Cindy and not Cliff that carried me.

I mutely waited, my vision hazed with exhaustion as Cindy bore me out into a street covered in light and tents. Where were all the police or fire department vehicles? There had to be dozens injured. The NLR ambulance Cindy carried me to seemed to be the only one in sight. What was going on? Nobody said anything as she slid me onto the stretcher.

"Get in, Cliff." she said, and he climbed up and collapsed into the rear seat that she indicated.

"Yes, Ma'am." Cliff laughed a bit, set his sword across his lap, and grabbed a fist full of hand towels from the shelf. "You should see the other guys," he commented as he attempted to wipe the blood from his hands. "I feel like I've been dipped in this stuff." After fighting in nothing more than a hospital gown and a sling, you couldn't tell either's original color.

Cindy stood on the back bumper looking between Cliff and me, nose wrinkled. "You two smell worse than you look, but that's not saying much. Let's get you both someplace safe." Stepping back, she shut the doors.

I roused myself from my stupor to protest when she reappeared, pulling herself into the driver's seat. "Cindy, we're not done. Andrew Millar's shade is downtown. We have to stop him there."

Cindy started the engine. "You're both done for tonight," Cindy said with motherly firmness. "Because of you two, they evac'd almost the entire hospital."

"Oh, is that why it took so long for us to get down the goddamn stairs?" Cliff blew out his lips.

"Those undead came down all the other stairways and staff barricaded the doors. With the elevators broken, the only way down was our stairway. You weren't simply waiting for the group you saved, but everyone on the floors below you," Cindy said, starting to drive.

I laughed, which turned into a tired cough, "And here I thought I was going to have to give a stern lecture to some poor patient about the meaning of running for her life. If OHSU is overrun, where are we going? Legacy?"

"I'm taking you both back to the house," Cindy said.

"Well, drop me off at my ma's," Cliff insisted.

"No," Cindy responded. Silence stretched as Cliff and I awaited an explanation.

"Uh, why not, Cindy?" Cliff twisted in his seat.

"There. Is. No. Emergency," Cindy answered, straining against every word.

A little flicker of adrenalin gave me the strength to lift my head and look towards her. She'd discarded her wig at some point and individual cords of muscle stood out on her neck. "C-cindy?" I asked.

"Return to your, stations." She vibrated with effort, bringing the ambulance to a stop at the end of the ramp down from the hill OHSU sat on. A left turn would take us towards the Ross Island bridge and across the river, a right into southwest Portland towards our firehouse.

"The hell is going on?" Cliff gripped a nearby shelf and strained to pull himself from the seat.

"Gah!" Cindy turned the wheel right, nearly collapsing against it. "Sorry, I can't! It hurts! Oh, Jebus, it hurts."

"Is it Andrew Millar?" I asked, "Is he forcing you?"

"Yes." Cindy drove on through the night. "There's a pack

of juice boxes in one of the lower cabinets, Cliff. Give them to Abby; I think she's dehydrated. I'll try to get you help at the station."

I clawed at the exhaustion holding me to the stretcher. Tried to sit up and only succeeded in lifting my head. That brought the length of my body into view. Not a single spot of my skin was not tinted red or had a fleck of gore adhered to it. Like Carrie after they'd dumped a bucket of pig's blood on her head, except they'd hit me with a second bucket filled with organ meat. But beneath that, my body had withered, my ribs protruding along my sides. Straining hard, I managed to peel one shoulder off the stretcher before failing to resist gravity and falling back. The effort left me panting, and I had to close my eyes as the ceiling lights started to spin.

Once they closed, I didn't have the strength to open them again.

* * *

"Abby! Abby!"

Something patted my cheek.

"Come on! Sit up a little."

Something soft pushed its way beneath my head before a sweet wetness stole into my mouth. I swallowed. Sustenance. My stomach burbled, waking into a painful life. *More.* My lips sealed around the plastic tube in my mouth and sucked until it had nothing more than air to give me.

"Good girl," whispered the voice. "Here's another."

My eyes fluttered open to find Cliff's face hovering over me; he'd wiped the gore from his face, but it only made his exhaustion and worry more clear. He tried to smile, but his lips remained compressed in a tight line. I sucked at his offered juice box as I looked around the room; we were in the firehouse's locker room. Me laying on a stretcher in the center, lockers to one side, showers on the other. An IV bag hung from a pole beside me, but the cannula had been removed from my arm already. "Cliff? What?"

"You've been out for maybe ten minutes." He glanced back at the door to the station. "Almost everybody's here. It was fine when we arrived, everybody swarmed all over you and me. Cindy explained to me there was a voice in her head that once it told her to do something, it hurt like fire until she did it."

"Contracts," I gasped through dry lips, "the employment contracts, he's using them to force everyone to his service."

"That... don't make sense, but whatever. We were trying to let you rest, but new orders came down a few minutes ago to be on the lookout for you. They are trying to resist the order, but they can't hold out long. We gotta be gone, and I can't carry you with my arm," Cliff said. "Can you move?"

My limbs all felt as if they'd been packed with lead inside and my lungs ached with every breath, an echo of the rebar that had been shoved through my chest. Not waiting for a response, Cliff took one of my hands and pulled me up into a sitting position, then turning, he draped my arm across his shoulders. With a grunt of effort, he stood, dragging me to my feet. I got a nose full of his scent, and my mouth flooded with moisture. With me nearly a foot shorter, he had to stoop down low. I amended that, my legs didn't feel full of lead, but Jell-O laden with lead; incapable of bearing my weight, they more flopped around than anything as Cliff made three shaky steps towards the door.

I swallowed back my spittle before saying, "Cliff, this isn't going to work." My stomach twisted like a wrung-out wash cloth with every breath I took.

Meat, wolf me demanded as my teeth sharpened.

"What I the hell am I supposed to do, Abby?" he snapped back at me. "I'm trying, here."

Hot warm meat. Clean, he smelled clean of disease. My guts roared with hunger. All I'd have to do is turn my head and bite into that shoulder. It'd be easy.

No. I jerked my arm from his grip and tumbled down onto the floor, with only enough strength to catch myself with my elbows. "Cliff. I'm starving." I could feel Luna's power flowing into me, but there was nothing for it to latch onto.

"My mom will feed you. Mom's good like that. Come on, please get up, Abby." Cliff's voice squeaked with panic.

Someone called out through the door. "Cliff! We're calling! We can't stand it anymore! Get her out of here!"

I looked toward the voice and saw the stretcher I'd been lying on. A simple wooden board with straps through holes running down the length of the board. Straps.

"Drag the stretcher." I panted, managing to half-roll to it. "Strap in my hips and tie the top pair around you."

"I've only got one hand Abby!" His voice a near scream.

"Do it or go without me!" I snarled. There'd be food in the kitchen, maybe there'd be enough to plug this sucking hole inside me.

"You are such a pain in my ass, Abby." Cliff stomped over, grabbed my ankle, and dragged me back onto the stretcher. I did my best to tie myself in as he dropped down behind me and struggled with the straps. With his hand and his teeth, he managed to get a knot in and loop the wide straps around his waist. "I don't understand." He heaved himself up to his feet, lifting the head of the stretcher up to a thirty-degree angle with the floor. The straps around my thighs constricted but held. "You were a giant badass werewolf not a half-hour ago," he huffed, nearly throwing himself through the exit door and into the night. "How do I have more stamina than you? I don't get it." He dragged me across the BBQ patio and grunted as he pulled me up into the narrow forest behind the station. "I should be riding you!"

I didn't answer. I didn't have answers for him. The well inside was agonizingly empty; summoning the ghosts had left me numbed emotionally, but now my body felt ravaged. *Food, meat,* wolf me repeated in my head, pacing around my insides like a starving animal. All I could do was breathe and smell the foul stench of the Rot creeping into the air. Cliff swore and struggled through the woods, around a house, and then onto a street. Sirens sounded from the north, and he swore louder as the tail end of the stretcher scraped across the pavement. "Hey! I don't suppose anybody wants to help a brother out?" He called out as the street sloped uphill. "Anybody?"

A distant wolf's howl cut against the sirens. Victoria's song. *We're coming. Hang on.*

Cliff slogged on, climbing the hill step by step. "That just figures. Nah, that's fine, I got it. I never liked this neighborhood, anyway."

Someone called out. "They told us not to leave our homes or we won't get through the night." A man stood on the balcony of a two-story apartment building that over-looked the road.

"Who told you that?" Cliff hollered back, not pausing.

We did. The sinister whisper came from either side of the road. *You are out after the Pharoah's curfew. Your blood is forfeit.*

"Ah, crap, man, I'm sorry. I got kids, ya know." A door slammed.

"Abby?" Cliff called to me, "You don't happen to feel a

second wind coming on, maybe? Because these three look less than friendly!"

From the deepest dark beneath the trees, three shadows stretched out into the road; they slithered through the air like snakes, bulbous heads on tails of darkness.

My crude ring pulsed with light as the shades approached. Cliff snorted and strained like the wounded animal he was, yet moved a little bit faster. What had Victoria said in the mausoleum? "We walk in Luna's name, she who shines brightest in the night. It is her work we do. You will not bar our path." I added a little growl to the end, feeling like a toothless terrier. The light of the ring steadied.

They stopped, hanging back about ten feet from my ring, and stood upright on their tails.

It is her, said the one on the left.

Her light flickers, observed the right.

Fetch the ones who wear the flesh, ordered the middle one, and the two that flanked it slithered off towards the oncoming sirens. It made no attempt to breach the light, instead it circled around us, laughing softly to itself. *You do Luna's work, do you? So do we. We both war against the children of dawn. To remind them that they are not as mighty as they believed.*

"Go away," I told the shade as it circled us. The sirens, definitely police cars, were almost to the firehouse now.

"Yeah! Take those creepy eyes of yours, and shove them right up your floaty ass crack," Cliff said between huffs of breath.

Why do you serve her when she is so weak, big man? the shade asked. *She hungers for your flesh. She drools over the scent of your blood.*

"Abby would never eat anyone!" Cliff said, slowing his pace just a bit. "Right, Abby?"

I gave a weak chuckle as I imagined the sweet taste of warm meat on my tongue. "I'd never eat you, Cliff."

"That's... a little more specific than I was expecting, Abby."

Still lying, the shade hissed.

"On purpose," I amended. "Can we talk about who precisely my diet includes after we get to your mother's?"

"That depends whether or not my mom's on the menu," Cliff huffed, but he didn't stop moving.

A hunger pang hit me so hard I cried out. "Stop talking about food!" I begged.

"Shit. Shit." The pace increased again. "Hang on. Almost there." Then, under his breath, "Shoulda dragged you to the bodega down the street, cuz Mom is gonna kill me."

The shade laughed.

"Cliff! What the hell are you doing?!" Sophie's voice split the night.

Mine. The shade slithered out of my vision.

Sophie screamed, "Get off me!" The thunder boom of a shotgun sounded.

Cliff bellowed his sister's name; the stretcher banged to the ground, slamming my head against its head pad. I twisted to see Cliff running up towards his sister. She clawed at her neck, hands passing through the coils of shadow around it. The shade's eyes glowed like hot coals as it choked the life from her. Cliff pounded through the twenty paces to her and delivered a savage punch to the shade's head.

It passed right through.

"No! Let her go!" Cliff swung again to the same effect.

In a moment, the shade laughed. *Wait your turn.*

I called out to him, "Cliff! Drag her back here!"

With a cry of fear and frustration, he reached down,

seized his sister's arm, and pulled hard. Sophie became a rope in a tug of war between Cliff and the shade. One step, two, back towards me and my bubble of moonlight. The shade released Sophie. In the span of her desperate gasp for air, the shade darted forward, wrapping itself around Cliff's neck instead. His good arm flailed as he spun around in a blind circle.

Digging long nails into the pavement, I reached out to wolf me but found no strength in her, only aching hunger. Reaching further I found Victoria, body ablaze with her swift power. She had crossed the bridge. Close but not close enough to help Cliff. "Towards me!" I urged him. He staggered two steps towards me before falling down on one knee.

Luna, Please! I prayed, pulling off my ring and tossing it up the hill. Its light guttered out as soon as it left my hand, but it hit the road with a ringing ting. Sophie, who had gotten up to her hands and knees, whipped her head up at the sound. Her head turned to track the ring as it bounced and then rolled up towards her.

"Hit it with that," I called at her.

She pounced on it. The instant her hand touched it, the entire street lit with a pulse of moonlight as if Luna had tossed down a thunderbolt. Sophie emitted a primal screech, springing up from the ground, her fist a blaze of silver fire that she drove up through the shade killing her brother. The flames scythed through it and the shade fell from Cliff with a wail of pain as it dissolved into the air.

Sophie didn't watch its destruction, she rounded on me with speed, making the beads on her braids clack together. Pale light shone out of her pupils that dimmed as she stalked over to where I lay. "I really hate you," she said as the last remnant of light left her eyes, and tossed me the ring.

It flipped down and stuck to the surface of my palm. "You saw Luna."

Sophie didn't answer, but bent to grab the straps and started hauling me up the hill. We swiftly passed Cliff, still on the ground coughing with his hand on his throat. "Come on, bro, shake it off and give me a hand with your girlfriend."

With a nod he slapped his hand against his chest, coughed once more, and swiftly caught up. His huge hand scooped up the tail end of the stretcher, and together the siblings swiftly crested the hill with me. The pair set a pace that had Sophie nearly jogging. The sirens were getting even closer now, and headlights shone on the power lines as we swung into the yard of a two-story house as the thin figure of Gloria, Cliff's mom, held open the door.

41

———

"Cliff! What have you done now?" Gloria asked, once she'd shut the door and locked it.

The house smelled of meat, young, old, and cooked. That's all I could see as they set me down. "Need some food, mama," Cliff said as I heard the breaking of a refrigerator's seal. I nearly drowned in my drool.

"Dear god in heaven, what happened to her?!"

"Here, Abby, chicken." Something was shoved into my hands. It didn't matter what it was; it could have been an arm. I shoved my face into it and bit down.

Meat. Glorious meat. Still a tiny bit warm. I tore off a chunk, swallowed. Felt it travel down my throat and fall through a terrible chasm inside me. My entire being rippled once it hit bottom. *Yes! Finally.* Then roared for more. Another bite, another swallow, bones crunched between my teeth, with every morsel tossed into the abyss, strength surged back into my limbs allowing me to shove more of it into my mouth.

"Damn, guess she likes your cooking, Gloria." A new voice laughed uneasily.

"She exhausted herself getting me out of the hospital. She saved hundreds of people, mama." Cliff said as the fridge opened again.

"Those are for lunch tomorrow!" Gloria protested as I tossed the plastic container away. I sat at a table, a very long dining table, in the center of the long room. Nearly a dozen meat, no people, all dark-skinned, stared at me from a set of couches and chairs arranged around a TV.

"Abby, here!" Cliff called and I turned to the sound of his voice, snatching an object from midair. Sniff, more food, sweet fat. I tore open the plastic bag and sank my teeth into the stack of salami. It tasted so good I would have howled, but it would have taken time away from eating. Whenever I found my hands empty, Cliff would toss more food at me as he attempted to explain what had happened to me, but he was wrong. Andrew Millar had succeeded, had killed me. Murdered me several times over. I figured it out as the chasm inside of me slowly filled, my body churning to devour its nourishment, finally quenching the pangs that had begun as I had run off that bridge. Healing from that had depleted my reserves and then the hordes in the hospital had inflicted a constant stream of minor wounds as I protected Cliff. By the end of it I had nothing left, my insides hollowed out.

First rule of werewolfing: if you've been injured, you must eat. I resolved to tell Victoria that, or maybe make a pamphlet, as I watched myself shovel the entire contents of the Gifford's double-wide refrigerator into my maw. The frozen turkey slowed me down a little; I had cracked it in half when someone shouted, "It's the cops!"

Dimly I knew that meant police, but I continued swallowing chunks of frozen turkey as the Giffords swarmed into action around me. Gloria ordered everyone to get the kids into the basement. Cliff called my name.

I ignored it all until a voice shouted through the walls. "Heeey, Lass! Guess who's back? How'd you like another round? Really shiny bullets!"

With that taunt, I came back to myself, a growl rising in my throat that sent Cliff stepping back. He seemed small; everyone around me had gotten smaller. My stomach whined as I placed the half-eaten turkey onto the kitchen counter. Human fear and stress filled the air; grief and the sour notes of the Rot hung beneath that. I stood, towering over their kitchen, in my hybrid form, my ears flattened against the ceiling. The white fur on my arms was still patchy and thin, and that space inside me still had room to fill, but it would be enough. It had to be.

"Abby! Go out the back," Cliff urged me and at the same time, I felt Victoria arrive and the gossamer scents of Secret and Rey.

We're here, she whispered into my mind, and with it she sent the image of three SUVs pointed towards the house. Their doors were splayed open, humans standing behind them, each leveling a long black gun at the front door. One, who had to be Scully, stood forward from the others, bullhorn in one hand and a revolver size of his head in the other.

Human me wondered how many of them were actual police forced into this; wolf me did not care. We couldn't let them hurt anyone in this house. Two versus a horde of guns, but it was better than one versus them. I couldn't go try to parley, he'd simply shoot at me, and I'd seen how ineffective modern walls were against bullets. I needed something truly bulletproof. Or I had to hit them before they saw me.

We flank. Ready, Victoria sent to me.

Wait, I urged her, imagining Scully causally wheeling and shooting her when she tore into the back line. I had to get him focused on me first.

My gaze fell on the half-eaten turkey and then the refrigerator. A large stainless-steel model, just wider than my shoulders. That would stop bullets and be big enough to crouch behind. I looked to where Cliff stood, next to an open sliding glass door more than big enough. This wouldn't earn me any points with Cliff's mother, but it might work. Holding a finger against the tip of my muzzle for silence, which spurred worried looks among all the humans, I went to the fridge.

"Haven't you had enough?" Sophie hissed at me. "What are you going to do about this?"

I grabbed the top of the fridge, dragged it out from the wall, wrapped my long arms around it, and lifted. Heavy, but carrying it wasn't nearly the strain I feared; my tail wagged trying to provide a counterweight.

"This isn't a takeout restaurant!" Gloria admonished me. "If you're going to run away, just go!"

I shook my head, but I had no time to explain to her that I wasn't running. Hustling as fast I could, I ducked out through the door as Scully shouted one more warning. Once outside, I heaved the fridge up higher, my hands grabbing hold of its far bottom corners, and carried it to the corner of the house. A driveway packed with cars ran down the side of the house. I howled out a challenge and charged.

"Be sharp, lads! She's coming around the side!" Scully screeched. Gunfire stuttered before I made it halfway; dropping the fridge to the pavement, I plowed my shoulder into it. Three SUVs parked on the street, and the house sat only three car lengths from the road, but only the leftmost SUV had a firing line at me. The fridge shuddered under the impact of bullets, the steel ringing as I pushed it forward. As soon as I reached the corner of the house, a fresh chorus of guns joined, including the cannonlike boom of Scully's pistol. I ducked down low, shoving my hands beneath the fridge as shrapnel pelted my sides.

Going! Victoria charged into their rear, and men shrieked with alarm.

Luna, give me strength. I heaved the refrigerator to the sky with every muscle I possessed. It arced into the air, doors opening like wings, shedding jars and containers of food.

"Heads up!" Someone screamed. Those who were not spinning to face the wolf in their midst, were lifting their heads to follow the fridge's flight. Including Scully. He fired two bullets into it before his gaze broke away and leveled at me. The throw had forced me to stand to my full height, and I was still lowering my arms as he brought the barrel down towards me.

Dead to rights.

A gleaming blade swung out of a ripple of air and chopped down through Scully's elbow. The gun went off as the arm fell; the bullet whizzed through my whiskers, parting my cheek fur. At the end of the blade was a fox in a kimono. Nothing human about Rey now, except that being about two feet tall, she wielded a straight sword taller than her with thumbless paws. Yet, she whirled the sword around and cleaved straight through Scully' knee before the fridge cratered in the roof of the center SUV. The moment unpaused, I took a single step, slapped my paw-hands against the ground and bounded across the lawn. Claws found flesh as I landed amid already bloody men. Victoria's golden eyes shone, smiling with bloody teeth. The corners of my eyes registered movement from either side as guns swung in my direction. I ducked low, grabbed the undercarriage of two SUVs and flipped them both onto their sides. Rot and blood flooded the night as I hurled the vehicle to the left and Victoria swept around it. Bone crunched beneath my feet; one stumbled back trying to lift his weapon, only for Victoria to clamp jaws around the back of his neck and bring him down.

With that I heard no more scraping of boots on pavement. I stood and peered over the last SUV to find only two slitted green eyes gazing up at me over a toothy grin. She clutched the silver shiv I had made in both hands. Her bare feet stood on the neck of a body as her little shoulders heaved. "Abby!" Crying my name with pure joy as she sprang up onto the roof of the SUV and launched herself at me. I caught her and hugged her close, despite a sinking realization that I truly was the world's worst parent. Good thing that little dress of hers appeared to be self-cleaning. Cradling her protectively as she purred against the nape of my neck, I searched for any more movement among the cop cars.

Safe now, Victoria reported, popping around the corner with a wag of greeting, her large ears pointed in different directions. *Shades fled.*

My heart lifted as I kneeled to thank her with many laps across the top of her head.

She whined in frustration and licked my nose. *More to say. Can't.*

I nodded, understanding. This... wolf speak was amazing, but limited to what wolves themselves could say.

Victoria bounced up on her hind legs and I hugged her, too. My pack had come to my rescue.

"Stop wasting time," Rey demanded, standing on top of

the same SUV Secret had jumped off of; I hadn't heard her at all. She still appeared as a very large fox with bright red fur, sword slung casually over her shoulder. Her features were sharp and pointed; the tiny fangs protruding over her bottom lip and the narrowed eyes gave her a vicious aura. The small kimono she wore did nothing to negate the malice she exuded, and fear prickled down my neck as I recognized it. Rey was channeling Reynard, her other parent legend, a master manipulator and casual murderer. The brightness of her fur hinted that she had plenty of power to spare tonight, too. "I'm not here for you." Her ears went flat. "I saved you and your overly muscled heart for one reason. Tell me who has Cindy bonded herself to? Right now! Who have I lost her to?" Hurt strained her words as three tails rose up behind her and stood like a scorpion's; I had no doubt of their sting.

It took an effort to pull wolf me back far enough to regain my speech in the face of that threat, but I managed. I considered calling her out on her loyalty oath, but it would probably only enrage her further. She had saved me from that silver bullet after all, no matter how she wanted to frame it. "Rey, it's not her fault. She's been entrapped. There were hidden clauses in her employment contract. That's why Victoria has to stay as a wolf for now; he has a hold on her human half."

Rey's vulpine features softened. "Entrapped? She didn't know?"

I looked straight into her amber eyes, "I will promise you, on pain of releasing you from your bond, that she did not intentionally bind herself to this Pharaoh."

"Then..." She sniffed, her aura of malice fading a tad, "You will take me to her. I will break this hold on her and bring her home. With me where she belongs."

"We're heading there next. I won't leave her behind." I turned to see Cliff and his family watching us, "Or anybody else who's helped us tonight." Scully would be back before too long. I hadn't punched him with my silver ring. And even if I had, I wasn't sure it would destroy him. Not with that huge hole on the bridge.

I set Secret down and she held my hand as I approached the Gifford clan. Cliff sat collapsed in a chair. Sophie and Gloria stood with their arms crossed. While Sophie scowled, Gloria held a guarded expression. Sophie didn't give me the chance to speak. "Just turn around. You don't bring any good to us. My dad died protecting you. Now you're murdering cops on our doorstep."

"They weren't cops, Sophie." Cliff said, his voice a spent whisper.

She rounded on him. "And you brought her to us! How-"

"Sophie, that's enough!" Gloria snapped at her and coughed. The fit stilled Sophie to silence. Gloria, then, was the source of the Rot I had smelled inside. "Let her talk," she finally managed after the coughing subsided, and looked expectantly at me.

I took a deep breath. "Thank you all very much for your hospitality, and I apologize for the damage. I will replace what I broke. But-"

"We're not safe here." Gloria finished.

"No one's safe on this side of the river, but friends of mine are going to be targeted. We're going to the firehouse next to rescue our friends and then get them out of here." I had no idea how we were going to do that; hopefully whatever method Rey had for breaking the contracts would be something we could use on everyone.

"Jesus on high, give me strength," Gloria muttered before pronouncing, "Alright, we're going with you."

"Mom!" Sophie protested.

Gloria responded with soft steel in her voice, "The devil you know. Get your dad's guns. Cliff, get up."

42

Gloria gave me a gray robe and then herded the rest of the family out of the house. A dozen people, including two kids about Secret's age. The three of them talked softly among themselves as Sophie distributed weapons to the adults. Each time they took a firearm, they'd look at me with calculation in their eyes. Staring at me, with my blood-covered hand resting on Victoria's head as she leaned against my hip. If it had just been us, maybe one of them would have taken the shot. Particularly the thin old man who'd claimed Scully's gun as his own; his stare lingered the longest, but as his gaze slid to Rey, he finally dropped his eyes. Rey paced impatiently, her colors brighter than the night normally allows, as she rested the flat of her sword against the back of her neck. A constant reminder that the world no longer worked the way it had a few months ago.

Victoria straightened as Cliff and Gloria approached; neither had taken a weapon from Sophie, but Gloria held a dark wooden cross in her hand. Cliff only held a can of cold brew which he took long gulps from. He didn't seem to even notice Victoria; his eyes were on Rey.

Rey stopped her pacing to watch him back. "Where is the sword of summer, Sir Knight? I cannot call you to service without it, and we might need you yet."

His grin gave a nervous flash of his teeth as he checked both my expression and his mother's arching eyebrow before answering. "Back at the station. I only had one hand, and needed it to carry Abby."

"You will retrieve it when we arrive," Rey said with cool detachment.

"Rey, I'm spent." He dropped his voice low.

"Then we are fortunate that I am not." The corner of her muzzle flicked upward in a brief smile before she resumed her pacing.

Wolf me growled; Rey had her hooks in two of my friends. Cliff's eyes met mine for the briefest second before he looked away.

"Abby, I needed her help to get the sword out of police lockup. You'd disappeared, and I didn't know if you were coming back." He gave a shrug with his left shoulder.

"Could have told me. What do you owe her?" I asked; no wonder he'd declined to go into Cindy's house with me.

"Haven't you learned your lesson about taking shortcuts, Cliff?" Gloria asked, her tone tender while shaking with barely contained rage. "Wasn't three years enough?"

"Mom, it's not a shortcut if it's the only road. If I hadn't had that sword I'd have died long before Abby got to me tonight. Now let's get moving. Stick close to Abby." He held his mother's gaze with little effort.

Gloria thrust that cross against her son's chest. Nothing happened. Cliff glanced down at it and chuckled.

"Just checking." Gloria closed her eyes and swallowed something back as she pulled the cross away. She turned to address her family, "Alright, everyone. As George would say, double check you got everything, and let's move."

"If anything gets weird, stay within ten feet of Abby." Cliff added.

Within another minute we were walking back down the road Cliff had labored on. Victoria ranged ahead, and I tasted the musk of Rey's glamor. The rain had stopped, but our breath swirled in the beams of the Giffords' flashlights.

We'd walked halfway back to the station when Victoria growled. *Danger. Shades.*

I touched my ring, but Rey placed a paw on my forearm. "No. Don't call to her. You're hard enough to hide without her shining through you."

"What do we do?" I whispered back. "This is my only weapon against them."

She snorted. "That is not a weapon; you are the weapon Luna is forging. Take this and strike it very softly." From within her sleeve, she pulled the teapot bell I had crafted for summoning the shades and pushed it into my hands. "Do not falter. I will do the rest."

With that she held her sword in her teeth and rushed down the street, disappearing into a bush.

I had plenty of misgivings as I turned the silver over in my hands, feeling its pull on my being, but I did as instructed. Tapping the spoon against the chime produced a soft *tik*.

tik

Tik

With every footfall I produced that soft atonal noise. Beside me, Cliff snapped his fingers; he peered at his hand curiously, as if not sure why he did it. It spread through the group, a beat that was barely a sound, skin meeting skin. Then Gloria's voice rose in a whisper of a hymn. The striking of the bell had brought the dead. Did this soft sound do the opposite somehow?

We were going to have a chance to find out; above the trees and houses that diverted the road off the direct path to the fire house, shadows twisted, free-flying ribbons of darkness against the gray clouds. My hair prickled as their gaze swept over my procession. Victoria crept between the houses, and found the ground thick with the scent of sweet rot. Mushrooms forced their way up through the wet mat of discarded leaves and pine needles. She pulled back, and I guided the procession around the bend, unwilling to risk anyone's footing through the forest.

We swung down around to the main street, and I noticed that thin black tendrils were creeping up the walls of some of the houses. My thoughts immediately went to the isolation colony, and my pulse crept into my ears. It only been a half hour since Cliff had dragged me out of the fire station, maybe an hour, tops. Surely it couldn't be that bad!

Gunfire answered my question, not just one; it sounded as if an entire war zone had appeared in front of the firehouse. Fear made the beat stumble as the entire group ducked down. The eruption ended as swiftly as it began, and I felt the itch of eyes. I hit the chime, *tik, tik,* but the spell of whatever we had been doing had broken and the group looked at each other warily.

I'll see, Victoria sent as she crept around the side of the building. *Clear, but,* and the same mix of rot and the blood of the one that had attacked us up at the house filled my mind. What had Rey done? Or had she screwed up?

Wolf me slipped down into my limbs, ready if needed as I stole down the last ten squares of sidewalk and looked down the street. Four buildings down, a police SUV and a large truck sat in the middle of the road. Both the cars and the surrounding buildings had been raked with bullets. Bodies lay slumped on the ground. I had the sudden mental image of a fox wielding a tommy gun. Above the scene, the shades writhed.

Close eyes! Victoria sent as something flew up into the cloud of angry shades.

My eyes shut in time, but the searing flash dazzled anyway before a sharp crack hammered my ear drums. A flashbang. When I could bear to open my eyes, the shades were gone and Rey strode by the door to the firehouse, gesturing for us to hurry. We hustled down the street along with whispered curses from Cliff's family. As we did, I couldn't help but look between the truck and the SUV. A circle of bodies, guns roughly pointed at each other.

Rey wasn't in the mood for explaining. "Open the door! Open the door!" Staring fixedly at the steel handle. I grabbed it and wrenched it open. She shot inside, a red blur of motion. "Cindy!" calling the name with such force that it echoed back. I huffed; I wouldn't be getting much more out of her now. We needed to know how long we had before the shades came back. Cliff took the door from me, and I headed in.

Except for the brightness of Rey's excitement, sour despair flooded the station. It made me hesitant to follow Rey's trail into the vehicle bay.

I heard muffled coughing and then voices:

"I'll raise."

"Call."

In the center of the room, four card tables had been set up and nearly every paramedic NLR employed sat at one. Drawn faces stared listlessly at the cards in their hands. Some eyes turned toward me as I entered, but most remained centered on their game.

Except for Cindy; a now humanlike Rey had wrapped herself around her, kissing her with a desperate passion. Cindy's eyes slowly closed as her arms wrapped around Rey, fingers threading up through her hair. The seal of their lips broke just long enough for Cindy to say, "Fold," before she rejoined Rey's affection.

A violent cough pulled my eyes off the pair and to Douglas, who wore a blue surgical mask. "Don't worry," he said and sniffed, "Still me. No voices."

"That's good," I said, smiling nervously, "Cards? It's like a real fire department in here."

That got some muffled laughter as the EMTs stirred from their funk a little.

Douglas turned back to the game and pushed a chip into the pile at the center of the table. "Call. That bastard told us to play cards in the name of the Pharaoh and now that's all we can do, Abby."

I was about to ask what bastard, but then I spotted the corpse on the ground, his head split open like a melon, blood and rot tendrils spilling from his head.

"Sorry for calling them on you. Hurts if we don't obey," Patricia continued, from the next table over. "Told us no one gets saved tonight. Dispatch is silent but the 911 system is logging a lot of calls. A few of us tried to drive for the bridge." She looked toward the three parked ambulances; one looked like it had hit a pole, "They laughed at that, but didn't try to stop us. The pain did, though. It's hard to drive when your chest feels like it's packed with ice.

Both Patricia and Douglas coughed hard, turning away from their tables. I looked down and found tiny black and purple mushrooms pushing through a crack in the concrete. Coop up a bunch of medics while a disaster happened, and they'd be a buffet for the Rot.

"Abby." Cliff spoke my name, and he stood in the door to the office, holding the Fey sword. "Can you give me a hand with this?" Inside the office he pointed at a pile of boxes. The employment contracts were still here. They hadn't been shipped to Legacy. "I'm thinking we light the BBQ in the back. Think that will work?"

"It'd better," I said, not having another idea. At least for those who hadn't pulled shifts up at the funeral. As I bent to grab a box, Cliff shut the door a bit harder than he needed to.

"So, you know how to do it now. That's Victoria out there, isn't it? Can she shift? Is she stuck?" Parts of his face quivered as he fought to maintain a neutral expression.

"Accidentally, we figured it out. Blood, bite and maybe a blessing." I smiled, feeling awkward. Wolf me perked up, paying attention, but didn't howl at the rest of me to bring Cliff into the pack. "She's not stuck, but if she becomes human, then she's in the same boat as everyone else. So, she has to stay wolf until... until I figure out how to end Andrew."

"Is your offer still open?" He asked, finally letting the pain show on his face. "Even with Rey's help, I can't imagine I'm going to be much use tonight. Those drugs didn't help with the Rot, either."

I set the papers down to give him a careful hug. "It's still open, Cliff."

More pack. Wolf me whispered excitedly as he squeezed back. His entire body trembled a bit, a sneeze might knock him over.

"Okay how's it work?" he asked.

"Not tonight. I gave Victoria a full pint of my blood over three months ago and noticed the changes only yesterday." I rose up on my toes and gave him a peck on the cheek.

"Three months? That's not quick enough to cure the Rot, Abby." His brows furrowed.

He had a good point, but I sniffed at his mouth to make sure. "Cliff, you don't have the Rot. At least not as bad as you did. With all spores around here, that might not last, though. I guess those drugs worked, after all."

He pulled away, shaking his head. "Abby, they didn't. I was coughing petty badly right up till…" He trailed off, eyes searching a space only he could see. "Right until the damn zombies tore down my door. Then I sliced through that mother as if it were warm butter." His grin turned on, which I hadn't seen since finding him in that hospital. "Just incredible. Like I'm a goddamn anime swordsman; next thing I know I'm cutting one in half who's trying to bite a nurse fending them off with a pile of binders. Then she's following me and we're pulling others out of rooms. I'm cutting, I'm cutting, but they keep coming. Then there's too many folks and I could only be in one place at once. I realized we were in trouble." His smile fell. "Bastards are getting wary and then, Abby, you showed up, looking straight out of a horror movie and totally beautiful."

Cliff was the only person I knew who would call a hulking gore-covered werewolf beautiful, and it made me smile. He'd be beautiful too, soon, as long he didn't get cold feet. Soon. Instead, I focused on the symptoms he described, "Sounds like you experienced euphoria," I whispered. "That's it. That how to counter the Rot." I hugged him again.

"Ow! Easy!" He winced. "What do you mean?"

Hugged him a little too hard, apparently. I let him go and grabbed the box again. "It feeds on despair, so euphoria must poison it! Come on. Let's go burn these things."

43

I found Victoria standing vigil at the door to the street, her long slender black body braced against the door, neck craning around its edge to stare up the street. *More coming. Gathering storm.* Next to her stood Secret, one small hand pressed against Victoria's side, her tail's tip twitching.

"How long do we have?" I asked.

Victoria shared the scent of the twilight's sweet rot, but it had a crackling quality to it that lifted hairs all along my arms and legs as if lightning were about to strike.

"Shit," I murmured; we didn't have time for much. "Seal the building. There's a couple canisters of salt in the kitchen."

Through our connection, a pack bond, I guess, I witnessed Victoria's wolf open the barest crack to the place where she'd sealed her human half. I wanted to pull her back; while her wolf's love and eagerness to help radiated, I missed the woman and our fumbling efforts to define what we were to each other. The crack closed and Victoria, her wolf, gave a huff of agreement.

"I'll help," Secret announced. "I'll show you the kitchen.

This way." She moved past me down the hallway before she finished speaking.

"Stay inside!" I hollered after her as she dodged around a few of the Gifford family, who had clustered in the hallway. They all got out of the way as Victoria followed her.

Secret paused at the kitchen door. "I saw how Rey hid us! I can do it, too!"

"Just be careful," I grumbled, hurrying down the hall myself. Ignoring Sophie's *you are a terrible parent* stare.

"Hey, there's four more boxes of these," Cliff barked at the bystanders, "Somebody give us a hand."

I let him press his family into helping and went outside. The wind immediately buffeted my too-large robe and slapped my cheek with wet drizzle. My bare feet hit a patch of black ice on the concrete patio. The box in my grasp fell onto the concrete pad. It burst open, spilling out a fan of manila folders in a line across the patio. Hurrying, I scooped them up and dumped them onto the small picnic table we called the smoking room, placing the one labeled Cindy Maveri on top. Then I turned towards the rusting BBQ grill. I opened it and paused. The grill had two black plastic dials and a red button; all instructions and markings were worn away. I turned a dial, but heard no hiss of gas.

"Shit. Don't let them get wet!" Cliff chided as he came through the door behind me.

"How's this thing work, Cliff?" I asked as I fiddled with the knob to no avail.

"You gotta turn on the gas first. Outta the way." He jostled me to the side and bent to twist a valve on the propane tank. Wolf me bristled, but I let him handle it as the grill hissed to life. The button clunked and the grill lit with a whoosh of flame. He grabbed the blackened grate off the top and tossed it aside. Taking the top folder from the pile, he laid it carefully into the grill and frowned at it as smoke drifted up around it.

The wind kicked up a notch, and I had to pull my robe tight to my body to stop it from billowing out. "Cliff, we need to do this faster."

He shook his head, "Gotta get it going first. Need it hot. Then we can pile it like logs. You ever built a fire in the rain before?"

Memories of camping with Jimmy burbled up, lying together listening to the downpour beat against the nylon. I shook them away. "No, I never did. Jimmy always did the fires." He opened up one of the files, started crumpling up individual sheets and tossed them into the grill, they caught immediately. I moved to help and soon the single folder was surrounded by orange flame dancing in the gusting wind.

A white something whipped around the outside of the patio, I jumped before I realized it had been Victoria, running with a canister of salt in her mouth.

"You never struck me as an outdoorsy type," Cliff commented with a smile, adding two more folders to the pile.

"Jimmy was a boy scout for a while. Camping with friends was a good excuse to get out of the house for a weekend. It's just that I didn't have any friends other than Jimmy," I said, not really sure why I was sharing that.

His smile faltered. "Ah, sorry for stirring up bad memories."

"My therapist taught me to call them soured. We had good times but where they led..." I shook my head in disbelief that I was talking at all to him about this.

"What he did wasn't your fault." He blew out his lips, letting them vibrate.

"You're wrong," I said, adding another folder to the pile;

they were burning now and there was more than heat coming off them, a tension radiated with the flames. "He couldn't have done what he did if it hadn't been for me. It's not really survivors' guilt when you hand somebody the weapon they used to kill your parents and others." I waited for the usual gut-twisting rush of guilt that came when I admitted all that, but wolf me stared back.

Now matters now, she said.

I looked up at Cliff, chewing the inside of his cheek. Mulling over how to respond to my admission? Considering half a dozen platitudes and jokes? Finally, he turned back to the flame, "We all live with what we've done. Or not, right?"

I gave a small snorting laugh. "Do you have some great dark secret you need to share before we try to sneak out of here with a storm of shades bearing down on us?"

He chuckled, "You got me beat on darkness. I did three years for embezzling three grand. Had an asshole boss, so I charged his profits an asshole tax. Everyone always assumes I was dealing drugs or beat somebody up. But nope. It's really hard to get an accounting job with 3 years of counting nothing but time. That's as dark as I get."

"You have an accounting degree? Why does your family think you can't add two plus two?" I asked, recalling all of his sister's snide remarks about stealing money.

"My family, half of them say they raised me better than that. That includes mom and dad, by the way. The others feel if I weren't stupid, I wouldn't have gotten caught." He shrugged. "So, weird question..."

But he didn't get a chance to ask it. The fire flared with icy blue flame, and I flinched as my entire chest rang like a struck gong. I fell back onto the picnic table's bench hard enough that the wood gave a warning crack.

"Abby?" Cliff's hand grabbed at my shoulder.

I opened my mouth to tell him I was fine, but the door to the building banged open. "Abigale Night! What are you doing?!" Rey screeched, eyes wide with horror. The grill flared again, that horrible ringing sensation hit me again, but it didn't actually hurt. Rey, though, she jerked back, shielding her eyes with her wide sleeves with a pained yip.

"Burning those contracts. There has to be a clause in them that holds everyone to Andrew. We're lucky they were still here, or we'd have to go to Legacy headquarters and burn down their archives. I would have asked you, but you were busy." I grabbed another folder and tossed it on the pyre.

"Contracts? Written contracts." Her wide eyes peeked over her sleeve. "He left them here?!"

A laugh rolled up out of Cliff, "My sister barely got everyone to sign them before everything went to hell. I wasn't going to ship them for her."

Rey stepped out onto the patio, shielding her eyes from the fire's light. "Yes, the Dead are not Fey. They are order and decay. Their agreements need to be held in a physical thing and have no life unless it's given. Wait." She cocked her head as if listening to a sound "That was Cindy's!"

"Well, yeah." I smiled at the Fey. "We started with that one."

Her amber eyes glowed, "Then all I need to do is show her euphoria, and she'll be free of this rot. I can do that." Rey zipped inside, little more than a red blur.

The wind moaned, and I looked up to see shadows slithering through the trees. They were here already.

How long would a circle of salt hold against all that? And if it held, how were we going to shepherd all these people out of it? The trick with my silver chime? Could it get us over a bridge?

"Abby, I can finish this," Cliff said. "Get everyone loaded into the ambulances and get out of here. If you rip all the equipment out, you should be able to fit everyone in."

I turned to him with bared teeth, "No one gets left behind." I pointed up at the sky. "One of those nearly strangled you."

He patted the Fey sword that lay on the picnic table. "Besides you, I'm one most likely to make it on my own."

"Cliff, your mother has the Rot; if we leave you behind what are the chances that she'll ever be happy enough to beat it?!" I said, staring him down.

"She'll be happy that her son finally did something right." He held my gaze, "They're hunting you. Not me. Get going."

The grill flashed as the flames consumed another contract. The ring of it made me blink.

"Go on," Cliff said. "By the time you're loaded, I might be done here."

"You'd better be," I growled at him and followed Rey back into the building as the flock of shades slithered closer.

Gloria and Sophie pushed away from the wall, the two women blocking my path back to the bay.

"What's going on?" Gloria demanded, chin thrust out.

"We're getting everyone out of here. Just have to get everyone organized and loaded up," I told them. They nodded with approval and allowed me past, following me into the bay.

"Alright, everyone!" My voice rang throughout the room, and about a quarter of the gathered EMTs looked up from their games: the ones freed from their contracts already. Except Cindy, whose seat sat empty. "We're breaking you all out of this pit and getting everyone to safety. We're going to unload the ambulances and pack everyone in. Who here brought a large car?"

"Why bother?" someone asked before coughing hard. I turned to find it was Patricia. She wiped her mouth and spat at the corpse that still lay next to her table.

"We're burning everyone's contract; you'll all be able to go home. To your children, Patricia." A chorus of wails interrupted me, and the garage doors shook. I touched my ring. "Worse comes to worst, I'll buy you time, like I did in the hospital." The corners of my lips pulled into the same expression I used with frightened patients.

"No." She cleared her throat and looked at me with eyes that were little more than pits of despair. "You think I don't know what this is? We're all going to wind up like those poor bastards you ripped apart. A city of the dead doesn't need an ambulance service. I'm not bringing this home to my kids." I didn't know Patricia particularly well, but I didn't need a deep connection to see a brokenness that had not been there before. Even if we spirited her away and poisoned the sickness in her lungs with a temporary happiness, those pits in her eyes wouldn't disappear anytime soon.

I simply stared at her, anger slowly cracking my insides. All these people, they didn't deserve this. That didn't cover it. The thousands out there who didn't deserve what they got, and I wasn't rushing out to save them. Life is unfair. But Patricia was different, part of this little tribe of people who swallow down the long hours and stupidly low pay to move people to places where they can get help. We all have different reasons; some of us are trying to pay a debt, others like the hours or the thrill, a rare few are simply out to do good. NLR paramedics were no more perfect or broken than any other of the dozen ambulance companies in the city, but they were my little tribe, my extended pack, and Andrew

Millar's grasping dead hands were not to be allowed to do this to my people.

They wouldn't meet my gaze; Patricia's bleak expression was reflected on every face. "We can cure the Rot. It feeds on despair; that's why you're all coughing. We don't like to be helpless. But happiness can poison it."

"Sure, that's gonna be easy to find in the rubble. All puppies and rainbows out there." Dobson laughed; nobody else did.

I stared at them all, this wasn't how this was supposed to go. Where was the anger? The incredulity at being controlled? Raising my voice, I told them, "You can't stay here. Breaking your contracts makes a noise. They are coming here. We have to fix that problem first."

Doc stood rubbing his chest and stifled a cough. "You got folks with ya. Take care of them first. Then if there's room we'll come with."

"You're all coming whether you want to or not," I seethed, "I'll stuff you in there like canned tuna if I have to."

"There's no way we can fit ten people in one of those ambulances." Sophie spoke up from the where the Giffords clustered near the entrance to the bay.

"You'd be surprised how roomy they are once we rip out all the stuff in them. Come on." I ripped a set of keys from the rack and tossed them to her. "I'll help."

The Giffords and I descended on the ambulances, frantically pulling out supplies and equipment first. Then I tore out the shelving. I had one completely gutted when Rey appeared, her red hair askew and damp, kimono hanging open as her eyes locked on me. "It's not working! You need to release me from my promise, now!"

I swallowed, feeling a storm of desperate emotions

crashing against me. "What's not working? And which promise?"

"Let me feed on her. I need to take her despair before it's too late. I can't get her to euphoria with the memories of what happened tonight weighing her down. It's too heavy!" Her eyes pleaded.

"I'm not dead yet, Rey." Cindy coughed, stepping behind Rey. "I feel better now that you're here." She was as disheveled as Rey, more so with her wig on crooked. Her eyes narrowed at me, "And what were you thinking bringing Secret here? Are you mad?"

Rey spun to Cindy, saving me from answering the question, "No you don't! You're even more worried now! I can't take but I see. I can always see into you. He won't take you from me! You care too much about all these people around you, strangers, even. You have to let that go! Let me sweep you away; then you'll be safe." She reached up to rest her hand against Cindy's cheek, stroking it gently, as if she feared Cindy's solid frame might crumble with the lightest touch.

Cindy smiled, gripping Rey's wrist, and holding it against her chest. "Rey, you can't have my depression, you're not made for it. It's not what you are. You should all go while you can."

"Cindy, none of us is leaving without you. We burned your contract," I said.

"Not the one I signed up at the funeral, Abby. Most of us worked at least a shift up there. He's not pushing on it now but it's weighing us all down," Cindy said.

Rey pulled on Cindy's head, forcing her to look her in the eye. "I can fix it! I can make you forget it. It is the weakest of bonds; I can free you of it, but you have to allow me in." She whirled to me. "I ask you one more time,

Abigale Night; release me from my promise. If you do that, I will owe you a solid favor. Another lifetime of service."

"No!" Cindy wrapped her arms down over Rey's chest and pulled her close. "No, Rey. That promise is what makes us work. Without that, you wouldn't be able to help yourself."

Rey growled, struggling against Cindy's grip; her hair entirely broke free of her bun and curved claws slid from her fingertips. A caged wildness ran through those eyes, and all semblance of humanity fled from the Fox Fey. Cindy held on to a fox the size of a Doberman, with a painfully thin frame that spoke of a long starvation. Her coat whirled with different textures, from vibrant red fur that only existed in storybooks, to inked-on hatch marks, red pixels, and the rusty color of Portland's natural foxes. A piece of every fox story eddied in her. The plush tails maintained their length, but the fur along them became patchy, some sections shining with new growth, and others thin or matted. Her long neck twisted to snarl. "Let me in! Let me cut out all the parts that make you hurt. Even if I cut the contract away, you still care too much! Let me take the screams you heard tonight. Let me take your pain."

Cindy, who flinched at the barest sight of my own fangs, leaned forwards and kissed that black nose. "If you took that part of me, then nothing would work. It's the part that lets me love monsters like you."

"I told you not to use that word!" Rey's growl ended as whimper as Cindy stroked her ears.

"It's a selfish love, if that makes it better. You give me things that no one else could. Not only nights where I can taste being beautiful, but you make me feel like the person I want to be when we close that door. Nothing else has ever made me feel like that, Rey. I'm a mess of a person and you make me whole." Cindy squeezed the Fox Fey tight and kissed her between the ears.

The fox struggled, her teeth snapping at Cindy's face and neck, seizing the fabric of her shirt and tearing it, but not injuring the flesh beneath. "I'm using you," she growled. "I've lied to you. You can't l-love a liar."

Cindy continued to stroke her. "Yes, I know. That promise to Abby is like living with a foot in a trap. And you told me everything that made her dangerous, marked me so she wouldn't pull me into her pack." Cindy looked up and smiled at me. "After the moon, when I saw Abby wouldn't hurt me, I knew you lied to me. It changed nothing. You were protecting me in your own way. I don't want to be a werewolf." Cindy turned her head to the side as a coughing fit wracked her, ending with her spitting a wad onto the concrete. While she coughed, Rey went absolutely still, her tails curling protectively around Cindy's body. No one said anything as Cindy stroked her from head to tails, then lowered her lips to one of the flattened ears and whispered. "You can't take any part of me, Rey, but I can offer you a stronger bond than any stupid contract."

"No, you can't. A mortal and a Fey... I'll destroy you." Rey's words crept out of the side of her muzzle, but her body squeezed Cindy ever more tightly, the one ear unflattening to receive the words.

"I love you, Rey, I love you, Rey, I love you, Rey. Three times seals it," Cindy whispered.

"And I you, Cindy Maveri." Rey's form meandered back to a roughly human shape so there was no awkwardness when their lips met, but she remained a skinny patchwork being. As the kiss deepened, the seams between the stories that made her tightened; a few mixed together while a couple appeared to wink out altogether. I felt the fire claim another contract, and they parted. "Now what will be, will be. You stupid human. A Fey's love is stronger than iron; it can change, grow and shrink, but it can never die." Rey let out a long breath and rested her cheek on Cindy's shoulder.

Cindy breathed, not coughing. "I can live with that."

"You have no choice in that now," Rey murmured.

The pair gave no indication they would separate soon. I stepped away, blinking back tears of my own. My arms ached for my own loves. Where had Secret and Victoria gone?

Here, Victoria's wolf answered my call. She stood in the doorway, teeth bared against the storm of shades that beat on the barrier she had circled the building with. Her ears straining to hear beyond the wails and moans of the undead, the growling of approaching engines. Serious, strong, ready to follow. I thought of that kiss as we broke into the mausoleum, the way coping with this wolf had made her giddy. Her want to be more than a member of the pack. How we didn't know if that would work, but it was a seed that I wanted to grow. I couldn't find out so long as Andrew reigned as "pharaoh." Even this safety was an illusion; I'd never been a full wolf longer than a few hours. Her wolf would tire soon, and she'd be vulnerable.

Some of the EMTs had shaken off their paralysis and drifted toward the ambulances, Dobson among them. He stared at the piles of medical equipment and supplies with longing. "Don't we need that stuff?" he asked.

"Not for this run," I told him. "We're still doing what we do. Taking people to where they can be safe and heal."

"We are?" His eyes finally focused on me.

"You are." I gave him a little smile. "I have a different job description right now." Acting on an impulse, I hugged him. He flinched but didn't push me away. He was far from my favorite member of NLR, but even with his rude mouth, he was part of this place. Part of the rhythm that had been part of my existence for the last five years. "I'm sorry about Mitch."

"Me, too. He wasn't himself," he said, suddenly sniffing hard. "I don't wanna go that way, Abby."

"You won't," I promised and meant it. Love could defy any bond, Rey had said. I loved these people, this place. I'd been focused on newer loves: Secret, Victoria, and Cindy, but it didn't alter the deep connection to here. More than the blocks that surround Cindy's house or the forest I ran through, I was rooted here. In Dobson, in Patricia, in Cliff, and in this room. They were my territory. Territory to be defended from the living and the dead.

"Uh... Abby. You're, uh, growling?" Dobson pointed out.

I let him go and stopped the possessive growl. "Everyone load up," I told the assembled people, and pulled my silver kettle chime out of the pocket of my borrowed robe.

"You think that whole trick with the chime will work again?" Sophie asked. She'd been hovering closer since I'd walked away from Rey and Cindy.

"Worth a shot," I said, tossing it at her.

She caught it, and frowned, "What the hell are you doing, then?"

"I'm going to pick a fight with a Pharaoh."

44

———

With each step I took towards the garage door, I grew more certain of my path. The earth beneath me gave a subtle vibration, acknowledging my claim on this place. There were no animals other than a few mice to answer my call, but the concrete offered a bountiful harvest of memories: the anxiety of a new shift and the happy exhaustion of a job well done. I slapped the open button on the panel. Rattling to life, the garage door slowly clicked its way upward. Outside, a wall of shadows writhed, held at bay by a thin line gleaming with pale moonlight. Despite the drizzle and the wind, the salt had not moved. A new magic, a new gift, a sign that even while the clouds hid her face, she watched, and we were not alone.

The salt circle looped out as far as the opposite sidewalk, giving us a buffer against the shades. As I stepped out of the building, Victoria and Secret did the same from the side door. Tossing off the robe, wolf me and human me drew together, pushing into my hybrid form. Secret, carrying my silver shiv, hid herself behind my left leg while Victoria stood to my right, her fur as black as the shadows that swirled around us. The pack I had. I tipped my head back to proclaim that this building, these people were ours, there would be no other claims on them. Victoria joined, her song rippling outwards; the line of salt blossomed with light, projecting a shimmering luminescent wall up into the sky. The specters screamed as their outlines burned with silver flames, their shadowy curtain parting. Beyond it nearly a dozen cars and trucks were coming down the road. Large, misshapen mounds stood in the backs of pickup trucks. Those would easily disrupt the line. I had to stop them.

Raising my ring to hold off the whirling shadows, I strode through the barrier, the world shrinking around me as I grabbed hold of the first car and flipped it up on its side. The metal body screeched in protest as I dragged it into the middle of the road. I was going for another car on the other side of the street when Victoria barked a warning. *Down!*

A whistle of cut air and searing pain lanced through my shoulder as I threw myself down behind the upturned car. Burning like fire and ice, I clapped my hand over my shoulder, discovering a shaft protruding from the wound. Another soft whistle above me and something tinked off the shining wall as if the light were made from concrete. It landed on the street, a silver shaft about a foot long bearing a wickedly barbed arrowhead.

"What is this?" The voice of Andrew Millar rumbled up from the pavement beneath me. Another arrow struck the barrier and bounced off. I huffed; I hadn't expected him to show up yet. I had to talk to him, but shifting was out while the silver tore at my being. More silver, more pain. I'd never treated an arrow before, but I knew the basics. Grabbing the shaft I twisted it, trying to reorient it away from the bone, but the soft metal bent like a disobedient nail. Damn it, why couldn't he use a wooden shaft for something? I tried to yank it out, but my fat padded fingers slipped on the narrow shaft. Couldn't quite reach it with my teeth, either. I needed a medic. With a low howl for help I retreated through the barrier.

The shade of Andrew Millar floated at the head of his column of horrors, his form shining that blue light that cast no shadows. Eyes blazing even brighter than they had been on the bridge. Around him a dozen of those silver arrows hovered like a swarm of waiting wasps. "You'd think two dozen violent souls carrying all the silver ammunition we could scrounge up could have handled two wild animals, but you seem to have more tricks than I imagined."

I growled at him.

He sneered. "I beat you on the bridge, and now I'm ready for you. Not so fast to heal from these, are you?" The arrows spun, their broad heads flickering in the dim light. "Even that one in your shoulder dims your light. So, you brought some sort of magic wall. It changes nothing."

Behind me I heard the soft *clang* of my teapot chime. They were going; I just had to keep the shade's attention. If I got close enough to punch him with the ring, then maybe I could drive him off. But I needed to talk. I dug claws deep into my shoulder, ripping through the muscles and tendons that surrounded the arrow. Roaring with pain I tore it all out along with the arrow, and tossed the gore onto the ground. Immediately Luna's cool presence flowed back through me, quenching the silver's burning. Yet my arm fell limply to my side, and I had to shove my working fist into the wound to staunch the bleeding.

Victoria danced away from me, with a yip of her own. *No hurt!*

Andrew laughed. "Now that is gruesome. How many times can you do that, I wonder?" The surrounding arrows spun, "Will you tear off your head after I sink one of these in your eye?"

I pulled in my muzzle. "Only after I put you back in the ground." The gong of a consumed contract rang out. There couldn't be many more left? I wondered, resisting the urge to look. If I looked, then they'd never get out. "See that line, Andrew? That's the border of our territory. You have no power beyond it."

He floated closer to the barrier, the flames of his eyes narrowing as if he had trouble seeing through it. "You are stealing from me. I own that business, bought it fair and square for over market rates. It all belongs to me. You're squatting on my property, and I will evict you."

False Pharaoh, Victoria sent.

I smiled at him. The numbness around the wound was fading, and the flesh itched as it reluctantly knitted back together. "You're a pitiful excuse for a god, Andrew, worried about deeds and contracts. You're no Pharaoh, nothing more than a minor demon of trapped clauses and paperwork."

Andrew lit like a cold bonfire. "This city is mine. Bought and paid for. The birth of my Kingdom!" He blinked out and reappeared right next to the barrier, his fist blazing as he struck out against it.

I took it for the opportunity it was. Leaping forward as his fist collided with the barrier, a blast of ethereal power seared through me but didn't stop my momentum in the least. His face registered shock as the back of my hand and the silver ring slammed through his transparent head. It splatted like a water balloon struck by a baseball bat, and he disappeared from my path.

Victoria yelped in alarm as I landed. *No!*

There where Andrew had first appeared, the silver arrows still danced. They blurred into silver streaks as they shot towards me one by one. The first struck my thigh as I tried to backpedal to safety. I got my arm up, blocking the second that came for my eye. The third sliced into my gut. Then Victoria raced across the line of fire, canister of salt held in her jaws, spreading a line of salt behind her, and the barrier sprang up in her wake. The remaining arrows bounced harmlessly off it. My world became a haze of pain as my leg buckled and I crashed down onto my side.

"Abby, you can't beat him like that!" Victoria cried out. I jerked my eyes open to find her, not her wolf, standing over me, missing nose and all. Her golden eyes filled with my pain and her own desperation. "Shit, that looks deep! Gah!" Her hands fluttered over my midsection. "Do I pull it out?"

I'll get it, I sent, or tried to; the three silver arrows made my internal river a raging rapid in all directions. Moving was marginally easier; while my right arm refused to move, the left did kinda move.

"Abigale! Don't you dare meatball that arrow." Cindy called out, and then she was there, unzipping a medical bag.

"Do we need silver scalpels to cut her?" Douglas dropped down next to my arm.

"No. You just need to be quick about it," Cindy responded.

"You're going to be fine, Abby." Patricia spoke with professional brightness. "You there, other werewolf person, could you hold her head, so she doesn't bite?"

I coughed a laugh. How to snap a bunch of paramedics out of anything? Give them an emergency to respond to. Victoria did as she was told, wrapping her arms around my muzzle and holding it close. "Abby, listen to me. Andrew's tied to his remains; it's still the seat of his soul. Unless you destroy his heart, he'll shrug everything off. Even trapping him won't work." Her voice brimmed with strain, her human voice. She couldn't be human; it wasn't safe.

Change. I sent to her with a pleading whine.

"I'm trying but she's tired and... I can feel him pulling on me." Her body trembled with effort, dark fur slowly spreading down from her hair line, jaw pushing forward.

Desperate, I searched for that connection, the lever I used to force her to change, but in the chaos of all the silver pulling at my essence, I couldn't reach it. I whimpered, tried to grab for her, and the EMTs cried out in response to the movement.

"Aaaaah! Abby, don't move! I've almost got it!" Cindy shouted.

"Hold her down! You guys! Stop standing there and help!" Douglas screamed at people they shouldn't be calling any attention to. A multitude of knees slammed down on my arms, pinning me to the pavement. Rey hissed at everyone to get back in the buses to no avail.

None of them saw Victoria sag, her features snap back to human, and let go of me. "I'm sorry. Thought it was easy money. I've fucked up so much, Abby. Gotta pay for it one way or another, I guess. It was nice to believe I had a future worth looking forward to while it lasted."

Tipping my head back, I attempted to snare her with my teeth, but another pair of arms forcefully shut my muzzle. Victoria stumbled away as if pulled by a leash attached to her neck. No, I howled, *Stop her! Somebody stop her.*

Secret appeared, standing beside my head, her green eyes clouded with worry. "I'm here. They're helping."

I dug claws into the asphalt in frustration. She didn't

understand, no one did but Victoria. No one stopped her from being dragged through the barrier. My body slumped, and a whine crawled up my throat.

"That's it, Abby, stay still. I know it hurts," Cindy soothed, but I barely felt more than a prick as her scalpel cut into my stomach.

Andrew's triumphant laugh twisted and stirred all the silver embedded in my soul. "There's the asset I want. She'll be a fine dog, maybe a tomb guardian? Take her back to the Mausoleum." He floated up to the barrier, peering through it at me and the paramedics. "You're all wasting your time. I've got a lot more where those came from. Melted down my grandma's silver. Maker spaces are very useful facilities."

No one responded to him, staying completely focused. Trading whispered requests for tools and bandages. Dobson pushed the arrow in my arm through and out the other side.

"Do you not hear me? She can't save you. Even if this barrier holds, you are on an island in the ocean of my kingdom. What do you think she'll do when she wakes up hungry? You'd be safer giving her to me."

"Got it!" Cindy jerked her fists up, and an arrow came out of my midsection in the grip of two giant forceps. Luna's flow within brought a fresh breeze through my body. "One more."

"Working on it, someone give me more light," Patricia answered as Rey slipped next to Cindy.

"There, she will recover. We need to go now, or I won't be able to hide everyone all the way to the bridge," Rey whispered into Cindy's ear.

"No," Cindy said, stuffing an anti-bleed cylinder. "We're not leaving her. Don't you have to be loyal to her, too?"

"She doesn't want you to die," Rey growled back.

Cindy whipped out a penlight and shone it on Patricia's

work area, "I don't want her to die. You can help or get out of the way, love. I'm working now. Pat, don't be so gentle; she can take it."

Jaw dropped, Rey staggered back from her lover and watched her work with three other paramedics to pull out the last arrow. Then all of them looked at me expectantly. They didn't understand that we'd lost already. I'd failed to protect my pack and I couldn't protect them from Andrew's knives.

And yet, when Cindy said, "Get up, Abby."

I did.

Secret hugged my leg protectively, offering her little strength. Cliff came up wheeling a cart loaded with labeled brown paper bags, the contents of the kitchen's fridge. "Probably not up to my mom's standards, but I figure you need a pick-me-up. Eat up. I'll watch the line." He reached beneath the cart, pulled out a Fey sword and looked at Rey, "Hey if you wanna power me up, now might be a good time."

Rey only stared at him, still in a sort of shock from Cindy's brush-off as I shoveled the food into my mouth.

"You are all making me sick to my nonexistent stomach!" Andrew boomed, turning back towards the convoy. "You! Mortals, shoot through this barrier!" The doors on the truck cabs yawned open.

"Gladly!" A voice answered behind me followed by the chatter of gunfire; bullets peppered the front truck and spider webbed its windshield. Five of the Giffords, led by Sophie, held the captured rifles to their shoulders and formed a firing line. The rest had gotten out of the ambulances, all holding firearms. The doors on the truck did not reopen.

Andrew howled with rage. "This changes nothing! You

have nothing. I have an army. I have thousands of people shouting my name, and I have this!" He held up help his hands and the glowing eyes pulsed. I heard the crackle of breaking pavement and couldn't help from looking behind me. A fissure opened in the center of the road back to the bridge, that would swallow a car, but worse was the mass of black threads that flowed up and over the edges. Twisting together into thick tendrils they spread across the street, over the sidewalks, and up the sides of the buildings. The pressed against the windows, splitting back into hundreds of threads as they forced themselves around the edges of the glass, which alternately yielded with sharp cracks or were lifted wholesale from the buildings. They housed businesses, but a human scream choked off as they darted inside a third-story window. "I will bring this entire neighborhood into the Twilight if I have to! I will spare no one." Andrew's voice boomed.

Cliff stepped forward and with a gleaming arc, cleaved through Andrew's legs. They fell away from his transparent form as utter shock made his mouth and fiery eyes form perfect circles before he screamed, shooting back from the barrier. He stared at Cliff in complete disbelief. His legs slowly reappeared, but his fire had dimmed.

"Finally doing something right!" Gloria shouted from the back.

Everyone laughed. In the middle of a dying city, they laughed at this creature whose greed led him to defy death. Rey had said I couldn't beat him without an army, but I had one.

A stream of hope joined with the flow of Luna's power, and strength surged through my limbs. I howled out to the night. *Victoria, we're coming.*

"AAAIEEEAYYAAAA!" An inhuman sound embodying utter frustration answered me. It came from a skinny patchwork fox standing on her hind legs in the middle of the street. She stomped on the ground, like child pitching a fit. "No! No! No! This is not how the story is supposed to go!"

45

———

"Rey! What's wrong?" Cindy rushed towards the fox.

"Stay back!" Rey thrust out her paw, and Cindy fell back as if she'd hit an invisible wall. "This is all your fault! I've been gathering every scrap of power to make sure this works, but you've undone it now! It would have been beautiful!" Her tails swished as she gathered herself up, the digits of her paws extending into a long finger. "A grand story! The rise of an evil king and the heroic sacrifice of Portland's noble wolf on behalf of a small group of survivors." Her eyes fixed on me, no longer a single color but whirls of dark colors. "I would have been free of you while being loyal to your end. I was so close." She bared gleaming white teeth at me.

Cindy staggered up to her feet and in a blurred motion, Rey coiled around her, body and tails acting like a snake's body. "Then we would rally the east in her memory. The best friend of the wolf and her lady fox. You would be a hero and the seeds I've planted in this city would grow me into its patron goddess. A war between the living and the dead would have been a story of my own. I could have discarded all these mismatched pieces, but you decided to die for her!"

Protesting with a snarl, I took a heavy step forward. *We had a chance;* I could feel it in both the earth below my feet and the pull of the moon above. Both had their eyes upon us.

She rounded on me. "Unless your goddess is going to come down here and fight beside you, this group will never reach even halfway to his citadel. They will run out of ammunition, you will run out of strength, and your hope will falter."

Laughter came from beyond the barrier. "Finally, a creature that speaks sense."

"YOU SHUT UP!" Rey's voice struck with the force of a thunderclap, and I got a noseful of her musk as her magic rushed over the street. Stalking up to the barrier, she growled at Andrew. "You are a god not worth urinating on. Your stolen power would have crumbled within months and your masters would have devoured you. They won't get the chance now."

"That's big talk for someone who knows they're doomed." Andrew glowered down at her.

A sly, vicious smile spread across the mosaic muzzle. "I never said we are doomed, only that Abby cannot defeat you without me. And now, by my bond of love and my binding of loyalty to Luna's First Wolf, I must march against you. Know fear, Andrew Millar."

I heard a quiet giggle below me and found Secret beaming a smile at Rey. She caught my gaze and whispered, "She's almost better than my momma."

Andrew drifted away from the barrier, eye flames flickering uncertainly. "What sort of creature are you?"

With a laugh, she closed her mouth and a voice burst from the very air.

Before the streams were covered in rock.

Before the first builder set a single stone.

A fox did rooooooooam.

One patch from her quilt like hide peeled itself from her back and sprouted another Rey, human with fox ears and a tail. She had oversized headphones on and a small mixing board at her hip. With the tap of a button, a beat joined the song.

So lux her pelt, the color of desire.

Hunters set to trap her and dry it by the fire.

But every snare she did spring.

Still, she roooooams!

Another Rey stepped with a bounce from a pixilated patch and spun into a dance that had her long tail chasing after her hips.

From the shadows of dawn and dusk

She calls this city her home

The moss pads her steps

As she roooooams

A large patch sprang off, unfolding into a woman in a white fox mask and clutching green stalks in each hand. Emerald green moss spread from where her feet touched the pavement as she joined the dance.

Brambles guard her den.

Leaves hide her trails.

In Portland's winter

Still, she roooams.

The song circled, building in volume, new notes joining the beat like new leaves sprouting from an old twig. Andrew backed further away, and I realized it wasn't Rey's voice crooning; too deep for that, it was Cindy's. It creaked lightly, but she soldiered on, belting out the story of a fox woven into life as Rey herself shed characters until she herself was a small fox with a single pink flower perched between her ears. The song snared the humans one by one, first bobbing their heads, then lending their voices to it.

She calls you now yip, yip, aaiieee!
To the city she calls her home.
Spring comes soon!
The roses will bloom!

With that verse, the building power rushed outward; it called to spring with a longing howl. It rejected Secret's and my wintery hearts, leaving us painfully sober as an ecstatic dance broke out. The black threads creeping up the walls of the firehouse began to peel away.

Andrew had floated backward to the convoy from the gathering storm of Fey magic. Can a transparent blue man look green? Because his expression was that of a man who'd been on one rollercoaster too many. "Make them stop! Shut them up!" He hollered at the men cowering in the cabs. Reluctantly, heads popped out of windows. I lowered myself, preparing to pounce.

Hold, wolf, Rey urged, and swung out her tails. The men sang *Yip, yip, Aaiieee!* As they fired their guns straight into the air.

"Give me those!" Andrew ripped the guns from their hands and more flew from the police cars to join his swarm. I pounced then, not on Andrew but on the unfortunate barrier car, ripped off a rear wheel, and threw it like a discus at the shade before he got all the guns pointed in the right direction. He gave a shout of surprise as the tire passed through his midsection, knocking a pistol from the swarm along with it. I didn't intend to let him get a grip on that; the door's plate came off as a single sheet. Leaping at him, I brought it down over his head, clearing away the majority of the guns with that single swipe; the crosswise second blow got the rest. He stopped cringing midway through that one, fixing me with his baleful stare. On the third blow that I made just in case he tried to float his weapons, he straightened and unnecessarily adjusted his tie. "I'm sorry, is that supposed to tickle? You seem to be under the mistaken impression that you can win, Abby." He held out his fingers.

I swung without looking, my metal panel swatting aside several silver arrowheads, sending them careening from Andrew's telekinetic grip. As his face distorted with frustration, I slammed a fist blazing with Luna's light into it. He recoiled like a flesh man who'd been sucker punched before blinking out and reappearing higher than I could reach.

"You can't win," he spat at me. "I thought it might be fun to bring you to heel myself. After all, just because you have access to a legion of undead doesn't mean you should rely on it to solve all your problems." His frown literally flipped upside down into a smile, "But I'll enjoy watching it solve you."

Rising higher than my reach, he disappeared. The swarm of shades, which had fallen back to spectate, suddenly churned into motion. Horns blew in the north, a low moan that traveled beneath my feet as much as it vibrated the air. It brought a wind that bypassed my fur and whistled through holes in my heart. The shades rushed down on me, a thick tendril of black miasma swirling with the malevolent stars of their eyes. I raised my ring against it; the torrent of souls scattered as a stream of water into the blades of a spinning fan as they struck the light. The shades screamed in agony as they burned, but still more bore down on me, driving themselves closer and closer to the source of the light. My arm shook from the pressure, and I grasped my wrist to steady it. I knew I should flee for the safety of the barrier, but every muscle I possessed strained against the force of the shades, locking me into this struggle.

Hold them! Hold the barrier, Wolf, Rey whispered in my head, *Every blow you strike is kindling for me to stoke this pyre.*

The barrier? I allowed my focus to stray for a fraction of a second; the shades surged close enough for me to feel their gasping cold on my knuckles, but I saw that this was only one prong of their attack. Thicker tendrils threw themselves against the wall of pale light, bowing it inwards. Victoria had woven that barrier, blending her talent with Luna's light. Without her, it frayed; even the ring I wore had shone more brightly in her hands. We were stronger together. How could I do this without her?

You are not alone, Luna whispered from my memories.

I know that, I thought at her. You are the light on my hand, you are the power in the barriers. Please gift me with more of your light tonight.

Yet the Goddess did not answer with a flare in the brilliance of my ring or by filling my thundering heart with renewed strength. She a gifted me with only a simple caress down my spine before resting her presence on my shoulder. *You have all my light already, my wolf, do not rely on me to conquer darkness.*

My arms shook as the shades inched closer to my knuckles. In desperation, I gave a strained howl for help.

Secret answered immediately, her weight thudding into the back of my calf, bracing against me. "Here, Abby." Strength flowed with her words. Her magic was not my magic, not Luna's, but it came with a warm determination that she would not let me fall. We had both sacrificed ourselves to each other. And we would not fall to this. The shades' advance stopped, but still they poured forth; those repelled from the light circling back into the storm of darkness. We needed some way to injure them.

"Leff! Heff! Um! Oord!" I called out Cliff's name the best I could with a muzzle.

But Secret understood. "Cliff, come here! Use your sword! Stop dancing and help!"

I didn't dare turn to see what he was doing, but heard him respond, "Uh! Right! On my way."

He ran up beside me, crossed into the space beneath my arms and shoved that gleaming blade into the path of the shades. The torrent parted on the Fey blade, the shades shrieking as they cleaved themselves in twain and then scattered in Luna's light. These shredded shades dissolved into nothingness as they tried to rejoin the storm. The tendril snapped back up into the sky as the song swelled. Luna hadn't been telling me that she was with me, she'd been reminding me to use those around me. With or without Victoria, the dead had to be conquered with a pack.

"I call my knight to service!" Rey called out as Cliff sagged back against me. The beat of the song vibrated through him. In an eyeblink he changed, He stood leaner; a mane of dreadlocks bunched into a tight ponytail sprouted from his formerly shaved head along with a twitching pair of black-furred fox ears. His right arm had been freed of its sling, sheathed in a slim bronze gauntlet. The rest of his clothing transmuted to a flowing red garment, trimmed with a sash of black fur across his chest.

"Whoa." Cliff stared at his hand, flexing his fingers, each movement on the beat of the Fey song pulsing through him. His smile was the sunrise over mount Shasta as he tossed his sword over to his right hand and stepped out away from me. The sword twirled, cleaving lethal arcs through the air, then as Cindy's voice belted out "*rooooams!*" he jumped as if propelled by her voice. He slashed down through another tendril of miasmic shades and the barrier's light destroyed them same as the first. "Awww, hells, yeah!" he shouted with a flourish of the blade.

The piles of flesh shaped like men dismounted from their trucks, coming towards us. They ripped up street signs and bicycle racks to use as clubs. Four came charging up on either side of the convoy. The same things Victoria and I had fought on the bridge. I growled a warning to Cliff and together we charged, my claws tearing up the pavement as he sped above it. Throwing my bulk at them, I punched though their line, claiming an arm as a prize. Beside me, he cleaved through one abomination, two halves separating in the sword's wake. I lost him in a whirl of blood and freshly dead meat. Secret clung to my back, the silver shiv severing reaching fingers as my claws and teeth tore meat from borrowed bones. Cliff's sword pierced the bubble of my melee, chopping through the leg of a flesh thing trying to clobber me with a stop sign. As it fell with a bubbling wail, it tried to backhand Cliff, but he had already leapt away, cleaving through another's head on the next beat. The red light of their eyes snuffed out before the head hit the ground. The last shade fled its body before Cliff could strike it.

"Witness!" Rey crowed from behind us. "A sword sharp enough to cut a soul! They will not rise again!"

The crowd cheered. Rey had reclaimed her human face and size; her long mane of red hair had turned into a rainbow garden of roses. The patchwork fur pelt was now tattoos along her back and arms. While her tails swished to the song, she addressed the crowd with one arm raised. "Death has overstepped its bounds tonight! Wreathed the city in despair! But this old Fox is here to remind you that life is always stronger." She shouted over the music. "Some of you know the fragility of life but also its tenacity. You see it in your gardens, in the coyotes that howl in your streets," she turned and winked at me, and then focused on Cindy. "In ill-advised love. See hope that this death can be beaten back. Look around." Her hand guided eyes to see that on every surface grew greenery, ivy now claimed the firehouse walls, the bare sticks of the dormant shrubbery had blossomed with purple flowers, and mossy tendrils crept from the sewer grates in the road.

"See your power around you. While my knight will slay the monsters, it is you who must pull the sickness from your land, from yourselves. Together we will plant life in the heart of this decay, uproot the shade that is spreading death. But you must give yourselves to the battle and decide to hope. Can you do that?"

"Yes." The crowd murmured, as I stared at Rey's back, at how she pulled this all into a vortex around her. Gathering power as she had in the club, but not gorging herself, instead channeling all it outward, through Cliff and into the ground.

"I can't hear you!" Rey taunted the crowd, and they answered more surely the second time.

"Can you kick some undead ass out of this city?" she snarled, and the crowd responded with a yes that echoed down the street. The area flooded with the scent of Rey's gossamer musk, the ambulance turned itself around, speakers sprouting from its sides while greenery grew from every cranny, shaping itself into foxtails and dancing figures. "Thrice sworn is thrice bound!" Rey crowed, "It's time to dance." She spun down to the ground, her back to the crowd, and held out her hand to the side, where Cindy took it.

They shared a deep kiss and parted as the chorus swelled anew. Everyone, whether they'd been a fit twenty-year-old or had needed a walker a moment ago, jumped into the air and whirled with a pulsing beat. They marched through the barrier, and the storm of shades whirled back towards the north.

Secret and I found ourselves in the middle of a music video, and the only ones who weren't dancing. That was okay; everyone in the hunting pack has a different job to do. At the lead, Cliff's sword flashed. He would defend the dancers, while we would strike at the enemy's heart.

46

The motley crew made up of paramedics and Cliff's family swelled with other Portlanders the moment it paraded out from the safety of the barrier. Greenery grew up from the feet of the dancers, new roots engaging in combat with the threads of the Rot that had been creeping over the street. The song grew past the need for words as Cliff led the way north, his sword a lethal baton. I strode beside him for a time, shifting to four legs to keep up. Secret rode low, kneeling between my shoulders, one hand with a death grip on the thick fur of my neck. Her other hand held the silver shiv against her hip. While the music did not sweep us into its embrace, by stepping to the beat I pushed myself into it, pulling its flow through my heart. The hidden power of the seeds waiting beneath the soil gathered in my fur and muscles, the scent of sweat and sap filled my lungs. It banished exhaustion, awakening a burning hunger in my belly and an aching need in my loins. In my mind's eye I exploded through a dense thicket to snap at a huge hog which ran squealing into Victoria's black jaws. As we ripped up the corpse, a red wolf joined us, herding a small pack of pups to the kill. We all tucked into the meat under the cool gaze of the moon, safe and satisfied. It made my heart howl. The song took my beatless notes, rolling it into itself, leaving me panting with want for that moment. That could be our future, and I mentally added a young woman with cat ears and a tail alongside the wolves. There, that was what I wanted. Maybe Cliff was that red wolf, maybe he wasn't but I would have that perfect moment someday, and the life that got me there. In front of us, more dead gathered in our way. The dead think they're hungry, they believe themselves to be parched, but they're only dim reflections of the living's appetites.

Cliff danced through the dead that challenged him, but he remained tethered to the song. Secret and I ranged, zigzagging across the parade's route, using teeth and Luna's light to herd the shades into the path of Cliff's sword. Their stolen bodies filled the air with bullets. None of them touched the blur Cliff had become, although I smelled his blood in the air. His laughter rang out between the buildings. "This all you got? Come on!"

A bullet stung my hide, but it only took a dip back into the song to fill my reserves. Secret took its energy to silence the click of my claws on the pavement as we scattered groups of shades who tried to sneak around the fox-enhanced blender that Cliff had become.

At one point, the hapless undead had set up a roadblock with a yellow school bus. The windows were crowded with gun barrels. Gathering the energy of the song, Secret and I burst through its back door, my body becoming a whirlwind of teeth and Secret's blade slashing. Yet the taste of living blood did not enter our mouths. Andrew had sent no humans to attempt to stop the swelling dance we protected.

Cliff veered from the road along the river and climbed

the hill to OHSU. While I worried the dark buildings would be perfect for snipers, we met zero resistance. I walked beside Cliff as we led a huge ribbon of people, all calling out against the darkness. The songs had shifted, other musicians had claimed microphones, but still Rey and Cindy bounced and grooved in the crowd's heart. Rey had grown to equal Cindy's height, her red hair and fur barely visible through the garden that grew in them. Besides that, she wore a flannel shirt, its sleeves rolled up to her elbows and its front open to display a scarlet bra. A very Portland fox.

Cliff stepped with a soft shuffle, the Fey sword twirling in his hand with the pulse beneath our feet. His smile warmed my fur as we came to the edge of the campus. Although he showed no sign of injury, the scent of his still-human blood wafted into my nose. Worry broke me out of the song enough to hear a competing one. The mournful tones of a dirge rose up at us through the trees that separated the campus from the city. It beat heavy and slow but roiling with power. Spotlights swooped on the underside of the cloud cover from the Millar Mausoleum in time with its tempo. Andrew had marshalled all the humans under his sway to sing him a dirge to counter our call to life.

Rey's voice flowed. *Our champions cannot fight this battle alone. Armies must clash. Andrew's power is drawn from the same place as mine. Life. Gods rise from both Twilight and the Dream. But only the moon, the earth, and the sun have power that flows from themselves. All else grows from the people of the Crossroads. Remember, sweet mortals, that a gift freely given is more valuable than any stolen gold. That dirge is a song that is chained to their hearts. Shatter their chains.*

Both songs cried out, their volumes rising, the swelling dirge to an eternal god against the boppy call of life. Secret and I rushed down the hill. At the foot of it, I saw them, a teeming crowd, a solid line of bodies standing three blocks into the city center. Running to the side, I found its extent, three blocks, four roads, swollen with people. They smelled of sick and fear, their faces covered in black veils or hidden in the depths of their hoodies. The crowd saw us, brandishing their signs with menace as their tones battled with our beat.

Our dance poured into the city like water and flowed down all four streets. Secret and I swam through them, searching for any sign of the undead, but only the living and their mournful song confronted us now.

The crowds met on Harrison Street. The mourners wailed in chorus; our dancers shook every body part they had. Competing noises and energies crashed against each other. The traffic lights exploded in a shower of sparks. Join us, the song of life called to them.

"Join us and see the glory of the Pharaoh," the mourners called back.

Back and forth they shouted and sang, the lights flickering in the buildings caught between.

A step started it. They postured, they shook, the energies piled against one another, dust rose into the air, demarcating the border between the two camps. A crack grew in the road. Our side needed an opening, a gap to fill.

I jostled Secret on my neck and felt her shift low.

"Ready," she whispered, and the tingle of her glamor washed over my skin.

With a howl, I charged the line. The mourners' cries of alarm and fear had broken them before I even burst through the horde. It broke behind me not like a wall but a dam, the song of life flooding in behind me. The mourners who dove out of the way to avoid my paws were quickly snared by the crowd rushing in behind me. With every step the dirge weakened as hope pounced on the fearful.

As I turned in a wide circle at the intersection, Andrew's voice boomed through the streets. "Do not falter! To oppose the Pharaoh is to invite death! Behold!"

The thunderous crack rumbled from behind our lines and our song wavered, pierced by screams. Leaping from the crowd, the song carried me up onto the roof of the building I stood by. There I saw a blazing pyre of blue hovering over 4th avenue, the outer street of the four we had flowed up. Andrew. But he wasn't shooting fire or raining bullets onto the crowd. No, he had torn a full quarter of an office building up from the ground. Groaning, it floated up to join him in hovering over the road. I charged at him, racing over the roof towards him, straining every-thing to cover two blocks faster than he could float the building. Cliff leapt up from the street, running along the wall; he'd been closer to begin with. Becoming that red blur, he launched himself just as the building reached its apex above the street.

Andrew's light flickered out a full second before Cliff's blade passed through the space where he'd been. As he passed beneath it, the building remembered gravity.

It crashed to the earth with a cacophonous groan, heaving up a great mass of dust. Screams of pain and terror rode in the cloud, tugging me towards the injured, but I skidded to a stop. The conflagration of power that was Andrew had reappeared on the other side of the three blocks we danced down, Broadway. His laugh pounded through the song as Cliff streaked towards him.

Distraction, growled wolf me. She was right.

Get him, Cliff, I silently urged my friend and tore myself

from my path, running away from the disaster as another building rose into the air. Towards Andrew Millar's heart.

Circling around to the rear of the municipal center and the smell of humanity thinned. These mourners had fewer of the deep hoods, and the song on their lips was a mumbled mess. They made no effort to stop me and Secret as we skirted their edges. Andrew's devotees battled on the other side of the city.

I had to do this as fast as possible, but beyond the reach of Rey's song, I couldn't afford to take a faceful of automatic gunfire getting into the Mausoleum. The mourning mob had smashed in a few store windows in their enthusiasm, and I snatched up some clothing. After a quick change in an alleyway, I led Secret by the hand towards the Mausoleum through a crowd that increased in density the closer we got. Still, using the flows and eddies, we made progress until I could see the pillar of stone that was Andrew Millar's temple to himself. A single block away from it, the crowd's behavior changed. No longer milling with the dirge mumbling from their lips; instead, they all knelt in supplication to their lord of the dead. Raising their hands over their heads before bowing to such a degree that their foreheads pressed into the pavement. Among these worshipers were men carrying rifles. They wore anything from cop uniforms, to security uniforms, to flannel, but they all had the same shiny new guns. They patrolled between the rows of the worshipers, their chests swollen with self-importance. Beyond them, at the entrance of the building, stood three guards on the east side, each gripping a spear. If Andrew had any silver left, I'd guess it was on the tips of those spears.

I knelt down to Secret's level. "What do you think? Can we get through with your magic?"

She squinted at the guards and nodded. "More eyes make it harder but it's the shades that worry me. They might see the glamor, if not us within it."

"Then let's give them something else to look at." Fear hung in the street, in every breath. These people had no real inkling what they were doing. Why they had been compelled into the street to sing this dirge. Primed for panic so long as I was brave enough to light the fuse. People were going to get hurt, but I didn't see another option. We needed a distraction, and I wouldn't risk separating from Secret again. "Okay, Secret. I'm going to do something, and then you try to hide us. While we're hidden, we're going to charge that door. Got it?"

Fangs appeared in her smile. "Gonna get Vicky back?"

"That's right, and everybody else. We have to get that heart," I said, turning so she could climb up onto my back.

Her arms encircled my neck, "Ready," she whispered, and I stood with a grunt. Without wolf me in my limbs she was heavy.

I waited at the very edge of the standing crowd, waiting for a guard to pace up towards me. He had a black AR-15 rifle in his hands, but also a pistol at his waist. I watched his feet so he wouldn't catch my gaze. He got within two paces and turned. I rushed out towards him, wolf me surging into my limbs. He gave a grunt of surprise as both my and Secret's weight thudded into his back. Hooking his neck with my left arm, I tore the pistol from his holster with my right. Jerking him backward, I whipped the pistol out towards the Mausoleum and pulled the trigger. The gun kicked in my hand with a hollow pop. The shrill scream of panic answered the second shot as all the worshipers leapt up from the ground in a wave of surging bodies. Spinning, I hurled my guard onto the ground and rushed into the back of the fleeing worshipers as the scent of Secret's glamor flooded the air. Secret and I ping-ponged off backs and shoulders as we ran with the crowd. More gunshots answered from up ahead, the crowd reversed, and we jammed up into a crush so tight that it lifted me. A mere twenty feet from the corner of the mausoleum's block. Wolf me growled, wanting to run out, but I pushed her back, letting her gift me with only a little strength to hold my ground as the sea of humanity tried to run in the other direction.

With a flash of ghostly blue, Andrew appeared above his statue's head. "That's it! Everyone Kneel!" He commanded. The crowd flinched but made no haste to obey. Too panicked for his hold to take.

His eyes flared, a wind passed through my body as he gathered power, and the statue below him shivered. They'd been worshiping the statue. *What if?* The thought was fragmentary, but my body acted. Planting my feet, I shoved back against the crowd and used a tiny fraction of space to take aim at the statue's face. *Dear Luna, give me one good shot,* I prayed, then hedged my bets by emptying the clip.

"I SAID KNE-AAAH!" Andrew stopped his command to slap a hand over his face, the gathered power splashing harmlessly out over me and the crowd.

The red marble features erupted into small plumes of rock dust, like hidden pimples bursting. Andrew could only clutch at his face as the crowd surged away. I ran with them and within ten steps they thinned out enough that I could see that a line of guards had formed in front of the doorway, but they had all obeyed Andrew's command, kneeling with heads bowed. Hanging onto Secret's arm with one hand and trusting in her magic, I ran for the gap in that line.

The closest guard looked up with dazed eyes as I

snatched the rifle from his hands. Running through the legs of the statue left me about forty feet from the framed entrance with the shades moving to block the doorway.

"I said STOP!" Andrew's voice boomed up from the very ground. The shades froze.

Which was very convenient for me; they didn't even move to dodge as I clamped the rifle butt in my armpit and opened fire. The glass door shattered and three of the shades crumpled beneath the spray of bullets.

With every step I pulled the trigger again, firing wildly into the building. It clicked empty, and I tossed it away a few steps before the doorway, scooping up a silver-tipped spear.

"No! No! No!" Andrew's frustrated scream shook the tile beneath my feet as wolf me flowed freely into my body. My clothes were beginning to strain and stretch as I emerged into the central chamber. Fortunately, Andrew had constructed it as a tourist attraction, not a fortress. But that would also mean that if I wasn't fast, Andrew's goons would come pouring in as soon as he got hold of his temper. Pausing to look around the room, Secret dropped from my back with a whispered, "I'm gonna go hide," followed by a rustle of fabric.

People were scattered around the chamber. A band of musicians in the corner. A long table had been set up in front of the enthroned statue of Andrew; near it I recognized the Mayor and the Chief of Police among a bevy of aides, who both looked up at me in horror. To the side of the throne sat Victoria in a folding chair as her "queen's throne." She dripped with golden and diamond jewelry in a tacky infusion of Egyptian and Hollywood chic over a white dress. It looked so completely wrong on her; the only black was her hair, and it lacked even a single red accent. She stared straight ahead, chest rising and falling with the rapidity of a woman running a marathon.

Seeing her, I forgot about what I'd come here to do.

47

Heedless of anything else I raced across the room, my wolf's worry pushing all my humanity away. *Packmate! Packmate!* But when she didn't react to my oncoming bulk, I skidded to a stop. *What wrong?* I whined, sniffing for a hint in her scent. I could feel her insides, her wolf, trapped and frantic.

"Is that what you came here for? Well, you can't have her. She's mine, despite what you've done to her face." Andrew spoke from behind me.

Victoria grunted as I whirled around.

I found the bastard floating in the center of the room, flaming eyes flickering with anger and frustration. He wouldn't have anything once I finished with him; remembering my plan, I leapt at the Sarcophagus lying between the now-abandoned table and the statue of the enthroned Andrew. My body flowing into my hybrid form, I sank my claws into the seam, and I tore off its lid. It hit the floor with a floor-vibrating thunk. Empty.

The inside of the sarcophagus was smooth red marble polished to the point that my wide eyes reflected in it.

Andrew's malevolent laugh filled the surrounding space.

"You really think I'd be that stupid! To leave my body where anyone could desecrate me?"

I growled, bringing up my fist and its glowing ring as my mind scrabbled for a new plan.

"Oh, that's very intimidating." He glared down at me; misty ephemera seeped from the spots where I'd defaced his statue. "That little ring of yours stings. Now shooting my statue, that was a fancy trick. Very clever, how'd you know that? Who told you?" The spear that I'd snatched up from the guard floated up from the floor to hang in the air beside him.

"He's under the statue." Victoria spoke through gritted teeth.

The point of the spear turned from me to Victoria. My body sprang to the side, long arm reaching out in front of Victoria as the spear hurtled down. The shaft brushed my fingers as it pierced Victoria's chest.

"Traitorous bitch! You are under contract!" Andrew howled so loud my ears popped. Pain bit through my own chest as she fell. Victoria's mouth opened in a breathless scream as I caught her and lowered her gently to the ground. A bloodstain the size of a coffee cup had already spread from the wound.

"T-there's a m-mechanism in the left elbow." She coughed, bloody spittle bubbling into the corners of her mouth.

No time for anything else; I had to get that silver out of her. I could feel it, her pain sizzling against my right lung. My fingers must have deflected it some. As I grabbed the shaft, a line of bullets stung across my backside. I clenched my teeth against this new pain and focused on Victoria. The silver was deep; pulling it out might nick the aorta, so it had to go through.

"Give me that spear!" I heard Andrew holler as I twisted the spear, feeling the point in my own chest.

Victoria's body arched. "Code, is T-I-W-aaah." Grabbing her shoulder, I drove the point though a gap between her ribs and out her back, then snapped it off with six inches to spare. The cold burning of the silver ceased, and numbness came. Healing wasn't as quick in human form, had to give her time now. First rule of trauma for werewolves is to get the silver out. Then stop the bleeding. Someday I'd put together a standard operating procedure. I snatched her up and ran off the dais, frantically looking for cover. None presented itself; the room was nothing more than a huge box with a central throne and decorative walls. Only the exit doors had any hope of relief from the gunfire ripping into my hide. My free arm smashed into the exit's push bar, it bent, opened a few inches, and slammed closed. To avoid crushing Victoria against the wall, I had to roll along it, briefly exposing her to the dozen guns firing in my direction. Andrew had three spears floating above his hand. One shot out for my head, but I ducked. Its shaft shattered on the marble above me.

"Take out her legs!" Andrew's voice boomed, "Hold her still."

I cradled Victoria with one hand as if she were a football and protected my head with my other arm as I raced along the wall. The only plan when I hit the corner was to leave Victoria there and start running toward the gunmen. Didn't get that far as a line of fire cut across an ankle and it went sideways, the shattered bone ripping flesh as I crashed down to my knees.

"Finally!" Andrew crowed. "Time to split a melon!"

"Vicky! What's the last letter of the code?!" Secret's voice suddenly echoed through the room.

I risked glancing under my arm to see Andrew pivot back towards the statue where a pair of black ears poked above the edge of its left arm. Victoria took a deep breath. "Y. Take it with you."

"Got it!" Secret sang, followed by a distinct ka-tink as a small oblong object was lobbed into the air.

"Shoo-"

The flashbang blasted the word out of Andrew's mouth with a concussive snap and a blinding flare.

My ears rang with a high-pitched squeal as I tried to blink away the hue-shifting afterimage of the flare. Partially cut off from sight and sound, my body loomed up in my perception. Throbbing across my back and side as muscle and skin sealed over the bullets. No time to wait for the healing. Had to move; Secret might shrug off the silver-tipped spears, but not steel bullets. Easing Victoria to the ground, I hobbled towards the center of the room on hands and knees. Had to give them all a target to worry about before they started shooting again. The dim light reflected on something on the floor; the spears lay there. If I could grab those... I reached out for them, but they lifted into the air. Andrew's transparent body flickered into existence, his formerly torchlike eyes now reluctant candle flames. The spears floated up towards his outstretched hand without hurry even as the ghost's mouth opened in a shout that didn't make it past the ringing. He grasped the first spear and pulled back to throw it, but not at me.

The entire enthroned statue of Andrew had begun to rise, supported by massive hydraulic jacks in each corner. Secret had slipped down into a depression beneath it, where Andrew's body lay in a golden suit trimmed with gems beneath a glass display case. Secret hammered at the glass with the butt of the sliver shiv. Cracks spread from the impact of each blow.

Andrew threw the first spear; it glanced harmlessly off the top of the display case. Secret gave a trill of excitement as she broke through the glass, opening a hole wide enough to fit an arm through.

I heard the thump of a beat as Andrew flew away from me, trying to get a better angle on Secret. I grabbed my ring. It slipped off my thick finger as if greased, so in the same motion I flung it. It spun through the air, brightening as it traveled before impacting Andrew's cheek. He flinched, spinning out of the ring's path and screaming loud enough that I heard him, "Die Already!" and threw the spear. It didn't come as a blurred streak, but as a pole bending back and forth as it flew. My arm already outstretched, I simply smacked it aside.

Fear dropped his jaw as my right ear popped. Sound rushed into my head, the competing beats of the dueling songs outside. The heavy, languid beats of the dirge seemed even slower against the heart-racing assault of Rey's call to spring. With him in here, Rey had been ravaging his worshipers. I grinned as panic widened his flaming eyes.

"Shoot the girl! Shoot the girl!" He screamed as his attention snapped back to Secret; she pulled his body closer to the hole and had thrust her hand into his chest.

Sluggishly, the guns raised in her direction as Secret pulled a pulsing mass of blackness from the corpse. The first pop sounded as she pulled her prize from the body and dove for the rear of the case. Bullets started flying then, shattering the glass and riddling the body. Andrew cried out with an anguished, "STOP!"

The gunfire ceased.

Secret popped up holding the black meat in her hands.

It made my heart soar to see her grin like that. "It's not nice to shoot at people. Only meanies do that."

"I agree." Andrew's voice had become a labored whisper. "Now why don't you give me that." He floated towards her, hands outstretched.

Secret opened her mouth to take a bite of it and he quickly backed off. "Because I'm the heart inspector and this one is way too heavy."

"Now, child, let's not be hasty here," Andrew said. "Give me that and everyone can go home."

"Because...." Her grin widened to rival that of the Cheshire cat. "My mother always taught me not to play with my food when I'm hungry. And I'm starving." With that she stuffed the entire fist-sized orb of meat into her mouth. With her cheeks bulging out, she tilted her head back, and the gulp echoed.

"Nuh-" was all Andrew got out before his mouth opened into a soundless scream, insubstantial hands tearing at his chest.

Secret's eyes popped open, slitted pupils shining with the same cold blue as in Andrew's eyes, her fangs glinting with predatory glee. "That's all mine now." Stretching out her black-furred hand to the writhing shade as a tendril of blue fire snaked out from his heart and lazily slithered through the air to gather in her palm. The flames of Andrew's eyes guttered out into empty holes in his face, and the brightness of his body faded to the point that he could be mistaken for an afterimage on your retina. But he didn't disappear, not entirely, as the last bit of power left him and his limbs fell slack.

The blue flame hovering over Secret's hand condensed down into a small luminescent sphere. Her fingers closed over it, her grin twisting into a grimace of effort as she crushed it. A bright flash showed the bones of her fingers as the power rippled down her arm and into her body. Her mouth opened to emit a long burp, and she opened her hand to display her empty palm. "Definitely stale, but all gone now!"

"No." Andrew stirred, form straightening, an open hole in his chest. "I'm still here. It isn't over. They still... call my name." He reached up, grasping at something invisible and pulling it toward him. His body became less transparent, but the sockets in his face did not reignite. "I can win."

All the guns in the room tore themselves from the hands of the gathered men to swirl around him. They fired all at once, sending the humans diving for cover, many joining the mayor where he hid beneath the table. Andrew's face contorted in concentration before finally snatching a single pistol from the whirling collection.

"You lost the moment you died, Andrew," Victoria called, and his attention snapped to her as she struggled to her feet, the bloody stub of the spear clasped in a clawed hand. "The pharaohs were worshiped in life and death. Your contracts and PR campaign were the poorest of substitutes." As she talked, Secret slumped back down behind the glass.

A shot interrupted her; it struck the wall behind her, about a foot from her face. She didn't flinch. "You betrayed me! Violated your contract that we signed in blood!" Andrew's shout was little more than a harsh whisper now.

Her smile turned fearsome with her sharp teeth, "The contract where I'm called on to attend, consult and advise you on matters of the supernatural. I did that, I came when you called, I told you that you were doomed. No obey was in there. Not even a non-compete clause. I didn't even need the whole 'love can defy any bond' thing," Her golden eyes shifted to me, "although it helped."

The gun cracked again, and her body jerked as she clapped a hand over her arm. "Tell me how I get it back. I command you."

"Lucky shot," Victoria hissed, "and I don't have to answer, without your Ba you're not Andrew Millar anymore. Nothing but ghost, a fading collection of emotions and memories. And I know how to handle ghosts." She fell to her knees and started drawing a circle on the floor with her bloody hand.

An inarticulate wail of anguish and rage filled the room. The guns dropped to the floor in a rain of metal and plastic. Andrew's form twisted in upon itself and disappeared; the lights of the building dimmed as the steel within the walls groaned.

Secret, in her cat form, pawed at my thigh and I scooped her up protectively. I hoped Victoria could back up her claim, but she had certainly distracted Andrew from Secret herself.

Victoria completed her circle and slapped her hand down within it. "Andrew Christopher Millar, I bleed in your tomb. In the name of Luna, I command you to stand in my circle."

You dare command a god in his temple! The entire building shook with his words; the lights flickered back and forth to darkness. With a shout, the humans snapped out of their trances and ran for the doors.

They snapped closed. *No one leaves here! Traitors, all of you! I will- I will...*

Victoria tsked, "Kill them? Collapse the building on us, Andrew? Then you'd have to share your tomb. Why don't you let them go and attend me? Maybe I can put you back in that husk of a body and you can be my zombie butler."

In response one skylight shattered, raining shards of

glass down onto us. I clutched Secret to my chest as the debris pelted my hide. My thick fur saved me from most cuts. The humans weren't so lucky. They screamed and pounded on the doors, "Help! Anyone!"

She roaaams! The outside world sang back through the hole in the ceiling.

Victoria laughed, high and long, her wolf out as far as it could be and still retain the power of speech. The white dress stretched taut against her wiry frame, dark fur covering her arms and legs; her predatory grin had a skull-like quality with her missing nose. Terrifying and beautiful with her golden eyes. "Abby, fetch me his skull. I've always wanted a talking bookend."

Never! A scream tore at us and one of the massive hydraulic jacks that lifted the statue tore away.

The humans shouted for help even harder. My ankles finally snapped back into their correct angle. Thinking of bashing a door open for the humans, I stood as the second jack snapped out of its place and flew directly at me. With a yip, I dodged to the side. Absent the two forward supports, the base of the throne splintered as the enthroned statue toppled forward. The torso snapped at the hips and the head rolled free.

"Oops. How will anyone remember you now? That's your last idol." Victoria shouted to be heard over the deep roar of rage that shook the building. The red marble tiles crumbled from the walls, their dust swirling into the center of the room; a cold wind tore at my fur and lifted larger chunks of debris from the ground. The roar continued to pour forth, whipping rocks and stones through the air, gathering them into a cyclone at the center of the building. Blows to my temples and nose drove me back to the wall where Victoria huddled, shielding her eyes by peeking through her clawed fingers. Her other hand immediately found mine and squeezed. "This is it. This is all he has left. One last temper tantrum and he'll never have the strength to bother anyone again."

Together, with Secret huddled in the crook of my arm, we watched flashes of light spark in the center of the cyclone, revealing the vaguest outline of a man floating at its center. Nothing more than spinning rage. Across the room the door opened among the humans, the doorway flooding with a golden light and the peppy beat of Rey's song. All the humans hurried through it, but it did not close. It stayed open and empty for several beats before a fox-eared woman stepped through, ears brushing the top of the doorway and six long tails fanned out behind her, following her like tethered clouds. Rey as I saw her last but more, still wearing the flannel, her tails and hair choked with greenery and flowers. Only her ears showed a trace of her red fur as she stepped into the cyclone.

The swirling dust and marble projectiles bent around her as if they didn't dare to disturb a single leaf that decorated her personage. "Ghost," her soft tone broke through Andrew's growl of rage. "Your followers all sing my song now. Not a single one offered blood for you, so I claim your resting place as my temple."

Temple? Fear bit through me. What was she doing? I pushed away from the wall.

Andrew didn't even respond to her as she raised her hands with a slow, twisting motion. The ground rumbled as the floor tiles lifted and vines crept out of the widening cracks, buds blossoming into moon-white flowers. They crawled along the ground, up the walls, and below the screaming ghost they twisted together into a spiraling shaft reaching up towards him. The vines split once they reached him, wrapping themselves around his transparent form. His roar shifted in tone from rage to a wail of pain as the force of the wind slowed.

"Now, now," Rey chided, "We hunted you as pack, it's only fair that I get my share of the kill." She turned her eyes to me for a moment, now the green of new leaves, as if to be sure that I was watching before twirling her hands once again. The ghost disappeared beneath the coils of the vines. Her tails lifted to allow two more people to stand beside her, a fox-eared Cliff, his sword sheathed at his hip, and Cindy wearing a red bridal gown, with a long train stretching out behind her.

Handing Secret off to Victoria, I took a cautious step towards them, Wolf me stepped back reluctantly, but I needed to talk. As I closed the gap, I felt Rey through the bond of our promise, or rather this Rey. And she invited me in, displaying the great rivers of worship flowing through her, far more than the amount that had almost killed her back at the club. Joy, bliss, gratitude, and everything else wrapped in her song moved through great gaps in her spirit, holes purposely sliced. Only because of the great flow did she maintain herself; once it stopped, she'd collapse. A windsock lacking wind.

The vines entrapping Andrew swelled, their green skin changing to a rough bark as it extended branches outwards. Cindy and Rey moved together.

Cliff stepped in front of me as I drew close, blocking my way with a shake of his head. "Not yet, Abby. Don't interrupt." He shouted to be heard over the music pounding in through the doorway.

"Let her come, my knight." Rey's voice slid under the beat as if it were a separate channel. "She can officiate."

"Officiate what?" I pushed past Cliff.

"Our wedding." Rey smiled without a trace of malice or slyness.

Utterly dumbstruck, I stared at her. They'd declared their love; why would a Fey want to be married?

"Please, Abby," Cindy had tears in her eyes. "We don't have much time."

"I d-d-" I protested, declaring I didn't know how, but suddenly the memories of the dozens of weddings I'd attended over my life came flooding through my mind. The words floated on the very top. "Okay."

An archway formed of thorny vines over the pair and bloomed into red and white roses. They clasped each other's hands and gazed deeply into each other's eyes.

"Do you have the gifts?" The words flowed out of me almost unbidden, I'd meant to say rings but the script in my head had a few edits.

"I have this ring," Cindy pulled small diamond solitaire from a pocket in her dress. "It was my mothers, and the act of giving it to you will give happiness and no small about of smug satisfaction." It slid on to Rey's finger without effort, and they both sighed in contentment.

"And for you, my Love," Rey whispered, reaching into her chest, "I can only give you what you already possess. My heart." She opened her hand to reveal a quarter-sized pulsating red gem, its many facets shining. "Keep it close to your own and a piece of me will always be with you. I regret that the rest of me cannot do the same." With a flourish of her hand the gem was set on a pendant attached to a gold chain which she swiftly affixed around Cindy's neck.

"I will never take it off." Cindy's words struck the tone of an oath.

They turned and looked at me expectantly.

Swallowing, I turned to Cindy, "Cindy Maveri, do you take Rey as your wife?"

"I do," she said with no hesitation.

Moving my gaze to Rey, I found an eagerness in her eyes and felt hunger through the bond. There would be consequences for this that I couldn't predict but then again, this entire night had nearly destroyed the city. We all would live with the consequences. "Rey of the Fox Fey, do you take Cindy Maveri as your wife?"

"In whatever state her soul exists, I do." A flash of predatory teeth, and they didn't wait to kiss.

"I now pronounce you wife and wife," I said after the kiss went on for a bit. Stepping back, I found that the mausoleum had transformed into a lush garden, with a towering oak tree at its center, its gnarled roots twisted into a stair leading up into a circular hollow within the trunk. I stumbled back from it, overwhelmed with the sudden immensity of it all.

Rey and Cindy parted, the last vestiges of Rey's original red, her ears, were turning green, the fur fading to the waxy shine of leaves. She took Cindy's hand and led her up the steps. "Portland isn't ready for a walking goddess," she called down at me. "But they need something to mark this night, to convince them that it was real, and to protect them from the Rot. In a few hours I will no longer be Rey, but in time Portland's new goddess of spring will grow from what I leave behind." She paused at the top of the steps as Cindy disappeared into the dark hollow. The corners of her lips turned up in that sly smile. "Our bargain is complete; I wish you luck when the courts come a-calling."

She turned to Cliff, "My knight, you are to guard us until the song dies away. Then, once you escort Cindy home, your service will be over. And you will be free to pursue your own desires. Good night and goodbye." Rey darted inside the tree, her tails curled up inside the hole and stilled. In a blink, there were only flowering vines on the side of the tree, no hole at all.

"What a night," Cliff sighed as he stepped in front of the tree and flashed his brilliant smile. "Hope that tree is sound-proof. I didn't sign up for babysitting a honeymoon." His foxy ears wiggled.

I heard a soft step next to me and found Victoria holding Secret in her arms. The mania had faded from her eyes, and she just looked tired. "Should we head home?" I asked her.

"No." She shook her head. "There's something I need to do first."

48

"Death! I'm here!" Victoria shouted up at the huge gash in the wall between the living and the dead. We were back in the center of Marquam bridge. The hole still dripped ichor into the river below, but shades no longer crawled from its depths to flee up into the sky. No one, living or dead, occupied the bridge. Emergency workers from the east side had retreated, and everyone who'd survived the night on the west side still cavorted in the spontaneous festival that had risen up from the ashes of Andrew's funeral as Rey's song played from the very air. So it was just me and Secret nervously staring into that abyss.

Victoria was busy shouting up at it, clad only in a blanket she'd pulled from a wreck. "What do you want me to say? That I'm sorry? Because I am. For this mess, at least. Vampire, too, I guess. I'm sure he's eaten people. He's sneaky about it, at least."

We waited, marinating in the silence. When I opened my mouth to suggest we try something else, the darkness rippled, and a voice slithered out. "I believe the term you are looking for is penitence, Victoria Quentin."

"You can call it whatever you want," Victoria growled. "What I want is for you not to drag me down into the Twilight when you think you can get away with it. And if you could please close this hole, that would be nice, too."

"You have made my purpose more difficult, therefore you will bare part of its burden. On nights your Goddess turns away from the Crossroads you will join me in the Twilight and assist me with my tasks. Do that faithfully, and I will not make any more attempts to shorten your mortal span."

Victoria swallowed. "That's three nights a month; I can handle that. How long does this community service last? A year? Two?"

"A year. Three hundred and sixty-five days in the Twilight."

I blinked; there were about 3 days of new moon per month, I tried to do the math in my head and gave up. "That will take more than a hundred years!"

"Yes," Death confirmed.

"Vicky, don't take this deal," I huffed. "The Twilight's not healthy to hang out in even for us."

She tapped her missing nose, "I'm aware of that, thank you. I will make my own deals, Winter Wolf." With that she squared her shoulders and stared up at the abyss. "You promise to keep that collar off my neck until I'm a permanent resident and I agree."

"You may find you pine for the collar's power before too long, but I grant you this." Death responded.

"Do we need a contract?" she asked, pulling her blanket tighter around herself. "Not sure where I'll find a lawyer at the moment, but there's gotta be a hotline somewhere."

Death scoffed, "We will forge our covenant after Charon fetches you, Victoria Quentin. I have already claimed one piece of you. Shirk your new duties, and I will claim more. I bid you adieu." With a creek of old hinges, the hole shut.

"Oh! That's how you do that," Secret said, squinting up at the space where the portal had been. Her fur along her ears and hands had lost its healthy sheen, almost eating the dim light; her complexion was paler as well. "I see the edges. It's like opening a gateway to the Dream in reverse."

I scuffled her ears. "We have to work on your timing, kiddo."

She mewed and pushed at my hand until I relented.

"Just closing it wouldn't have changed anything, Abby," Victoria said, biting her lip. "He let all those shades out tonight because you didn't leave me with him. I had to give him something and... and." her eyes strayed to my feet before lifting to my eyes. "Anyway, do you even realize how naked you are?"

A laugh rolled out of me as I shrugged. "I've gotten used to it." I'd gotten used to a lot of things in the past couple weeks.

"Abby, you're ridiculously cute naked when you're not covered in gore." Her golden gaze dipped down and not submissively.

Suddenly feeling quite warm, I resisted spinning on my heel like a startled mouse. I turned with a slow dignity to stare out at the city lights reflected on the surface of the river. Her arms closed around my shoulders and her warmth pressed into my back.

Packmate, Wolf chuffed happily, then Victoria kissed my cheek, and wolf me amended, *mate maybe.*

"I think it's time I took you home," I told her, twisting around in her grip to stare into those gold-flecked eyes.

"'Bout time," she murmured, before our lips met and I

drank in her dusky scent. As she twisted to deepen the kiss, I broke away on a playful whim. "Wha-"

"Catch me if you can." I licked her cheek, grabbed Secret, shifted, and broke away in a sprint. Got to the end of the bridge before a howl of pursuit rang through the air. She raced up beside me before I made it to the bottom of the ramp, nudging my shoulder with uncomplicated affection. Her form swelled and stretched until we stood shoulder to shoulder, wolves the size of horses. Opposites, white and black, muscular to lithe, my silver eyes smiling into her gold. Together we tore through the empty streets. Secret stayed quiet, but I could feel her purrs as she clung to my neck.

As we passed through the border to my territory, we let our human sides go entirely, becoming smaller and sleeker. Over and under fences we went, following the scent trails of the smaller residents. I flushed out a rabbit, and she snapped it up, tossed the squealing meat up into the air before breaking its neck with a decisive crunch. She carried it over and set it in front of me. I bent to accept the gift, only for Secret to launch herself at it, using my head as a springboard. Both Victoria and I huffed with canine laughter as my adopted pup playfully attempted to claim the entire rabbit for herself. Eating it together, the white fur of my muzzle contrasting against her black, all three of our scents mingling with that of the meat, a lonely part of my heart filled, and I had to howl to the cloudy sky. She joined me, and together we sang to the fading night.

Clouds parting like an opening eye, Luna gazed down on the three of us; still waning towards the half moon, she regarded our pack as a napper with one eye open. The soft breeze held her smile, and I felt the caress of her touch run down my back. A shiver closed my eyes. As they opened, I found Luna before us, an arm around each of our necks.

Her silver face slid into the thick muzzle of a bear as she whispered, *I am pleased to witness this auspicious night. To behold a single voice become a chorus is a blessing even to me.* She squeezed us to herself with the same strength that moved the oceans, and she slipped away as suddenly as she'd appeared. Victoria and I both staggered until our bodies leaned against each other for support.

"Merf," Secret commented from below, seemingly unimpressed by the Goddess' presence. Chuffing, I grabbed her scruff and tossed her into the air.

She yowled and landed claws first on my back. I took the deserved pain with grace and shouldered Victoria hard enough to knock her out of her tongue-hanging stupor. There was so much more to show her. We visited each of my markers and slowly made my territory ours. The local Coyote pack paid us homage, and we took turns chasing each other through the park that butted up against the neighborhood until we all froze as the wind brought us the tantalizing scent of a nearby deer. A white stag stepped through the underbrush and bellowed in challenge. We chased it for hours, almost getting our teeth into it before it leapt out over a ravine carved by a stream and disappeared, not even a trace of its scent remaining.

We sprawled on top of one another in the forest as dawn came on a new day. Secret resting on my ribs, my head resting on Victoria's black-furred thigh. New challenges were coming, more all the time, but so long as I could have moments like these, I'd face whatever this changing world offered.

****

The Full Moon Medic will continue in Soul Shock.

To be notified when it's complete and receive news and bonus stories, please join my mailing list.

ACKNOWLEDGMENTS

Thank you for reading! At the time of this writing I am mentally happy dancing because the light at the end of the tunnel turned out to be exit and not the light of an oncoming train. This book took forever to decide what it wanted to be and them transformed into a hulking beast of a novel. I'm very proud to bring it to you and I hope you enjoyed it. Abby and her little pack will return soon, there will be larger time jump, months this time. Summer's going to be harsh for Winter's Wolf. (Insert evil laughter here)

Many people provided comfort and assistance as I stumbled, walked and slogged through the dark tunnel of crafting this novel. I want to highlight the heroic assistance of my copy editor Andrea, who, when I was about a month and a half late giving her the novel, got the job done in record time. My spouse Amanda served as a very needed sounding board and shoulder to cry on when I believed Abby and Victoria wanted me dead. My author friends such as ML Spencer, Virginia M, Dyrk Ashton, Matt Presley, JC Kang and so many more provided encouragement and commiseration. WWCO provided needed fun tangents and doodles. Also, the two brave souls who took a look at an unedited draft and assured me it wasn't terrible, Aria and Mr. Hobbit. Thank you to Podium who are publishing the Audio editions of the Series.

And thank you to everyone who's let me and others know that you're enjoying the Full Moon Medic series. The response to the first book has been overwhelmingly positive and I'm looking forward to many long years of torturing- err, spending quality time with Abby and Secret. Please continue to support the series, leave a review and share it with your friends.

Daniel Potter

ALSO BY DANIEL POTTER

The Full Moon Medic Book 1: Emergency Shift

The Full Moon Medic Book 2: Midnight Triage

* * *

Freelance Familiars Book 1: Off Leash

Freelance Familiars Book 2: Marking Territory

Freelance Familiars Book 3: High Steaks

Freelance Familiars Book 4: Aggressive Behavior

Freelance Familiars Book 5: Pride Fall

Rudy & the Warren Warriors (a Freelance Familiars short story)

* * *

Rise of the Horned Serpent Book 1: Dragon's Price

Rise of the Horned Serpent Book 2: Dragon's Cage

Rise of the Horned Serpent Book 3: Dragon's Run

Rise of the Horned Serpent Book 4: Dragon's Siege